RUNAWAYS

RUNAWAYS

Etta Grace

First Edition

Gold and Grace Publications LLC

Hebron, KY

2025

With Illustrations by Quinn Siarven

ISBN 979-8-9987631-0-6 Hardcover

ISBN 979-8-9987631-1-3 Paperback

First Edition

Gold and Grace Publications

www.ettagraceauthor.com

To My Siblings

Table of Contents

THE STORM 2

THE DISAPPEARANCE 9

THE SEARCH 15

THE PREPARATIONS 22

THE WEASEL 27

THE MEETING 33

THE CHASE 39

THE PORTAL 45

THE AMBUSH 52

THE CAPTURE 59

THE TEST 67

THE REVELATION 74

THE TRUTH 78

THE EXPLANATION 85

THE TRANSFORMATION 92

THE PUNISHMENT 101

THE LADY 112

THE DECISION 120

THE TWINS 127

THE SCOUT 132

THE GLAMOUR 139

THE CHANGELING 147

THE TARGET 157

THE SWITCH 164

THE OFFERING 174

THE VACATION 184

THE NAMER — 191

THE TRAINING — 200

THE DEPARTURE — 207

THE ARGUMENT — 214

THE MAZE — 222

THE APPROACH — 229

THE TROLL — 237

THE CONFRONTATION — 245

THE ACCEPTANCE — 252

THE RECONCILIATION — 256

THE ESCAPE — 260

THE HERO — 268

THE SACRIFICE — 278

THE NAME — 283

THE RELEASE — 287

THE RETURN — 298

EPILOGUE — 306

ACKNOWLEDGMENTS — I

GLOSSARY — IV

ABOUT THE AUTHOR — VII

FOLLOW ETTA TO LEARN MORE! — VIII

CONTENT WARNINGS — X

COLOPHON — XI

Chapter 1:
The Storm

HANNAH'S CLOSET DOOR creeeeaaaaks open. The sound rouses Hannah from her half dreaming state, and she blinks the sleep from her eyes as she reaches for a flashlight. The door swings slowly, revealing a pale, nightgown-clad figure staring into her dark room with haunted eyes. Hannah pulls herself up to greet the trespasser with a weary smile.

"Are you sleeping?" the girl whispers.

Not anymore obviously, but it doesn't matter. Hannah clicks on her flashlight and pulls back the covers. "Cecelia, are you alright?"

Cecelia's terrified expression softens as she scrambles across the room and clambers into Hannah's bed. She pulls the covers over her head so she looks like she's wearing a ghost costume. Hannah pats the bundle of blankets and takes her little sister's silence as an answer. Cecelia's alright, now that she's safe with Hannah.

"Did you close the passageway?" Hannah asks. Their farmhouse is a rickety old building, full of odd corners and false façades. The wall between their connected closets hides a trapdoor large enough for a small child or a cat. They don't want their pets running around the house at night, though, so Hannah double-checks that Cecelia locked the hatch behind her when she came through the closet.

Cecelia's face pokes out of the blanket and nods solemnly. Hannah gives her a satisfied smile; then, as drumming rain rolls over the roof, she clicks off the flashlight to watch the lightning that follows.

Gasping, Cecelia claws the flashlight from her hands with urgent ferocity. Hannah flinches as her sister's fingernails rake her skin. The beam flickers on again beneath Cecelia's face, pointed upward. She gives her older sister a fearsome scowl. The light catches the curves of her features and turns her childish pout into a mask of anger.

"What are you doing?" Hannah asks, rubbing the marks on the back of her palm. "You always want to watch the storms. Last week, I had to pull you back from the windowsill before you fell because you said you wanted to pet the wind."

Cecelia shakes her head. "The wind spirit isn't a friend tonight."

Hannah lets silence fall between them as thunder rattles the window panes. Cecelia's always believed in faeries and ghosts and other such nonsense, but she's never *feared* them before. She narrows her eyes at her sister, but lets the matter drop. Shrugging instead, she rolls onto her stomach and reaches for the nearby bookshelf, letting her fingers dance over the spines as she reads the names. "Fine then. I'll read you a bedtime story until you're calm enough to go back to sleep, okay? What do you want to hear? Robin Hood? Treasure Island? *Fairy Tales* . . . I think we left off on The Pied Piper?"

Cecelia shudders. Hannah glances over her shoulder and re-examines her sister's huddled form, her frightened face, then stops and frowns, concern knitting her brows. "What's the matter?"

"Don't say his name."

"Whose name?" Hannah turns back to the shelf where her fingers rest over the creased cover. She pulls it off the shelf and flips open to the ribbon bookmark. The page shows a colorful illustration of a figure leading rats into a river, a horde of children following behind.

"We shouldn't draw his attention," Cecelia says.

"Is that what you're worried about?" Hannah asks, trying her hardest to sound concerned.

"Can't you hear it?"

"Hear what?"

"His pipe on the wind." Cecelia shivers again. "It's deafening."

If Hannah strains her ears, she can imagine the howling of the autumn storm as keening, discordant music. A lightning flash illuminates the room in stark black-white contrast. Is a pale mask peering through the window?

She doesn't have the chance to answer before Cecelia whispers, "I hope you don't. You only hear him when he's coming for you."

Now Hannah shudders. Adults dismiss her sister's ramblings out of hand. They call them flights of fantasy, childhood foolishness, only a phase. Kids who consider themselves too cool for make-believe taunt her as well. Hannah has always hated how much those comments hurt her sister. She's vowed to humor Cecelia's eccentricities, even if she doesn't believe the stories herself.

Besides, Cecelia always listens whenever Hannah explains the cool plants she finds or how to tinker with Dad's tools. Whether they're collecting samples for her field journal, making a tire swing for their willow tree, or building instruments out of recycling, they're a team. If Cecelia's dreams aren't hurting anyone, then what right does Hannah have to call them nonsense?

Cecelia bites her lower lip and twists the sheets into her fists, trying and failing to keep tears from welling in her big brown eyes. Hannah wraps her arms around her sister's small, shaking shoulders.

"I promise, I won't let him take you."

Cecelia melts into her arms.

"That's right!" Hannah continues. She frees one hand from the embrace and points a finger in the air. "If he wants you, he'll have to climb to the second-story window in the storm. But we'll grab the broom and beat him back! We can scatter blocks on the floor to make a minefield so he can't reach us. And we can sic Hobbes on him! Remember how he caught that grass snake last summer?"

Their orange-striped cat guards the door to her bedroom from his favorite napping spot—the pile of clothes on top of her dresser.

"The Piper will run away, *begging* for mercy!"

Cecelia finally gives her a slight smile. Hannah congratulates herself as the younger girl gathers her resolve, slips off the covers, and retrieves the blocks from the closet. She scatters them on the wooden floor with a clatter that sends the shadowy form of their black cat, Inky, shooting from under the bed into the hallway. Hannah winces at the noise, hoping the racket won't wake their parents. Cecelia follows Inky into the hall, retrieves the broom from the linen closet, and places it by the bed, a ready defense.

Downstairs, their Newfoundland dog, Willow, barks at something crashing in the night. Cecelia scrambles back into bed with her.

"It's just raccoons in the trash bins again," Hannah says. "Willow guards us like we're her own pups. We'll be fine." She flops back onto her bed and glances at the clock. "Stars above, how *late*." She pulls a pillow under her head and shuts her eyes as another flash of lightning brightens the room.

Cecelia shakes her before she has the chance to slip into darkness. "Did we leave out milk and cookies for Hazel?"

Hannah cracks an eye. "Yep. One vanilla wafer and your chipped tea cup. We used cream tonight, remember?"

Cecelia wholeheartedly believes their home belongs to a brownie—a small fae who cleans their rooms at night and appreciates offerings in return for her services. Without fail, someone or something eats the treats by the next morning, but

Hannah guesses Mom takes them away after they fall asleep to avoid ants. Or maybe Dad snatches them. He's always had a sweet tooth.

"Mm-hmm. Say goodnight to Mr. Spider."

"G'night," Hannah mumbles for good measure.

"Did you push socks under your bed for the shadelings?"

"The dirty ones, sure." *Shadeling* is Cecelia's word for sinister shadow monsters under their beds, and she insists they're only appeased by nest-building materials. It's a good enough excuse for not doing her laundry. Mom will chide her if she finds out, but Hannah promises herself she'll take care of the chore in the morning. Now, she wants to sleep.

"I gave them my fuzzy blue ones. It's cold enough." Cecelia says.

"The shadelings deserve fuzzy socks?"

"Well, I'm not giving them my special blanket, and they need soft nests so they don't climb into my bed," Cecelia explains yet again, as if her logic is the most obvious thing in the world.

Hannah smacks her with a pillow. "You're the shadeling, climbing into my bed like this."

"Am not!" Cecelia sticks out her tongue and pulls Hannah's blanket closer around herself.

Hannah rolls her eyes. "You're not even using your own blankets!"

Satisfied, Cecelia settles into bed and curls into Hannah's side. "Thank you for letting me steal yours."

"Uh-huh." Hannah puts an arm around her and points at the clock again. The numbers blink, showing 12:00 am. "Go to sleep. We have a busy day tomorrow: chores, homework, trick-or-treating, and then the Petersons and some other people from church are coming over for a Halloween party. If we don't get our rest, I'll pass out before dessert, which would be *tragic*."

"Don't remind me about Halloween," Cecelia answers through a yawn. "Can you sing for me? I still hear the pipe. Sing the one about the woods. Please."

Hannah doesn't want to press the issue any further, so she sings. Her voice is only good for campfires, showers, and lullabies, but right now, it's all Cecelia needs. Hannah doesn't know where they had first learned the words to the song, but she gives them her soul.

> *Leave it dense and let it wild,*
> *God's own playground for a child.*
> *Oak and maple, birches thick,*
> *Wineberry bush with thorns that prick.*
> *Creeping ivy, mossy stone,*
> *In the woods lies Oberon's throne.*
>
> *Nectar scent on summer's eve,*
> *Wand'rers know not how to leave.*
> *Starlight shines through painted sky,*
> *Owls aloft watch passersby.*
> *Crickets chirp, frog choruses sing,*
> *Titania's Dance in faerie ring.*

More lines await, but her brain has grown too fuzzy with approaching dreams. Whatever Halloween brings, she and Cecelia will face it together. The fright of the night's fairy tale fades as the thunderstorm runs out of anger. Rain beats in rhythm on the rooftop, lulling her into slumber. She slips into humming, then soft snores.

Chapter 2
The Disappearance

HANNAH AWAKES WHEN the sunrise streams through the window and splays its rays over her face. She rubs the sleep from her eyes and rolls onto her back to smile at the morn. Canadian geese clamor in the distance. They always stop at the pond across the street on their journey south for the winter.

Branta canadensis, she says to herself. When she had learned scientific taxonomy in biology, it had inspired a special interest in memorizing the Latin names of the plants and animals in their backyard. Hannah makes her best imitation of honking at them in return before stretching and smacking the flashlight onto the floor. The clatter reminds Hannah of her visitor the night before, as she reaches down to set it back on the nightstand.

Cecelia's not in bed, but that's not unusual; she's the earlier riser of the two. The clock tells Hannah it's 7:30 am. As the smell of bacon drifts up the hall, Hannah throws back the covers and swings her legs over the edge of the bed to join her sister downstairs.

She shouts as she stubs her toe on a sharp block, forgetting last night's escapades and paying the price with pain. Stifling curses, Hannah tiptoes around the rest of the blocks to reach the hall. She slides down the creaking banister and alights on the landing a moment later.

As expected, Mom stands at the stove, scrambling eggs and listening to the morning news over the radio. Her brown hair sits in a ponytail, and she's wearing part of her Halloween costume—the same witch's dress she's been wearing every year since Hannah was a baby—over her gardening jeans. Mom stays home with the girls while Dad goes to work, but they all pitch in to take care of the animals and make breakfast before getting started on the day's tasks. Hannah moves to the cabinet to get plates, falling into the natural morning routine.

"Good morning, Mom."

"Morning, baby. How'd you sleep?"

"Alright. Cecelia had me up late."

Willow rests with her head on her paws in the middle of the walkway. Hannah scratches the big dog on the butt with her toe, which pokes out of the front of her sock, before setting the table. Mom clicks the radio to a music station; bluegrass guitars and banjos join the background noise of the sizzling food and the *whirrrrrrrrrrrr* of the box fan.

"That storm was something else, huh? It's still drizzling," Mom says as she flips bacon in the pan. "Dad said we might have lost some shingles—I hope we don't have to get the roof replaced. Why did Cecelia keep you up? She normally loves storms. What was wrong?"

"I dunno. She was being weird." Hannah finishes the plates with a shrug and moves onto the silverware.

"Did she say anything about her incident?" Mom asks, lowering her voice below the music.

"No, you know she never talks about that."

Mom sighs, but she puts on an apron and a smile. "You excited to go trick or treating?"

"I'm so ready! I got all my Stegosaurus plates cut out of cardboard, and Dad helped me spray paint them last week. According to my research, I think the colors are accurate. Do you think there will be any other scientifically accurate dinosaurs?"

Hannah's project has been commandeering the dining room table for weeks. Luckily, they normally eat in the kitchen. She'll have to clean it up before their guests arrive.

"Maybe not, but that'll just make yours extra memorable. Just remember, we need to rake leaves before the party tonight."

When Mom brings up the party, Hannah grimaces. "Is it too late to cancel that?"

"How come?"

"The adults are going to ask why we don't go to 'real school,' and I don't really care, but it bothers Cecelia," Hannah argues. She fills glasses of orange juice and removes the toast when it pops.

The sisters had dropped out of the local public school after a single disastrous year of enduring bullying and starting playground brawls. Now, Mom teaches them at home. Hannah learns more when she doesn't have to endure the crowds or the schedules, the sitting still or the flickery buzzing lights, and the constant pressure to keep up her guard around her peers. Plus, she can make epic dinosaur costumes. At home, she and Cecelia can be weirdos together, in all their shy, socially awkward, nerdy glory.

Their justification had only grown after her sister's accident last year, after which Cecelia hadn't been the same: timid and flighty, hiding from peers, and refusing to speak with strangers. After that, the constant gossip had become unbearable. Their uncomprehending neighbors still ask "polite" invasive questions. Cecelia plans to disappear as soon as their guests arrive, making herself as scarce as Inky in the myriad of hiding spots in the house.

"That's not your problem to handle. You'll have fun once you're playing with the other kids, and if Ms. Tina is nosy, you tell her to talk to me or Dad, alright?" Mom says.

Hannah sighs, but she knows it's too late to change the plans now. "Speaking of which, where is Dad?" she asks, settling into her chair to enjoy her breakfast.

"Gathering eggs. Can you feed Snubs after breakfast?" Mom serves the cheesy eggs and waves a spatula at Cecelia's empty spot. "Now, go call your sleepyhead sister. I won't have her eating cold food."

"What do you mean? She's not awake?" Hannah thinks back to the flashlight, the blocks, the empty bed, trying to remember Cecelia returning to her room. "I assumed she was outside helping Dad."

"She never came downstairs, and I've been up since seven."

"Hmm. Maybe she went back to her room to sleep in? I'll get her." Hannah pushes her chair away from the table, scraping the legs on the wooden floor, and scrambles up the stairs to rap on the doorway to Cecelia's room. "Hey! Up and at 'em!"

No answer comes from within, so Hannah throws open the door to Cecelia's darkened room. "You're gonna be late for breakfast. Mom made your favorite, but if you don't hurry, I'll eat it all!"

Even her taunts don't earn an answer. She pulls the blinds open with a flourish and tugs the covers off the bed, then freezes.

Cecelia isn't there. She'd arranged the pillows in the lumpy form of a sleeping girl, but the child in question is missing. Hannah's chest tightens as the implications settle over her, but she gathers her resolve and starts searching. Maybe she's already hiding.

Hannah checks the bathroom and the upstairs linen closet with no luck. They call it the Dark Room because they sit inside with only flashlights, telling scary stories until someone calls chicken and cracks the door. Cecelia usually wins. She has a terrifying imagination. Last night she must have frightened herself, imagining monsters under her bed. Inky sits on the third shelf up, though Hannah cannot fathom how she got there. She picks up the black cat, who meows with annoyance.

"Have you seen Cecelia this morning?" she asks, gazing into her pet's wide green eyes. She receives only an indifferent blink for an answer, so she sets Inky on the ground and lets her streak off to find a new hiding spot. Hannah double-checks her own room, even cleaning her socks out from underneath her bed, but to no avail.

Retracing her sister's steps from the night before, Hannah crawls through the passageway back to Cecelia's room. In the year since her incident, Cecelia has let the space stagnate. She'd always been the more artistic of the two sisters, but dust had gathered on her craft desk. Her artwork had been taken down, shoved into an opaque plastic tote under the bed, next to locked instrument cases. When Hannah had asked why she'd abandoned her hobbies, Cecelia couldn't give her an answer.

Curiosity gets the better of Hannah. She glances over her shoulder and crouches to pull out the tote from under the bed. Cecelia would be furious if she caught Hannah snooping, but if her younger sister is really missing, Hannah needs to know what's in this box. She cracks the lid and pulls out the first slips of paper. Familiar paintings of the family that used to be hung, but in each one, Cecelia has scribbled blue over her face. Why?

Hannah pulls out drawing after drawing, each with the same marks, before finally emptying the bin. More puzzled than ever, Hannah returns the drawings exactly in the order in which they were placed, and tries to shove the tote back under the bed, but it knocks against something else. Lying on her stomach, Hannah reaches under the bed and extracts a shoebox that had been hidden behind the other tote.

This one contains drawings Hannah doesn't recognize. A tree on fire. A wiry figure with dragonfly wings carrying a flute. A mask at the window. They're unfinished and warped with frustration, sloppy strokes of the pen turning into angry scribbles in the margins, paper crumpled, paint smeared. Hannah frowns with concern as she flips through them. Cecelia's been hiding her nightmares?

Mom calls from downstairs. "Hannah? Where are you? Breakfast is almost ready!"

"Coming!" Hannah shouts back. Her gaze lingers on the last painting, the mask at the window, before she shoves the failed artworks back into their shoebox and slides both boxes under the bed again. Nobody needs to know about her spying.

Standing, Hannah moves to check the window. The sill is freshly damp, causing chips of green paint to flake off the old wood beneath, and the rusty latch hangs open. Hannah jams her finger trying to force it down, ripping her nail in the process.

How could Cecelia have opened this window on her own? It always sticks, and Dad has to ease up the sash with a healthy dose of oil every year.

Did she climb out the window? And during a storm? It's at least a thirty-foot drop to the ground with no convenient trees or ivy or drain pipes to climb. If she'd tried to jump, she'd have ended up as a heap of gashes and broken bones. Cecelia must have left the window open in her fear and carelessness last night. Hannah's stomach twists with an unwelcome lurch as she locks the window, then rushes downstairs two steps at a time.

Hannah announces the news as she slides into the kitchen. "She's gone!"

Chapter 3

The Search

HANNAH'S NEWS BRINGS breakfast to a screeching halt. Mom switches off the radio and turns to her elder daughter, eyebrows raised.

"Gone? Gone where?" Mom asks.

"Who, Cecelia?" Dad asks at the same time, stomping the mud off his boots at the door. Mist shakes off his curly black hair and beard, and he looks over the top of his glasses, which are fogged up from coming into the warm house.

"She's not sleeping in either of our rooms. Her window was unlocked, and I looked everywhere else upstairs," Hannah explains.

"She didn't sneak outside when I wasn't looking?" Mom asks Dad. He shakes his head. Mom flicks off the stove, slams the pan of bacon on a trivet, and abandons it on the counter as she calls around the rooms downstairs for her daughter.

Hannah joins her, even though the mounting tightness in her chest tells her their efforts will be fruitless. She runs through their best hide-and-seek spots—an odd corner where the back porch addition doesn't match up with the original house, the cubby under the main stairs, the awkward set of wooden spiral stairs behind the kitchen pantry leading to the basement. All empty. She troops to the mudroom and checks the back door. Locked. There, she finds her father inspecting the clothes hanging out to dry.

"Her coat and shoes are still here," Dad says, checking the rack.

"She doesn't wear those half the time anyhow," Hannah informs him.

"But in late October, after a rainstorm? There's frost on the grass between the mud puddles."

Hannah can't understand why a nagging thorn sticks in the back of her brain. Why would Cecelia leave without even writing a note? She should know better.

Hannah decides her discomfort is nothing more than annoyance and absentmindedly bites the torn nail of her thumb. Mom comes back into the kitchen and flings her apron onto the closest chair.

"After what she went through last year, any other child would give up wandering, but not Cecelia!" Mom says. She wrings her hands and triple-checks the coat rack. "This is the third time since the incident! I don't understand her."

"Last time, we found her hiding in Snubs' pen. Maybe she'll be close," Dad says, in what he must think is a comforting tone. It doesn't put Hannah's anxieties to ease. He gives Mom a kiss and grabs his heavy work coat and Cecelia's jacket from beside the door. "We'll find our girl."

"She can't have gone far without her coat, right?" Mom asks.

"Hopefully. I'll take the car into town and ask if anyone's seen her walking along the street this morning."

"I'll search the neighborhood with Willow and see if we can find her scent. Hannah, stay near the house and check the gardens and animal pens. Keep a lookout, in case she comes back before we do." Mom keeps her voice even and her face calm, but

Hannah senses her growing anxiety in the jerky movements of her normally deft fingers as she fumbles with the leash. Hannah nods her acknowledgment and wraps her bleeding hangnail in a napkin as Mom continues muttering under her breath.

"Cecilia should know better than to wander off without telling us where she's going. We've talked about this dozens of times. How do you ground a kid with her head in the clouds?"

Hannah scowls at the neglected skillet of bacon cooling on the counter, and feeds a piece to Willow, who emerges from under the table. They've all lost their appetites with worry, even if Mom and Dad won't admit it. When they think Hannah isn't listening, she catches a whisper. "If we can't find her by noon, we'll call for help."

Hannah's heart speeds up, imagining a missing-persons rescue in their backyard. Too many people poking, asking questions, turning over every corner of their yard. The flashing lights on their cars, and maybe even the buzzing of helicopters. She remembers last year, when Cecelia had gone missing for a week on one of their family camping trips. During a hike, Cecelia had fallen behind, and in the few minutes before Hannah noticed and warned their parents, her sister had disappeared without a trace. they'd doubled back and searched the entire trail, but when they couldn't find her, the park rangers had called for a squad to track her, leaving Hannah terrified and helpless.

She hopes they find Cecelia before their parents have to repeat such drastic measures.

What if Hannah solves the mystery? She'd be a hero for bringing her sister home. Heroism is about cleverness, right? Were there any clues pointing to Cecelia's destination? The hidden paintings are Hannah's only hint, and they're clear as mud. Cecelia left no note, but why hadn't she? Has Hannah lost her sister's trust? Cecelia had come to her last night during the storm.

The storm.

Snippets of conversation come back to Hannah.

The wind isn't a friend tonight.

Don't draw his attention.

The pipe on the wind, it's deafening.

The lullaby about the faerie courts. The troubling drawings shoved under the bed.

These signs could all be the products of Cecelia's overactive imagination, but any of them could be motive enough for a confused child to venture into the forest on a whim. And on the wild chance supernatural beings were pursuing Cecelia, she could be kidnapped at this very moment, trapped in a troll dungeon, or turned into a rat! Hannah turns their interaction over in her mind and weighs the possibilities, skeptical but unwilling to discount the theory.

"Can I search the woods?" she asks, interrupting her parents' hushed conversation. They turn to her with gaunt faces.

"No." Dad shakes his head. "Mom said to stay here. We can't have you wandering off, too. If she comes back to an empty house, she might leave again to search for us. Besides, we never cleared the trails. We'd have two lost daughters."

"Cecelia would never go into town alone," Hannah argues. "She's wandering in the forest somewhere, if she's not in the house or the yard."

"Don't be ridiculous," Mom says, tying on her stomping boots. "It's too dangerous to go hiking alone."

"You could search the woods with me!"

"The forest is so overgrown she wouldn't make it past the tree line at the edge of the pasture," Dad says. "It's not like a state park with premade trails. She would have had to follow the road because it's an easier path." He speaks kindly, but treats Hannah as only a foolish child. "Especially if she ran away this morning, she could only be a couple miles away. We'll be faster finding her if Mom and I split up the search."

Mom finishes her preparations and gives Hannah a serious *'this is not up for debate'* look. "Promise me you'll stay here. She might be . . . I don't know, climbing a tree or something. That one maple you like at the edge of the driveway—I'll check there. She'll be back before we know it. You welcome her home and make sure she's safe until we return. I trust you to stay in the house alone, big girl, okay? It'll be alright, Hannah. Promise me you'll stay put."

"I promise, Mom," Hannah lies.

Mom plasters on a smile which doesn't reach her eyes, and Hannah gives her a solemn nod. Dad squeezes her shoulder once then straightens and grabs his keys. Despite the words of reassurance, fear writes creases in their mother's brow and bows their father's shoulders as they leave on their missions.

In a minute, Hannah's standing alone in the kitchen. Against her better judgment, she searches the house for clues twice, hoping Cecelia's just playing a one-sided overachieving game of hide-and-seek. Counting to thirty, Hannah shouts, "Ready or not, here I come!" and begins her search, looking beneath every bed and in the cramped spiral staircase connecting her parent's room to the den. She looks behind the shower curtain and in the gap between the couch and the wall, where they'd pushed it to hide the hole they put through the drywall while roughhousing. She looks through the basement, where they stack wood next to the stove, and in the attic, where she turns over every cardboard box full of decorations, desperate to find more and more obscure potential haunts.

No Cecelia.

Hannah returns to the kitchen and flops onto her chair to wait. She positions herself across from the window so she can watch the woods as the wind rustles the branches. What if Cecelia hurt herself in the forest? A squirrel scampers past and tries to steal birdseed before sliding off the pole. The clouds billow and fade. What if she broke her ankle in a ditch and she's lying there, defenseless?

Leaves drift from the trees and pile themselves against the deck. Hannah taps her fingers on the table in time with the clock.

Dou-bles. Dou-bles.

Tri-pl-ets. Tri-pl-ets. Tri-pl-ets.

She passes half an hour in this way as the shadows shift across the table. What if a bear mauled Cecelia? Unlikely, but Hannah can't help herself from worrying.

A mockingbird sits at their feeder, careless, and she glares at it through the window. *Mimus polyglottos.* Bored. Bored. Bored. Why can't she help? She's more useful searching, not sitting and waiting.

The nervous energy builds from tapping to shaking her leg to leaning back on her chair until she falls backwards with a clatter. Hannah picks the chair up, straightens it, and starts pacing laps around the kitchen. After another minute of boredom, she directs the energy into something more useful: clearing the uneaten plates of food from the table. Mom will lecture her for the lack of initiative if she gets back and finds the kitchen a mess. Cleaning will help pass the time and stifle the cruel hypothetical questions springing to mind. Hannah scoops up the dishes and moves to the sink before stopping in her tracks.

There's a message scrawled in a dusting of spilled flour on the hardwood floor. It couldn't have been there earlier. She passed through this room a dozen times during her rounds, and there had never been flour on the floor. There's none on her socks, and Hannah has been sitting at the kitchen table for the past half hour, so Cecelia can't have done this if she were hiding in the house. Hannah leans closer to the writing, afraid to breathe on it and ruin the careful lettering scrawled in spidery cursive.

The Piper tried to take her. Follow the song to the Seelie Court. I'll clean up the mess. —Hazel.

Their house brownie is real? Hannah sits back on her heels and takes a deep breath as she tries to come to terms with this new discovery. If it's an elaborate prank, she has no better leads. Not after Cecelia's fear last night.

In the woods lies Oberon's throne.

Cecelia had feared the Pied Piper last night. A child's nightmare, but now...she's not so sure. What if something hunted her sister?

Titania's dance in faerie ring.

Was Hannah too ignorant to understand the real threat in her sister's words?

Hannah stands to her feet and gazes toward the forest again. The mockingbird still sits on the feeder, but it doesn't eat the seeds. It stares back at her, expectant. The trees loom at the edge of the pasture, dark and full of secrets. The words of Cecelia's song drift through Hannah's mind as she recalls her parent's instructions to stay put and wait for their return.

"What do you want?" she asks the bird.

"Pay the Piper," it says.

Hannah drops the plate she'd been holding. It shatters when it hits the floor, but she doesn't care. *Mockingbirds can talk*, she tells herself. It's a normal fact of life. There's nothing magic about mimicry. It's in their very name. Except they usually mimic other bird calls, not human speech.

"Where did you learn to say that?" she asks.

"Pay the Piper." The mockingbird doesn't use any voice she recognizes. Did a stranger teach it, or did it speak for itself? Of all the phrases it could learn to speak, why this one? Why now?

"What do you mean?"

"Pay the Piper!" It screeches and then flies off without eating the seeds. Hannah can't help but notice it flies toward the woods. She takes a long breath and makes her decision.

Her parents should be worried. Neither of them knows what's at stake. They mean well, but they won't find Cecelia near town, and they won't heed Hannah's warning. Hannah must be clever if she's going to find her sister. It's up to her to be the hero.

Faeries or not, Cecelia's in danger. Hannah will bring her home.

Chapter 4

The Preparations

HANNAH RUSHES UPSTAIRS to her room, sweeps away the blocks still cluttering the floor, and snatches the book of fairy tales from her bookshelf. Even if she doesn't believe in faeries, if she's going to go looking for trouble, she wants to do it the right way. It can't hurt to research them, especially since she can't explain the flour message or the mockingbird. At least, not yet. Eager determination replaces her anxiety, and she takes a deep breath before flipping through the pages.

Each story claims new facts regarding the fae folk: they wear the color green; clothes worn inside out confuse the fae's True Sight; humans need enchanted lenses or stones with holes to be granted the Sight and discern through glamours; red string might ward them away; cold iron burns them; and one must never eat their food, lest they slumber for a hundred years.

Hannah constructs a careful plan. She tosses her pajamas in a heap on her bed and pulls on her favorite red-and-black striped sweater, inside out. Next, her cargo pants—lots of pockets good for carrying supplies. From Cecelia's art stash, she snips several lengths of red embroidery floss and braids two friendship bracelets. The first goes in her pocket for Cecelia; the other she ties around her wrist, using her teeth to finish the knot.

Cecelia always told Hannah she'd be binding bad luck if she tied the bracelet on herself, and she would be doomed for that luck to come to fruition were she to cut the bracelet off, instead of waiting until it unraveled on its own. Hannah shuns her sister's warning. Necessity requires her to make do with the resources she has, even if it comes with bad luck. She'll just have to be twice as clever to make up for the helping of hazard.

Dismissing the memory, she drops the rest of the spool in a pocket for safekeeping. She owns nothing iron, but she packs her steel pocketknife and a first aid kit, hoping it will be enough. Then her fingers drift over her spyglass. Her parents had given it to her as a Christmas gift last year, and it's one of her most prized possessions. The antique has a wood barrel and brass couplings that telescope to the full length of her arm. The maker engraved delicate swirls as decorations in the wood, and it comes with a stamped leather case to protect either end. She hates the idea of losing it or scratching the lenses in the forest. It should stay home.

Hannah peeks out the window. Mom and Willow are only specks on the horizon, and tracks from Dad's truck lead out of the driveway. She remembers her lie, promising her mother she'd stay near the house. They'll be absent most of the morning. Maybe they won't notice her having snuck out.

What else does she need? If she's taking this rescue mission into her own hands, she'll need to be prepared. She snatches the flashlight off her nightstand so she won't have to follow any will-o'-the-wisps without a light of her own. Extra batteries too—they always die when you need them most. As she turns to leave, she grabs the spyglass anyhow. Something tells her she might need it.

She slides back downstairs and makes her way to the kitchen, where she notices the flour message swept away, along with the broken plate. Further confirmation of the house brownie's existence. Hannah still hasn't *seen* Hazel, so she's not ready to accept they have a faerie living in their home, but it *is* Halloween, and so she whispers a small thanks, just in case.

Hannah takes the last of the fresh bread from the table and puts it in a bag along with a chunk of cheese and sausage, then tucks the snacks into her knapsack. She fills up one bottle with water and one with lemonade. If they offer her treats, she will offer her own. There must be magic in the breaking of bread between humans and fae, she is sure.

Oh, and she needs something to make a trail, other than breadcrumbs, to avoid a Hansel-and-Gretel situation. Chalk won't work because of the rain. She grabs a notebook and pencil instead. Maybe she can make a map as she explores. For markers, she could steal pebbles from the gravel driveway, but she doesn't want to slow herself with an armload of rocks. Hmm. She searches the kitchen for an alternative.

There! Their seashell collection from last summer's beach trip sits in a glass bowl on the table as a centerpiece. Those aren't heavy, and the shells will be recognizable in the forest. Hannah dumps them into a plastic baggie and zips them shut. She's careful to leave behind Cecelia's favorite—a chambered nautilus, *Nautilus pompilius*—as she doesn't want to lose it.

Satisfied she has everything she needs, she pulls on her mucking boots by the door. While dad took his winter gear and Cecelia's sweater into town, he left his forest-green jacket. Hannah squints between it and her own dark-red woolen coat. If she wears his, it'll be the right color, and she could share it with her sister. The choice is obvious. Hopefully, the wards and lucky items she carries will not only be enough to help her find the fae, but keep them from hurting her when she does. She snatches the jacket and throws it on over her red sweater, then pushes up the sleeves so they don't cover her hands. Her satchel is out of space for Cecelia's shoes, so Hannah ties the laces together and slings them to hang around her neck. She wonders how Cecelia walked to Faerieland barefoot.

All set?

One last precaution. She scrawls a note for Cecelia in their secret code. It's a series of swirling strokes and flourishes her sister had invented and taught her for pranking their parents and visitors. Hopefully, Hannah will get more notes in this script soon. For now, she writes:

We went out looking for you. I'm in the woods. Stay put if you're reading this. We'll be back before dinner. Love you, Hannah

She hangs the note on the fridge with a magnet that holds a picture of them as babies, dressed up as faeries for Halloween. They shared a resemblance then. Hannah's hair is still dark and curly, and she keeps it cut in a bob around her chin, but Cecelia grew her straight hair to waist-length. They have the same brown eyes and freckled faces. She does not miss the irony of the old costumes. She wasn't looking forward to the party this morning, but now she hopes they'll still be able to go trick-or-treating and carve jack-o'-lanterns tonight. She writes another note for her parents in normal English letters.

I think Cecelia is missing in the woods. She was talking about faeries last night and it's Halloween. I'm going to bring her back. Don't worry about me. I promise we'll be back before the party.

Love, Hannah

She tucks it next to the other note and inspects her preparations once more.

All set.

She slams the door shut, jumps over the two front steps, and lands running. As she rounds the back of the house, Hannah passes their chicken pen and does a sharp about-face, remembering they need to be fed. She throws them a handful of grain, and as they flock around her, she squats to whisper to them.

"I know Dad checked on you earlier, but did you see her leave?"

A black hen snatches grain from underneath a red one, and Hannah shoos her to peck somewhere else. "Onii, don't steal Amber's snack! You're no help. No treats for the thief chicken."

Onii *squaaaawks* her discontent, and Hannah sprinkles more food on the ground. "Don't tell anyone I spoil you," she says, standing up to check for any tracks of Cecelia's passing around the pen. There's only the chicken scratch and her father's huge boot prints, so she continues toward the pasture where she finds their miniature horse, Snubs. Hannah ruffles his mane and double checks his shed for her sister.

No Cecelia.

Hannah sighs and turns her steps toward the line of trees at the end of the pasture. She climbs over the fence then faces the woods. They loom over her, and the ground slopes up to show one path leading through the underbrush. She takes a deep breath, says a prayer to her guardian angel, then forges ahead.

Chapter 5
The Weasel

THE WOODS AREN'T otherworldly or cursed. Overgrown and creepy, yes, but heaps of soggy leaves and mucky paths are mundane problems. Oak, maple, and birch trees tower so close together that their bare branches might scratch holes in the sky. *Quercus, Sapindacae, Betulacea*; dozens of species grow together. She doesn't have time to stop and identify them beyond the familiar lobed leaves and genus names as she wanders. Thorns of wineberry bushes tug her clothing as she hikes along the narrow trail, and twigs snap with a sound like cracking bones when she shoves through a tight thicket. Leaves underfoot rustle loudly, and she catches herself glancing around as squirrels charge through the debris. The unfamiliarity is intimidating, more than the prospect of finding anything paranormal. She dreads the poison ivy more than the Pied Piper. *Toxicodendron* is only identifiable by its fuzzy vines at this point in the season, having lost its leaves of three.

Her family doesn't own these woods and they don't know who does. The maps show the property lines disappearing somewhere into uncharted land, and their distant neighbors never venture close enough to clarify. As far as Hannah knows, they are wild and wonderful.

She'd wanted to explore them long ago, but their parents had warned about wild animals, and fixing the old house kept them too busy to blaze trails. Besides, they'd forbidden exploring after Cecelia's incident last year. Hannah ignores the twinge of guilt in her chest as she reaches the end of the beaten path. She'll be back soon.

This deer path chokes thin with weeds after a ten-minute walk, and there's nary a mushroom circle or lost sister in sight. This is where they pick berries in the summer, but the fruit is long gone. The damp smell of rotting logs lingers from last night's rainstorm. Now what? She pulls out her notebook and scratches a quick map.

"Where do faerie kidnappers hide little girls?" she asks aloud. "Well, Hannah, you're not a faerie kidnapper, but you have to think like your opponent. It's chess," she answers herself. "Not that I've ever been any good at chess."

The story says the Piper leads the children into a cave. Other stories say you can enter Faerieland by walking widdershins around a hill seven times. The fairy tales say "widdershins" means counterclockwise, so she'll walk in a left-handed path around the slope of the mountain and keep an eye out for any strangeness that might lead her closer to the goal.

She beats her way through the brambles, following the deer trails that offer the least resistance. Cecelia most likely followed the same route. Even if she overcomplicates simple actions because of her superstitions, Hannah doubts even her weird little sister would blaze a trail for fun. Besides, it's unlikely she'd make it far without tools.

For all her flawless logic, Hannah finds no footprints in the damp earth, barefoot or otherwise.

Burrs snag Hannah's pants as her boots squelch in the mud. She tries to memorize the details of her surroundings as she marks her passage with the seashells, only using them when necessary. One goes in the crook of a tree trunk where she veers off the path. She sets another on a mossy boulder when she loses sight of the way she came. She rations them, unsure how far she'll be able to travel before she runs out.

The path takes her uphill, around the bend in the mountain. She enjoys the sun filtering through the last of the leaves still clinging to the trees, warming her against the late fall chill. She crunches through the litter of the forest floor and whistles a melody Cecelia composed last week that's stuck in her head. Both of them love having background music and they often make their own songs, bandying the tune back and forth and making each other laugh with ridiculous rhymes. She leaves off in the middle of a phrase, no longer having the heart to hum without her duet partner.

As she walks, she wonders. How old are these trees? Their trunks are so wide, she cannot wrap her arms around them. What history have they witnessed as saplings? If Cecelia's stories are true, which ones do the sprites call their home? Do the boulders guard fossils, or do they represent the ruins of an ancient city? Why do they stand guard where they do? Were they pushed here by glaciers or moved by the work of giants? Could they be the back doors to a dwarven fortress under the mountain?

Her imagination supplies stories as an explanation—and a few spooks when she hears unexpected noises. They entertain her for a short while as she scrambles over the enormous rocks, but she knows they will not satisfy her need to know the truth. She wonders if her inventions unwittingly contain reality, but must content herself with wondering.

By midday, frustration weighs on Hannah more than her oversized coat. Her feet hurt, and despite the autumn chill, she sweats from the exertion of the uphill hike. Had the mountain been this tall when she set out from home? If this entire trip turns out to be a waste of time, she'll give Cecelia an earful.

Hopefully she'll have the chance to give Cecelia an earful. She wishes she could fast-forward time to the end of this journey, that she could fly above the shadow of the trees, that she had as much confidence or as many clues as she thought she did when she left home.

The seashells run out at a small ledge overlooking the slope, but the path continues—narrow and overgrown as ever. Hannah pauses for a breath. If she doesn't return home, will her parents worry? Should she turn back now, choosing the path that ensures her safety but leaves her sister at risk? Is she going to turn around now, when there's no one else to save Cecelia from the monsters? She can't imagine what the Piper would do to a child, but Hannah refuses to let Cecelia languish without *trying*. How can she call herself a protector if she can't save her sister from a stupid storybook villain?

Besides, there's still a lot of ground to cover. What if Cecelia's stuck in a tree, or hurt after twisting an ankle on the wrong rock? How can Hannah imagine herself a hero if she stops her search now because she ran out of stupid seashells? Heroism is about bravery, right? How would she be able to face herself in the mirror, knowing she'd proved a coward?

She refuses to quit now. No matter what these woods throw at her, she will keep moving. She has to do this. For herself, and for Cecelia. Hannah takes a deep breath and a determined step over the invisible threshold between home and the wide, wild world beyond.

A scream shatters the sylvan silence.

She spins to find the source of the screech and stomps off the path, following the sound and flattening bushes along the way. What if that's Cecelia? There's only a thin line of brush between her and the next clearing, where she finds a knitted tumble of limbs and tails and teeth.

It's a weasel, locked in mortal combat with a swarm of brown rats. *Rattus norvegicus.* They surround the poor animal, trading bites and scratches with human-sounding screams. The weasel fights valiantly, but its energy wanes, sapped as it bleeds from a gaping wound along its side. It chomps the leg of one rat, which falls away, but another jumps on its back. The smell of desperation whips the others into a frenzy.

Echoes of her parents' warnings sound in her mind, that the woods are dangerous, and she should never touch wild animals, especially not angry ones. Hannah watches, paralyzed for a moment, but when the rats band together to overwhelm the helpless weasel, she cannot stand idly by. Hannah knows injustice when she sees it.

She snatches the nearest branch she finds and swings. Her boots stomp forward, intending to shake the earth beneath her feet. She shouts over their squeaks, fury overpowering her fear. A few of the rats scatter. One rat charges for her ankle. She bashes it away like a hockey puck, and it scuttles off to avoid another attack. The weasel twists around, clamps its jaw around the skull of the last foe, then falls exhausted beside its dead attacker, panting with pain.

Hannah approaches cautiously and drops the stick to let it know she poses no threat. It lets her near, and she finds a large, dish-shaped leaf, places it on the ground next to the animal, and pours out some of the water in her bottle into the makeshift bowl. The weasel laps it up then sniffs her hand. She guesses he's a male by his size and the musky scent he uses to mark her.

"Hey there, little critter. Are you alright?" Hannah coos. "My, my, they gave you quite the nasty wound there. Here, let me help."

She douses the wound with water, and he hisses in pain at the contact but does not bite or scratch her. The water washes away the blood and dirt, and he places his front legs on her jacketed arm, long enough for her to cut away the fur and bind the gashes with bandages from her first aid kit. Hannah's not sure if she's doing it right for an animal but figures that having something to stop the bleeding is better than leaving him alone. Her dad's thick coat keeps his claws from scratching her skin, and before long, the weasel makes a happy chitter and curls into the soft inner layer of the coat.

"You're a scrappy little fighter, huh?" Hannah tells him. "I think you're a least weasel. Such a silly name for something so brave. A little *Mustela nivals.* You act so tough, but you're sweet. My cat Hobbes is a lot like you."

He regards her with what Hannah assumes is an inquisitive stare.

"I'm gonna call you Kit-Kat. How's that?"

Kit-Kat chirps. He sounds joyful, and she takes it as agreement.

"You like that name? Me too." Hannah pets him on the head with one gentle finger, then sighs and gently scoops him out of the jacket, setting him on the ground. "I probably shouldn't have named you. It isn't smart to get attached to wild things. You need to find shelter, and I need to find my sister. Goodbye."

When she rises and walks back toward the path, Kit-Kat follows her, limping but keeping up with her strides. Hannah grins, happy for the companionship. She offers to pick up the animal, but he only lopes a couple paces alongside her, so she lets him move at his own pace, mindful that he's still wild. "What do you think of faeries?" she asks her new friend.

Kit-Kat can't reply, so she answers herself in a high-pitched voice, mimicking his tiny size. "If they exist, I think they're a bunch of cowards! They're hiding, even after you've searched all this time!"

"That's right," she says in her own voice. "In fact, I bet I'm the only human to ever set foot in these woods for hundreds of years! They ought to be better hosts. It's indecent. I even brought my own snacks for teatime."

"Perhaps that's the problem," Kit-Kat answers as he scurries over a fallen branch with some difficulty. "You're too well-prepared."

"How could I be too well-pre—" Hannah cuts herself off mid-sentence, mid-step, as realization hits her like a bucket of cold water to the face. She spins on her heel to stare in disbelief at her weasel friend.

She hadn't said Kit-Kat's line that time.

Chapter 6
The Meeting

"**D**ID YOU SAY something?" Hannah asks Kit-Kat.

He doesn't answer, of course. Hannah does a sweep of the forest and, upon finding no anomalies, turns back to Kit-Kat and gives him a good long stare. He hops forward and scurries along the path, rooting among the leaf litter.

"Who goes there!" she calls to the surrounding forest.

Nothing answers her. Kit-Kat disappears briefly, before popping up on a boulder farther away. He cocks his head at her, as if waiting for her to follow his lead. She sighs. The mockingbird could speak because it was a mockingbird, even if it had said something weird. A weasel is a weasel. He couldn't have made any comment.

Then who spoke? Is Hannah's imagination playing tricks on her after walking for so long? Without Cecelia to keep her company, she must be losing her mind. What if someone's following her, or she's journeyed far enough to run into another person? Maybe the mockingbird came back to taunt her again? Or perhaps she's found the fae? Hannah follows Kit-Kat, keeping a sharp eye for the true source of the voice, be they friend or foe.

The statement nags at her mind. She thinks back to the stories, in which witches cheat poor unsuspecting maidens who wish away their lives and promise too much in repayment. Too well-prepared? Who says that? Does that mean the faeries fear her? A ridiculous idea. For all her preparation, they're far more powerful than she. But she wonders. And wishes.

She wishes she knew who owned the voice. She wishes Kit-Kat could speak and provide her some companionship. But most of all, she wishes she had the power to save Cecelia. The idea of a skulking specter scares her, and she can't shake the feeling she's being watched.

"I don't know what to do, Kit-Kat. This isn't working. I'm getting nowhere and I think the trees are spying on us," Hannah says.

Kit-Kat ignores her and scurries under a log. She shouldn't mind, since he's not her pet. She can't expect him to follow along by her side like Willow. Yet she mourns the lack of company as she continues past the log. Back to talking to herself again.

"I guess if the trees are watching me, it means I'm getting closer to Faerieland," Hannah tells herself.

"Oh dearie, no! You're still quite lost!"

That voice! Someone else is speaking to her, and it's not Kit-Kat. The voice is low and melodic, and so close she jumps out of her shoes. Hannah whirls around to search for the source. Her mind isn't tricking her, but the fact is not a relief.

"Show yourself!" she shouts to the barren path and rustling leaves. That way leads home. She could turn back down the mountain and follow the seashells. Can't she?

As she completes her turn, she realizes with growing dread that dozens of paths spiral from where she stands. How hadn't she noticed the others branching off in every direction? She stands frozen, staring at the new trails. How to continue now? Which way is home? Fog rises around her feet, mist choking out her vision beyond the bend in the hill. Any familiar landmark vanishes to the blur.

Stupid. Stupid. How did she wander into one of their traps? She was so careful, so . . . prepared. Her pulse races in her ears as she shoves her hand into her satchel to seize the flashlight. It's not that dark, but the sunlight barely reaches through the murk. She fumbles with the switch, and when the light flickers on, the thick clouds filter the beam, turning the world dim and pale gray. Fog curls around her head, and the light cuts a thin line through the mist to land on a shadowy figure. She moves toward it, at a loss for what else to do, and squints past the shifting shapes in the haze.

"I said, show yourself!" she shouts.

The clouds part before her as she stumbles forward. Propped against a tree is a rail-thin figure wearing the motley clothes of a medieval jester. A tattered robe swishes over a forest-green tunic and silly-looking double-dyed tights. The outfit was topped with a brimmed cap, complete with a red feather. Emerging between slits in the cloak, translucent dragonfly wings twitch with anticipation, flashing rainbows as the struggling daylight fractures through the condensation on their filmy surfaces. Prismatic shards of light flicker, reflections from silvery earrings dangling from pointed ears. The figure holds a length of wood in one hand, but Hannah's gaze doesn't linger there for long. Instead, her eyes are drawn to the haunting theater mask that covers his face—pale as death with hollow black voids for the eyes, nose, and mouth. The expression twists like warping clay into a surreal smile.

"Ah, you've found me!" he says in a cheery tone. "But I'm not the one you want to find, am I?"

It's a faerie! All the stories are real! The realization sends Hannah reeling, and she stumbles backward, tripping over a root, landing on her butt in the soft leaves. How did Cecelia know the truth? What was she trying to tell Hannah last night? Everything Hannah saw today, everything she tried to deny, the mockingbird's warning, the house brownie, Hazel, all of it. All true!

Suspicion replaces her shock as she comes to her senses. She scowls at the figure as she scrambles back to her feet and brushes her hands on her pants. She found a faerie! The small part of her that still held out in disbelief crumbles. There's no chance Cecelia wandered off and got lost. The Piper stole her. She's in real danger. Though the eerie fellow is not a welcome sight, she's relieved that at least she has a lead, something to chase besides indistinguishable woods. Finding the faerie puts her one step closer to her sister.

She squashes the voice in the back of her head that warns she hadn't found him, but he'd found her.

"You're one of them! One of the fae."

"Am I?"

"Of course you are! You conjured the fog and shifted the paths."

"Did I?"

"You're not human, like me," Hannah explains, feeling as though she is talking to an especially dense adult.

"Are you?" his voice warps, warbling on the faint wind and pitching higher to resemble Hannah's voice. She shudders. It's unnatural. Even on recordings, she hates hearing her own tone echoed at her.

"Stop that."

"Stop what?"

"Answering my questions with questions. Knock it off," she says, feeling her cheeks flare with annoyance. "Do you know where my sister is?"

The faerie doesn't answer her query. He stares at her with cold, empty eyes for a long moment. Then he throws back his head and laughs. It is a strange, cold-hearted, raucous thing— an approximation of a human laugh, one with no joy or mirth or humor behind it.

Hannah shudders. She hates her fear. This faerie will not intimidate her, not when he is her only lead toward finding Cecelia. Steeling her resolve, she tightens her grip on her pocketknife.

When he finishes enjoying his one-sided joke, his head swivels around to face her, and he holds up a bony, clawed finger. "I know the things you seek. Are you prepared to pay the price? The secret things of the world earn their cost." The fake smile distorts into a sinister stare.

Hannah pauses as her mind races ahead of her mouth. What does she remember from the stories? He doesn't ask an unusual question, but it strikes her as odd. Do real faeries even follow the stories' rules? Before she can gain his information, she needs the answer to a different question. "What do you offer me, and at what cost?"

"Ahh." He hums, reverting to the smiling face as if it's a preset on a machine. "I offer you the secret knowledge of this forest. It contains guidance to wherever your heart leads, and the graces of enchantress queens to unlock its powers. Come with me. You will learn whatever you set your mind to."

A tug of doubt dampens her excitement, but Hannah cannot ignore the anticipation building in her chest. This might be her chance. With knowledge of the faerie forest, she could find out where the Piper took Cecelia. With enchantments, she could track her sister, take on the monster, and bring her sister home safe.

"You've already passed my tests by traveling so far and freeing the weasel from the rats. In doing so, you've proven your character," he continues. "You'd be a fool to pass up such a powerful ally as myself."

If she doesn't take his deal, she may wander—and wonder—forever, alone, helpless, and ignorant in a harsh wood. But if she makes a contract with this being? Dreams of exploration without the threat of harm flash before her eyes. She stands on the precipice of an incredible opportunity. The land would be open to her and Cecelia. They would be able to go on so many marvelous adventures! It might be worth the risk. He seems nice, if he's rewarding her for saving Kit-Kat.

"What do you want from me?" Hannah asks tentatively. Where is Kit-Kat, anyway? She hasn't seen the little mustelid since the fog rose.

"All I want is your name," the faerie says casually, leaning forward to shake her hand.

Hannah hesitates long enough for her gaze to land on the object in his other hand. The fog has thinned as they've talked, revealing a pipe. The musical instrument resembles a recorder made of dark wood carved with a warping, spiraling design. Recognition flashes through her mind and dread knots her stomach.

"Are you prepared to pay?" he asks her.

The mockingbird's warning flashes through her mind. Hannah has played the fool.

Are you prepared to pay the Piper?

Chapter 7
The Chase

HIS IS A trick! Her foe stands before her and she hadn't even noticed! She had been about to sell her soul to him with a smile. Why doesn't he play his instrument? If he's here, where is Cecelia? Disgust and anger replace Hannah's fear. She takes a menacing step forward, intent on wiping the condescending grin off his smug face.

"You stole her! Give me back my sister!"

The Piper's demeanor switches from friendly trader to cheated dealer in a second, his grin melting into a sneer, wings twitching. "Your sister belongs to me."

"She belongs at home! Return her to me, at once!" Hannah lunges for the instrument, but the Piper raises it above her head, growing twenty feet in size, scraping the trees' canopies as he taunts her.

"You can join your sister! My court offers many wonders for wards who play by my rules," he promises, raising the pipe to his lips.

Hannah can only gawk as the first note plays, but something tugs her back. A jerk on her pant leg trips her before she makes another move. She shakes her foot with her next step, but sharp claws dig into her socks. She spares a glance at her shoe.

"Kit-Kat!"

The weasel chirps before scampering off. He stops, turns, and jerks his head, gesturing for Hannah to follow, then rushes back to pull on her pant leg again. Her friend has returned to guide her to freedom! As Hannah turns to follow Kit-Kat, she remembers Cecelia's warning from the night she went missing.

You can only hear him when he's coming for you.

Hannah breaks into a sprint as the Piper's song begins, ringing loud and clear in her ears.

"I don't need your help!" she shouts back, and though thrilled with terror, she hopes she sounds triumphant in her escape.

The tree cover grows dark, and the brambles edge closer. They spring to movement at the sound of the flute and grasp at her legs, trying to pull her back toward the Piper. The keening notes curl over the wind, reaching her loud and clear. She shakes her head at the haunting music, but her steps falter.

Trapped between the notes are secrets Hannah could only dream of. The tune tells of terrific sights—trees of fire, moonlight made into marzipan, stars captured in crystals. Her sensations blur together, smelling sweet spiced cider, honeysuckle nectar, and ambrosia, in the spaces between the notes. Maybe the Piper's price wouldn't be so high. Not if she hears the end of the song. Not if she unlocks the answers in the melody. It's so close now, she has to stop—

Kit-Kat barks at Hannah to keep up, shaking her from her trance. She stumbles but does not fall. She screams against the music until her own voice drowns out the tones. Exhausted, she stops for breath at a gnarled tree.

The Piper's hollow face peers at her from a frown of twisted knotholes in the trunk. She screams, stumbles back, and runs again. His power shifts the ground, jabbing rocks into her feet. Bugs swarm around her head, and eyes blink from every leaf. The winding string of notes twists the dying wildflowers around her feet. She hides behind another tree just long enough to catch her breath before starting headlong down the path again.

Which path? Who knows? Who cares? Kit-Kat leads, and she follows. She must escape the Piper. She runs until she outpaces the music. Until she outruns the choking vines and swarming bugs. Until she outruns the fear that she is being watched, hunted, trapped. Until her legs give out underneath her, and she collapses in a heap on the soft cover of pine needles.

Kit-Kat flops beside her, blood seeping through the bandage Hannah had tied around him, the run reopening the wound from earlier. They have to hide before the Piper catches up. She searches for a hiding spot, but they've fled so far up the mountain, the gaps between the trees are wide and sparse. She scrambles for the nearest patch of scraggly underbrush, lays belly-down on the ground, and pulls branches on top of her.

"Kit-Kat! Down here!" she hisses, and the weasel crouches beside her. Hannah hides him among the branches, too. They wait as the fog moves in on them. This time, she prepares for its disorienting effects. As the mist and darkness envelop them, Hannah's vision swirls, but she digs her boots into the dirt to ground herself, and she shoves her fingers into her ears so the pipe's song can't burrow into her mind.

The horrible, wonderful, beautiful song.

The haunting melody warps into a wailing screech. A rustling joins it as thousands of footsteps scatter the debris of the forest floor. Thousands of throats let loose a high-pitched whine. Rats sweep through the clearing in a feral, hungry wave, coordinated as if dancing to the Piper's twisted music. Hannah dares to take one finger out of her ear to reach for her pocketknife. She flips open the largest blade as the tune worms its way into her brain.

She can't remember why she opened the knife. Why is she laying on the ground in the dirty woods with pine needles in her hair? The rustling of the leaves adds such a depth to the enchanting music. It's so peaceful. She wants to lie here and nap. After such a long journey, her exhaustion crushes her. Contentment awaits, if she follows the music. She will be with Cecelia! Why does she have a knife?

"Let go of the knife," the music urges her. It knows best. Let go. Let go.

An angry hiss next to her ear disrupts the spell. Growls and pressure drive her back into the present as Kit-Kat pounces on her back. A rat squeals in pain as the weasel's teeth fling it from her neck. Hannah flinches as another rodent rakes its nails into her jacket and digs its wet nose into her ear. She jabs sideways on instinct. A squeal. The knife comes away red and slick.

A shudder runs down Hannah's spine as she hears Kit-Kat wrestling another rat. Where did they come from? How did they find her? Are they going to eat her alive? She drops the knife and plugs her ears again.

"You'll get hurt! Stop that!" she hisses when Kit-Kat vanquishes his foe. The weasel settles, still ready for a fight, stationing himself between his charge and the swarming servants of the Piper. They killed the first two scouts. The rest of the horde scurries around the clearing, but without guides, they lose the trail on their quarry and spread out to search.

"Hide," she pleads.

Hannah's guardian refuses to lower his defense.

The tune fights past her attempts to block it, but without the full effect of the magic, Hannah resists succumbing to the trance. She squeezes her eyes shut and focuses on the rough ground against her cheek. It anchors her to reality. As the controlling charm passes over her, the rats move on in their hunt. They return in the direction they came, without noticing Hannah's hiding spot. She can't help a twinge of sorrow as she listens to the music go and strains her ears to catch the last shreds.

But go it does. After waiting an eternity, the forest quiets enough for the bones of the mountain to creak. She stays still. Only when she tires of waiting for the trees to grow does she dare breathe a sigh of relief. She emerges from her bunker and brushes needles from her curls as she scans for rats. The forest answers with serene silence. She pulls out her water bottle, takes a long drink, then lets Kit-Kat have some. They need rest, but Hannah still looks over her shoulder. Just in case.

Chapter 8
The Portal

WITH THE DANGER avoided, Hannah patches Kit-Kat's bandage and tries to collect her racing thoughts. Her mind puzzles through the Piper's words, even as it struggles to accept the Piper's reality. He said she could join her sister in his court, if she followed him, but Hannah knows now she can't trust the Piper's lies. He claimed to be willing to reward her for saving Kit-Kat from the rats, but the rats had belonged to him all along! Of course they belonged to him, the Rat-Catcher of Hamelin. She's such a fool.

What had she been planning to do against such a legendary figure, capable of bewitching a whole town full of children? Did she really expect to march up to her sister's captor and demand he let her go? She has no scheme to outsmart the tricksy fae. Hannah's as good as dead the next time the Piper comes to call. She can't help but wonder if he had let her get away, just for the sake of the game. All her gambles have brought her no closer to finding her sister. Hannah's cheeks flush with shame and anger at her weakness. What has the Piper done to Cecelia? Hannah's lost the wide-eyed girl who looks up to her for guidance and follows her lead in every silly scheme. Now what can she do to save her sister?

She had thought she was "too well prepared." Was that a trick, too? Hah!

Hannah shakes her head and stands up. It doesn't matter now. She needs a new plan to find Cecelia, and wallowing in self-pity won't do her any good. Why did he kidnap the children in the story, and how did Cecelia know he was coming for her? Why did the Piper want Hannah's name as payment? She has more questions than when she left home, and even fewer answers.

Taking a minute to gather her bearings, Hannah realizes she's far off the beaten path. Heavy branches of ancient pine trees cloak this part of the forest in darkness. Stunted underbrush clutters her way, not enough light reaching the forest floor to allow its growth. The heavy blanket of rust-red pine needles muffles her steps. The angled ground tells her she's near the top of the mountain. Beyond that, she's lost.

She turns to Kit-Kat, expecting the weasel to lead the way yet again, but he's vanished. She tries to stifle the growing anxiety and calls his name, but gets no reply. A surge of regret closes her throat. Did she scare him away?

Hannah forces herself to remember his nature as a wild animal. She can't fault him for fleeing after being attacked a second time. Naming him only made him seem tame, and she'd lured herself into a false sense of security about the weasel. He owes her nothing, and she can't expect his loyalty. She misses the small, ferocious beast, nonetheless.

She realizes now she will have to face the woods alone. Panic bells go off in the back of her brain, her parents' warnings coming to mind. She fidgets with the knife, flicking it open, then shut, then open again. How long has she been gone? All morning or all day? How can she continue when she doesn't know where she is? Her parents will have noticed she is missing by now. Did her mother cry? Is her father scouring the woods for his daughters? Part of her hopes he'll find her, but another part hopes he'll stay home. What if the Piper attacks them too, the unaware adults that they are?

She could sit down, build shelter, and wait for rescue. She's read *My Side of the Mountain* enough times to know how to build a lean-to. Her parents won't wait to call for help, and soon, search parties will storm the woods looking for both lost girls with dogs and helicopters. Who knows how long she'll have to wait. It's best to stay put, so they won't have to search far.

But she still hasn't found Cecelia, and now that she's met the Piper himself, Hannah knows her sister's fears were well-founded. She had heard his music when he was coming for her. Faeries are real and they have taken her sister. She's the only one who knows the truth, and she needs to bring Cecelia home.

A plan forms in her mind as she takes a second evaluation of her surroundings. The Piper might have captured Cecelia, and if so, he must have hidden her well. But if Cecelia had escaped to the Seelie Court, Hannah needs to also find her way there. Oberon's throne lies deep in the woods, and Hannah is deep indeed. Debris streaks the ground where the rats swarmed. First, she'll try to follow their path to find her sister. If she's stealthy enough, she might escape the Piper's notice long enough to execute a rescue plan. She will not be a puppet following the Piper's orders, but a spy. Their roles would reverse. She likes the idea of turning his own tricks on him.

Before charging off headlong, Hannah figures she should get perspective on her situation. She stands, stretches, and looks around for something to use as a vantage point. Soon, she spots a pine with thick branches, low enough to reach. *Pinus strobus.* Naming it grounds her whirling emotions in comforting familiarity. Hannah prefers maples for climbing and she cringes as she gets a palm full of sticky sap, but she pulls herself upward regardless—hand over hand, limb by limb—until she reaches a gap high enough she can see most of the forest floor.

No paths or signs break up the blanket of trees, nothing points toward home. She climbs higher, above the tops of the other small pines, to reach the light of day. The sunbeams warm her face, and she takes a moment to catch her breath and enjoy the pleasant breeze as the pine needles rustle around her. There's a gap in the distance, where the branches don't crowd together, creating a blank space in the canopy. A clearing? Her curls brush around her ears as the breeze toys with her hair and tickles the back of her neck. She squints and leans forward, filling her lungs with the spicy scent of evergreen, and she thinks she might jump, pet the wind, and fly. Her hand slips off the branch as she reaches for the horizon.

For a single terrifying moment, she's falling. She imagines falling, crashing through every branch, landing in a heap of broken bones. Self-preservation snaps her to her senses. She pinwheels her arm and regains her grasp on a nearby branch as her heart jumps in her chest. Her breath comes in shallow gasps, and she clings to the trunk for dear life until her adrenaline stops racing.

You're not a fae. You don't have wings, you idiot.

She avoids looking down and remembers she has her spyglass—a much safer way to get a closer look at the distant clearing. She slips it out of her bag, careful not to drop the precious item, and brings it up to her eye to investigate.

Where there was only a vacancy before, a splash of gold-red leaves rises above the dark forest's greens and grays. Hannah lowers the spyglass, and the strange tree disappears. She raises it again, lowers it, raises it, checking three times before she believes what she's seeing. Through the lens, the magical tree towers above all the other pines by stories, a giant among saplings, spreading thick branches ablaze in unique autumn colors that have persisted long after the other deciduous trees have lost their raiment for the winter. It's still too distant to make out details, but it's there. A beacon.

And since when was her spyglass enchanted with True Sight? If only she had realized its secret power sooner. This tool could have saved her precious hours wandering around the woods. Now that she knows how to use its abilities, she'll find Cecelia in no time!

Hannah memorizes her position and the direction of the enormous tree, making a few marks on her notepad to figure out her orientation relative to the shadows and the sun. Then she crams her pad and spyglass back in her bag and scrambles down the tree as fast as possible to set off into the woods. Hannah zips up her coat and pulls the hood low over her face so she's cloaked in the drab green, hoping it will help her blend into the surrounding forest. She follows the zig-zagging path of rat tracks through the trees beside the trail, being careful not to ruin the fine marks and stepping around any snapping sticks.

The new objective gives Hannah energy, and she picks up speed as she learns to recognize the signs of the Piper's passing. When she looks through her spyglass, she sees unfamiliar vines where they should not grow and trail markers on the trees in a script that reminds her of the code she uses with Cecelia. When she gets too close to the vines, her senses warp with a smell she cannot place at first, but comes to recognize as pungent urine and rotting fruit. After a while, she learns to recognize the lingering scent of his awful magic. Phantom whispers of the music play at the edges of her perception, but when she turns to find the source, there's nothing there.

She shudders when she finds traces of the Piper, but she reminds herself that knowledge is power. Now, she knows what to expect from her foe. She has the Sight. Through her spyglass, she finds the secrets of the fae. Soon Hannah sprints headlong toward her goal, driven by the satisfaction of solving the puzzle. This run fills her with exhilarating confidence. She is not a scared, lost little girl fleeing a bogeyman. She is a hunter.

As the forest thins before the clearing, she skids to a stop at the threshold. She retreats to the safety of the tree line and sits on her heels to observe from her hiding spot. The pines grow thin and stunted as she nears the border. Someone had taken care to mark the ground with flat rocks forming a pathway around the edge. So close to the faerie circle, she doesn't need the spyglass to see magic's imprint on her surroundings. Here, the magic smells of honeysuckle and spiced cider–sharply different from the Piper's magic. Bright red-and-white toadstools growing between and around the cracks in the stones beckon, delectable or deadly. They might be *Amanita muscaria*, but she can't be sure it's not a lookalike.

In the center of the faerie ring stands an ancient tree. Gnarled roots protrude from the soil, and mushrooms cling to the outside bark. The trunk of the tree is hollow and striped with burn marks, the clear result of a lightning strike. The opening must measure a couple feet wide, big enough to fit a child. Despite the damage, maroon and vermilion leaves flutter like wildfire against the surrounding drab winter branches and evergreens. Metallic gold sparkles along the autumn leaves' edges and veins, and when Hannah looks closer, she realizes they're actually *on fire*, but not consumed. Sparks dance along the blades without burning them.

She doesn't recognize the species, and she doesn't think she could identify it, even if she had all the guidebooks in the world. Not a bird chirps, not a leaf rustles, not even a whisper from the wind breaks the silence. Despite the vibrancy, this place is deader than the dormancy of winter. Beautiful, but wrong. All wrong.

Dappled shadows dance across the mossy green ring. Hannah blinks at the brightness as brilliant sunshine cuts through the leaves. The sun rises high overhead, proving she hasn't lost time, and she enjoys a sense of smug satisfaction.

For now. Once she crosses into the faerie circle, there's no telling if time will slow or speed up or keep passing at the same rate as in the human world.

Hannah creeps forward until her toes bump the edge of the stone ring. She tightens her grip on the straps of her backpack, her senses snapping back to her as she finds herself terrified at the implications of what she's found. It might be a trap. Another trick of the Piper, more cunning than illusions, luring her into a false sense of security. But he is nowhere in sight, and no flute music invades her mind. She snatches a twig from the ground and pokes a pale, bulbous mushroom. It puffs under the impact, stinky and green. She holds her breath and tries not to breathe in the spores, hoping she didn't attract his attention.

When no rats descend to rend her into shreds, another thought occurs to her. If the Piper didn't make the clearing, who did? Hannah recalls the message in the flour, written by the house brownie, Hazel.

Find her in the Seelie Court.

Can Hannah trust the strange but friendly creature who has lived under their noses for years? Could the answer lie within the faerie ring? Maybe Hannah will find allies, or perhaps Cecelia escaped the Piper's grasp! After all, the Piper lies.

Hannah sits back on her heels again, considering her options. She pulls her spyglass and inspects the tree more closely through its magnifying lens, but notices nothing new or any less strange. Nothing but trouble will come from blundering into the ring. She could sleep a hundred years like Rip Van Winkle, or journey to a new world like Narnia where she won't be able to return home. It could lead her closer to her sister, or straight to her enemies.

But the ring is such an obvious sign. She's been hunting for faeries, and now she finds herself on their doorstep. If she had found this ring before she met the Piper, she wouldn't have hesitated stomping into it. She likely got the fae's attention by poking the mushroom anyhow, like ringing a doorbell. This is the lead that she needs, no matter how much it frightens her.

Her stomach twists inside her as she makes up her mind, and it takes effort to straighten her shaking legs into a standing position. She doesn't want to go on adventures anymore. She knows she's not a warrior or a cunning mage. There's only a slight chance she'll survive another encounter with the Piper. But Cecelia's still missing, and hope rings its promise across the border of the faerie ring.

Her sister needs a hero. Hannah's not as clever as she thought she was, but heroism is about boldness, right? Even though the faerie ring makes her hands sweat and spine prickle with terror, she must be bold for Cecelia. Hannah takes a deep breath to steady herself and steps forward.

Chapter 9

The Ambush

WHEN HANNAH CROSSES the threshold, the ground lurches beneath her feet. A groan fills her ears as branches erupt from the dirt around the border. They writhe and twist around each other, forming a wall behind her, encircling the clearing.

She's trapped.

Someone pounces on Hannah—a small, scrappy child, all sharp elbows and knees, bears down on her with a fury. The attacker wears a rat-shaped mask that covers the top part of their human face. Hannah shrieks and ducks on instinct, missing a punch aimed at her temple. She drops the spyglass on reflex, and there's the sickening sound of shattering glass as it hits a flagstone.

The next punch catches her in the stomach, and she staggers backward as it knocks the wind out of her. Hannah gasps for breath as panic seizes her lungs and she lands against the tangle of thorn bushes that hadn't been there a minute ago. Barbed hooks catch her jacket like Velcro and hold her in place. She flinches as one digs into the soft skin of her neck above the collar. Urgency pushes a scream from her throat. How did they grow so quickly? And who is this random child attacking her?

Hannah rips her sleeve free from the thorns. On instinct, she claws for the child's mask, catching the edge under the chin, and tears it free. The child shrieks, the high-pitched sound painfully piercing Hannah's sensitive ears, and jerks her face away. Hannah doesn't get a glimpse of her features, but she stumbles away as the child winds up for another punch. Hannah runs, desperate to win this sick game of tag, and her attacker follows without bothering to retrieve her lost mask. Hannah's feet skid on the soft moss, causing her to slip. She lunges, rolls, scrambles to her feet, and takes off again.

Her strides are longer than the girl's, and she keeps her distance for a short time. They round the clearing as Hannah looks for a gap in the thorns. Finding none, she dashes for the massive tree to put an obstacle between them. She hazards a glance behind her. The girl reaches for Hannah's jacket as her back presses up against the trunk. Hannah spins, and a fist slams against the wood as she whirls behind the obstacle, putting it between them. They fake lunges back and forth, but with the tree in the way, the girl can't get close enough to hit.

Hannah's mind races, searching for an escape or an advantage. She needs the high ground. When the girl lunges right, she dodges left. Ignoring the hollow tree trunk, which would trap her in a corner, she leaps for the nearest branch and dangles for a moment, fingers slipping. She braces her feet against the stepped fungi, crushing them beneath her boots as she pulls herself up, climbing as fast as her arms and legs can take her.

The girl grabs for Hannah's ankles as her feet swing out of reach, then follows behind, but Hannah is too fast. She jumps to one branch and climbs higher. The feral child clambers up the opposite side. She works her way around the trunk, but Hannah swings lower, and they continue their dance above the ground.

The girl growls in frustration and stops chasing. They can't fight up here—at least, not with fists. The moment of hesitation gives Hannah the chance to catch her breath and study the girl's face through the branches. For a moment, recognition dawns in her mind. Is that Cecelia?

The girl looks young, maybe ten, about the same age as Hannah's sister, and the features match perfectly. But as Hannah takes in the rest of the child's appearance, the resemblance falls apart. Her hair is wavy, black, and cut in a bob similar to Hannah's own hairstyle. Cecelia's was always long, and the matted, choppy sections imply this girl cut it herself with something dull. It takes more than a night in the woods to tangle hair like that.

She wears an elfin costume: an oversized beige tunic with dagged edges, tied at the waist with a knotted belt. It slips off one shoulder, showing a scar snaking from her neck down her back before slipping under the collar. Her gray cloak has a cowl but it slipped back in their chase. The garment is threadbare with ragged edges, and Hannah wonders how she moved so easily through the tree without catching it on branches. Loose brown breeches are frayed at the hems and knees, where holes have worn through the fabric. Despite the chill, she goes barefoot. Poor thing must be freezing beneath all the dirt caked on her arms and legs.

Besides, Hannah knows her sister, and Cecelia would never attack anyone. She's the type to run away when she's scared, not pick a fight. This little lost child isn't her sister. Hannah's been so fixated on finding Cecelia, she lost all reason during her panic. But that begs a better question.

"Who are you?" Hannah asks.

"I'm a weapon." The girl shrugs and reaches into her pocket, but Hannah can't tell what she pulls out through the burning leaves. Hannah hadn't considered the embers when she'd climbed up the tree, but as she brushes past them, she realizes the flames are as cool as creek water.

The girl scowls. "You must be new here."

"Why are you fighting me? I never hurt you!"

"Don't matter. You're the target."

"Did the Piper send you?"

"Who else would? I missed the first little imp, but you ran straight into my trap." The girl gives her a wicked smile. "He'll reward me."

Hannah stifles the panic that arises from the threat. "But why does he want us? Where's my sister?"

"Sister?" The girl crouches on the branch and reaches into a leather pouch at her waist. "I don't mind the Piper's business."

When the girl pauses on the word, Hannah seizes on her hesitation. Maybe she could be an ally. "My sister is a little girl, like me. Your age. Dark-brown hair, like mine, but longer. Barefoot and wearing a nightgown. She disappeared last night from our home."

"Even if I knew, why should I tell you?"

Hannah groans in frustration and tightens her grip on the branch. *Be calm*, she tells herself. As long as the girl keeps talking, she's not attacking, and Hannah might gain valuable information.

"Did the Piper steal you, too? I'll help you escape. Stop this, and let me help you," Hannah pleads.

"Don't say such stupid things," the girl says through a gap-toothed sneer. She raises her arm in an arc, and a zipping sound grazes past Hannah's ear. A sharp burst of pain hits her thigh a second later. She winces and jerks back, losing her balance on the branch she's holding.

Hannah bites back a shout as her stomach plummets with gravity's pull, but she catches herself on a branch in time. She uses the momentum from her near-fall to swing herself to safety. She crashes into a thick branch, clinging to it for dear life as her cheek presses against the rough bark. The girl raises her arm and whips a strip of leather over her head. She has a sling.

Another stone misses Hannah by an inch. Cursing, the girl loads her weapon again.

Cover. Hannah needs cover, the high ground only a liability now. Hannah braces herself against the deep hum of the sling as it sings in her ears. Two, three, four more projectiles slam into the wood with hollow *thunks*. The leaves spark and release embers as the girl moves to a higher angle. Hannah shifts in sync, keeping the trunk between them as cover. How long can she keep up the dance before she missteps? She's a baby bird that will break its wings when—not if—she falls.

Her foot slips on a thin branch, and fall she does, stomach slamming against it as she drops a few feet before catching her weight.

"Stop this!" she begs, groaning as she rights herself.

The girl only responds with a low, angry hum. She stows the sling in her pocket, pulls out a small pouch, and slams it onto her branch. A black dust erupts from beneath her, before something green and winding emerges from the bark. The fine seeds take root. Tendrils curl around her feet, anchoring the girl in place. Then the seeds sprout vines that shoot along the branch toward Hannah.

Hannah tries to dodge, but they're too fast. Tendrils snap around her arms and legs, trapping her in an instant. Hannah jerks her hands away to grab the knife in her pocket, but she can't reach it in time. The girl's humming changes pitch, and the vines yank Hannah's arms above her head. Hannah is suspended now, dangling above the hollow of the tree trunk, limbs tethered like a puppet. The humming pauses when the girl gives a cruel laugh at Hannah's terror and pain, stopping the plants movement with it, then the droning resumes.

The girl controls the plants with that noise, Hannah realizes, the same way the Piper controls the rats with his music. Hannah's wrists and shoulders wrench with each pull of the vines. Tears prick at her eyes, but she can't escape.

Metal clashes in the distant forest. Tangled in the vines, Hannah can't turn to see the source of the new sound. The girl freezes, and her humming cuts short. Hannah glances downward to check how far she'll fall. Too far.

Several figures, alien and armored to the hilt, charge into the clearing. Hannah can only stare as they take off and swarm toward the girl, insectoid wings and metallic blades flashing. They're as large as humans and moving as fast as wasps, circling to surround Hannah and her attacker.

The girl glances from her quarry to her pursuers then flees. The vines follow and launch the girl from the tree, who swings out of the faerie ring and into the woods. She flies between two of the flying beings, tumbles across the ground, and regains her feet at a run. In a moment, she disappears into the woods, her cloak fluttering behind her. Thorn bushes arise from her footsteps, blocking anyone from following her path.

With their puppet master gone, the vines suspending Hannah loosen. She clenches her hand into a fist, grasping for an anchor, but without the song to animate them into action, the limp plants slip around her wrists and retreat out of reach. She hangs in the air for a sickening instant of stomach-dropping horror before the gaping maw of the hollow tree trunk swallows her whole in its darkness. Hannah screams.

She falls.

And falls.

And

  F

    A

   L

 L

  S

deeper than the tree is tall, plunging into the earth below, gasping as she braces herself for an impact that doesn't come. Dooooowwwwn the rabbit hole like Alice into Wonderland. Heart racing, hands grasping, feet kicking, then—

CRASH!

Chapter 10

The Capture

HANNAH LANDS IN a heap of leaves, but the fall knocks the wind from her lungs, and her chest aches as she tries to gasp for fresh air. Her arm twists underneath her body and her shoulder screams. Her head pounds, dizzy from the impact. She can't move, not yet.

She waits for the pain to fade, and it does, replaced by exhaustion wrapping around her like a shroud. Something slimy wriggles over her fingers and she twitches it away. She would let herself slumber among the rotting leaves and earthworms if she could, but her anxiety prevents her from succumbing to the earth.

Whatever she'd expected when she crossed the threshold, it hadn't been *that*.

She begrudgingly blinks open her eyes to assess her surroundings. She's in a deep pit, a cavern beneath the tree's roots. A pinprick of light shines above her from the trunk's open hollow. Was that whole clearing a disguised portal to this underground entrance?

She squints at the distant daylight. No bodies block out the sun. They're not following her through the Portal Tree, so she assumes the fae guards, or whoever they were, have chased Hannah's attacker away from the clearing.

Hannah shifts her weight off her arm with a throbbing ache. *Too many questions.* She's free for the moment. She needs to escape while she still can.

Can't panic. Stay calm. Survive. Roll over. Keep moving. Keep searching. Stand. Don't black out. One step at a time. Find Cecelia. Dust off. Get home. Have dinner.

No. Too many steps. Back up. Reach for the flashlight. Flick it on. Stand up.

Stand up.

Stand UP!

A tunnel opens before her, and though she can't see beyond her own nose, it's her only way. Hannah tries to lift her arms above her head and moans as her shoulder pops back into place. She could try climbing out, using the tree roots as handholds, but it's too far, and she's not sure her aching arms could pull her without risking another fall. Besides, she would only emerge into the battle above. Of course, by following the path before her, she's venturing into unknown dangers.

She doesn't care. Walking is easier than climbing.

Hannah takes a deep breath that fills her cramping lungs with musty air and makes her chest and back ache. Her feet burn from hiking, and her knee throbs, whether from the exercise or the fall, she isn't sure. Despite the pain, she can stand steadily, so she can keep going. Onward, for Cecelia.

The tunnel ceiling rises enough that Hannah can walk upright as long as she crouches beneath the occasional rock or tree root. She pulls her pocketknife out and wields it in her free hand, more for comfort than for any real defense. Choking fear still clings to her like tendrils, but the small weight in her hand brings her slight relief. She's not defenseless.

She reaches a dozen paces into the tunnel, before a hand clamps around her wrist and wrenches the knife from her grasp.

Hannah screams at the unexpected touch, but the sound dies as another hand clamps over her mouth. Yet another grabs her flashlight and pulls her arm behind her back. Someone pushes her forward, and she stumbles over loose dirt. She writhes, trying to break their grip. The hand over her mouth earns a vicious bite. She clamps her teeth into a twiggy texture and bites down like a dog. The assailant howls and lets go of Hannah's face, but grabs her by the collar of her jacket instead.

Hannah's elbow jams into the dark as her flashlight clatters to the ground. Where had they come from? Too many strange hands grasping, tugging. Restraints bind her wrists as she's dragged forward with a rough pull.

"Let me go!" she screeches as soon as she gets her mouth free of the hand.

Her captors don't respond as they tow her out of the tunnel and into a cavern lit by lanterns hung on the walls. She struggles against the guards until she sees their forms for the first time: two fae with long pointed ears and camouflaged features that make Hannah's eyes shift in and out of focus. It's impossible to tell where their flesh ends and the armor growing from their bodies begins, a tough chitin layered with leather.

Hannah needs these faeries to help her, not arrest her. She needs a different strategy. To show she's not a threat, Hannah stops struggling, and the tall fae holding her right arm stumbles.

"I come in peace! You startled me! I'm sorry I fought. I'm scared. Help me," Hannah pleads, hoping against hope that her voice doesn't shake with the tremor of an approaching meltdown.

The shorter guard on her left scoffs. She has a sturdy feminine build, dark brown skin, and long hair, drooping with wisteria. It's bundled into purple locs and pulled away from her face so she can fight. Her white wings are speckled with gray, like the cabbage butterflies that live in the garden.

"Tell that to my black eye," she grumbles. A bruise spreads around one eyelid, and viscous tears, like the ooze of an ink cap mushroom, drop from her lashes. The other eye shows a green iris around a horizontal pupil, like a goat's. Hannah should remember their scientific names, but she's too preoccupied to recall them now.

"I'm sorry," Hannah repeats with an exasperated huff. "Don't grab me without warning next time. I'd like to see you keep a cool head when you're ambushed in the dark."

"What were ye doing, nosing around the Seelie Realm, spy?" interrogates the tall one, bending over and pointing a bony finger under Hannah's nose. Hannah can't tell if it's a piece of armor fit over the fae's hand or the exposed skeleton itself. The guard's curly red hair is piled into a bun that teeters with every gesture, and when she sneers, her teeth are fanged. Acorn earrings swing with each syllable, and oak leaves swirl in asymmetric patterns down her tabard.

"I'm not a spy!" Hannah protests. "I'm human."

Short Wisteria juts her chin out. Hannah assigns the guards names in her mind, and guesses she's a woman from the long leafy hair and the treble voice, like a bird chirping. "Like the Taken the others chased off—a spy. Which Master do you belong to?"

Hannah vehemently shakes her head. She knows nothing about spying or masters. Her voice only wavers a little when she argues. "What? No! I'm here for my sister. She went missing last night. Did you take her?"

"Nay, we don't take changelings anymore. Ye got the wrong court," says the one Hannah's dubbed Tall Oak. Her voice is lower and gruff, with an old fashioned accent Hannah can't quite place.

"I don't know what that means," Hannah cries. "The stories don't make sense anymore. I'm lost and tired, and I only want my sister back." She slumps to her knees. They must deem her pathetic enough to release, because Tall Oak lowers her bony finger with a sigh and gestures to Short Wisteria to let her go. Hannah doesn't run.

"You caused quite the ruckus," Short Wisteria says, looking her up and down.

Now it's Hannah's turn to scoff. "I don't suppose you would have revealed yourselves without one? Not even if I asked nicely, with tea cakes?"

Tall Oak laughs. "Aye. Most likely not."

"We make it a point to avoid your kind," the other responds.

"Always wanting wishes."

"And spying."

Hannah makes a petulant frown. "I swear I wasn't spying. I was searching. Big difference. I was trying to be found."

"Hrm. That ye were," Tall Oak says flatly.

"Will you help me?"

"We'll bring you to the Monarchs and let them question you. You're quite the curiosity, you are," Short Wisteria explains.

Hannah looks at her own disheveled outfit. She wonders if they mean her mismatched clothes or the fact that she looks and feels like a soiled handkerchief left out in an autumn storm. She scrubs tears off her wet face with the dirty sleeve of her jacket, hoping it doesn't leave a stain. "Thank you."

The guard rolls her eyes and pulls her ahead. So much for their truce.

Hannah follows along, forcing herself to dampen her expectations with patience and caution. Now that she isn't fighting for her life, she takes the chance to observe her surroundings. The cavern is spacious—so large, Hannah forgets they are underground. They follow a walkway made of flat paving stones that cut through a carpet of moss. Glowing spots hang from the ceiling to provide light, the sprawling undersides of the mushrooms that outline the faerie ring. The damp, musty air works into her lungs despite her deliberately shallow breathing. She imagines greenery growing inside her chest.

The guards lead Hannah from the cavern through a dark tunnel that twists one way, then another. She reaches out with one hand to follow along the wall, and they don't stop her. It does little to help her sense of direction. The walls of the tunnel branch out into varying pathways, and they turn so many times, Hannah is sure they must have retraced their path at least twice. Seashells in the woods won't help her out of this maze.

Something roars. The distant thundering grows louder, while her captors force her ever forward. Hannah does not dare to slow her steps, even as dread knots in her stomach. But the earth beneath their feet takes a sharp slant upwards, and they emerge from the mouth of a cave behind a waterfall.

Resounding water echoes off the rocks, and Hannah lets out a sigh of relief as she realizes the roaring was never a monster. Mist spraying her face, she rounds the barrier and emerges into a forest of blazing red. Autumn leaves grace the branches of trees that tower amidst lumbering giants, who shuffle with the *CREAAAAKK* of bones and stone. Gryphons make nests atop the crags and ridges on their backs. Hannah cranes her neck to bask in their presence.

A million twinkling stars hang in the dark sky, unrecognizable constellations in a myriad of colors. A galaxy of fireflies flash their dancing lights. The stone path continues before them, lined with late-seasoned wildflowers that grow as high as her waist. Garlands holding golden lanterns draw moths that flit around the troop; one of the insects even lands on her hair. Hannah can't stifle a laugh of delight as it perches on her head. The species is foreign to her, with filmy, bright blue wings and fuzzy antennae. When the bug flits off, Hannah catches Tall Oak grinning at her from the corner of her eye.

Soon, they approach a palace enthroned amongst the trees. Alabaster rises in a pattern more like lace than stone, creating bridges between branches and courtyards within clearings. The white structure, marbled with brown streaks, melds with the surrounding bark, and Hannah shrinks back from what she assumes is a massive web before recognizing that no spider wove this masterpiece. It buzzes with the voices and movements of a crowd assembled for a ball.

The guards march her up the front steps and into a ballroom filled with fae. Again, Hannah wonders how their insectoid wings don't stick to the pillars. She touches one and finds the sparkling substance is cold, smooth rock, not spider silk. Perhaps this trap is more metaphorical.

At first glance, it looks like a masquerade party—figures dressed in ornate costumes designed to impress. But as they spin, Hannah can't tell which features are fake and which belong to their faces. A few faeries gawk at her, while others revel in their mad dances, thoughtless to leaving Hannah and her escorts space to pass. The fragrance of magic makes her head swim. Music soars and twists into impossible shapes, a lively tune that winds around her and pulls her into its intoxicating thrum.

What if the Piper is here? With his mask of a face and mismatched costume, he'd fit right into the motley crowd. Hannah scans the scene, but with their fungi crowns and flower gowns, she can't tell one faerie from another. He might be whirling among the dancers, or hiding among the dozens of musicians in the band. They play dulcimers and harps, lutes and lyres, drums of all sorts, and of course, pipes and flutes. Any one of them might be the Piper in disguise. The music carries the jaunty beat of the dance, multiple melodies twisting together, but Hannah can't enjoy the performance.

It's too overwhelming.

Stop.

Stop everything!

Hannah shoves her fingers into her ears and resists the urge to scream and crawl out of her skin as the attention and noise grates into her brain. Sinking to the floor with a sob, she blocks out the urge to twirl to the tune—too many colors, too much noise, too many people! She doesn't want to dance with them! She doesn't want to be here! The Piper's coming for her!

The guards grab her arms, and she shrieks at their unexpected touch. She tries to bat them away, but their firm grip pulls her from the ballroom. As they move away from the source of the sound and the smell of magic, the urge to fall into step fades, and for the first time, she appreciates her guards towing her toward their destination.

Chapter 11
The Test

THE GUARDS DRAG Hannah, still shaking, into an antechamber, then let her go. She still hasn't recovered from her meltdown. All her senses reverberate with an overload of input; every muscle aches, and her head throbs. She pulls her hood over her head and curls into a ball, hugging herself tightly to ground herself.

"What's the matter?" Short Wisteria asks.

"The music," Hannah chokes out. "The Piper's after me. Help."

"The Piper?" Tall Oak leans down so she's peering under Hannah's hood, looking her in the eye. Hannah flinches away as she continues speaking. "We won't allow *him* to hurt ye here."

"If the Monarchs allow you to stay, the Seelie Court will help you escape him," the other guard assures her. "You just need to pass their test first."

"A test?" Hannah feels her stomach drop with dismay.

Tall Oak shrugs. "Dunno what they'll have ye do. It's different for everyone."

"If your intentions are true, you'll pass through," Short Wisteria intones.

"Are ye ready?" Tall Oak rests her hand on the doorknob of the throne room.

Hannah shudders, takes a deep breath, and nods. She squares her shoulders, throws back her hood, and prepares to meet the Monarchs, as the two guards march her into the throne room. She must be strong. For Cecelia.

The room ripples with magical energy: waves of warm and cold air and sweet and spicy scents roll over Hannah, sending goosebumps up her arms. Two seats stand atop a raised dais in the semi-circular space. The Queen sits distinguished in a silvery celestial gown. She has a wild look in her large golden eyes, and her skin is marbled indigo and violet. Black hair spills like clouds of ink over her shoulders, and a tiara of diamonds forms a constellation in her curls. Her wings are those of a luna moth, *Actias luna*, huge and pale green. She holds a glass of a chocolaty liquid in danger of spilling over the rim, as she picks delicacies from the nearest tray.

If the Queen embodies the night, the King personifies the day. He is sprawled sideways, knees kicked over the armrest of his throne. Dark freckles spatter his face, sunspots on pale yellow skin framed by a tousle of gold-red curls. He wears a crown made from a wreath of ivy. His wings match those of the monarch butterfly, *Danaus lexippus*.

How fitting, thinks Hannah with a wry internal laugh. He wears a plum-colored robe and sandals that dangle from his feet. One hand holds a glass of sparkling champagne, and the other, a leg of meat. He laughs with a doting attendant, and his dark eyes flash with enjoyment.

When he notices Hannah, he waves the meat leg at her to come forward.

"What do we have here?" hums the Queen.

Tall Oak leads Hannah up with a sharp salute, lifting her dappled gray-brown moth wings high and proud. "We found this one trespassing in the sacred Portal Tree after fighting the Taken. She said she's looking for her sister, so we told her we'd let you decide her fate."

"Well done, soldier!" says the King. "What fun, what excitement! A wonderful opportunity!"

Hannah shudders to wonder what that means. She steps forward, abruptly sober and wary.

"May we have your name, little one?" the Queen croons. Hannah sets her jaw. She prepared for this. The Piper taught her a valuable lesson. She knows better than to trust these powerful beings, no matter how nice they might seem at first.

"You may call me Maria," she answers carefully. There are millions of Marias in the world, and they bear a good name—a safe, powerful, beautiful one, but not hers.

"Let us offer you these sweet cakes then, Maria," the King says. A platter materializes out of the air, overflowing with luscious tarts.

"I humbly decline, for I had my meal at home."

They grin, an identical, sharp-toothed grin. "What do you seek from the Seelie Court?" the Queen asks.

"My sister."

"Which sister do you want?" the King asks.

Hannah shakes her head at the ridiculous question. "Mine."

"My dear," the Queen purrs, "you'll have to be more specific than that."

Yes, Hannah needs an exact request, lest they pull a horrid trick on her for their amusement. Lest they endanger Ce—her sister. Best to avoid even thinking about her name in their presence. Who knows if they can read minds? She won't tell this king and queen about her meeting with the Piper. The less they know, the better.

"I believe your people took my sister during the thunderstorm, between midnight and seven this morning. She spoke of the Piper's flutes on the wind. I couldn't hear his music because he wasn't coming for me. But she had vanished by the next morning. I wish for her freedom, to return to our home and our parents."

"You wish, hmmmmmm?" the King muses. "We do not owe you a wish, but yours is a noble plea."

Hannah's heart leaps with hope.

"Why do you seek her here?" the Queen asks.

Why? A million reasons, but should she reveal her heart now? Hannah ventures for a safe answer. "Because our mother and father will be cross with us if we return late for dinner."

"Why?" insists the King.

Hannah's stomach turns as they press into her with a driving tone. The Monarchs' façade of indulgent amusement drops, leaving behind hard, angry eyes. Is her request so unreasonable?

"Because she left without a word, and I am worried about her."

"Why?" hisses the Queen.

"Because I miss her. Because I love her."

They give her those same sharp-toothed grins again. Hannah wants to slap those smiles right off their silly little faces. She holds her breath for an agonizing moment.

The King finally answers with another question. "How will you know her when you cannot call her by name?"

Around Hannah appear a dozen figures—girls identical to Cecelia. They gaze at her with wild, desperate expressions. She shrinks back, but another materializes behind her. Hannah scowls at the ring of imposters as she recognizes the illusion. One Cecelia will be the true sister, trapped in the game. The others? Phantoms meant to lead her astray. She has to choose.

Hannah closes her eyes and takes a deep breath to steady herself.

"I know her by her footsteps, when she creeps into my room at night to watch the thunderstorms." Each Cecelia takes a step toward her, menacing. Three of them sound wrong—too heavy. Cecelia tiptoes to sneak up on her older sister. Hannah snaps open her eyes and, with a wave of her hand, banishes those impostors into puffs of smoke.

"I know my sister by her laugh, when I tell her a terrible pun," Hannah says. The girls laugh on command. She can't tell apart individual voices, but a few remain silent, refusing to join in the imitation. Hannah had said nothing funny to warrant a laugh. Banish. Vanish. Smoke.

"I know her by her competitiveness, when she jumps off the top of the maple tree to beat me in a race." One flinches at the idea of breaking bones, but her sister never hesitates at great heights. Banish. Vanish. Smoke. Down to two.

"I know her by her kindness, when she sneaks our cats and chickens and horse extra treats, and not just the cats, but the shadelings and the house brownie too, even though nobody else believes in them." One of the Cecelias rolls her eyes when Hannah mentions Hazel the house brownie. The other keeps her gaze fixed on the ground, hands twisted together behind her back.

Hannah banishes the last impostor without a second glance. One Cecelia remains. Hannah locks eyes with the girl through the smoke, squinting through tears. "I know my sister," she says, relief choking her voice. "And she knows me."

With a flick of the King's wrist, the test ends. Conjured wind cuts through the smoke. The figure that stands opposite Hannah has the same dark-brown eyes and dark hair that glows golden around the edges in the candlelight. She doesn't wear the same nightgown as the night she left home. Instead, she has a new dress, simple but flowy in its design, embroidered around the hems. It's paired with leggings and tall boots that curl at the toes. Hannah could excuse this, but she has *pointed ears*. Blue lichen that climbs up the side of her face and circles her brow breaks the familiar picture. Wings sprout from her back, blue when they're open, brown with orange eyespots when they're closed.

Yet she is unmistakably Cecelia when she tackles Hannah in a hug.

Chapter 12

The Revelation

ECELIA IS A changeling. She is a faerie. She is not supposed to be a sister.

Conflicting feelings war in Cecelia's chest as she clings to Hannah and buries her face in the soft sweater that smells of home—woodsmoke from the stove, Mom's bread, stray cat hairs tickling her nose. She'll never share those things again— the Seelie Court is her home now—but she cannot deny the comforting familiarity. She never thought she'd see her safe, steadfast elder sister again, but she'd made her peace with her decision when she had first arrived in Seelie.

How is Hannah here? Cecelia's stomach sinks, knowing the human's presence will bring nothing but disaster, even as she clings to her. Cecelia's mortified to show her true face. Why must it hurt to be known?

She never meant to face the consequences of her actions. Her lies...

"I'm sorry," Cecelia whispers. What else can she say? "I love you."

Cecelia knows Hannah by her posture, by her voice, by her tears. What will she say to the apology when Cecelia's sprouted wings?

An arm awkwardly but gently wraps above her drooping wings and around her shaking shoulders. Cecelia leans into the embrace and lifts her face to give Hannah a relieved smile. Yes, she knows her sister by the protective barrier placed between her and the Monarchs.

Applause interrupts their reunion.

Queen Titania claps while King Oberon dabs at his eyes with a yellow handkerchief made of rose petals stitched together.

Hannah jerks away from the hug and fixes the Monarchs with her most withering glare.

Cecelia slips her hand into Hannah's and squeezes. *No, please don't antagonize the Monarchs. They are kind, but not nice. Powerful, but not safe.* Cecelia wants to believe they'll be better than the Piper, but her panic is too deep-set to ignore.

"What a wonderful show. How touching," Queen Titania says.

"Tests all passed with flying colors," King Oberon says with a mirthful wink at Cecelia.

Hannah opens her mouth to say something—a protest, a demand, or a question, but Cecelia can't let her older sister make a fool of herself now. Hannah came to save her; now she must save her unwitting human sister from undoing the impressive effects of passing her trial. Until they receive a promise, Cecelia can't be sure they'll be safe. It's up to her now. After all, who between them believed in faeries?

Cecelia steps forward and makes a deep curtsy, casting her eyes to the floor as etiquette lessons and survival instincts alike guide her movements. She cannot say the Piper taught her nothing, though his music was a harsh instructor. *Appear non-threatening. Show respect. Offer only what you will freely give, but no less than they deserve.* She'll play their game and win.

"Seelie Monarchs," Cecelia says with the practiced reverence of a princess from their storybooks. "For our performance, may I ask a boon?"

"Yes, my child," the King answers, grinning. Hannah shivers. Cecelia offers her warmest smile to the King in return.

"I appeal to the protection you granted me when I arrived, and ask you to extend it to this Seeker, as a refugee of the Unseelie, your enemies."

"No harm nor trap shall befall her while she remains within our realm," the Monarchs promise in unison.

Cecelia pauses a moment, head still bowed, as she parses their statement for any hidden threat or loophole, but she finds none. It's a genuine promise; the Piper will not be able to reach them in Seelie. So long as they stay here, they'll be safe.

With time, perhaps Cecelia can come to trust them. One encounter isn't enough to reverse the Piper's influence on her mind. She hates the cloying paranoia that ruins her thoughts, though evidence shows the Seelie Monarchs hold none of his malice. Satisfied, she sweeps into another curtsy. Hannah, begrudgingly, does the same.

"Will you hear another request from your humble servant?" Cecelia ventures, eyes still lowered.

"Look at us, dear heart. You need not cower among friends," Queen Titania croons.

Cecelia could never consider herself a *friend* to such powerful beings. Ward or ally, perhaps. But their warmth sets her reservations at ease, and she's grateful for their cooperation.

"I know not why the Seeker is here, but she is a stranger to your realm," Cecelia says with a side eye to the human trespasser. "The Piper claimed me for a changeling and brought me to the human world when I was only a weak sprout and had no choice. If it pleases Your Highness, she would appreciate an explanation of the faerie courts."

She's directing Hannah's attention away from herself. It's best if Hannah learns the basics from someone else; Cecelia has enough to explain already. She peeks through her curtain of hair to see Hannah raise a skeptical eyebrow. Guilt and embarrassment squirm through her chest. Cecelia cannot lose her composure now. There will be enough time for answers, now that the Piper cannot reach them.

Wait, Hannah. Cecelia thinks. *Wait and trust.*

King Oberon gestures to the nearby attendants, who bring seats for them. Hannah all but falls into hers. Cecelia rearranges her wings several times before she's comfortable, slotting them through the specially constructed chair-back. She's out of practice using them. The Monarchs wait for her to stop fidgeting before they speak again.

Chapter 13

The Truth

HANNAH'S WORLD SHAKES.

The survival panic halts long enough for her to understand the unthinkable reality that sits before her, but that only sends her into shock again. Cecelia is a faerie. She's one of *them*. She tricked their family. She lied to Hannah. For twelve years, they had grown up together and she'd never known the truth! Were they ever sisters?

Catching her breath, Hannah studies the strange features. The faerie's wings—Cecelia's wings—sprout from her back, slipping through two slots in the back of her new dress. Her long, pointed ears flatten against her head in an expression Hannah can't understand. That face woke her in the mornings, made weird looks from across the table at dinner, accompanied her every waking day. Familiarity makes the differences that much more uncanny. Hannah sees now that the spidery blue lichen on her temple and cheeks is not a tiara or ornament but real fungi, growing out of her skin, leaching across one side of her face. The surrounding flesh is pale, flaky, and sickly. Hannah instinctively recoils from the eerie sight.

Had she miscalculated? What if she'd chosen an impostor from the group? If Hannah had failed her test—but no—the sorrow and guilt in her sister's voice are too real to ignore.

Cecelia is a faerie, and she can't come home.

Hannah is so lost in her own thoughts, she misses the rest of the conversation between Cecelia and the Monarchs. Before she can react, they're bringing chairs, so she resigns herself to staying. Her knees lock up when she tries to take a step toward the seat, and she stumbles forward, catching the back with one hand to steady herself before collapsing. Hannah contemplates untangling her muddy shoelaces and stretching out her sweaty socks, but decides against such crude behavior in the presence of the Monarchs.

She watches with a passive, slack-jawed stare as Cecelia stretches then refolds her wings around the chair. They flash from dull brown to a brilliant blue, then shut, showing orange eye spots. *Blue Morpho menelaus.* Hannah's fingers twitch, tempting her to reach out and tug, as if the wings are a flimsy Halloween costume that might rip away. Imagining Cecelia's cry of pain, she instead crosses her arms over her chest as she braces for the Monarchs' information.

The Queen begins, "The Seelie Court treats humans with indifference."

"Some indifference, setting up this circus for me," Hannah grumbles.

The Queen notices and narrows her yellow eyes. "Not you, sweetness. Mortals, as a concept, are rather tedious."

If anyone calls her "sweetness" or "dear" again, Hannah might start biting people.

"Our realms exist next to the human world, separated by barriers we maintain through exerting our magical wills. We prefer to keep our secrets and let you live your lives without intervention. When one of you is brave or foolish enough to stumble into our realm, you understand, we must take precautions to determine if the individual means harm to our home and people. You, child, pose us no threat."

Hannah uncrosses her arms and slips her hand into her pocket to wrap her fingers around her knife. They're right; she's harmless, and she's furious to admit that humiliating fact. A child with a slingshot bested her. Hannah grits her teeth and resolves to make herself a threat.

"Faeries live for thousands of years, barring direct force," Oberon says, as if reading her mind. He leaves out how one might, hypothetically, accomplish such a feat. "We want only to enjoy our time, to live alongside the humans, animals, and plants that share this world as stewards and guardians.

The Unseelie Court is a counterpart to ours. These fae feel entitled to use their longevity and power as an excuse to trample anyone they consider beneath them. Queen Mab rules over the four Masters who play with mortal lives as if they are but toys. The Piper is one of them."

"And you belong to him," Hannah says with a sidelong glance at Cecilia.

"No," she whispers, her voice slipping into scorn.

"The Seelie Court opposes their vile deeds," Oberon says, ignoring the sisters' exchange, "so they consider us the enemy. Long ago, we warred with each other."

Hannah shakes her head. "What's the point of war when both sides are practically immortal? Why not just ignore each other for all eternity?"

The Queen leans forward in her seat and clenches her fist. She speaks through a disdainful scowl that reveals fanged teeth. Hannah wonders if she was a warrior herself, once upon a time. "We fight to defend the innocent and weak from those who would seek to make slaves of all. A passive approach does not appease those who seize control at every turn. Though perhaps you imagine war differently, our current conflict is not waged on battlefields." Now she leans back in her seat and brushes a stray wrinkle from her skirt, returning to a composed aura. "These are battles of the mind and of the soul. The Unseelie are hypocrites who won't risk their lives for their own cause. So, they take proxies. People."

"You mean both sides take humans to fight for them?"

"We give our soldiers a choice," Oberon says. "When honorable people, who want to protect and serve, come looking for answers, we test them. Our court supplies the just and noble with powers, magic weapons, and blessings of luck, wit, and kindness. You know them as the folk heroes of magnificent feats.

The other Unseelie Masters take wards in different manners, but the Piper steals human children and uses changelings as spies."

Hannah's eyes widen as she understands the King's meaning. She glances at Cecelia, whose wings flutter as she shrugs. Hannah bites her lip to keep herself from saying anything hasty. She waits for further explanation, but Titania refuses to elaborate and gestures for them to rise.

"The changeling should tell you her own story," the Queen instructs. "You may discuss in private. The courtyard is available, as is the small cottage where she's been staying. You will find it further along the path. Do not fear the movement of time in our realm, for every hour spent here reflects only a minute passed in the human world. Rest well, and if you have more questions when you wake, you will find answers in the library."

Cecelia rises with a curtsy, and Hannah copies her with a clumsy bow before her little sister grabs her hand and drags her from the throne room into Faerieland. As much as she dreads the next conversation, she doesn't resist, eager to leave behind the King and Queen. Cecelia must have explored already, because she leads them on with a determined stride.

They emerge into a glittering courtyard paved with mother-of-pearl, reflecting the light of millions of twinkling stars. Garlands drape over fluted stone pillars, dripping with gemstones. Fountains spring from the center of the square, throwing fractal rainbows and iridescent gleams to play off the walls. Hannah's breath catches in her throat as she gazes at the spectacular sight, mesmerized by the moonlight.

"Beautiful, isn't it?" Cecelia sighs beside her. "We're safe here. They promised."

"No, *you're* safe here." Hannah digs in her satchel for the snacks and water bottles. She slumps to the ground and sits cross-legged, right there in the courtyard. Relief granted for the moment, she tears off a chunk of bread before giving it to the changeling sitting across from her, not looking at her fungi-encrusted face.

"Will eating this food bind you to the Human Realm?" Hannah asks.

"It binds me to you."

"You're bound to be grounded for life when we get home. I'm sure we can fix . . ." Hannah trails off, gesturing at the transformations. She takes the red friendship bracelet out of her pocket and ties it around Cecelia's wrist to match her own, then leans in close to whisper. "There. Now, tell me what's going on. Why was the Piper trying to kidnap you? How did you end up here? Did the Seelie steal you instead? Do you have an escape plan?"

Cecelia swallows her bite of bread and twists the friendship bracelet, as if trying to figure out where to start. "The Piper didn't take me," she whispers. "I ran away."

The gut punch of betrayal makes Hannah's stomach turn. Her head swims as the implications settle over her. She was supposed to bring Cecelia home, but now . . . now she questions whether this changeling had ever considered their farmhouse as her home. How can a faerie live in the human world? Had she ever been happy with their family?

"It was the only way to escape," Cecelia says. "Why did you follow me? I warned you about the Piper—now you're involved, you know?"

"I . . .I don't understand."

"The Piper tried to claim me—to drag me back to that awful place. His ward tracked me. If I slipped away—too risky—couldn't say—you'd intervene—stupid plan—" The words tumble from her lips so quickly, she runs out of breath and gasps before starting again. "But you made it to Seelie. As long as we stay here, the Piper will never find us, and we'll be okay!"

Hannah's heart breaks as Cecelia turns to her with a tearful, hopeful grin. She shakes her head, reality reasserting itself with distance from the intoxicating sights and sounds and smells of the palace. "I wanted to bring my sister home, but I don't even know what's real anymore. Tell me something only Cecelia would know. Just to be sure. Please?"

Cecelia's face falters, mirroring Hannah's own heartbreak. "When I broke Mom's favorite china plate from her grandmother last Christmas, you took the blame for it and couldn't play with your gifts for the whole morning because you wanted to make sure I had a fun holiday. And you never told Mom and Dad the truth, because then I would have gotten in even more trouble for lying and escaping the punishment I deserved."

It's true, and Hannah isn't sure if that hurts more. The overwhelming exhaustion takes her, and she laughs and cries at once, pulling Cecelia into another hug. She needs to know her sister is real. Cecelia radiates warmth, solid and familiar in her arms. When she pulls away, she gives Hannah her most relieved smile and stands, but Hannah doesn't move. She can't help but shatter the joyous reunion with another painful truth.

"Cecelia, we can't stay. I can't stay. This place is *dangerous*."

"Only if you leave the Seelie Court! The Monarchs gave us their word."

"And I'm supposed to trust them? How am I even supposed to trust you, when you lied to me about being a changeling for the past twelve years?"

Cecelia crosses her arms. "That's not fair."

"Okay, then. I don't trust those tyrants because they put me through a dozen Cecelia imposters for their own entertainment. I don't trust this place because I hiked ten miles to get here, and I don't want to get lost or attacked by an assassin girl with a slingshot again. I don't trust you because you're the Piper's changeling, and he nearly bewitched me on the way here!" As she speaks, she ticks the offenses off on her fingers, runs out of fingers, and then switches to the other hand.

"The Piper almost got you?" Cecelia's voice rises to a screech, and she ignores the rest of Hannah's concerns. "Tell me three times true. Did you meet him?"

"Yes. I did. Truly." Hannah struggles to keep the bitterness from her tone. "We were *sisters*. We shared every secret and scheme. At least, I thought we did! So, fine! Maybe I'm not being fair. I'm sure you have a valid reason for running away, but we were so, *so* worried! Cecelia, what were you *thinking*?"

Cecelia doesn't answer, she only holds herself and stares at the floor.

Hannah's words taste leaden in her mouth. Thinking about the Piper, she's seized by a restless need to move, to run, to escape. It sends a jolt of electric adrenaline through her muscles, even though nothing threatens her. Despite her protesting muscles, she pulls herself to her feet and stretches.

"Well? What other surprises do you have for me?" If Hannah needs to move, she might as well move toward answers.

"What? No! I want to hear your story first. Are you sure you're okay?"

Hannah doesn't answer that question, because a truthful answer would hurt Cecelia more. Part of her wants to spit out the fire burning up her stomach and scream, *NO! You're not my sister, and I'm not okay!* But when she looks at the familiar face, she cannot muster the will to unleash such a cruel accusation. When she looks at Cecelia, she doesn't see a monster, just a concerned, remorseful little girl.

"I already told you what happened," Hannah says flatly. Then she sighs and rubs her eyes with the palms of her hands. "I'm exhausted. The Monarchs said something about a cottage? Let's go there, if you think we can trust them. Then I want an explanation."

Chapter 14

The Explanation

ECELIA CHOOSES NOT to fly but to keep pace with Hannah's weary steps. She sets her jaw as they pass from the courtyard through a copse of trees, moving toward their cottage for the night. It's a lovely evening to bask in the starlight. Cecelia can't lose herself in this forest, unlike her dreadful experience last year. Here, the wildflowers would point her toward the cottage, if she asked. She has yet to think of it as a home, but she longs for it to become so. For once, no eyes prickle the hairs on her neck. She can trust these trees.

Hannah keeps her eyes cast toward the ground as they hike along, following Cecelia's lead. Cecelia tries not to pull too far ahead of the half-dead Hannah, even though she's barefoot. If only she could run away from this confrontation. Hannah's shoulders hunch with tense frustration and she stomps her boots with every step, releasing her annoyance in a palpable aura. They walk in silence for a while, the discomfort between them growing ever more unbearable, until Cecelia finally finds a place to begin, knowing full well how ridiculous it will sound.

"Until last year, I didn't know what I was."

Hannah snorts her derision. "How did you not know you were a faerie? Let me guess. Magic."

"Well, you didn't figure it out either. The switching spell worked." Cecelia gives a helpless shrug.

Hannah echoes the gesture with a mocking shake of her head. "Of course not! I don't live in your body. You seriously expect me to believe you didn't know you had wings and mushrooms crawling out of your face? The magic keeping you disguised from us was totally outside of your control this whole time?"

When she mentions the mushrooms, Cecelia's cheek itches, and she raises a hand to scratch at it before shoving it deep in the pocket of her dress. "Yes. Kind of? I knew I was different, but I wasn't consciously faking . . . It's all fuzzy. I remember in dreams, mostly nightmares."

"And you never thought to mention—"

"The Piper uses *children*, Hannah! Of course I didn't understand my nature as an infant. Only that I hurt, that my nightmares haunted me, and that you were warm, and kind, and safe." She can't bear Hannah's anger. If Hannah feels pity, Cecelia can survive her scrutiny, but not anger.

Hannah only shakes her head and holds up her hands for a pause. "If faeries live for thousands of years, how old are you really? I thought you were my little sister, but you must be some ancient trickster."

Her tone is so indignant, Cecelia gives a wry, mirthless laugh. "I've only seen twelve summers. Truly, still a child."

"But shouldn't you still be a baby by fae rules?"

The lichen growing from Cecelia's face trembles as she winces. "I'll be lucky if I live long enough to come of age at a century."

"What? Why?"

She gestures to the web of filament seeping into her pores and climbing along her skin. "An uninfected faeling of my age would still just be a nymph. But I have the Piper's Plague. It makes changelings age at a convenient rate, so he can swap us with mortal children. He takes the humans to train as fresh soldiers to fight the Seelie. The curse erases the sick fae's memories and disguises them with a shapeshifting glamour to be replacements and spies. We're not meant to have lives. Not of our own."

Somehow, saying it out loud makes it worse. Now the pulsing, burrowing pain is something Cecelia can't ignore. She scratches at the lichen, pulling a bit off her skin. It feels like ripping off a scab, a satisfaction that only lasts so long before it aches.

Hannah turns pale, and her voice trembles, soft and scared when she speaks again. "You're . . . you're going to die soon?"

Sooner than she should. Hearing her fate spoken out loud settles foreboding around Cecelia's shoulders like a burial shroud. "I won't rot away tomorrow," she says, trying to keep her composure as analytical as a doctor's note. She doesn't know the day or the hour of her demise, but then again, who does?

Hannah scrubs her hand on her pants to rid herself of the contamination.

"It's a curse the Piper puts on his wards. Nobody here can catch it. It's not contagious," Cecelia says quickly, noticing the gesture. The assurance doesn't seem to abate Hannah's paranoia.

"Aren't you scared?" Hannah asks.

"Yes." That's true, at least. Fae can't tell blatant untruths, but her life's been a lie of omission. Now, she isn't leaving anything out of her story, no matter how humiliating.

"Does it hurt?"

"It's nothing you can fix."

Cecelia shuts her eyes and takes a shuddering breath, knotting her fingers in her skirts to resist the ever-present burning. She feels Hannah take her hand and give it a squeeze, despite her repulsion from a few seconds earlier. It's just as much a comfort as it ever was, and the relief is a reminder that Hannah should never have followed her here. Now that she's involved, she needs to understand the consequences.

"I don't fear death or pain as much as I fear the Piper," Cecelia says. "He used to be like me, but he somehow survived, and became a Master in the Unseelie Court, either by making a deal with Queen Mab or the Devil himself. They say the rot obscures his true features so much, nobody knows who he once was. But it doesn't matter. In all the stolen years he's lived, he's grown warped into what he is now. If we survive long enough, we'll lose our own features, forget our own names and faces, and fade into shells for him to control when he finally steals our faces. I belonged to him, even if I didn't know it until last year. When I learned the truth, I ran away to escape that fate."

Hannah's face goes drawn and pale. "If you didn't know you were a faerie, how could you be a spy?"

Cecelia blinks to make her point. "My eyes and ears were not mine alone. I only needed to live undetected, like a hidden camera. I had no name for the presence in the back of my mind or the feeling of being watched."

Hannah dutifully follows Cecelia as she shudders and continues at a breathless pace, eager to finish the painful memories. "The memories are clear now, since I've arrived in the Seelie Court. He can't reach me here. But in the Human Realm, he can still hold power over me. I knew he had other wards, but I never met them. I'm starting to remember flashes from the Unseelie Court, now that my mind is free. Hunger. Cold, barren rooms in an endless maze. The constant music."

Hannah flinches at the word "music." Good. She must learn caution.

"One night, he led me through the woods. I trembled in the cold air and tripped and skinned my knees on the trail. We came to a house, and I don't know how he brought me inside. I just remember the transformation *hurt*, and then . . . nothing. So many years passed with no contact from the Piper that the Unseelie Court became a distant thought. I pushed it away. All the rest of my memories are just growing up like any other kid, even though I knew, deep down, I was the mismatched piece in a set."

She's wringing her hands now, keeping her eyes on her feet, though she knows Hannah's watching her. What's behind her eyes? Fear, disbelief, resentment? When Cecelia recalls her past, it hurts as much as digging into an infected wound to extract a splinter. She'd lied to everyone and to herself about the ugly truth buried inside of her. Now she's caught, an impostor and a thief, ashamed and awaiting the judgment she deserves.

Judgment comes in the form of a hug. Cecelia's composure breaks again as she dissolves into heaving sobs, and Hannah rubs circles into the space on her back between her wings.

"Shh. Shh. It's okay. You're not wrong," Hannah whispers. "I'm sorry. I'm sorry I yelled at you."

Cecelia sniffles and pulls away from the embrace. Their conversation comes to a lull as they come to the cottage where she's been staying, nestled in the boughs of a tree with a rope ladder dangling from the landing. Cecelia raises her wings as if to fly, then thinks better of it, and climbs up to the landing, Hannah following after. When they reach the porch, Cecelia fishes a tiny, intricate brass key from her dress pocket and slips it into the lock. It gives a satisfying click and swings open with a creak that reminds Cecelia of the squeaky front door in the home she abandoned.

"I've been staying here," she explains, as Hannah enters and finds a cozy one-room arrangement with a lit hearth at one end. It's a wonder the fire doesn't burn down the tree, but Cecelia appreciates its warmth and gentle crackle.

"For how long?" Hannah asks, making a circle around the cottage. A bunk bed sits on the right side, and a spare bed faces it on the opposite side of the room. Perhaps this used to belong to a different family. There's a small table with three chairs in the center of the room.

"Only a couple days, in Seelie time. I left shortly before dawn because I wanted to wait for the storm to pass, but I couldn't delay any longer. Flying was a bad idea. I'd never learned how. Then the Piper's ward tracked me the whole way to the Portal Tree, so I tried to shake her but lost valuable time."

"The crazy girl with the slingshot?"

"Yeah," Cecelia shudders, recalling the *thunk* of the stones against the trees as she fled, and her wings tearing against the thorns. "Since I arrived, I've just been resting here." She had lacked the spirit to explore as she picked up the pieces of her life.

Hannah dumps her bookbag, coat, and boots on the ground while Cecelia does her customary check of the cabinets and under the beds. She finds no creeping monsters, but pulls out the box of tea she'd found when she'd arrived. Hannah declines a mug, declaring she'll need to find untainted water to refill her bottles. But she pulls up a chair to the fire and collapses into it. Cecelia can't argue with her paranoia, so she doesn't try. She pulls up a chair beside Hannah and sinks into it, nursing her warm drink as a floral aroma rises from the steam. In the clear mug, it swirls purple, then pink, then blue, shimmering with golden flecks. Hannah might fear losing time to the foreign food and drink, but Cecelia's a faerie. She belongs here, right? She can't go home, so what does it matter?

Hannah pulls off her socks and lays them on the bricks, then stretches out her feet and wiggles her toes.

"Those smell awful," Cecelia says with a laugh, plugging her nose.

"I'm so sorry I don't smell like roses," Hannah says, sticking her tongue out. Cecelia makes a fake gagging sound, so Hannah pokes Cecelia with her foot.

"Now you're smelly, too."

"Noooo, how dare you!" Cecelia shoves Hannah's foot off her knee and breathes in the steam from her tea. Though it's nothing Cecelia recognizes from the human world, it tastes amazing anyhow, like sorrow and solace mingled together. For a moment, the familiar bickering lets them forget their worries, but then Hannah's face grows somber again.

"How do you know all this, if he wiped your memory? When did you learn the truth, and how did you find this place?"

"You remember my accident last year?" Cecelia makes air quotes around the word "accident."

"When you got lost for a week on our hiking trip? Mom and Dad were worried about that happening again when you went missing this morning."

Cecelia cringes at the reminder. "We passed too close to a border. It was dusk, and all that separated the mundane park from a pocket of the Unseelie domain was a small stream. I don't know if the border was there first, and then people built the park around the portal, or if the border moved later to prey on travelers. It doesn't matter."

The recollection comes back to Cecelia in full force, a memory she had tried to keep at bay for the past year as the call of the Piper's music had become louder and louder. She stares into the flickering fire, feeling the present growing distant as she gives in to her story.

Chapter 15

The Transformation

THE FLAMES DANCE and take shape as she speaks. She's not sure if it's an idle manifestation of her magical will, or the passive magic of the Seelie Court forcing the fire to take on the role of a living storyteller.

"It was a humid August day with thunderstorms brewing," Cecelia says. "I stopped to walk down to the stream, took off my shoes, and stood ankle deep on one of the large flat stones. The water was so cold, my feet went numb. Mom and Dad kept walking. I think they were rushing to make it back to the campsite before the storm, and they hadn't realized I'd slipped off, so I fell behind. You were around the bend, and I thought I could catch up, but I forgot any idea of rejoining our family when I started to hear the music."

The fire dispels the image of a wispy figure standing in a river of embers as a spectacular split of wood sends sparks shooting into the air. They crack and fizzle to match the rhythm of Cecelia's lilting speech.

"The sound of the Piper's flute followed me for as long as I could remember, though I didn't know it belonged to him. It had always been a phantom melody, something I would hum when I wasn't thinking. I knew it belonged to my past, and it scared me.

But that didn't stop me from straining to hear just a few more bars when I woke up from a dream. When facing the unknown, it's up to you to decide if the mystery is hiding a beautiful or a frightening truth. I could never decide which the music was to me.

"Until that day." Cecelia bitterly remembers the innocence she'd so recently lost. Though she knows she's still young, she could never go back to being that carefree little girl, exploring with her sister, unaware of her true purpose. If she hadn't discovered the truth about herself that day, how different would her life be? Cecelia shakes her head to dismiss the thought. It does her no good to dwell on hypotheticals, and the sooner she finishes the story, the less painful it will be to recount. Hannah nods along as she speaks, recalling the same mundane camping trip, before Cecelia's fate changed forever.

"What started as a whisper grew into a murmuring tone that carried over the water from upstream, as if I could only hear it by standing in the water. The notes wove around me like a net, and without a second thought, I started wading toward the source. Finally finding an answer I needed as much as I needed to breathe.

"Thunder shook the hollow, and the rain started pelting down without warning. I should have resisted and turned back then, but something colorful caught my eye on the other side of the stream, and I was too curious to tear my eyes away. I moved to get a closer look. At first, I thought it was just a stray toadstool, but as I drew closer, I realized it was a wild rose."

A furl of yellow flame spirals from one of the burning logs; a dead shrub comes back to life from its desolation. Cecelia murmurs, and Hannah leans in closer to hear her soft words. She's told no one about this experience before, and her lips guard her deepest secrets out of habit. She cannot force the words out in anything more than a whisper before her throat threatens to choke up and reduce her to sobs. But she swallows and begins again.

"The rose seemed . . . familiar, somehow. If you had asked me at the time, I might have said I knew it from a storybook, but in truth, it called me by name. Why did it know my name? As I drew nearer, I realized it shouldn't have been growing there, and though my conscience was screaming at me to leave such strangeness well enough alone, I wanted answers more. I climbed onto the opposite shore, picked the rose, and put it in my hair.

"That's when I pricked my finger on the thorns.

"On the pad of my thumb was dark blood, not red, but black. I bent over to wash my hand in the stream, and the water was still. Despite the current and the rain, the stream's surface was smooth as a mirror. A face I didn't recognize looked back at me." Cecelia shivers, and dark red flares consume the yellow rose. She had been whispering before, but as both the storm and the story grow with intensity, her voice rises to a near-belt, straining against the song that clamors in her mind. Her voice aches, and tears prick her eyes as Cecelia remembers her terror.

"I felt the transformation as I crossed the border. If butterflies go through such pain emerging from their chrysalises, then I do not envy them. My skin stung as wings sprouted from my back, and the Piper's Plague exposed itself. I tried to wash it away. The rain kept coming down, but every time I tried to submerge my hands, the river froze, the surface like a mirror, reflecting a face I didn't want to see."

The flames illustrate the scene, creating a writhing figure that erupts with smoke and embers, a torrent of ash cascading around it. Hannah looks away, and Cecelia's relieved when she turns away her gaze. The truth burns in Cecelia's chest, an ember flaring as she breathes each new word of her story. After she's carried it for so long, smoldering and filling her with soot and ash, the pain of burning away the husk of the person she used to be is liberating.

"The music tormented me. A pounding drumbeat inside my head, a cacophony of singing, screaming, and howling, cut through by the strident sound of pipes, clear and close. My memories unfurled along with my wings, as the glamour that was laid during the switching spell fell away. The Cecelia I knew drowned, flooded by fear, caught up in a Current of my past, filling every hidden crack in my mind and shattering the secrets. I squeezed my eyes shut, but my vision fractured into a kaleidoscope of half-remembered dreams I could now recall with vivid clarity. Moments from our past, seen through a second set of eyes, seen through my eyes, processed by a separate presence that took up residence in the back of my brain. I realized the truth and the curse of my being all at once. The Piper's attention snapped onto me, and I recognized the weight of his gaze for the first time, as my head throbbed. He knew I knew now. He was coming for me.

"I fled. Stumbling, sprinting, trying and failing to fly, trying to lose myself and run so far away, he would never find you. Thorns attacked me as I fumbled through the sudden darkness of the Unseelie Woods. The thunderheads blotted out the sun, and I threw myself from ledges in leaps that should have broken bones. Lightning struck a nearby tree, and it crashed into my path. I dove and barely skirted underneath the charred and smoldering bark. The smell of mud, decay, and smoke clung to me, despite the rain. When I finally collapsed under the shelter rock overhang, he was waiting."

Cecelia remembers how a flash of lightning starkly illuminated his displeased face, the chill of his fingers tapping her on the shoulder, gripping her by the arm to prevent her from running off. She squirms and rubs at her skin to brush away his phantom touch. Hannah scowls and balls her hands into fists.

"He congratulated me on my secrecy, but said it wasn't the right time for me to "join the swarm." Since I was aware of the connection now, I could tell when he watched me—watched through me. He needed me to complete my mission. I would never have a moment of relief from his surveillance. He warned if my family ever found out what I was, they would..." Cecelia's voice catches, and she gives Hannah a pointed glance before staring back into the flames. "He said they would betray me, if—"

"We would never!" Hannah interrupts, but her voice doesn't sound confident. What if she had learned in any other circumstance, without the cushion of worry or the assurances of the Seelie Monarchs? If she'd caught Cecelia spying, would she be so charitable? She hasn't been very kind since learning the truth.

"He made it clear, you weren't my family. You never could be," Cecelia says, the words loaded with months of concealed insecurity and subtle accusation. "The Piper had constructed my entire life. I belonged to him."

"Do you believe him?" Hannah asks.

"I didn't want to believe him," Cecelia answers, skirting the question. "I mourned for something that was never really mine." Hannah doesn't keep pushing, so Cecelia stifles her nausea and continues. "When the Piper first planted me, he cared less about the family and more about the house Itself. The last owner had worked with the Seelie before we moved in, and remnants of their presence still linger—passageways, shadelings, Hazel the brownie. I'd already found everything he'd needed, and he'd grown tired of those trivial matters. Once I knew what I was, he wanted to use me to my . . . fullest potential." Cecelia hisses the last two words through clenched teeth.

When Hannah holds her hand for comfort, Cecelia clings on tight so Hannah can't let go, so she has to listen to what comes next.

"He wanted me to betray you," Cecelia sobs. "He wanted me to bring you to him as a new ward, and he promised that when I returned to the Court, he would reward me. So, he sent me back. But time passes differently in the Unseelie world, where it bends to the will of the Masters. To me, only a few miserable hours had passed, but by the time you found me on the road, I'd been gone for a week."

Hannah's eyes grow wide as she puts the pieces together, and she tries to pull her hand away. "When the Piper tried to trick me, when the girl in the tree attacked, was that all a trap? Did you lead me here on purpose?"

Cecelia keeps an iron grip on Hannah's hand. "No!"

"The Piper said the Seelie stole you from him!"

"He was lying!"

"How do I *know?*"

"I've known what I am for a year. I've been trying to escape for *a year!* Hazel taught me the lullaby about how to find the Seelie Court. If I couldn't bring myself to sacrifice you, the Piper would come to the house to collect me. Either betray the family or invite a demon like him into the home. I had to run away to protect you. I never expected you to follow me! The Piper just saw an opportunity and took advantage of it."

Cecelia lets go of Hannah's fingers now, and Hannah puts her face in her hands with a long-suffering sigh. "You're a fool, you know that? I would follow you beyond the ends of the earth."

Shame and gratitude twist in Cecelia's stomach. "I know."

Hannah takes the poker and jabs at the fire, behaving as mundanely as she would in the human world, despite her best efforts to goad the flames into fireworks and fury. Cecelia's mind blanks with fatigue as she watches Hannah mess with the embers.

That's it. Her story's over, truths told and splinters pulled. She gives herself over to homesickness as she takes in the familiar sight. If she forgets they're sitting in a treehouse, she could imagine Hannah stoking coals in the basement stove, throwing fuel on the fire of Cecelia's current heartache.

She loved the old house, full of strange nooks and crannies. In the end, it had held nothing valuable to the Piper, but Hazel's cookies and help with tidying her room had been invaluable to Cecelia. The little brownie had only revealed herself after Cecelia realized the truth about her nature, but she'd become a treasured friend and trusted confidant in the short time they'd known each other. Cecelia misses her, and their cats, and Willow, and all twenty-seven chickens. She misses their dad— Hannah's dad—telling them bedtime stories, and their mom— Hannah's mom—tucking her into bed at night.

That's not her life anymore.

Hannah's white-knuckled grip on the poker slips, and she nearly burns herself on the hearth. Muttering and grumbling to herself, she banks the coals, puts down the tool, and scowls at her scraped skin. Then she turns to Cecelia with a frown.

"Why didn't you tell us?"

"You wouldn't have believed me."

"I'm here, aren't I?" Hannah spreads her arms to make a point, gesturing at the picturesque surroundings, then at Cecelia's new appearance. "You could have *tried.* I would have believed you. We could have found some way to protect you or . . . or something, I don't know."

Cecelia squirms but doesn't respond. Hannah makes it sound so easy. She doesn't understand the paralyzing fear of discovery, the paranoia of knowing your every movement is subject to scrutiny. Even now, her very appearance raises ire. Focusing her effort into her magic, Cecelia shapeshifts, folding her wings into herself and letting her hair fade to its old, dark shade. She covers the lichen and changes her face to fit the human girl Hannah knows and remembers.

Hannah looks away instead of watching the transformation, but when it's complete, she sighs and puts a hand on Cecelia's shoulder. "We can figure out how to fix this tomorrow. You're safe. That's all that matters. If I ever see that Piper again, I swear I'll snap that instrument into pieces for what he did to you."

Cecelia gives Hannah a grim smile, part of her thankful for her sister's protectiveness, part of her bittersweet as her eye twitches from the shapeshifting. Even though Hannah knows the whole truth now, Cecelia's still hiding her nature for the human's comfort. Even in Faerieland.

"If we can trust the Seelie Monarchs about time passing differently here, does that mean I can take a nap without getting stuck for a hundred years like Rip Van Winkle?" Hannah asks, eyeing up the bed.

"You're probably safe." Cecelia doesn't have the energy to explain temporal displacement right now, and she scarcely understands it herself.

"I'll risk it," Hannah mutters. Before, her posture had been tense, wired with anxiety and fidgety with anticipation. Now, that energy has given way to weariness, and Cecelia suffers another pang of guilt, as Hannah drags herself out of her chair to stretch and move toward the bed. There's a soft nightgown folded on the pillow. Hannah inspects it, because she always checks to see if new textures will be okay for her skin, even in the Human Realm. Cecelia never realized how she had ached for all of Hannah's little habits when she spent the past evenings lying beside empty beds.

Eventually, she decides the clothing is acceptable, and changes. Cecelia watches the ritual with muted contemplation. "If I remember correctly, Rip Van Winkle got really drunk on fae wine and gambled with the Unseelie, which is always a recipe for disaster. You're not that dumb."

"Gee, thanks for the vote of confidence."

Cecelia laughs as she climbs onto her top bunk and rests back on her pillow, hands behind her head. "This place is freeing. My mind is my own, like I can think without brain fog for the first time in my life."

"Really? And all this time, I thought it was just fluff in your head."

"Hey!" Cecelia's outburst is indignant and amused, not offended, as she tries to keep the tenuous truce between them intact. She can't tell if Hannah was joking or trying to insult her. After a moment, she adds, "I missed you. I'm glad you came for me."

There's a long pause from the lower bunk. Is Hannah still angry, or just sleepy?

"I'm glad I found you," Hannah finally says, sighing as she rolls over and pulls up the covers. "Goodnight."

"Goodnight."

All is peaceful after that, with crickets singing in chorus outside and the fire crackling as it goes out. For the first time since she'd learned of the Piper, Cecelia slips into a restful sleep, without dreams full of thorns and piping music.

Chapter 16

The Punishment

THE TAKEN CROUCHES between two large boulders, trying to make herself as small as possible in the darkness between the mossy boulders. Her breath comes in gasps after her reckless escape from the Seelie sentries. They can't reach her anymore. Bits of vine cling to her hands, and she peels the splinters from her palms with her nails.

What a cursed disaster. First the runaway gave her the slip. And she'd almost captured the human girl—a pathetic thing wrapped and packaged like a fly in a web, ready to be returned to the master spider. She should have checked for guards before crossing into the portal. It seemed like a clever risk with a handsome reward.

Mab! Stupid. Careless. Arrogant. The Taken hits her head with her palm and knocks her elbow against the stone. It hits the nerve, and a shock of pain shoots through her already sore arm, prompting another string of muttered curses. She puts her head in her hands and only now does she realize her mask is missing. Oh no! At first, she only cared about winning the fight, but now she's lost both her quarry and her disguise. Her face flushes with shame for exposing such a dangerous secret to her enemy, but it's too late. The damage has been done.

She's picked an awful hiding spot, but it's too risky to go back for it now, in case the guards circle back to look for her. So she must wait. The stones slope low over her head, forcing her to crane her neck and curl her spine to fit. Her muscles ache, and her butt hurts from sitting on the sharp rocks. All the same, it's peaceful. The only sound beside her quiet breathing is the distant rustling of a grungtuttle burrowing for worms. She's not thrilled about sharing her cave with one of those, but as long as she doesn't spook it, she should be fine.

Even in her contorted position, she's tempted to nod off to sleep. She watches the winter trees sway in a breeze, their bare bark clattering and chattering above the whistle of the wind. Winter strikes hard in the Unseelie Court, and the Taken's threadbare cloak barely keeps out the chill. The opportunity to find new clothes doesn't arise very often when she's let out of the maze on missions, but once, she had stolen a sweater from a human's drying line. It was her most treasured possession for a brief afternoon, but the Piper confiscated it as soon as she'd returned to the Unseelie Court, so she never tried to fend for herself again. Though the Taken is used to the cold, she's thankful for the shelter. She rubs her hands on her arms to keep from freezing solid where she sits.

Several minutes pass, enough that she's sure the guards have taken care of the intruder. She could leave now and go make her report, but she tells herself it's worth it to stay here, for just a little while longer. If she's still as a gargoyle at noon and silent as a spirit, maybe the Piper won't find her this time.

She wishes she had troll sweat-slime to wash off the sticky-sweet Seelie scent and disguise herself from the swarm's sharp noses. Mud will have to do. She rubs it on her arms and bare face, squelching it between her fingers in a satisfying squish, drawing swirls and patterns on her skin, pretending it's the war paint she's seen other wards wear. She hates the swarm, with their nasty little claws, their wet snouts, and course whiskers, with their cold tails, and their—

Chittering.

It's still distant, an incessant squeaking of a million voices, screeching and whining and yelping in pain as the Piper jerks their little minds to suit his will. They're looking for her. She's supposed to report when she's captured her quarry. The stupid upstart changeling girl was supposed to report, too, but she ran away from her duty. She'll pay for that. The Piper never excuses such extravagant disobedience. The Taken failed to capture the changeling, so she was supposed to capture the other human girl, who'd followed her to the Seelie Court. She failed at that mission, too.

Should she run? No. That would be a death sentence. She's not any braver than the runaway changeling, who's trying to hide. When the rats find her, will they punish her for cowardice? It doesn't matter what she does; eventually, the Piper will find out she failed.

It's not fair! If those stupid Seelie guards hadn't interfered, the girl would be hers! Too many attacked her at once, and if they'd captured her, she'd be breaking the first rule. The only rule. *Don't go into Seelie*. They're the enemy. They'd kill her. The Piper will understand why she ran. He has to, right?

The screeching is close now. Their footsteps rustle the leaves to the right of the Taken's hidey-hole. There's no use staying here any longer. At least the stones had protected her from the scouts.

She moves to the edge of the cavern and tries to make it seem as if she'd been waiting for them to arrive. The rats gather around her ankles, each vying to get the first bite and prove they were the one that found her. She kicks them away, grimly enjoying the satisfying thud as the ball of her foot sends the soft bodies flying.

The Piper arrives soon after his swarm. His cloaked figure warps the forest with the might of his presence. Trees wither and bend as if they're bowing at the waist. The other wildlife flees as his mantle passes through the thickets of brush, cloaking them in shadow. A thick fog stains the sunlight into a wash-bin gray. His thin form towers over her.

He can choose his size. The Taken has seen him shrink to walk among humans before, but he likes to make her feel small. Fear, more than willpower, keeps her frozen in place, even though everything in her tiny body screams at her to hide again. She knows his wrath will be worse if he finds her avoiding him. The Piper's pitted eyes sweep over the forest before landing on the Taken, fixing her with a stare of disappointment that burns into her conscience.

"Where is the sister?"

He speaks softly, but the depth of the words still rumbles in her chest. The Taken doesn't know what a sister is, but the Piper keeps using the word. She doesn't think it means what he thinks it means. Maybe it's a connection between the changeling and the girl who escaped, but she can't imagine why they're looking for each other. Regardless, the "sister" was the Taken's target, and she has nothing to show for herself.

"The Seelie took her," the Taken says, trying her best to sound angry and confident. Anything to justify herself in his eyes. "Too many guards—at least six of them—all armed to the teeth and chasing me. I had to get away, and she slipped into the Tree."

"You let her reach the Portal Tree?"

"I knew she was trying to find the Seelie, so I thought if I waited for her there, I would surely find her. It was faster than searching the whole wood. And I was right. And I almost had her too, right until—"

"Almost is not good enough!" he roars, and the Taken flinches. "How dare you allow them to take two from me?" He grabs her by the cowl of her cloak, like a misbehaving kitten, and lifts her off her feet. She digs her fingers into the collar as it digs into her neck. "You useless whelp! They're out of reach now. We must return to the stronghold. And you should know better than to lose your mask, foolish child."

He drops her to the ground, then flings a new mask at her, identical to the last. It's shaped like the face of a rat, fashioned out of carved and painted wood, embellished with fur and whiskers.

The Taken quickly pulls it over her face, as the Piper whirls on his heel and flies off, leaving her with the swarm. She stumbles forward, as every step she takes, he outpaces her by seven leagues in the magical boots he wears. Her lungs are strong but she pants with the exertion of following as the rats nip at her heels. There's no use in asking how far they have left to run; she gave up trying to make sense of time and space long ago. She's seen other humans spend years among the Unseelie Court, never aging a day, then wither into dust as soon as they step outside, gaining hundreds of years in a moment. The Piper's power preserves her, despite the time she's spent in the faerie world.

At least, it preserves her age. It doesn't preserve her from his other torments.

A step misplaced on loose gravel sends her tumbling to the ground. The Piper whirls on her with a hiss. She's too much of a hindrance to maintain this pace under her own will. No. No! Not the flute! Inside her mind, she screams, but the Taken knows better than to beg for mercy. The Piper relishes their begging cries.

She tries to stand, to prove she can persevere through this test, to earn his esteem, to show she's worth his time. Her legs wobble under the exertion, and he raises the wicked instrument to his lips. The first notes sink into her, and she's lost to the song, conscious but no longer in control of herself. He drags her forward, faster than her muscles can bear. She stubs her toes and endures scratches all over her skin as she's buffeted against brambles. The Piper's control drags her into a headlong sprint, far beyond her natural capabilities, yet she can't even flinch.

It's obvious when they cross the forest between the Human Realm and the Fae world to reach the Unseelie lands. Dread rises in the Taken's throat as they approach. Here, everything cares only about itself. Herd animals like deer wander alone; no mycelium network connects the webs of roots, leaving the plants exposed to wither and die. The soil erodes, yielding to uncaring gravel. There's no softness, no wilderness—just sterile, half-dead things kept from true release, forbidden from the relief of oblivion.

The Taken's favorite beasties are the trolls that could eat you in one gulp. It's fun to taunt them when she's bored.

The Piper's lair is a labyrinth made of enormous granite stones near Queen Mab's palace. Though the Taken has lived here all her life, she still doesn't know how to navigate the cursed place. Every time she's entered or left, the Piper has guided her steps for the sake of secrecy. As they cross the threshold, the Piper squeezes her eyes shut and tugs her this way and that, through an impossible series of twists and turns that leave her exhausted and confused. Eventually, she's dumped in a cell and allowed to open her eyes.

There's another child here, a boy, just as grimy and frightened as she is. He wears the same style of mask, so she doesn't recognize him, even with his mousey brown hair and lanky frame that curls in on itself. None of the wards may interact with each other, unless the Piper arranges it, which he does on rare occasions. Only when the cell door is shut does the Piper finally lower the flute from his lips.

The Taken's body sags with the release, pain screaming back to the forefront of her mind. She stifles a moan. *Don't show weakness.*

The boy sniffles. Doesn't he know the rules? Stupid child. She doesn't correct or comfort him. Better for him to draw the Piper's ire and hope he forgets all about her.

"Report your failure," the Piper demands of the whimpering ward.

"It wasn't my fault! I swear! I almost—" He cowers into the corner and holds his arms above his head in supplication, voice rising to a whine.

"Almost isn't good enough," says the Piper. "I am sick of excuses."

The Taken cringes at the echo of their earlier conversation. Is this it for her? Is this how she meets her end and joins the swarm? No, the Piper's attention is still on the boy.

"I'm sorry, I'm sorry, I'm sorry," he moans. "Give me another chance. Just one more."

"How many have you let go?"

"Three, sir. Only three."

"You're out of chances." The Piper raises his flute to his lips, and the Taken stands frozen where she is, too terrified to cower. "You will sing your last song."

A tone screeches from the instrument, a dizzying cacophony of notes tumbling over each other, eager to escape and wrap themselves around their target. The boy's eyes grow frantic as he realizes what this means, before he seems to give up all hope. He had been kneeling, begging for compassion, but now he slumps against the wall, all strength sapped from his crumpled form. The notes ricochet off the stone walls, echoing and amplifying into a noise that hurts the Taken's ears and leaves her with an awful headache. There's no sense of melody or harmony, but somehow the boy knows the tune.

He sings using the True Voice, the one the Taken uses to command plants. But this time, the voice doesn't target some helpless animal or unwitting scrap of vegetable. He turns it on himself, chanting his despair. The wordless series of sounds tells the Taken everything she could want to know—and a great deal she doesn't—about his suffering and terror. Music tears from his throat, and the vocalizing grows raw and hoarse as the song reaches a desperate crescendo. The Taken feels it rise in her chest, clawing at the air in her lungs, trying to slip off her tongue, but this transformation is not meant for her.

The boy's singing turns to squeaks as his nose morphs into the snout of his mask, melding together above needle-sharp teeth. His limbs shrink and curl inward while his nails grow into claws. A tail sprouts, pink and grasping. Hair grows all over his body, poking through the clothes, and his whiskers quiver. His size diminishes until he's three feet from the tip of his nose to the tip of his tail—still a rodent of unusual size compared to any wild rat. Any sense of recognition is gone from his eyes as he— it—nips at the Taken's sleeve. She finally comes to her senses and jerks away, crouching back into a corner to put as much distance as she can between herself and the transformed animal. She's extremely conscious of the rodent face that covers her own, how easily her features could meld with the mask in the same transformation. Now she understands why the Piper makes them wear these things. It's not just for disguise, but for this twisted purpose. She squashes the urge to rip it off.

The Piper's song lingers a moment longer, before the room falls silent. The Taken realizes she's gasping for breath and tears streak her face. She tries her best to wipe them away under the edges of the mask, while the new pet distracts her Master. He antagonizes it for a few minutes by poking and prodding it to run around. When the Piper finally grows tired of playing with the beast, he turns to watch it scurry away before he faces her again, an ominous grin cutting across his warped features. He wears a new face now, the one he just stole.

"How many have you let go?" he asks.

The Taken swallows her fear and stands. "Two, sir."

He leans down to her level, cupping her face in his hands. They're cold and bony as he pulls away her mask long enough to wipe away her tears. Then he replaces it tightly and takes her chin, tilting her head so her eyes meet his—vacant and probing. "I'm giving you a fair expectation, child. Three tries are customary. They should be more than enough to subdue your targets."

"Yes, sir. I understand, sir." She tries very hard to keep her lip from trembling.

"I'm sure you will not disappoint me as that one had. You're a smart girl who can see reason. I test you to sharpen you into something better. I protect you from the Seelie, who would soften your mind and mettle. I saved you from the humans, who did not understand your potential. You must be strong, little one."

It's praise she's seldom heard before, and it's a kindness and a relief after her failure today. "Thank you. I'll be better," she whispers.

"Among the Unseelie Court, I will make you wonderful and terrible, if you can prove you're worth the effort. Either you will win power and respect from me, or..." He gestures to the pathetic rat, shuddering on the far side of the room. It's a small room, so it's not very far at all. "You will join the ranks of your peers who lacked ambition."

With that, the Piper sweeps out of the room. The Taken doesn't move to follow him, as he waves his hand in a deft gesture and the stone shifts to create bars over the door. He doesn't say when he'll be coming back for her, or what her next assignment will be, but he never does. Rytchic, the kitchen imp, will bring her food. Probably. For now, she's alone with the transformed ward, and she can finally rest.

She tries her best to make herself comfortable on the wooden slats that serve as a bed. A hard bed is far better than moldy, scratchy straw. The terror recedes to relief as she accepts her new roommate. It's just one rat. She hates sharing the space, but she knows how to deal with them. She's not one of them. Not yet.

And she never will be.

This next mission has to be her best. She won't waste her last chance. There's not another option.

Is there?

Her mind wanders back to her encounter with the human who got away, to her own brief moments of freedom sitting in the cramped cave. The weird girl had barely cared about her own safety; she kept asking about her sister. The Taken thought her a fool for not fighting back. She would have been an easy mark, had the Seelie not intervened. Why should they save a human trespasser? It makes no sense to her. How do they survive without a Master like the Piper?

The Piper claims the Seelie are feebleminded, weak, and unfit to rule the fae, but the Taken has seen the world outside of the Unseelie Court. It's not a soft world at all. She loves the forest, for it's as wild as she is, and she can't force herself to believe the Piper's harsh reality is the best the world offers. The Seelie must be strong to control the Portal Tree, and they'd fought her back, after all. They must have something the Piper isn't telling her about.

The bond between the human and the runaway draws her attention again. Something about the brief conversation with the human compels the Taken to revisit it in her mind, again and again. The crazy girl had offered to *help*, despite the danger and her urgent quest. She'd offered an escape. What if the Taken had—

No. She mustn't think such treasonous thoughts. Not if she's going to be strong enough to prove herself to the Piper. Dreams are for star-addled fools like the girl in the tree. The Taken hopes the time will come soon for her third mission.

It had better be a rematch.

Chapter 17:
The Lady

THOUGH HER EXHAUSTION runs bone deep, Hannah tosses and turns throughout the night. Thorns and music taunt her dreams. Her growling stomach and aching shoulder wake her every few hours, ensuring she never drifts away into the land of rest and time forgotten.

She bolts up, escaping the nightmare, losing the mysterious girl running away from her. It takes a panicked second to realize she isn't in her own bed, and another three to remember where she is and how she came to be here. Morning light filters through the windows, illuminating the faint glow of floating dust motes. She lies on her back and tries to slow her gasping breaths as she gazes at the bunk above her.

At home, she has her own room, and she doesn't sleep in a treehouse. Hannah rubs her eyes and confirms that none of this nightmare belongs to her dreams. She isn't sure whether she should be relieved or upset by this realization. She groans and pulls the pillow back over her head.

Shuffling comes from the top bunk, then the sound of Cecelia's voice. "Good morning, sleepyhead."

"Nrrrghhhh."

"Come on, let's get ready!"

"How long have you been up?" Hannah peeks one eye out from under her pillow. Cecelia lies on her belly and hangs upside down over the edge of the bed. A tangle of hair hangs from her head, desperately in need of a comb.

"A while."

"Go back to sleep. Five more minutes." Hannah grumbles and smacks Cecelia with the pillow.

"Can't! We have too much to explore today! Besides, the Monarchs told us to go to the library last night, and we're late enough as it is." Cecelia throws the pillow back at Hannah and clobbers her in the nose.

"Grr."

"Grr, yourself."

"I will consider rising from my eternal slumber if you offer me pancakes."

"Fresh out, sorry. Maybe the library will have some." Cecelia swings down from the top bunk and pokes Hannah in the shoulder.

"That's ridiculous. It's a library!" Hannah swats her away, so she moves to the table, where her empty tea mug from last night has been replaced by a bowl of fresh fruit. Maybe the cottage has a house brownie of its own.

"Look, you're the one who refused to eat anything." Cecelia says, plucking one of the mysterious fae fruits from the basket. She turns it over in her hand, inspecting the ripe purple flesh, before taking a bite and letting the pink juice drip down her chin.

"Fine. FINE. I'm up, you white rabbit."

Hannah kicks herself out of bed and stumbles bleary-eyed to the table to empty her bookbag of any unneeded weight. She's still sore, especially in her left shoulder, where the mystery girl's vines had dangled her by the arm above the hollow of the Portal Tree. There's little she can discard, so she repacks her gear. There's a clean change of clothes set out for her: brown sturdy fingerless gloves, loose-fitting pants that button at the ankles, a loose red shirt, akin to those Hannah has seen in books about pirates, and a green hooded cloak. She's grateful to discard her sweaty, muddy hiking clothes, and the style suits her.

Hannah dumps the pebbles out of her boots and swings the bookbag over her uninjured shoulder, ready to face the day. Cecelia offers to take it, but Hannah sullenly refuses her offer as they open the front door out into the faerie landscape.

The sun has risen on a new day, painting the mosaicked stepping-stone path in shades of red, orange, and golden light. A strong wind blows through the whispering trees, and when Hannah looks again at the leaves, she realizes they're almost transparent, like shards of stained-glass windows. The breeze toys with Cecelia's long hair as they walk, but she keeps her wings hidden away, and Hannah wonders why she doesn't fly. The same little girl who'd always wanted to "pet the wind" stays grounded, even now that she has the freedom to take to the skies. Did the Piper take that from her, too? Hannah mulls over the story from the night before, its troubling implications settling in her stomach like soured milk.

"What's the matter?" Cecelia asks. "You're staring."

Hannah hadn't realized she'd been glaring into the back of Cecelia's head as the younger girl led her along the path. She averts her eyes to the ground with a shrug.

"Last night, you said all the stories about faeries are true," she says. "But then why haven't Dad's old iron tools ever burned you? And why didn't my pocketknife deter the Piper?" It's still in her pocket, and she rubs her fingers over the handle to ease her nerves.

"Remember, the switching spell made me fit in among humans. *True* fae burn on cold iron—or cast iron, a metal that people haven't wrought or turned to steel, like your knife. But for me, only some tools hurt, and I never had a scar."

"You flinched away when we worked on carpentry projects. I thought you were afraid of smashing your finger, but never a burn."

"Touching them felt uncomfortable, like an allergic reaction, or other unpleasant textures, but not enough to draw the connection. You wouldn't say you're 'burned' by sticky surfaces, or tags in your shirts, even though you don't enjoy touching them."

Hannah grimaces when Cecelia mentions the feeling of squelching goo beneath her fingers, then nods. Sensory aversions are a feeling she can understand. She rubs her fingers along the soft felt on the inside of the jacket to dispel the uncomfortable feeling, but Cecelia is right. She wouldn't call her distaste for such a texture the same thing as being "burned" by it.

"The Piper is also so powerful, I don't think any simple knife would hurt him," Cecelia adds. "I don't know what you were hoping to accomplish with a multi-tool."

Hannah rolls her eyes and fires off another question. "His power—with the flute and the rats and the mind control—how does that work? Is all music dangerous?" She leaves her secret fear unspoken: *what if he controls me?*

Cecelia hesitates for a long moment, humming an idle tune as she tries to collect her thoughts. After a few bars, Hannah recognizes it as Hazel's lullaby. Eventually Cecelia answers, "All music has power. It's a universal language. It inspires people to dance, moves them to tears, but the Piper corrupts that power into control. Plants and animals are easiest, like his thorns and his rat swarms, but he can control anything if he knows its true name."

"So, he has your name?"

"My bond with him is more complicated than that," Cecelia deflects. She falls silent again as they reach their destination.

The path leads them into a stand of trees with striped white bark. Strips of it flake up, revealing pink underneath, and Hannah knows that if she peeled it back, it would remove in smooth sheets. Paper birch trees. *Betula papyrifera.* The recognition of a familiar name makes Hannah feel a little better, despite all the strangeness of the last day. The path branches toward each tree, and when Hannah steps up to one, she realizes that on the inside of each strip of bark are tiny letters written in a familiar script—Cecelia's code. Faerie writing. Hannah can't help but laugh when she realizes the entire forest is the library—each tree is its own shelf full of books. *Paper* birches. Who knew?

The birch comes to life, smiling at Hannah from a knothole. As the library spirit moves, the leaves that make up her "hair" rustle, and a branch rattles as she moves her arm. The dryad librarian pulls the strip of bark off its trunk and offers it to Hannah, who steps back, startled. She holds out her hands to refuse and shakes her head. The dryad takes back the paper, reattaching it to the collection from which it came. And waves a leafy hand at Hannah as she retreats back to the main path. Cecelia, wearing a pleased grin, leads on. Hannah realizes the tree faerie must care for all the books being kept here, and she smiles too, knowing the knowledge is kept in good care.

In the middle of the grove is one birch that towers above the rest, its trunk as thick around as a skyscraper. The path leads them around the curve and brings them to a door nestled between two roots as thick around as an adult human. Cecelia opens it into a huge, hollow room.

Following her inside, Hannah blinks to let her eyes adjust. Organically growing lanterns set with crystals illuminate the marbled wooden walls. They're striped with red, brown, and white rings, showing the tree's growth over millennia. The faeries have carved out the space in the middle, placing stairs that go up, up, up in a spiral along the outside, cubbies cut into the outer wall to hold scrolls of the birch bark.

A table with oversized toadstools for seats sprouts up from the middle of the room. A salamander curls up around a simple ceramic teapot to keep it warm. Maps, scrolls, notes, and inkwells surround the teacups. When Hannah sniffs the air, a scent like vanilla tinged with magic fills her nose, and she can understand why Cecelia likes it here.

"Cecelia! You escaped!"

Hannah's wonderment falls to dismay when she recognizes two of the three figures standing around the table. The King and Queen are here. Hannah narrows her eyes, wary as the third person greets her sister, then she almost faints from both relief and surprise.

There is another human in Faerieland.

A middle-aged woman circles the table, her pale face beaming. Her vibrant, red-gold hair drapes over her shoulders in two braids as thick as ropes and long enough to reach her knees, woven through and tied off with green ribbon. She's wearing a modest habit that belongs in a medieval painting, and Hannah briefly wonders if she's wandered back in time. Something about the tilt of her head or the spark in her eyes seems friendly.

Cecelia darts to the woman, tackling her in a hug that spins them around. Joyous laughter rings through the space, even as she backs up a step and curtsys. "Lady Brigid!"

"I'm thrilled you made it to the Court safely. Your timing must have been perfect, bless all the Saints and Choirs." The Lady takes Cecelia by the shoulders and looks her up and down before tucking a stray strand of hair behind her ear.

Hannah's jaw drops at the exchange. Cecelia hides with Inky every time their parents invite adults over. Why is this woman different?

"I rushed to make it here during the storm, since I knew the portal would open on Halloween," Cecelia says. "What are you doing here?"

Lady Brigid's smile wanes but doesn't slip. "My business with the Monarchs is a grave matter, but it can wait a moment. I'll make us tea." With this, her gaze comes to rest on Hannah, who doesn't bow. She hasn't the slightest clue of who this woman is or why they should curtsy to her, though she gives the King and Queen a curt nod to avoid getting smited on the spot. Queen Titania responds with a coy wave while King Oberon continues poring over documents.

"You must be the Seeker," the Lady says with a welcoming tone and a lilting Irish accent. "King Oberon and Queen Titania have told me much about you, and I'm pleased to make your acquaintance." She beckons Hannah to sit at the table. Hannah appreciates no one has found or shared her name, and she gives Cecelia a questioning look as she sits as far away from the Monarchs as possible.

Cecelia accepts a mug and stares at it, refusing to meet Hannah's eye. "After the Piper found me last year, he left me lost in the woods. Lady Brigid found me and led me back to the road, where the rescue team found me. She offered to bring me to the Seelie Court, where she told me they would take in runaway changelings. I refused. The Piper's threats were too fresh, and I was desperate to go home. Eventually I realized I had made a mistake, and I couldn't stay in the Human Realm. At that point, I had to wait a year before the portal would open again and I could escape. You know the rest."

Hannah scowls. So *this* is the woman who's responsible for this mess.

That's not fair, she thinks immediately. The Piper is responsible for this mess, and Hannah should be thankful to Lady Brigid for helping Cecelia, though a small part of her can't help but blame her for ruining the life Hannah used to know.

The Lady hands her a cup of hot water, and Hannah says "Thank you," because it seems like the polite thing to say, but she's at a loss for how else to react. She has so many questions now, it feels like her mind might explode. Her hunger and thirst might also be to blame for her headache, and she scorns the temptation of tea. Still, the stranger's wise eyes make her feel warm and safe, and Hannah hopes this is not a cruel trick to lure her into a sense of complacency.

"It is only Earl Grey," the Lady assures her. "I am no fae thing."

She holds up the tea bags for Hannah's closer inspection. Seeing such a mundane box from the grocery store —still sealed, even better—is comforting, and somehow, Lady Brigid had even picked her favorite type. Hannah looks to Cecelia for confirmation. Her sister takes a sip from her own mug, then sighs with satisfaction and nods.

"I promise, she's safe."

Hannah lowers her guard and takes the tea, thankful for the opportunity to make it herself and avoid the tainting of magic.

"Lady Brigid may not be a "fae thing"' but she holds an invaluable role in our court," Queen Titania says. "Occasionally, lost humans, runaway changelings, and reformed members of the Unseelie Court will find their way here and decide to stay, aiding us in our work. Lady Brigid manages and mentors this group, which we call the Powers."

King Oberon continues, "The Lady herself bears a special gift, which is what brings us to this conclave. She is a seer."

Hannah's eyes widen, and she glances at the box of Earl Grey sitting at her elbow. Is that how Lady Brigid had known it was Hannah's favorite type of tea?

Lady Brigid nods, as if reading her mind. "My abilities led me to find Cecelia that fateful night and allowed me to see her true nature through the glamours which hid her from your eyes. However, I am afraid Cecelia is not the only reason I've traveled to the Court today."

Cecelia shrinks in her seat, and Hannah leans forward, expectantly, bracing herself for the worst. What kind of grave prophecy worries figures as powerful as the King and Queen of Faerieland? Lady Brigid folds her hands solemnly.

"This Hallows Eve, the balance of the world will shift once again. Children, you must decide your own fates, but we cannot stop the actions of the Courts. Do you understand?"

Hannah sullenly sips her tea and refuses to meet Lady Brigid's intense gaze, feeling helpless and out of place in this room of commanding entities. How can she choose her fate when the forces of the world march all around her?

Chapter 18
The Decision

QUEEN TITANIA HOLDS up one scroll they had been reading. It's covered in watercolor illustrations, showing a cyclic procession of figures marching toward a pit, a distinct figure leading the way each time. Hannah recognizes the Piper first, with his multicolored outfit and the music-note motif coming from the instrument he holds. He's followed by a rat king—nine rats with their tails knotted together. The other cycles show a wolf, a woman dressed in white, and a cloaked figure with nine shadows. In each cycle, Queen Mab stands over the pit, gleeful.

Queen Titania gestures to the scroll as she explains, "Ordinarily, the might of Queen Mab would rival our own, but the Unseelie Court seeks to gain more power by journeying to Carterhaugh Forest and sacrificing a soul to Hell once every seven years. Rather than choosing one of their own, the Masters compete to offer a human ward that will please Queen Mab, hoping to win prestige."

Hannah's stomach sinks. "Like the Piper's wards. This is like the story of Tam Lin."

"Tam Lin was lucky. While he lived, he sometimes visited the Seelie Court, but he always stayed home on Halloween, and rightly so," Lady Brigid says.

"You met him?" Cecelia asks.

After the insane couple of days she's just lived, Hannah's unsurprised the character from their fairy tales is real, and that this human has lived long enough to interact with someone from the medieval times.

"His wife, Janet, was lovely, too. She saved him through love and trickery." King Oberon smiles softly, as if lost in a memory, but his expression quickly sobers. "The night of their attempted sacrifice is long past. This cruel game will take place again this year."

"You can't just let them sacrifice a person to Hell!" Hannah interrupts. "This is completely ridiculous! Can't we stop them somehow?"

"We try. Some years, our diversions are successful. We can help the offering escape and intervene to stop the ritual. In these seasons, we keep the Unseelie at bay, while humanity remains unbothered," says the Queen.

"In the seasons that we fail," King Oberon adds, "we must rally our forces and rise to meet the stronger foe. For seven years, we remain vigilant and defensive until their magic wanes. For this reason, we've already begun preparing a team to perform the counter-ritual. Including Lady Brigid."

"Won't you go yourselves?" Cecelia asks, her voice sounding slight compared to those of the King and Queen, whose very existences reverberate in the surrounding space.

"We dare not risk the temptation," they say in unison.

Queen Titania speaks next. "Should we near the diabolical source and fall victim to its false promises, as the other Masters have, there would be disastrous consequences for the world."

Putting a comforting hand on Cecelia's shoulder, Lady Brigid gestures to the documents and maps on the table. "I've thwarted a few of their attempts in the past, and I've foretold as much as I can to help the Monarchs prepare. Halloween is tonight, as humans reckon time, but we have about a month in the Seelie Realm."

Hannah crosses her arms. "Why are you telling us this? Do you expect us to join you?"

"Heavens, no." Lady Brigid shakes her head. "This is not your battle to fight, child. We tell you because you should know Piper's movements. This knowledge may influence your decisions, and your decisions may influence the Piper's agent. I can see some possible futures, but none are guaranteed."

"Then how do we get home with all these monsters on the prowl?"

"You need only to ask for an escort to the border to be delivered to the Human Realm safely," King Oberon says.

Hannah's heart leaps at the news. "Well then, let's get going!" It seems so easy. They've seen the Seelie's kindness so far. Maybe she should give them the benefit of the doubt. But the warning look in Lady Brigid's eyes makes Hannah pause before she can rise from her seat.

The Queen says, "We can promise you safety as long as you stay within our influence, but as soon as you leave our realm, we cannot protect you from the Piper's fury anymore. He considers you stolen property, a failure in his system, and will stop at nothing to reclaim you."

Hannah shoots to her feet and slams down the teacup so hard, hot liquid sloshes over the edge and burns her fingers. She flaps her hands until they're cool and dry and sticky. "I thought you said coming to the Seelie Court would set you free!" she says, whirling on Cecelia.

"I said I would be safe, not free!"

The King addresses Cecelia, his face an apologetic mask. "Here, our medics can treat the Piper's Plague and restore your long life. Other escaped changeling teachers can help you relearn magic, but you must stay here to take advantage of that aid. There's nothing more we can do."

With that, the Monarchs gather their papers and exit the library. Their passive magic goes with them, leaving the room hollow and cold.

Hannah can't contain her boiling anger at Cecelia for concealing another lie, another half-truth, another omission that puts them in more danger. Her face flushes with embarrassment for not recognizing the false promise sooner.

"Isn't there any way to break the spell and force the Piper to leave us alone?" she asks.

Lady Brigid gestures for Hannah to sit down again, which she does, pushing the teacup away and crossing her arms.

"One way," Lady Brigid says. "You can only break the Piper's power over the two of you if you break his power over all *three* of you."

Three.

A missing memory. Hannah scowls as she realizes the person of whom Lady Brigid speaks. The reason for the replacement changeling.

"The one that was Taken," Cecelia whispers. Her voice wavers with fear and dread as she corrects herself. "The one I stole. The one he still controls."

A human girl, Hannah's true sister, switched by the Piper and forced into his service. A shudder goes down Hannah's spine when the idea comes to her mind, like choking thorns climbing their way up a bush.

"Does she look like you?" Hannah asks Cecelia, her chest tightening.

Cecelia shakes her head. "I looked like *her*, at least, until I learned the truth about myself."

Hannah thinks back to the baby picture on the refrigerator that she used to hang her notes. The matching dark hair and dark eyes and lopsided smiles. She thinks back to the girl who'd attacked her, how she'd mistaken them at first, sporting such similar hair and eyes. The girl trained to grow thorns and vines in seconds. It's a guess, yes, but it's one that feels right, like the universe knows the truth of her words before she says them and gives them due weight when she speaks.

"I met her," Hannah says, solemn silence settling over the table. Lady Brigid watches them both expectantly. "I met my *real* sister, and I left her behind."

Cecelia flinches. Her words were cruel, but Hannah doesn't care. Tears well in her eyes. Lady Brigid puts a comforting hand on her shoulder, but Hannah pushes it away and lays her head in her arms on the table. The mounting pressure threatens to crush her. She wishes she could unleash her fury and frustration, but it's not safe, not appropriate. Not here. The fire eats up her stomach, and there's a heaviness in her shoulders where wings aren't. Unyielding gravity tethers her to the ground, and she longs for the freedom of Cecelia's flight.

Hannah doesn't want to be a fae thing, not really, but her legs ache from walking, a blister rubs raw on the back of her heel, and her back cramps under the weight of her backpack. She is only fourteen, and she is tired, and she is mean. She wants only to wake up in her own bed and find that this was all a dream. To wake with Cecelia safe and sound beside her, human and real.

But that would leave an emptiness between her and Cecelia. Now that she knows the Taken is missing—stolen, captive—the guilt of leaving without her would eat Hannah alive. The paranoia of looking over her shoulder for the Piper would leave her dysfunctional. She would wait with dread for Cecelia to run away again, this time never to return. The girl they left behind would be alone, scared, and vicious. Cecelia would be a stranger in a foreign court, forced to watch her family fall apart from afar.

Can Hannah travel further into the unknown danger that awaits her in the Unseelie Realm? The idea of fighting the Piper is so daunting she wants to scream. The betrayal still stings, the lies still cast wicked doubts that whisper into her ear, and the questions still fill her head with fog. How can she, so woefully inadequate, rescue her sister, the one who is truly human and real? Which possibility scares her more?

Cecelia and Lady Brigid let her have her cry, and she wishes Willow were here right now to headbutt her elbow and lick away her tears. She wishes she could bury her face in Mom's apron and feel her father's steady hand on her shoulder. She wishes she didn't have to make this decision alone. But her mother and father and Willow are not here, and Cecelia sits across the table, awaiting an answer.

Hannah musters what little confidence she can from the crumbs of Mom's cooking in her bookbag, Dad's oversized coat, and Willow's hair still clinging to her pants. When she finally looks up at her companions, the Lady's gentle, affectionate look almost makes Hannah burst into tears again. She misses her mother so much. She hopes her parents won't worry about them.

"While the Unseelie Masters distract themselves with the Tithe, the time is keen to strike," Lady Brigid says. "If you should choose to venture home, or delve into the Unseelie Court to find the Taken, your opportunity draws nigh. If you choose to remain in the Seelie Court, we shall afford all comfort and care during your stay." Her tone lets Hannah know she won't judge them, no matter what they decide.

"No, that's madness! We can't go back into the Unseelie Realm," Cecelia protests. "That's just as ridiculous as Hannah coming here in the first place! Besides, that girl is *dangerous!* She nearly killed me on my way here! Hannah, she attacked you! She's a lost cause."

Hannah glares at the changeling sitting across from her. As the eldest, Hannah has always been the planner and the spokesperson. She wants to scream at Cecelia, maybe even slap her, for having the audacity to insist on what they should do after she'd run away, leaving Hannah in the dark. Cecelia had condemned an innocent child to a life of torment with the Piper, and now she refuses to fix her mistake? After what she has been through, shouldn't she be even more willing to rescue the Taken? Hannah is too angry to form words, much less make such a big decision.

Does Cecelia deserve her rage? Hannah hurts in so many ways, but the physical ache in her arm is only because her true sister attacked her. And she had no choice, with the Piper as a Master. The Piper was Cecelia's Master, just as much as the Taken's. Glaring into Cecelia's guilty face, regarding the web of lichen denoting doom for her young soul, Hannah recalls the horror stories she'd shared last night. The protectiveness in her heart reignites.

Cecelia had no choice. She'd never had a choice, and as soon as she'd gotten her chance, she'd fled to keep them safe. This isn't her fault.

Hannah takes a deep breath to keep her voice from cracking and tries to wipe her bleary eyes and runny nose with a handkerchief offered by Lady Brigid.

"Obviously, we're going to rescue my sister," Hannah declares, forcing her voice to sound more confident than she feels. Cecelia opens her mouth to protest, but Hannah's already turning to the Lady for answers. "What do we need to prepare?"

Chapter 19

The Twins

HANNAH HEARS THEIR next destination long before they reach it. The clanging of metal on metal and shouts of enthusiasm ring through the canopy as they pass through the glade of paper birches and into a field of wildflowers, before reaching a training ground. They descend a grassy hill with seats for onlookers, then pass an armory and guardhouse, where some faeries lounge off-duty. A carved wooden fence rings the dirt floor of the arena, and four massive oak trees at each corner cover the whole area in dappled shade.

Two people spar with each other, kicking up dust and flicking swords in more of a dance than a fight. Hannah forgets her mission and her frustration for a moment as she's enraptured by the fencing practice. The combatants laugh as they trade blows, neither seeming to get the better of the other. The blades flash too quickly for Hannah to see the subtle movements. There's a brief pause as they recover for breath, before lunging at each other again.

One pivots to get a better angle but hesitates a moment, distracted as they notice the girls observing. The other takes advantage, flipping their opponent's blade away to gain the upper hand. The sword rolls on the ground near the onlookers, and Hannah stops the hilt under her boot. She picks it up, grinning with excitement as she feels the balanced weight in her hand. She slashes and lunges, clumsily mimicking their flashy fighting style.

Both fighters approach, pulling off their helmets to reveal smiling faces. They look identical, young adult men with athletic frames, tan skin, and mops of curly brown hair plastered with sweat to their foreheads. Neither have wings.

"Well, what do we—"

"—have here?" they ask, one finishing the other's sentence as if it were the most natural thing in the world.

With their helmets off, Hannah notices their strange ears—more pointed than hers, but shorter than Cecelia's long, expressive ones. A small but significant oddity. They're nearly, but not completely, identical—their eyes are mismatched, one green and one brown, their hair parted to one side, a scar over one eyebrow—but each is a mirror image of the other. One has a green right eye, the other, a green left eye.

"These are a Seeker and a changeling," Lady Brigid says, gesturing to Hannah and Cecelia, respectively. "Girls, meet the Semivera twins, Matteo and Marco." Again, Hannah appreciates that the Lady does not reveal their names, giving her the chance to share it on her own terms. The twins must not share the same hesitancy. It's not as if Hannah could control them by name, anyhow. She wonders if they use codenames for safety here.

"Matteo and Marco are members of the Powers. I'll let them decide how best to teach you, while I arrange other preparations for your trip and get in touch with our scout, who will inform us when the Piper's attention diverges." Turning to the twins, she continues, "These girls will bring home their Taken sister in two weeks. They'll need to protect themselves against the swarm."

The twins salute in sync. "Of course, m'Lady," says one.

"We'll have them trained up in no time at all," says the other.

"Though we'll ask the fierce one to put down the blade—"

"Before she puts it through one of us," the one to Hannah's left finishes the exchange with a wink. She lowers the point of the sword to the ground but doesn't hand it back to the strange pair just yet.

The fierce one. She likes the sound of that.

Matteo—she thinks the one to her right is Matteo, but she can't remember now—leans against the fence and props his helmet under his arm. "First, we must ask how you plan to persuade the Taken?"

"For we can caution you this: it isn't your decision to make."

"It's the Taken's own choice to take herself back."

"You cannot force that decision."

"And she may not be easy to persuade."

Hannah's gaze bounces back and forth between them as they trade phrases. She wonders if this is part of their special ability or if they'd rehearsed it to disorient her. Awfully tricksy fae behavior, for all their unsettlingly human appearances. She gives the sword an annoyed flick and shrugs off one of the oversized jacket sleeves to show a blossoming bruise on her shoulder, ugly blues and purples forming the shape of a rose with her veins blossoming along the pale canvas of her skin.

"I know the Taken is tough," she says. "She can command vines, and she's a crack shot with a sling." Hannah doesn't mention the prospect of facing the Taken's magic again terrifies her, and that she hasn't the slightest clue how to convince a child so entrapped to turn away from the Piper's power.

"Oh, dear! Let me see that." Lady Brigid prods the bruise with a gentle hand. Hannah squirms but doesn't pull away. Her examination complete, the Lady nods with satisfaction as she pulls a small bottle from a fold in her robe. It contains a green shimmery salve stopped with a cork. "Our apothecaries enchanted this salve, but it will only speed up the healing for your bruise. Will you allow me to rub it into your shoulder?"

Thankful for the treatment, Hannah nods, watching as Lady Brigid smears the ointment on her injury. When she uncorks the bottle, the medicine smells of earthy herbs and petrichor. The paste chills her skin, but the purple color recedes almost immediately, like paint washing down a sink. When Hannah rolls her shoulder, there's no pain. Lady Brigid caps the bottle and puts it away, turning to Cecelia as Hannah folds her coat and sets it aside.

"Did you learn the Piper's trade?" Lady Brigid asks. "Can you fight against his changelings, using their own songs against them?"

Cecelia shakes her head, and her face falls into a mournful expression. "I might have once, before he chose me to take her place, but the switching spell gave the Taken any abilities I might have had. I can only control the glamour. Perhaps I could learn more with time?"

"I'll find you a teacher," Lady Brigid says with a nod before taking her leave.

Hannah waves her sword impatiently. "First, we should figure out how to not get stabbed or shot. Actually, do you have other weapons? I don't think a foil will do me much good against a wall of thorns. Maybe a machete would work. A REALLY big one."

"Did you bring a weapon?" Maybe-Matteo asks, raising an eyebrow at her arguments.

Hannah digs in her pocket and pulls out the grimy pocketknife, then tosses it to him for inspection. He grins and catches it, then vaults one-handed over the fence and ducks into one of the buildings. The other one laughs again and ruffles her hair as he steps around to correct her posture and stance. Soon, the first twin emerges carrying a cleaned and sharpened pocketknife, as well as more equipment for the two girls. Hannah springs to don her new uniform, eager to begin training and cram as much knowledge into her head as possible. Cecelia takes her place across from Hannah, falling into a halfhearted fighting stance.

Before they're even allowed to touch the weapons, Hannah and Cecelia run through stances and setups, blocks and strikes, punches and kicks. Hannah's knees scream as she drops into another position. Her shoulders protest as she deflects another blow over her head, and liquid lightning streaks through her nerves as a strike hits just right on her forearm.

Despite the pain, Matteo's praise of a parry well-executed makes her chest glow with confidence for the first time since arriving in the Seelie Court. Hannah decides she likes the twins' smiles and how they give them away so freely.

Chapter 20

The Scout

FTER A FEW hours, Lady Brigid reappears with food. She spreads out a blanket to turn the training ground into a picnic spot, and they sit cross-legged right there. Hannah conducts a thorough examination of the meal before daring to touch it, finally relinquishing any hope of returning home on time. It's been a full day since she's eaten anything, and after so much physical activity, she nearly faints as soon as she stops moving.

The spread Includes yellow squash flowers, stuffed with a savory meat and roasted until they're brown and crispy, then dusted with flaky powder that tastes salty and sweet at the same time. There's also a salad that isn't made of lettuce but some new faerie plant that Hannah doesn't recognize, tiny blue flower petals, and bright purple carrots. Cecelia takes a slice of fluffy bread and spreads on it an amber jam and peanut butter. Hannah eventually follows her example.

The others don't force Hannah to eat, but they encourage her to take care of herself and assure her dozens of times the food will not trap her here. Those are Unseelie tricks, and they've enchanted nothing with more than healing charms. When Hannah bites into the sweet apples, she cannot tell if they taste so exquisite because they're magical, or if she's so starving that anything would taste delicious.

As they're eating, Hannah's mind wanders back to the Taken—not just her sister, but all the Piper's wards. Would it be easier to convince her real sister to return home if they all rebelled together? Strength in numbers could be an asset, especially if all the wards are as vicious as her Taken sister. How brilliant—how brutal—it would be to turn the Piper's own training against him. She can only imagine the reasons the Taken would have for craving revenge.

The more she considers the possibility, the more she grows to like the idea of freeing the lot. With the hellish sacrifice as a distraction, they could charge the hideout and break all the chains, then escape into the woods together. Hannah imagines leading their triumphant return to Seelie. She dreams of a little sister treating her like a hero. This time, she'll prepare herself. Heroism is about strategy, right?

"Where do the Taken wards live?" Hannah asks, giving voice to her idea. "Cecelia described a prison of some sort in Unseelie territory. Can we find my sister and the other wards there, then rally the group and bring them back?"

Lady Brigid gives her a puzzled frown. "You should avoid entering the Piper's labyrinth at all costs if you want to return with your own life intact. Most likely, the fight will come to you before you travel too far past our borders."

"We could sneak in," Hannah insists, defensiveness flaring. She should get to voice her idea, at least. "There's got to be some kind of back way, right? If we timed it right, we could be in and out in no time, and bring all his soldiers back with us. We'd cripple the Piper's power in this big war you keep talking about, and it seems obvious these kids don't want to fight for him."

As she explains, Hannah watches Lady Brigid's expression change to one of gentle bemusement. Hannah doesn't like that look. It's the same look Dad gives her to soften the blow when he says "No" to Hannah driving, even though she's already tall enough to reach the pedals. It can't be that bad of an idea, can it? It's such a simple strategy—perhaps too simple. If it's such a straightforward solution, why haven't they tried it already? There must be something Hannah's missing.

"The nature of each changeling bond is unique to the individual," Lady Brigid says. "The fundamental magic is the same, in the way we compose every song of notes and chords, but there are hundreds of thousands of ways to combine them in song. To unravel the spell for each child, you would need to locate both the changeling fae and their human counterpart, then persuade both to forgo the Piper's powers and their existing lives. Each needs to find their name. Cecelia saw how her deal would eventually consume her. Very few possess the wisdom to discern reality from the Piper's lies."

Cecelia picks at her food throughout the exchange. When she's described as wise, her face reddens, but she does not respond. Is the Lady implying Hannah is foolish by comparison? Perhaps. Now that Hannah thinks twice, her stupid idea sounds like a storybook scheme from a silly girl far out of her depth.

"Forget I said anything," Hannah grumbles.

"We're here to answer questions," Lady Brigid says as she puts a hand on Hannah's knee. "Do not be ashamed of your ignorance."

It's a gentle letdown, but a disappointing and sobering one. Hannah may not know everything, but she knows this—the faerie world is harsh. Though Lady Brigid is kind enough to forgive her rash ideas, Hannah cannot afford to act on assumptions, and her lack of understanding will get her killed if she's not careful.

"It's fine," she lies. "So, we can't rescue all the kids. I'd just hoped we could reunite more families with their lost siblings, that's all."

"We do what we can."

"But it's never enough, is it? You said the Powers is an elite group. And Cecelia went on and on about how the Monarchs are so powerful. It seems wrong that I'm the only one who wants to fix this." Hannah shoves the rest of her bread in her mouth, trying and failing to find solace in her sandwich.

"That's not fair!" Cecelia says, finally showing the audacity to speak up. "You don't seriously think you can single-handedly stop a war that's been waging for eons?"

Of course Hannah cannot do that, but Cecelia's condescending tone makes her bristle. When she opens her mouth to respond, Lady Brigid speaks before she can get a word in.

"I know you want to save the world, but sometimes, you cannot even save yourself." She lays a hand on Hannah's elbow and furrows her brow, leaning closer to make her point. "If the best you can do is claim minor victories against the dark, then that is enough. Never lose the desire to strive for perfection, but always know you will never reach it." Her voice is soft but stern, and it leaves no further room for discussion. "Do not fall into discouragement. Saving one lost child may not seem like it matters in the grand scheme of the universe, but it will matter to her. Persist, for your sister."

Hannah bites back her tears of frustration and the bitter unsaid words on her tongue. She stands and turns to the twins, ready to train again. They've been sitting apart to let the girls have their space, and now Hannah realizes another tiny figure has joined the party. She dashes over and drops to her knees to embrace her weasel friend.

"Kit-Kat!"

The weasel scurries across the floor, twists around Hannah's arm and across her shoulders, and pushes through her curls to nuzzle under her chin. She scratches him behind the ear and laughs, all her cares melting away at the sight of her friend.

"Where did you go, you little devil? You scared me when you ran off. I thought you were hurt! I'm glad this bandage stayed on, or else you'd *really* be in trouble."

"You know him?" Marco asks with a twitch of his head.

"Is he yours? He saved me from the Piper!"

Kit-Kat only gives Hannah an indignant chitter and jumps off her shoulder, running over to Lady Brigid. He stands on his hind legs before her, like a little soldier at attention, and chatters something the Lady seems to understand. She nods and pulls a few smooth twigs from a fold in her cloak, laying them out in a specific pattern on the picnic blanket. Hannah picks one up to inspect it, noticing runes carved into the wood, before Matteo bats her hand away and places it back down. She keeps her hands to herself as Kit-Kat scampers from one stick to the other, contorting and jumping in intervals. Eventually, he finishes his dance, bows, and then darts off to steal jerky from Matteo's plate.

"What was that all about?" Hannah asks as Lady Brigid gathers the tools.

"He's one of our scouts. He's reported that after the Taken retreated from the Portal Tree, after the guards seized Hannah, she lurked away from the northern border until the Piper seized her, and they both retreated into Unseelie territory. She hasn't been seen since then, but right now, the Piper patrols the South. Other swarms and agents patrol the other cardinal directions, waiting for you girls to emerge."

"How on earth did you get all that from . . . that?" Cecelia asks now, peering over Lady Brigid's shoulder at the runes.

The Lady points at a few different symbols. They're different from the faerie letter code that Hannah recognizes. "It's a shorthand system we taught him to aid our communication. A vast improvement from the dirt scratches, if I say so myself. His claw-writing is terrible. Almost as bad as yours, Marco. I never should have let you teach him."

Matteo clears his throat. "Our mother diligently instilled in us the importance of excellent penmanship."

"We only half-paid attention," Marco adds.

"And we do not share that skill equally."

Hannah shakes her head, as Kit-Kat returns to her lap. Checking the bandage, she sees the scratch he earned in battle is almost healed already. "I knew there was something different about you. You are way too smart to be just a normal weasel. Are you secretly a faerie, too? With my luck, I'd be two for two."

Cecelia sticks out her tongue at Hannah, who ignores her. The twins just laugh at the exchange, and Matteo gives her an approving smile for the medical care. He retrieves a pale yellow tincture from a knapsack nearby and gives her a few drops to put on the wound. Kit-Kat's torn flesh knits itself back together far faster than any natural process. Hannah smooths over the fur and kisses it, prompting a rumbling purr from Kit-Kat's throat.

"We don't truly know how the critter came to be so clever," Matteo says.

"Before we knew the nature of our bond, we were searching for a portal for the Seelie Court around an old haunted house at sunset on the Spring Equinox," Marco says.

"Well, I found the portal," Matteo proudly states.

"And I got lost," Marco amends with a sheepish grin.

"Critter found us and led us here to the Lady." Matteo picks up the banter again without missing a beat.

"And the rest is history."

"Kit-Kat is a far better name than Critter, though."

"More descriptive."

"Sweet and snappy."

Hannah scoffs, as she's sure there's far more to the story than their brief explanation. As the Semiveras chatter, Kit-Kat curls up inside the folds of her discarded jacket. Hannah's about to ask them to elaborate when Lady Brigid speaks up.

"I believe the Monarchs bestowed this Power upon our musteline friend," she says. "Every time I ask, they refuse to confirm this. I suspect King Oberon thinks it's a tremendous joke. I can't rid myself of the little devil." Despite the disparaging nickname, her voice is warm with affection.

"Lady, you know you love him," Marco says, scratching the weasel behind the ears. Kit-Kat fluffs up with a self-satisfied chirp.

"He's an admirable scout, indeed." She directs her next instruction to Kit-Kat. "After you rest, please continue patrolling the border, without causing undue risk to your safety, and return immediately if the Piper's guards leave an opening or you spot Hannah's Taken sister."

Kit-Kat nods in acknowledgment before returning to his nap. Hannah arranges the surrounding fabric in a comfy bed for him before dusting off her hands and standing to resume her training. The assurance that Kit-Kat is safe and working on their side puts her mind at ease, and the sustenance gives her renewed strength to face the mission ahead.

Chapter 21

The Glamour

WHEN HANNAH RESUMES her training with the twins that afternoon, Lady Brigid shows Cecelia to a different clearing instead, far enough away from the training grounds that their antics will be out of earshot. Exhausted by the physical exertion and frustrated by Hannah's attitude, she's glad for the escape and the opportunity to learn a trade better suited to her skills. Changing her appearance back to her human form had only made things worse. Guilt twists in her stomach, making her glance over her shoulder toward the training grounds again.

The role of Hannah's sister was never hers to claim. Hannah had never been good about eye contact growing up, but all day, she's refused to even glance at Cecelia's face, even during training. And Cecelia can't blame her.

She hates her own face, these days.

The Seelie Court accepts her, but she doesn't belong here—at least, not yet. The spells that come naturally to Seelie fae fail Cecelia before she even forms the will to cast them. Simple things, like tossing a bauble of light or catching slips of starlight in her hands, are impossible for her because of the switching spell. Now, they're going on this mad mission to the Unseelie Court before the most dangerous night in seven years. A few weeks of training won't protect her. All she has is her glamours, as pathetic as they are.

"Here we are," Lady Brigid says, leading her into a small clearing. "I shall leave you with your capable teacher and return to fetch you for dinner."

Cecelia glances around the grove. She doesn't see anyone.

"Should I just wait?"

Lady Brigid gives her a coy smile in answer, then sweeps away back the way they came. Cecelia shrugs and settles herself cross-legged in the soft clover. When a few minutes pass with no sign of her instructor, she lies down to watch the clouds. They don't roll past like they do in the Human Realm—here, they're living things. Wisps of cirrus play on the wind, chasing each other around like a game of tag, while cumulonimbus friends lounge and puff rings to each other. She waves. One forms a hand from its mass and reaches down as it drifts by, like she might trail her hand in the water when on a boat. It caresses her face with one giant finger, then tickles her belly, the touch as soft as a feather and cool as the dew. It sails off with a smile, leaving her dress damp.

Cecelia giggles and shuts her eyes, enjoying the feeling of the sun on her skin. Maybe her teacher won't arrive, and she can take a nap instead.

An acorn hits the middle of her forehead.

"Ow!" She sits up and inspects the offending nut, rubbing at the welt and cringing as her fingers accidentally brush a spot of the Piper's Plague that grows on her face. It's hidden beneath the glamour, but it's still there, and the illusion unravels. She doesn't take her hand away, instead working her torn-up fingernails under its edge. She scratches at the border, pulling the offending film away to expose the raw skin underneath. It aches. She doesn't realize what she's doing until inky blood runs down her temple and stains her fingers.

She pulls her hand away with a resigned sigh. The angry wound will sting all day now. Why can't she learn self-control?

After so many itches, she should know that giving into the compulsion always results in worse aftermath. The familiar reprimand cycles through her head as she searches for something to wipe her face and hand. As her fingers brush the mossy bed, they cross the acorn again. This time, it gives her pause.

What is an acorn doing in a grove of maples? She's not as good at identifying plants as Hannah is, but even she understands that's not right.

She looks again and notices something she'd overlooked before—the slightest shimmering of glamour around the edges of a faerie's figure, otherwise camouflaged against the bark. How long had they been there without revealing themselves? Is this her teacher? Is this a test?

Cecelia throws the acorn back at them, and it sails in a smooth arc before a near-invisible hand snatches it out of the air. Then an arm shifts and emerges into vision, the rest of the body coming into focus as the fae lets her glamour drop. She's a gangly dark-skinned woman with a bob of curly red hair and a sly grin. She crushes the acorn between two fingers, scoops out the meat on a sharp nail, eats it, and drops the shell before swinging down to the forest floor. As she reaches Cecelia, she pulls a handkerchief out of her pocket and extends it to the bloody wound. Cecelia shrinks back at first, until she realizes it's being offered as a gesture of apology.

She takes it gratefully and mops up the mess she's made of her face. It's damp with a sweet ointment that soothes the burning. What an embarrassing first impression. As she cleans the scar, Cecelia studies the fae who must be her teacher. She has amber cat's eyes, bony fingers, and gray moth wings. Part of her uniform seems natural, as if her skin is tough chitinous armor, like an insect's exoskeleton. The gaps are filled by leather and linen, all styled with greenwood patterns to break up her silhouette. She looks like a perfect soldier.

Then Cecelia notices the familiar blue lichen growing along her hairline. This fae also has the Piper's Plague. She is—or was—a changeling. The infection is faded and tiny compared to the ridges marring Cecelia's skin, and she can't help but stare at the saved fae—almost healthy, grinning at her.

"Lavender salve stops the itching," the fae says. "My name's Quercu."

Maybe it's Hannah's paranoia rubbing off on her, or a lingering result of the Piper's influence, but Cecelia doesn't share her name. She knows the Seelie Court is safe, and that no one will control her using it, but somehow, it still doesn't feel right to use it anymore.

"Pleasure to meet you, Quercu." She butchers the pronunciation.

"No, no, it's *k-where-coo*."

"Quercu," she corrects awkwardly. "You are kind . . ." She folds the handkerchief and puts it in her pocket, "And patient."

The fae's features shift away from the camouflage. Her face is angular and mischievous, her skin is nut brown, like the acorn, and her build, though lanky, is as sturdy as any oak. "No use in waiting 'round anymore. Let's see what ye can do."

Cecelia focuses and lifts her shoulders, letting her wings reappear as easily as shrugging off a coat. In the same moment, her ears lengthen to a point, and the rest of her fae features emerge from the disguise.

Quercu raises one eyebrow, unimpressed. "Is that all ye got?"

"I learned nothing else. I don't know where to start."

"You can copy the face of a girl you've never met before, so why don't you try copying the face of someone else you know? That's easy," Quercu says. She picks a nasturtium and munches on the spicy flower, looking bored.

It seems like a straightforward task, and Cecelia wracks her brain for options. She's not eager to steal more faces. Feeling impish, she chooses the most convenient material to study, and focuses. Cecelia squeezes her eyes shut, willing her magic to mold her features into their new forms. It's uncomfortable at first, but relieving, like stretching a tight muscle or cracking her knuckles, working out the soreness of disuse. When she opens her eyes again, she knows she's transformed into her teacher.

Quercu pinches Cecelia's cheek. Cecelia sticks her tongue out in response, but grins at her success despite herself. Her clothes didn't transform, but she's happy with her results.

"Don't get cheeky with me," Quercu says with a tone that tells Cecelia she intended the terrible pun. "Now make yourself scarce. I want ye out of my sight before I reach thirty."

"I'm sorry." Cecelia reverts to her natural form, tired and stinging from the sudden rejection. She ruined her only chance already. Her face feels sore and melty from the rapid change, like a wax candle left out in a sunny window, and she's ready to retreat until she can put her nose on straight again. Ashamed, she stands and turns to leave the clearing.

Another acorn hits her in the back of the head and she spins around.

"That's not what I meant, dandelion fluff fer brains." Quercu rolls her eyes with a wry smile. "Hide." She covers her eyes and starts counting again from the start.

Oh. It's a game. Cecelia's cheeks flush with embarrassment, and she rushes for the trees. Her wings get in the way as she climbs. She tries to lift herself enough to reach the next branch, but she's out of practice. She had never learned how to fly growing up in the human realm, and in the year since discovering the truth about her nature, she'd continued hiding her wings. She still doesn't know how to use them properly, and the useless things only beat at the air and make the leaves rustle around her, but do nothing to release gravity's hold on her.

With difficulty, she makes it into the boughs and tries to hide herself amongst the leaves, mimicking Quercu's disguise from before. How is she supposed to make herself into something without the shape of a human or fae? Should she change the pattern of her skin and her hair? Which way should she make the leaves grow? Should she make them look like they're printed on her skin, like they're woven into the fabric of her being, or should they sprout up from her arms and legs to hide the form of her body instead? She puzzles over what to do with her dress and tries to remember how Quercu hid her rugged clothes when she hid in the trees. She flushes with frustration, the same way she had lost her temper when she couldn't work out how to fix a ruined sketch. Before she can replicate the disguise, her time runs out.

Quercu doesn't open her eyes when she reaches thirty. She only stands, spins on her heel, pitches an acorn, and hits Cecelia in the arm. Merciful Monarchs, please let Quercu stop the onslaught of acorns. Only after hearing her yelp of annoyance and surprise does her teacher open her eyes and grin, crossing her arms in smug satisfaction.

"I know imitation is the highest form of flattery. Ye must really love me to try my own tricks twice," she jokes before her tone turns serious. "I appreciate the compliment, but I don't like my students to be teacher's pets."

Cecelia slumps under the reprimand. What else was she supposed to do?

"Well, it didn't work. You found me right away," she grumbles, climbing down from the tree. "I need some kind of reference. It's too hard to come up with the right disguise on my own."

"You have yer references right there," Quercu says with a puzzled expression, gesturing to the tree.

"That's not what I mean. I can't make a glamour from just the surroundings alone. It needs more structure, or it'll fall apart when I think about it too hard. I can't."

Cecelia sits among the flowers, letting her discouragement pull her down. Quercu strides over to her and takes Cecelia's small, soft hands in her bony, weathered ones. Cecelia frowns and refuses to meet her gaze.

"No, ye need to grow beyond copying now," the older fae says.

Cecelia lifts her eyes to glower at Quercu. Isn't that all changelings are good for? Copying other people and things? "How come?"

"There's not always something around to copy. Sometimes, ye need to invent yourself into something *new*, depending on what the situation needs."

"That's better than stealing people's faces, I suppose. I don't want to be a liar anymore, but I don't understand how to disguise myself as a plant."

Quercu lies down among the flowers and vanishes among them. "Glamour isn't a disguise or a trick. Did ye ever notice in yer years with the humans, ye never really *lied?* We fae don't do that. We'll stretch the facts, omit parts of the complete story, work in loopholes, even change reality—but never lie. Ye aren't concealing yourself in the flowers. Ye need to *be* a flower."

Somehow, that's worse. A half-lie is still a lie. Cecelia's false life still hurt Hannah. There's no taking back what she did, and she hates the reminder of who she was. She doesn't know what she wants to be now, but she's pretty sure she doesn't want to be a flower. She hates the Piper, but without the role he instilled overshadowing her life, there's nothing left to fill the void of purpose.

Exasperated, Cecelia picks a daisy and rips off the petals one by one. Quercu sits up and tucks a clean flower into Cecelia's hair, giving her an encouraging smile.

"Shapeshifting isn't supposed to be a limit. It's not just a tool, it's an art," she explains. "Ye can use it to express yerself."

When Quercu mentions art, Cecelia recoils and scowls. She stares at the mangled bloom in her hands and releases a sob. "That's the problem. I can't do that anymore."

She searches around for a branch and starts drawing in the loose dirt of the path, misshapen sketches of Hannah and the

Taken. "Before I learned the truth about the Piper, I loved to create. My art covered the walls of my room. I wrote my own songs. It's been a year since I found out I was nothing but a fake, and *nothing* I've made since then has worked! Ugh!"

She scuffs out her drawings in the dirt with the heel of her boot, cracks the stick in half, and throws the pieces into the tree line.

"Yer too wrapped up in yer twisted self-perception," her teacher says, shaking her head. "It's like yer magic is a ball of yarn, all tangled up in a little snarl. Unravel it. Glamours require careful weaving, and ye can't cast one with a knotted string of self."

"If my magic is so broken, then this is all hopeless!" Cecelia snaps. "You're a changeling, too. How can you do this when your magic is no more powerful than mine?"

"This isn't about power. It's faith, dear. Know what ye are first. Believe ye can become what ye want to be, enough to make it true. The glamour will form itself in the gap and grow beyond the original."

"I don't know what I am! I'm not Cecelia anymore," the Changeling screams, surprising herself at the outburst but giving into the grief. "I can't be Hannah's human sister. I can't be one of the Seelie. I'm just a knot of snarled magic. A blurry copy that came out all wrong. I'm a liar—a bad liar."

Something in those words cuts deep to her core, a sharp truth that carves out whatever was left of the girl she used to be.

The Changeling does what she does best. She runs away.

Chapter 22
The Changeling

UERCU IS QUICK to grab the Changeling's arm, but she's quicker to flee. Her steps crush the moss as she tears herself from her teacher's grasp and sprints across the clearing, summoning her wings and desperately throwing herself into the air.

A gale sweeps her above the trees, where the breezes beat her in frantic swoops and circles. A gust throws her toward the earth, the force threatening to rend her weak, unused wings. She crashes in an oak close to the meadow, caught in a knobby hollow. She wants nothing to do with oaks or acorns anymore, and she goes to leap out of the tree again, when a branch creaks and bends under a faerie's weight. The Changeling whips her head around to see if she's been followed.

Quercu's perched on the branch above her, of course, but this time, the other changeling carries none of her cocky bravado. This expression is one of sympathy and concern. "The Piper's done vicious work on ye."

It's spoken from experience, from understanding. The Monarchs were nice to the Changeling; Lady Brigid's been unfailingly kind; the twins, friendly. Hannah—for all her barbs—still cares enough about her to journey into Faerieland on a whim. But none of them feel their souls fraying at the edges, torn between three worlds. They don't wake crying as their life saps away to a parasite. None of them fear the Piper's swarm of rats as much as she does, their skittering feet and sharp teeth clambering to reach her in her nightmares. They don't feel eyes on their neck or hear phantom music in their dreams.

Quercu does. Her acknowledgment breaks the Changeling's composure more than anything else. *He broke me too*, she quietly means.

The Changeling chokes back a sob. "Yes." She doesn't run, or turn to face Quercu, but fixes her eyes on the horizon. Where else does she have to go? There's no other realm where she can run to find answers. She shrinks into herself, helpless.

"Ye have yet to learn the hardest lesson of our kind. I'm sorry I didn't realize, or I'd have started with this . . ." Quercu says. She takes a deep breath before asking, "What is your name?"

"I don't know. I'm just the Changeling. That's all."

Instead of more instruction or scolding, Quercu settles back in the crook of a branch and starts picking more acorns to replace the ones she'd thrown from a little pouch on her belt. "My name is Quercu," she says, as if to remind herself. "I've been Quercu for two-hundred and thirty-seven years. My sister won't return."

The Changeling doesn't respond, still trying to salvage the shattered pieces of her identity. She can't go back to being who she was. Some part of her mind dimly attends her teacher's words.

"I replaced an only child in the Human Realm, so I didn't have any other siblings to worry about. Just the Taken sister I replaced. Ye probably think I'm lucky. Your Seeker— meaningfully or not—has done a sorry job of complicating things. If it were just ye, leaving would have been easy, right?"

"I still hurt my—" the Changeling cuts herself short, about to say "my mom and dad," but they don't belong to her anymore. "I still hurt Hannah's parents."

"Ye miss them."

"They're not mine to miss," the Changeling sniffs. "What about you?"

Quercu hums thoughtfully. "I don't miss my human folks, not one bit. They were an awful lot. Didn't have a single clue about my faerie nature. They just thought I was odd. Hated me for it, too. I embarrassed them. In public, they raised their voices against me. Behind closed doors..." She lets her voice trail off as a dark expression of memory clouds her face. "Less said 'bout that, the better. Cruel folks. When my mind finally snapped, I didn't think twice about running off, and I never looked back either. Whatever fresh hell waited for me in those woods had to be better than what I left behind."

The Changeling's eyes widen. Quercu's story drags her out of her depths of pity and self-loathing long enough to feel astonishment at her words. Her misery almost becomes a blessing; at least she can mourn something pleasant, now lost. Her teacher had nothing worth grieving.

"They sound almost as bad as the Piper."

"Worse. The Piper is a wicked thing by nature, all twisted up inside for as long as fae memory, which is lengthy, indeed. Perhaps he wasn't always that way, and there's a tiny kernel of good somewhere, frozen deep within his being. I'd like to believe that's true. I have to believe that's true, because my sister is still with him. But it's neither here nor there, 'cause when the Piper got ahold of me, he was already a wretched thing. I could never expect kindnesses from that miserable old hack. Parents, though...they're supposed to love ye." Quercu's voice is bitter, even with the age long past. "I loved them, for all it's worth. Even visit their graves once a season, but it's a gloat. I survived them, and I outlived them, the fae that I am. But in the end, I hope their souls found eternal rest. They didn't know what they were doing."

"And your sister?" the Changeling asks, morbid curiosity overwhelming her sorrow. "She's still alive?"

"Alive and kicking. Nearly finished me last week, but oh-ho, was I clever! Hopped on that spite bear she sent after me and rode it clear across the river, back into the Seelie lands, where the poor old girl shook me off and trooped back home to her cubs.

The Changeling's eyes widen and her mouth gapes for a second as she processes that not only had Quercu ridden an angry mama bear across a river last week, but that Quercu's sister could control an angry mama bear. That would take mighty magic—a powerful song.

"Your sister's still with the Piper? Still attacking you after two hundred years? No human lives that long."

"The Piper's power sustains her. She's one of his most vicious fighters, the most successful of the brood, so she's avoided becoming part of the swarm."

"The swarm..." the Changeling shudders. "He threatened to transform me if I failed to bring Hannah to him. I fear he will, if I ever step foot outside this place."

"Yer still planning to rescue your Taken?" Quercu asks, cocking her head.

"*Hannah's* Taken," the Changeling corrects with a bitter sigh. That was the plan, Hannah's foolhardy, arrogant plan. Just march into the depths of the Unseelie caverns, wave a sword around, and ask her to come home. Of course Hannah thinks it'll be as simple as the storybooks. She's already made an animal companion of Kit-Kat; she's halfway to becoming the heroine of a different tale. But that's not the way this world works, and the Changeling wants no part of it.

The Changeling's mind swims. If someone as capable and tough as Quercu couldn't persuade her sister after two hundred and thirty-seven years, what makes them think they can accomplish such a feat in an afternoon?

"Why?" she asks, dumbstruck. "Why does she stay?"

Quercu fetches some strips of jerky from another pouch at her belt, and holds them out to the Changeling, who takes one. Quercu chews on her snack with a pensive expression before finally answering.

"I barely knew my own name. I'd only picked it the day before. Gave myself no time to even scab over the open wound of ripping off the last name, much less grow into a new one. The day after I made it to the Seelie Court, I went after her, and I'd made the wrong first impression. My parents taught me a lot of ugly habits. I didn't know better, but I thought hollering and threatening was the best way to get someone to listen. She didn't have a reason to like me any more than the Piper."

Quercu sighs again, long and tainted with regret. "We've been in a feud ever since. 'Twas not my finest moment. It thrilled her to dominate beasts to her will. Little things back then: bugs, mostly. But I tell ye, it's hard to make a convincing argument when a swarm of yellow jackets is after ye."

"It sounds like you tried your best."

"Aye. It was a rotten best, but it was all I knew."

"But in all the years since, she won't hear reason?"

"Ehh. It's become like a game now. We can sit and joke, have conversations about many meaningless little things, but the minute I try to ask her name, she's after me again. I go looking, she sets traps. Some are crueler than others. As her power grows, so does her stubbornness."

"And yours."

"Aye," Quercu says with a wry chuckle, before her expression settles to solemn concern again. "I tell you my story so you don't make the same mistakes I did. It's easy for me to go after her again and again, hoping against hope one of these days she'll come home with me. I'm only risking my life, and it's only my choice to make. I come back to Seelie, and the time I spend in that wicked realm washes away like sand in a river. Yer Seeker complicates things. I want at least one of ye to know, you'll be on the losing side of time."

"That's time we don't have to waste making mistakes and driving the Taken away," the Changeling says, catching Quercu's meaning.

Quercu gives one serious nod. "So, now you understand why I have to ask ye. What is your name?"

The Changeling squirms under the intensity of her stare, the weight of the question. She fights the urge to run again, as unwelcome memories clamber for attention in the back of her mind. It's easier to forget. If she's honest about being a liar, at least she doesn't have to bear the guilt anymore.

"I don't know. Not anymore."

"Then tell me who you are."

"I'm the Changeling. That's all I know. I'm lost and scared. Hannah doesn't want me to be her sister or her parent's daughter anymore, but I don't want to disappoint them in failing this task. I'll die if I return to the Piper, because he won't forgive my treachery. Finding the Taken terrifies me. I know nothing about being a faerie, and the powers I do have are useless to the Seelie cause. I don't belong anywhere." She pulls her knees up to her chest and rests her chin on her arms, unwilling to look into those piercing eyes any longer.

Quercu flutters over and tilts the Changeling's head up by the chin. "Hey, hey, hey, who said anything about not being useful?"

"I can't do proper glamour, you said so yourself." The Changeling jerks away and slaps Quercu's hand.

"Just because ye haven't figured it out yet doesn't mean we're kicking ye out. Ye don't have to prove yer worth to anybody here. Yer welcome, on account of ye being a person with dignity and enough good in ye to not be a hazard. Yer twin and my twin would both be welcome here, same as any other, if they'd find their names and stop their violence. Ye think I arrived being able to do all this?"

The Changeling goes to wipe her face on her sleeve, remembers she still has Quercu's handkerchief, and uses it to dry her tears. For all her rough manners at first, Quercu is kind.

"I have so much to learn," the Changeling says. "About myself, about everything."

"Ye don't need to know yerself right now. I'll keep asking yer name, in case ye find one, or remember who you want to be. But for now, all I'm asking is that ye listen. I'm willing to teach, if yer willing to learn."

The Changeling nods.

"Alright then. Now, what is your name?"

The discomfort still nags at the hole in her soul, but this time she expects it and it's easier to keep her temper. "I don't know."

"Who are you?"

"The Changeling. A student. Hopefully, one day, a member of the Seelie Court."

The Changeling twists a strand of her long hair between her fingers as she speaks. It's black, like Hannah's. Growing it out, forgoing the imitation of Hannah's close-cut bob, seemed like a rebellious thing to do. As she leaves that part of herself behind, she remembers she always liked the idea of having pale hair, like the elves in the stories, beautiful and pale as the moon. White with ancient age, not doomed by the Piper's Plague. She closes her eyes and imagines the change. It's not too hard to picture. She's seen people bleach and dye their hair before in the human world with chemical boxes from the store that always made her eyes water.

When she opens her eyes, the strands she's braiding look like she imagined. She drops the plait and laughs in disbelief, runs her fingers through her hair and pulls it around herself to see its transformation. The pale strands catch the autumn evening light and reflect a soft gold. Quercu gives her a look of approval.

"That's a lovely look on you," she says, pulling a small mirror from a pocket in her skirt and holding it up for the Changeling, who scarcely recognizes herself. It comes with a giddy rush of fear and joy. Quercu takes back the looking glass and lets the Changeling finish her braid.

Quercu stretches, letting her wings flutter in the breeze. "Let's quit the glamours for the day. Would ye rather learn to fly instead, seeing as we're already in a tree?"

The Changeling makes the mistake of looking down, realizing they're well over fifty feet above the ground. She tightens her grip on the branch. She had tried to fly only once before—when she'd left home on the night of the thunderstorm. Hazel had distracted Willow, so she could make her escape while the Teagan family slept. In the early morning, she had slipped out of Hannah's bed, through the passageway, and into her own room. Bidding farewell to the familiar surroundings, she had burned herself flicking open the iron latch, kicking out the screen, and in a single, terrifying decision, had thrown herself from the second-story window, trying to glide on unused wings as the rain and wind tossed her like a leaf in a hurricane. She had lurched and tumbled over herself, banging into obstacles and plummeting toward the earth, before swooping into the thunderheads, then dropping to the earth again in the distant woods, all sense of direction lost from her muddled head. The storm had hidden her from the Piper through the morning. She'd fled from the Taken, reaching the Portal Tree only shortly before Hannah had followed her.

She hasn't flown since.

Quercu extends a hand to her, and the Changeling's nerves run wild as she risks the fall.

"I'm not ready," she says, her breath catching in her chest. Is she ready to abandon her final tethers to the ground, the last illusions of being human? Can she trust Quercu enough to catch her? Can she trust herself to do it, when she doesn't even know who she is? She feels like a caterpillar in a cocoon, halfway to emerging from the goop of her former self, halfway to becoming something on the other side of metamorphosis, but she doesn't know what yet. Her wings haven't finished unfurling, and she doesn't know if they will bear her weight. She's just a mess of awkward pieces, but she's still designed to take flight.

The Changeling lets Quercu take her hand and lift her, so she's standing on the branch with her toes hanging off the edge. Quercu stands beside her and gives her a reassuring smile, the dappled sunlight playing over her face through the leaves, and the breeze tousling her red crown of curls. The Changeling wants this kind of freedom, this joy, the reckless abandon that comes with the confidence Quercu possesses.

"It's a beautiful day for a soar, and no amount of waiting will make you brave," she says.

The forest floor is so far away, but the Changeling shudders, squeezes Quercu's hand, and gives her a nod.

Quercu shows her how to place her wings and beat them with ease, but like with glamours, the technical points matter less than the intent.

The Changeling breathes in the fresh fall air, filling her lungs with the scents of flowers and her freedom. They step off the branch and catch the breeze. A gentle updraft lifts them above the branches into the tie-dyed sunset sky. She skims along the clouds, smooth as a satin embrace, tinted magenta by the sunset, as soft and sweet as cotton candy. When she sees the earth so far below, she panics, falters, and starts to fall. But the friendly cloud spirits do not drop her, buoying her aloft with a path of her own. Venus, bright and clear, shines like the first evening star, hanging at the edge of the sky, dusky blue with the approaching night, bright and close and smiling. The other planets and stars join her in a twinkling chorus of laughter and song—a true song, not the Piper's false claim to music, but a layering of voices in agreement, echoing and building into a harmonious refrain that tells the Changeling, *You are not alone.*

The Changeling doesn't notice for several moments when Quercu lets go of her hand. When she realizes she's aloft on her own, she shrieks with astonishment and delight but does not falter. Quercu allows her to take the lead, and she follows the fraying threads of fate and folly that led her here, circling the Portal Tree and the palace, the treehouse, and the training ground. From here, the world's problems seem so small; she dreads returning to them, but she's different now.

The Changeling can be anything. Anyone! Whoever she wants to be, in an instant, can be a façade as fickle as her moods. She'll have no true face. Of course, it will take time to learn her craft, but one day, she will wield her glamours as efficiently as the twins wield their weapons. She's free.

Even if it means throwing away her old name.

Chapter 23

The Target

HUNGRY BUT EAGER, sore but satisfied, Hannah drags herself back to their treehouse after the day's training. The smell of dinner and the promise of rest help her pull herself up the ladder, her absent sister only an afterthought. When she cracks open the door to their cottage, she almost doesn't recognize the creature tending the hearth.

The fae's hair is flaxen and shimmery, woven with plants Hannah can't identify. Lichen wreaths her brow, edges her ears, crawls across her face, and clings to her eyelashes, but instead of a dull gray, it's a vibrant blue. Worst of all, her eyes are hollow: black sclera, golden irises shining within. Hannah tightens her grip on the knob, resisting the urge to slam the door shut on the interloper. Despite all the changes, she recognizes the Changeling by the tilt of her head, the slant of her shoulders, the shape of her smile.

"What do you think?" the Changeling asks, twirling lightly on her toes.

"It's...different," Hannah chokes out as she closes the door behind her. "It's new."

The Changeling droops upon hearing the reservation in Hannah's tone. "You don't like it."

"No! No, I like it fine. It's a nice look on you," Hannah says dumbly, mimicking the courtesies her mother had given her when she first cut her hair with craft scissors. She drops her gear next to her bed, takes a bowl from the shelf next to the fireplace, and starts scooping her dinner from the pot. "It's just different from how I remember you, and it'll take some time to get used to, but it's ok, Ce—"

The name catches in her throat, heavy on her tongue. She tries to force it out a few more times, but a powerful magic prevents her from pronouncing—or even thinking—it. At the sound, the Changeling flinches.

"What's wrong? Why can't I—"

"I don't want to be that person anymore," the-Person Who-is-not-Her-Sister answers with a shrug. "It's a stolen name. You said yourself, I'm not your real sister, just a changeling. So, you can just call me the Changeling, at least until I come up with something else."

Of course, she's not Hannah's real sister, but hearing her say those words brings a special sting. This logic does nothing to quell the churning unease Hannah feels at all these sudden changes. The Changeling *would* throw out the one shred of familiarity left to her in this strange Faerieland. Hannah could never hold onto her.

She understands, though. Everyone here calls Hannah "Seeker" because she refuses to tell anyone her real name. She thought she would get used to it, but the nickname still feels wrong. She hopes she doesn't lose herself, now that both her sisters are little more than nameless strangers.

But she's still an older sister, and she can't bear to see the Changeling cringe away from the implication of her name, so Hannah sighs, nods, and agrees.

The Changeling smiles, revealing sharp teeth that weren't there this morning. "Thank you for understanding," she says.

And with no further words on that topic, she gets ready for bed. Hannah goes through the motions of eating alone as a numb unease settles over their little cabin.

Hannah's days pass in a blur of training and avoiding the Changeling. In the evenings, she sometimes tries to strike up conversation but finds she can only speak of her mission, and she's too tired to make other pleasant conversation. The usual topics of home, classes, chores, and Halloween all seem so distant and hollow. The Changeling can't—won't—return home, so there's no use dwelling on it. Hannah wonders if she'll be able to return to the mundanity of classes and chores after experiencing the splendors of the Seelie.

She does her best to bury her annoyance. Though she can tell not all is well with the Changeling, the younger girl doesn't want to talk about it, so Hannah doesn't pry.

Matteo and Marco, to their credit, stay to guard their charges and trade off as sparring partners for her. She observes their flowing and ferocious moves and learns the slight idiosyncrasies in how they speak and carry themselves. She tries very hard to identify which twin is which at a glance, and failing that, she asks which is which again, then focuses on hearing, rather than seeing, the difference. Matteo's voice is deeper than Marco's. He speaks in serious tones, clears his throat after every sentence, and gives careful advice with a firm but gentle touch. His brother exaggerates moves for the sake of illustration, and his jovial attitude lightens the mood. Both share tics like blinking their eyes a lot and snapping their fingers when something excites them, but they're still different people once she gets to know their mannerisms.

Hannah tries a dozen different blades, and at the end of the trial, she takes up her new weapon. True to her initial request, it looks an awful lot like an oversized machete. Only one side of the slightly curved blade is sharp, and it has a curved crossguard that protects her hand from any attacks that might slide down the blade or cuts coming from the side. The twins explain in their bandying speech that it's meant for quick slashing cuts in close quarters. Usually, using it on greenery would dull the blade, but the dwarven artisans had enchanted it to keep its edge. Marco calls it a falchion and praises her choice, drilling her until he stops dueling her left-handed out of pity. Though she's satisfied with her growing skill, she doesn't want to cut down any members of the swarm, much less use it in self-defense against the Third.

Lady Brigid leaves for a time with the Monarchs to gather materials for the ritual that will stop the Unseelie sacrifice. Before her absence, she teaches Hannah the letter-stick code and tells her to keep a sharp eye out for news. A few days later, Hannah arrives at the training ground early to find their scout frantically scratching a message in the fine dust. Hannah drops to her knees and pulls the spare set of scrying twigs from her pocket, dropping them before the weasel so Kit-Kat can mark the coded letters, which glow at his touch. *Ward. Northeast Border. Piper and Piper Swarm Missing*, Hannah reads.

"Good boy," Hannah says, giving Kit-Kat a pat on the head. She scoops the sticks into her palm and plops the weasel into the pocket of her oversized jacket, then dashes off to find the twins. When she tells them the news, they tell her to fetch the Changeling and Quercu, and when she returns with the girls, they've abandoned their practice equipment for their weapons of choice. Marco has a falchion of his own, a dagger in his boot, and a pouch at his belt filled with "surprises." Matteo carries a bow and a quiver of arrows, a seax knife, and a small throwing knife in a double-sheathed belt. Both wear cloaks that shimmer and soften their edges into the environment.

"What are we doing?" the Changeling asks as she sees the twins' change of gear. She's covered half her arm in clover, interrupted mid-transformation by the summons.

"It's time," Hannah explains breathlessly. "Kit-Kat reported the Taken's off the northeast border. Let's go."

"Now?" the Changeling screeches. "We're not ready!"

"She's out there, but the Piper's missing in action. I read it myself. We can take a few minutes to prepare, but we shouldn't wait too long. What do we need—"

The Changeling grabs Hannah's arm, stopping her mid-sentence. The clover brushes against Hannah's skin, and she tries not to jump at the strange feeling of a hand covered in greenery like a glove. Her grip is vice-tight, her voice strained. "The Monarchs told us we'd only be safe as long as we stayed in Seelie, and their power is stretched thin right now, *remember?*"

"It'll be safer if we stay close to the border," Quercu says, drawing a battle map in the dirt with a stick. "Don't let her lure ye out. Let us take point, and you stay between the three of us Powers, ye hear? At the first sight of danger, we'll duck back into the safe zone,"

Hannah tries to pull the Changeling into their circle, but she shrinks back, shaking her head so hard flower petals fall from her hair. "No. I can't do this." She takes three steps away from the huddle of warriors, into the shadows of the early morning forest, before turning tail and fleeing into the forest.

"You coward!" Hannah screams after her.

"Let her go. It's too dangerous for her in her current state," Quercu warns, stepping in front of Hannah, "Besides, yer right. We have little time. I'll talk to her later."

Hannah growls her frustration, but snatches up her weapon and follows her mentors to the northeast border. The landscape turns from grassy meadows into desolate fields of blasted stone. She can see why the Changeling hates this place, but that's all the more reason to rescue the lost children the Piper has trapped here! What a selfish brat!

At the edge of Unseelie territory, they come to a moat filled with a gurgling, caustic liquid. Across the divide, at the end of a narrow stone bridge, stands the target.

It's not Hannah's sister, but a young woman with short curly red hair and dark skin, wearing a beaked and feathered mask. An echo of mockingbirds flocks around her head. *Sturnus vulgaris.* An army of squirrels position themselves around her feet. Genus *Sciurus*, but Hannah doesn't bother identifying the species. She curses at herself. Did she read Kit-Kat's message wrong? This must be an assassin, meant to lure them out early. Stupid. Stupid!

Quercu tenses, flares her wings, and hisses, "She's mine."

"Come and get me!" teases the target in a sing-song voice. Her mockingbirds flock across the moat to dive-bomb the party, and Hannah flails her blade helplessly as the beaks peck her exposed neck and hands. Quercu charges across the moat, transforming into an eagle to chase off the mockingbirds. How do they know each other?

"Get behind me!" Marco starts across the bridge, putting Hannah between himself and Matteo. The mockingbirds start mobbing him instead. With a *thwip* of the bowstring, Matteo tries to pick off the mockingbirds harrying Quercu, but they're too fast. The flock surrounds her and mobs her to the ground, where she transforms into a bobcat and snaps one of them out of the air, before reverting to her changeling form.

"Nice welcome ye got for my friends," Quercu says through teeth bared in a menacing grin.

"Nice of ye to bring 'em," the target answers with a sneer. She sics the squirrels on Marco, who makes it to the end of the bridge and carves through the first wave, keeping them from reaching Hannah, who's still in the middle of the bridge. He's distracted when one bites his ankle, then another climbs his leg, and the second wave evades him. Hannah stumbles as they charge her, and she nearly falls off the bridge.

The moat water splashes her pant leg with a hiss. She screams as her foot slips and the liquid burns her skin, but Matteo's arm catches her and pulls her back to safety.

"I gotcha," he says, but it's Marco's voice that speaks. He staves off her attackers with his seax knife and calls to his brother for a retreat, switching weapons with a smooth hand-off when they pass each other. It's surprising enough to snap Hannah out of her fear, and she regains her grip on her falchion.

Quercu slashes her way free from a vine, her arm a bear's paw, but she looks up when she hears Hannah's near miss. "Get her out of here. My sister and I need to have a lil' chat."

The twins don't wait for Hannah's agreement and they all but drag her back to the Seelie Court, despite her shouts of protest. Their mission failed.

Chapter 24
The Switch

A FEW MINUTES later, they stumble into the training grounds, Matteo supporting Hannah by one arm. Her leg burns from the acid splash, but she can only focus on the battle. They left Quercu behind! The twins should be helping her, instead of saving Hannah's clumsy self.

"Steady, steady there." Though Marco had been holding her a second ago, it's Matteo's voice that says the words. He helps her to the ground, pulls a flask of water from his belt, and dumps it over her leg, washing away the stinging agent. There's that switch again! Hannah gawks at them for a second as her brain parses the speech a second too late.

"Are you alright?"

"Is Quercu going to be ok?" Hannah asks, embarrassment and anxiety reasserting themselves now that the peril has passed. They ran away! How could they have left their ally alone like that? Especially after calling the Changeling a coward. Hannah's a hypocrite.

Marco speaks, placing a hand on Hannah's shoulder. "She'll be fine. That's her sister. Quercu is the changeling of a human–Taken pair, like the Changeling and your Taken sister."

"They've been fighting for over two hundred years."

"This is old hat."

"What happened today isn't your fault, but maybe let us look at the letter-sticks next time," Matteo finishes.

Hannah relaxes a little, knowing they didn't leave her for dead. But there's so much she doesn't understand, so much weighing on her shoulders. How is it Quercu has failed to bring her sister home for *two hundred years?* The rift between Hannah and the Changeling is growing, culminating in their fight this morning. How can she mend her broken relationship with the Taken if she can't even understand the Changeling? Will she have to face the Taken alone? If this morning is any omen, her next mission is shaping up to be a *disaster.*

"Is something else bothering you?" Marco asks her. She's lost track of which voice is coming from which body now. Is it rude to point that out? She gives up on trying to guess and puts her head in her hands.

"Uh..." she says intelligently. "I thought your voices switched? It caught me off guard."

They turn their mismatched eyes on each other with a knowing grin, and whoever's sitting next to her gestures for her to relax. "She's a quick one," Marco's voice says.

"Took ol' Jack a good two years to notice us swapping."

"Jack doesn't care about anything but himself."

"How—how on earth are you doing that?" Hannah asks, dumbfounded.

"How is harder to explain than *why*," Marco replies with a laugh.

"We're half-switched changelings," Matteo says. "How much do you know about the Piper's switching spell?"

Hannah knew the twins had a changeling quirk, but now she regrets not having asked sooner. At least she can get a straightforward answer to one of her questions. She replays the conversation from the night she arrived in her mind. "The Changeling told me it hid memories in her mind, like locking something away in storage. It also caused the glamours that let her shapeshift into a human."

"She educated you well," Marco quips. Hannah gives a derisive snort. She's sick of calling her prodigal sister the Changeling, but she understands the necessity of protecting her name. Hannah still hasn't shared hers. To the twins' credit, they still haven't asked.

"The Master that meant to change us—" Matteo says.

"Was not the Piper, but one of his lesser bogeymen," Marco says. He waves his hands and says "booogeeeyyymeeennn" in a spooooky voice clearly meant to make Hannah smile. She's too puzzled to be entertained by his antics.

"A bogeyman with less experience in his heinous craft," Matteo says. "He didn't finish the switching spell because our mother caught him."

"It left us with no useful ability to perform magic and without the freedom of an unchanged human child but inextricably tied to each other."

Hannah holds up her hands. "Wait, wait, wait. You mean you're each half-fae?"

"Less like we're half of each, and more like we're neither of either."

"We can't do glamours, and we don't have powers."

"Nor can our past Master see through us—"

"Nor can we pass through life unawares—"

"For we've always had the Sight."

"And we switch places with each other, which is strange—"

"Even by fae standards. Lady Brigid didn't know what to do with us when Kit-Kat first brought us here."

Hannah loses track of which voice is which as the twins finish each other's sentences. Their synchronization is mesmerizing, and she wonders if this is how they're able to fight so well. Each movement rolls into the next, as fluid as a reflection in a mirror, if the reflection had a mind of its own. But Marco isn't a reflection of Matteo, nor is Matteo a reflection of Marco. How do they maintain their identities when impermanence is their very nature? It feels wrong to think of them as a unit, but if they're literally inseparable, is that really her fault? She can't imagine being connected to the Changeling like that. Maybe they are a little mad, after all.

"Don't you ever get dizzy?" Hannah asks.

"Never," Marco brags.   "Oh, all the time," Matteo says.

They speak at the same time, contradicting each other. Rubbing his temples, Matteo shoots Marco an annoyed look, but Marco continues, ignoring him. "We've experienced this since we were children. The comfort comes with practice. It didn't take us long to realize we're the only twins with this oddity."

Hannah counts the words as he speaks and realizes he's made out three complete sentences, instead of just a fragment. "Can you control it?" she asks.

They look at each other for a moment, and some unspoken communication passes between them.

"You explain," Marco says. He falls into an at-ease stance but remains near-motionless throughout his brother's explanation. His fingers tap on his arm, and Hannah recognizes it as a fidget to help him focus.

"We learned, with difficulty," Matteo says. He kneels beside her, puts a hand on Hannah's shoulder, and continues speaking in the same voice. "Switches are involuntary, like itches, or sneezes. We can tell when one's coming, and they happen more frequently if we're stressed or tired. Imagine we're boating on a river, floating toward rocks. It's less effort to dodge the rocks than to paddle upstream. We would rather control our actions when the switch happens, to avoid raising people's suspicion, instead of trying to control if the switch happens. Right now, Marco is keeping our boat in place by holding onto a branch, so I can speak this long uninterrupted, but he can only hold on for so long before tiring."

"Like most identical twins, folks usually can't tell our bodies apart. We're used to people confusing us," Marco says. "Learning to reorient after a switch is vital, in case it happens during an important conversation, an exam, or a fight. Covering for him is still pretending to be someone I'm not, but it takes less effort to lie than it does to explain ourselves to everyone who catches us during a switch."

Matteo shakes his head. "Half-truths, not lies. We share so much between us, it's more like a play, being the understudy for the other's role. Learning each other's lines through long hours of rehearsal. If it makes it easier, you can call this body Matteo, regardless of which I currently occupy."

Hannah studies both faces, letting herself memorize Matteo's creased brows and Marco's laugh lines. When she remembers how she reacted to the Changeling's shifted features, she feels a flush of shame. The sudden changes pushed Hannah away from the sister she remembered, which hurt, but the Changeling isn't wrong for wanting a change. Hannah decides to apologize later. Somehow.

"No more lies," she says. "You might be used to half-truths and assumptions, but I care about getting this right. You shouldn't have to pretend to be someone you're not."

Matteo gives her one of his gracious smiles. As she's looking into his eyes, she notices the flash, and then Marco stands from kneeling to ruffle her hair. Matteo relaxes from standing at attention.

"Thank you, Seeker. It means a lot to me." Matteo glances at his twin, who nods and matches his smile. "To both of us."

"Would you want to fix this somehow?" Hannah asks. "Maybe the Monarchs...I'm sure you've already asked..."

Matteo grimaces. "They have the power to separate us, and sympathy for our situation."

"But it would be like trying to untangle a piece of woven fabric, to separate the warp from the weft."

"We're so intertwined that our minds would unravel like an unfinished hem."

They resume speaking in exchanged phrases, but this time Hannah follows the conversation without losing track of the speaker, focusing on their tones, their expressions, their postures. A dozen tiny tells distinguish them from each other.

Marco unbuttons the collar of his uniform to give himself room to breathe while they rest from their training. He sits next to Hannah and stretches while Matteo cleans their gear.

"The Monarchs gave us the choice. At the time...it was tempting," Marco says. His tone is still bitter, but if their current state is any clue, Hannah already knows how this story ends; that he didn't get his way.

"We disagreed. Is it worth sacrificing sanity for individuality? To risk losing our memories, shaking our core instincts, for a chance of expressing ourselves?" Matteo explains. He takes Hannah's falchion from her and wipes off the mud and debris before oiling it and sliding it back into its sheath.

"Perhaps we're already insane, and losing our current perception of reality would actually move a step toward true sanity," Marco says. He returns to his joking tone and punches his brother in the shoulder. Hannah suspects this was a point of contention at one point, but he seems at peace as he continues. "But in the end, we decided it would be too dangerous. We'd be useless and ill after the separation for God only knows how long—days, weeks, months, years. Maybe even the rest of our lives. As infants, the mind is so malleable—"

"And no one expects anything of a baby—"

"So the switch was unnoticeable. It's why the Unseelie change young children, not grownups. But now, if we were to go through an un-switching, we'd be upsetting everything in our lives until we could recover. If we were to recover." There's a twinge of fear in Matteo's expression, and Hannah understands. So little of his life is his own. What if he were to lose even those shreds to a broken mind? He would rather protect the identity he has, as intertwined as it is with his brother. Would Hannah do the same in their situation? She can't decide.

"We have assignments at school and duties within the Seelie Court as part of the Powers. We have Lady Brigid, who found us at our lowest, explained all this, and trained us with ways to cope. We have siblings back home that need us to come home safe and sound at night, friends in town on our fencing team, parents who love and understand us the way we are." Marco finishes his set of stretches by tumbling into a handstand.

Hannah grins despite herself. "Your family sounds wonderful."

Matteo reaches into a pocket on the inside of his uniform jacket and pulls out his wallet. Hannah leans over, resting her head against his shoulder so she can see the pictures he pulls out of a plastic sleeve. They show a large family with dark skin, dark eyes, and dark hair in various stages of professionalism devolving into silliness. Matteo points to the faces as he introduces them.

"That's Mama and Papa in the middle. Our older sister, Julia, and her husband, Andrew. She's expecting, but she won't tell us if we're going to have a niece or a nephew yet. Our little sisters, Isabel and Agnes. Joseph is the toddler on my shoulders. And the baby's Anna."

"How old are you, Seeker?" Marco asks. He drops out of the handstand, rolling into a somersault, then lies on his back to rest.

"Fourteen."

"We're twenty. You're Aggie's age." Matteo says.

Marco laughs. "Oh, they would get along like a house on fire—I'd love to see the antics you'd achieve if put in the same room for five minutes. The Unseelie Court wouldn't stand a chance."

Hannah studies the girl's face and finds a fierce glint in her eye that she likes. "Thank you for sharing this with me."

"Of course, Seeker."

Upon hearing the title, she hesitates, then gives them a shy smile. These two friends have shown her nothing but kindness and respect. If they feel safe enough to share their family and names with her, it seems only fair that she does the same.

"My name is Hannah," she says quietly, carefully folding the picture back into the wallet and returning it. "Hannah Teagan." A pang of homesickness brings tears to her eyes, and she blinks them back as Matteo slips the wallet back into his pocket, next to his heart. Marco reaches over and hands her a handkerchief. The twins bow their heads in acknowledgment of the name freely given. Matteo puts his arm around her shoulders in a side hug.

"Hannah, you'll see your family again."

The action is so protective and familiar—something she'd done for the Changeling dozens of times. She's always been the protective one. Is this what it's like to have someone looking out for you?

Thinking of all their siblings back home, a sudden gratitude strikes Hannah for the twins acting as older brothers for her, too.

She sniffs. "I don't know how I'm going to explain everything to our mom and dad. I thought the Changeling was my only sister, but I don't even know if she wants to be part of our family anymore. Stupid sprite won't use her name. Won't let *me* use her name. Every time I try to call her, it gets caught in my throat. She wants nothing to do with the Taken. It hurts to even look at her." She gestures to the empty training court, choking back a sob. "You seem to have everything figured out. How many of them know the truth about you? About all of this."

"Our parents know," Matteo says, "since our mother caught the faerie who tried to switch us. Mama still sends us with biscotti whenever we come to Seelie, and Papa carries so many fae wards he's a walking arsenal. They don't like our expeditions, but they understand its something we need to do. I think Julia has her suspicions. You can't hide anything from her." Matteo rolls his eyes.

"Big sisters, amiright?" Marco says with a wink. Hannah laughs despite herself. At Matteo's mention of food, he gets up from the floor and rummages in their bags for snacks.

"The others understand we're . . . odd. They recognize on some level we're not like any other set of twins, but they don't have the context to understand the whole truth about the fae. It's easy for us, being switched as infants. Our family watched us grow up this way, so they don't know anything different." Matteo gives Hannah a sympathetic frown. "I don't know how you'll be able to explain bringing home a third child."

"Or losing their impostor daughter," Hannah grumbles. "What am I going to do if she refuses to come back, or she gets hurt, or she comes back . . . changed? Like this? I understand she's a faerie, but how will she live in the human world with us, and with the Taken, if we bring her back?"

Marco hums as he munches on a piece of jerky and hands a piece to Hannah. "If you can convince the Taken to return with you, the Monarchs could reverse the switching spell safely. It would effectively change your family's memories. You would believe you grew up with the Taken, and the Changeling would believe she grew up in Seelie. The Taken would have the Changeling's memories of growing up with you. It's every bit as seamless as the first change erasing the Taken from your mind and replacing her with the Changeling. The same would apply for your parents."

Hannah's stomach twists at the description. She hates the idea of fae playing more games with her mind, but it seems like the easiest option by far. There's no way she can convince her parents of the truth without evidence, and the Changeling is too much of a coward to face them herself. The Taken might fight them all the way home, or run away from their home, preferring the Piper she knows to the unknowns of a human household. Besides, it doesn't seem like the Changeling even wants to go home. She's playing enough in the Seelie Court to prove she's happier here than she ever was in the Human Realm. It'll be easier to go through the un-switching if they distance themselves now. Hannah can't miss a stranger. That's all the Changeling will become.

It's all she ever was. The sister she'd known was a lie.

"Thank you for your advice," Hannah says. "I've bothered you with too many questions, and I'm sorry about the messed up mission this morning. Where do we go from here?"

Matteo glances at the sky, holds up a hand to measure the distance of the sun from the horizon. "It's late enough. Take the rest of the day off. Rest. You've been here six days, in Seelie time. Tomorrow, take a holiday. Explore Faerieland. Spend time with the Changeling. You've trained enough to protect yourself, and I can promise no harm will come to you here."

"Besides, if anyone thinks to touch you, they'll have both Lady Brigid and the Monarchs to reckon with."

"And us."

"Aye, and us. We're scarier than both the bosses together."

Marco continues, "We'll talk to Quercu, but if you can convince the Changeling to come by overmorrow, we'll start training her with weapons, too. Now enjoy your day off. You've more than earned it."

Hannah smiles and nods. She's not eager to see the Changeling again, but her stomach growls as she strides off into the trees. The conversation drained her more than the battle, and she's looking forward to collapsing into bed tonight. She'll need her rest for what comes next.

Chapter 25
The Offering

HE TAKEN DOESN'T keep track of the days passed in her cell. She went mad trying to keep a tally on the wall a while ago, and she doesn't intend to revisit that experience anytime soon. The meals come when they come; she eats the bland food without fuss, then pushes the empty trays under the door. When she's tired, she sleeps. When she's awake, she stretches and paces.

She practices the True Voice when she's bored. The only other living things in the cell are some weeds that grow between the cracks in the floor and the rat. She tries to expand the weeds, pushing their roots into the stone to pry the stone apart. But they're weak little things, and they can't widen the seam, no matter how harshly she demands it of them. She never thought the pathetic plants would be strong enough to break the prison, but the insolence of the roots makes her angry, enough to tear them out with her fingernails and throw them across the room. The rat stirs when the roots hit it, then it eats them, for lack of other food. She hadn't shared her supper.

The Taken turns her attention on the rat, suppressing the tiny, inconsequential twinge of guilt that reminds her the rat used to be a boy. She doesn't know what his True Name used to be—and the Piper's taken it away, so using the True Voice does nothing to control it. It squirms as she tries to grasp the edges of its song, but eventually she gives up and returns to sitting sullenly on the bed.

At some point—hours, days, or weeks later, she hasn't the slightest clue—Rytchic the kitchen imp comes to the door. As the Taken moves to accept her tray, she realizes he's not carrying one.

"Where's dinner?" she demands. "Stop messing with me, you awful little—"

"Meeting time! Meeting tiiiiime!" Rytchic screeches.

The Taken steps back from the door, surprised, as Rytchic fumbles with an enormous, jangling set of keys. He has pointed ears that usually stick straight up and look like horns in silhouette, but they're quivering and pressed flat back against his skull now. His bloodshot eyes dart around, frantic as he searches for the right key. His barbed tail flicks anxiously, a half-butchered fish still speared through on the end. The Piper must have grabbed him from the middle of cooking to send him on this errand. The Taken groans with impatience, and Rytchic sticks his forked tongue out at her before finding the right one.

"Off with ya! Off with ya! Down the hall and to the left with ya!"

"Where am I going? What's going on? By Mab's beetles, I swear—"

"Meeting tiiiiiiiiiiiiiime!" he screeches, smacking her with the fish to get her moving before beating his holey wings and moving to the next cage to release another ward.

The Taken steps out into the hall and joins a throng of other children and rats alike, all moving in the same direction. They're all as exhausted and grimy as she is. Some are a few years older and have begun their transformations. The successful wards get to wield more of the Piper's power and have their own small slaves with them—usually rats, but sometimes the occasional crow or bat or snake perch on their shoulders. They get to choose the animal forms that mask their faces to distinguish them from the rest of the subordinate wards, all wearing identical rat masks, marking them as part of the swarm. The Taken steers clear of these chosen ones, wearing faces that represent the creatures they can control.

Some of the other children are tiny, only toddlers, and she remembers being that small and confused, not knowing anything of the outside world. Most keep their gazes lowered. None try to make conversation.

As she joins the crowd, she finds herself swept into the current of bodies marching toward their destination. Best not to question, best to keep her head down and avoid the others, but the Taken finds her curiosity overwhelming. It's so rare they're allowed to roam outside the cells without being blindfolded, and she tries to memorize the turns she takes. As the hoard of children nears its destination, another smell overtakes that of sweat and fear. Mold and rot, but not the hearty, earthy scent of the wild forest. This is putrid, stale, and raw. Underneath it all, the barest hints of sulfur and malice grow stronger.

The scent dislodges a memory, and the Taken realizes with a sinking feeling, she knows exactly where they are going. In her memory, there's only been one other march like this, and it didn't end well. She tries to stall her steps, but she's pushed forward by an older ward with a beaked mask who steps in time to a music they all know, a resigned, apathetic expression plastered over her face. This one's got a mockingbird perched on her shoulder and a raggedy squirrel curled up in her hair. The Taken sets her teeth and holds her breath.

Their procession finally empties into an arena—an open space with a dais at the center and seating in a circle all around. The Piper's wards filter into their sections and file into their seats, organizing themselves according to his music permeating their minds. The Taken doesn't fight it and sits next to the ward with the mockingbirds. Each of the older wards takes responsibility for a contingency of the younger ones with rat masks, and the Piper stands before them all, conducting the children with the proud air of a general surveying his troops. His rats surround his feet, of course, the ever-present honor guard. The rat that shared the Taken's cell leaves her side and scampers forward to join the swarm. She can't help but feel a little sad at seeing her only company leave.

The music stops once the children take their seats, and the Taken slumps, now free to observe. Nobody talks to their neighbors as the rest of the arena fills. The Piper represents only one of four Unseelie Masters, each with their own wards, each with a unique method of controlling them. The figure in the center terrifies the Taken too much to pay them any mind. It's a dark night. The stars are obscured by the heavy clouds that never dissipate from above the Unseelie lands, but the moon is allowed, only as a spotlight for the Queen.

Queen Mab. Right now, she's enormous, dwarfing the other larger-than-life members of the Unseelie Court, but the Taken hears legends she can shrink herself to be no larger than one's finger to sneak around at night. Supposedly, she takes joy in antagonizing humans in a million little ways, wreaking havoc on their lives in all the minute bothers that ruin a day. Her chariot looks like a hazelnut shell, spider legs forming the spokes of its wheels. She wears a dress of filmy web silk with armor overtop, so powerful she can scorn the iron that burns most fae. A whip hangs at her waist to drive the beetles that draw her chariot, creatures black and shiny and big enough to bite off a child's head in one snap of their oversized mandibles.

The Taken regrets cursing by the Queen's name. The Unseelie Court bows to Queen Mab's beauty and malevolence. She shapes their lives as the dispenser of their power. All love her, and despair.

If she's here, it can only mean one thing: the Tithe to Hell.

The Taken has experienced this gathering once before, when she was a small girl, but it still left a lasting impression on her mind. It was the only time she had ever seen the Piper cry. Every seven years, the Unseelie Court makes a living sacrifice to Hell to continue using their powers, but they never sacrifice one of their own. At these gatherings, the Masters bicker and simper before their queen, vying to gain her favor and a larger sliver of the new power. And they argue about which wards would make the best offering. It's a great honor, they say.

The Taken doesn't remember which Master won, though the Piper had come away with a meager portion. She does remember the last offering's screams as they dragged him away. They echo in her ears now, fixing her to her spot in blank terror. The Taken doesn't know how the Masters pick their offerings.

Last time, she had been so young, they hadn't considered her at all. But now? She's on her last chance. Will her position save her or doom her?

Queen Mab raises her scepter. It's made of bone and has contorted, frowning faces carved into it. "Who will bring forth their offering first?" she asks, her voice ringing clear over the hushed assembly. They waste no time on formalities here. They all know the reason they're gathered, and none of them deny her authority or the contract at hand.

The Monster steps forward to begin the ceremony. Right now, the Monster wears his favorite form, that of a wild black wolf, taller at the shoulder than any grown man, his snout twisted into a permanent snarl with enormous jagged, sharp teeth that jut out from between the lips.

"I bring a warrior," he growls.

On cue, a burly man steps forward from the pack of bodies behind their Master. His long brown hair is shaggy, and he has bushy eyebrows. A long tongue lolls between sharp teeth. His strong form demands attention. At the ends of his arms and legs, he has large paws instead of hands and feet, with larger claws. He carries a massive ax slung over his shoulder and prowls before the assembly. The Taken gets the impression the Monster has trained him for this moment his whole life.

"Entire towns fear his rampage. He ruins flocks and leaves the bodies to waste. The fences he wrecks, and the orchards turn to ruin. Should any unlucky traveler cross our borders, he dispatches them cruelly and with no haste. The silver blood of thirteen slain Seelie stains his hands!" the Monster declares, and the ward brandishes his weapon like he's daring the crowd to doubt the claims.

The rest of his wards howl, yelp, and growl their approval, either proud the Queen might choose one of their own or thrilled they weren't the one to be picked. Most of the Monster's wards can't shapeshift their whole bodies or exert control over when they shift; their changes are temporary and incomplete. Some sport claws and teeth, their forms furry and backs hunched like wolf-men. Some wear wings—feathers sprouting from their arms, instead of the insectoid wings that gracefully slope from faeries' backs. Others whip anxious tails or clatter horns with each other in head-butting contests.

The Taken scowls at them and recalls the Piper's disparaging words after their last meeting. Savages and beasts. Without control, they are no better than the animals they become. As much as she hates bowing to the Piper's whims, the Taken considers herself lucky to be among his wards.

Queen Mab regards the Monster's performance with an unimpressed gaze and thanks him for his offering, before moving onto the next of the nobles. It's not a dismissal, just an acknowledgment. She'll consider each of the offerings before choosing.

The Monster and his wards return to their seats to await her judgment.

The White Witch stands on a chariot of ice, which levitates on a mass of swirling icy clouds. She's serene, but everyone knows her wail is the shrillest of her hosts. A ghost with a glowing pumpkin head drives the wind. His name is Jack, and he's an awful prankster, always nipping at the Taken's nose and trying to start snowball fights. But he tells funny stories, and he's helped the Taken find shelter, so she isn't sure what to think of him.

Behind them trail the cavalry. Her wards are an eclectic mix. A few lost children she's lured with promises of sweets, knowledge, or royal treatment, but then she freezes their hearts until they're as cold as she is. Most are adults, taken for their arrogance or vanity, hearts already as hard and brittle as ice. They're called the Wild Hunt, and every winter, they tear through the night sky, terrorizing the world with their screams and taunts. Some ride emaciated horses, others run in a pell-mell sprint. All of them have blackened, frostbitten fingers and toes.

The Taken would never admit to spending winters curled in terror in the smallest corner of her cell, hoping she doesn't catch their attention. It's known the Unseelie Court makes a game out of playing for keeps with their wards, and if she's stolen away to another domain, that Master will trap her forever.

The White Witch drags forward a woman with unruly blonde hair and a dark look in her eye.

"I bring a Regret," the Witch says, her voice high and hoarse. The woman carries a blade like a sickle, carved from ice and fused to her frostbitten hand. She glares at the assembly and tries to speak, but the only thing that comes out is a screech, her words stolen by her mistress.

"This woman neglected her family and grew bored with her labors at home, so she fled to the Faerie Realm for adventure. The weak Seelie only offered her peace, not the glory and freedom she sought." The words come out as a sneer. "We gave her freedom for a night."

"For a night! For a night! For a night!" screams the Wild Hunt in chorus.

"But that kind of welcome costs. She didn't pay, and she wouldn't work, so we set her free, just as she wanted! She returned to her family, but they didn't want an unfaithful wife. They turned away from the negligent mother. She's truly free now, without their weight pulling her down. She's free to fly across the night sky! Feared and awed!"

The woman screams and tries to attack the White Witch with her sickle, but the ice blade shatters in her hand. The poor waif staggers back, terrified of what her failure means.

The Witch summons a blast of freezing air, which knocks the offering to her knees. She steps back, leaving her offering on the floor with the bear-boy. Her host of angry ghosts wails and shrieks as Queen Mab thanks her and the ceremony moves on to the third member of the Unseelie Court.

The Penumbra steals shadows. She's little more than a shadow herself, cloaked in black tattered robes and veils that obscure her face. Nine long shadows stretch from her feet in every direction, regardless of how the light hits her. It's said she can transport herself between any shadow, and the Taken has spent many long nights praying she doesn't choose to visit. All her wards look pale and waifish without shadows of their own. Keeping their eyes shut against the offensive moonlight, their silence is deafening compared to the clamor behind the other two Masters.

"I offer a servant," the Penumbra whispers; despite her hushed tone, her voice carries to the Taken with ease and makes all her hairs stand up on end. The Penumbra beckons forward a stick of a boy. He's a little older than the Taken, all lanky knees and elbows, shoulders hunched, head bowed, sandy-blond hair washed out against his sallow skin. He says nothing. His posture betrays no emotion. He doesn't even raise his eyes to meet Queen Mab.

The Penumbra snaps her fingers once. The boy steps into one of her nine shadows and disappears, turning invisible and reappearing in another shadow near Queen Mab, where he offers her a vial filled with shimmery green scales. She takes it and holds it up to the moonlight for inspection, then grins. By the time she turns back to the servant, he's disappeared again, retreating to the Penumbra's side.

"Your Majesty," the Penumbra lets the demonstration and the bribe speak for themselves. She steps back. Unlike the others, her group expresses their enthusiasm through a silent bow.

The Piper doesn't call any of his wards forward. The Taken's stomach drops, and she balls her hands into fists so tight her palms bleed as her nails cut her. Who will it be? He makes a bow to the Queen and pauses for dramatic effect before he speaks. The Taken can't tear her eyes from him. He faces away from the wards. His wings twitch, though his posture remains dignified, and the Taken guesses he's enjoying their terrified suspense.

"I propose...a runaway."

The Taken's heart stops. He can only mean one of two people—the one she failed to capture, and the sister that came after. Both would deserve this fate, but neither is here due to the Taken's weakness. What does that mean for her?

When none of the wards step forward, Queen Mab drums her fingers on her bone scepter and leans forward until she's bending over the assembly. Ravens flutter their wings and rats scuttle their feet, but the Taken stays very, very still.

"Can you produce this runaway?" the Queen asks, quirking an eyebrow and tapping one sharp fingernail against the glass vial the Penumbra offered.

"It will be a game!" the Piper exclaims with a grand gesture, and everything in the Taken's body recoils. *One more chance*, he had told her. Is this it? He gives a hum, and she feels the tug in her stomach pulling her to obey his wishes. She mindlessly stands and on shaking legs walks forward.

"The changeling's counterpart will bring her in, either as hunter, or as bait. Won't it be a prize to wrench one from the Seelie's clutches and put her back where she belongs?"

The Taken bows when she reaches the Piper. A game. Her mind races. How can she do this when both girls escaped into the Seelie Court? Why would they come after her? What reason have they to leave a place where they're beyond the Piper's grasp? Does this mean she'll survive? Every muscle in her body quivers with fear and anticipation as she waits for the Queen's response.

"And if she fails? Why should we allow you to play your little game, when we have other offerings prepared right now?"

"Then you can take the failure," the Piper answers with a casual shrug. "But if you let me play, you may take both the runaway and the human sister that followed her. My spies tell me they won't travel without each other, so you'll be able to take two sacrifices. Either way, you win a prize, and entertainment in the process. I only ask that you consider me favorably when you distribute the power."

The Taken can't breathe as the Piper lays out her fate. Queen Mab considers his offer. The other Unseelie Masters and their wards chatter about the drama of it all, the audacity of the Piper to come without a gift, the spectacle of a game, waiting to see if she'll reconsider them. Queen Mab finally makes up her mind and holds out her hand.

"Deal. I will stall the halls of Hell to pay the Tithe. Work quickly."

The Piper kisses her bony fingers before stepping back and sending the Taken back to her seat. "We will not disappoint, Your Majesty," he croons. She waves a hand to dismiss the assembly, but the Taken doesn't even notice the crowds rise and filter out of the arena. Her mind fixes on one fact.

She cannot fail.

Chapter 26

The Vacation

THE CHANGELING ISN'T at the treehouse when Hannah returns that evening. She washes off in the outdoor shower near their lodgings and changes into one of the clean sets of clothes Lady Brigid found for them. Then she cleans their room, prepares dinner from the fresh vegetables in the community garden, dishes up a plate for the absent Changeling, and settles down to wait. Her stomach growls, but she lets the food cool and the stars emerge in the firmament of the heavens before she's willing to have dinner alone.

When the Changeling finally returns, her glamours look normal this time, except for the blonde-brown hair streaked with vines. She looks like she's been crying, but she doesn't confront Hannah about their argument earlier. She only takes her seat across the table and puts her head in her arms.

"Quercu made it back to Seelie in one piece," she mumbles. "She told me to tell you not to worry."

"I'm glad she's alright. Did her sister—"

"No."

"Oh."

They sit in awkward silence for a while. So Quercu had told the Changeling about Hannah's failed attempt at leading a rescue mission. Hannah's still angry the Changeling abandoned the fight, but she has a different quarrel to mend tonight. Hannah shoves the plate of lukewarm food across the table and launches into the speech she's been rehearsing for most of the afternoon. "I'm sorry I acted weird about your glamours."

The Changeling raises her head from her arms, eyes wide with surprise. "I don't understand. First you were angry when I looked like the Taken, and then you hated me when I made myself look like someone different. I can't seem to do anything right."

"That's why I'm trying to apologize," Hannah says, holding her hands up in surrender. "I acted weird. You can do whatever you want. Just try not to catch me off guard, ok? It's super cool if you can give yourself dragon wings, but don't breathe fire at me or anything. Every time you're in the room, I never know what to expect."

The Changeling stares at Hannah for a second, then laughs and transforms her blue morpho butterfly wings to draconian ones, shimmery and blue. "I can do this, but I can't breathe fire," she says.

Hannah sits back in her chair like she's reviewing a fashion show. "Give them a flap for me."

The Changeling beats them a few times and rises into the air above the table, spinning for effect. Hannah gives her an approving slow clap. "Can you do a red-tailed hawk next? *Buteo jamaicensis.*"

She lands, standing on the table, and transforms again. Feathers ripple along the edges of the wings and she gives herself the iconic tail feathers, striking a pose.

"Hmm. Not bad. B+ for scientific accuracy."

The Changeling rolls her eyes, laughs, and transforms back into her fae form, stepping off the table and joining Hannah for dinner. The tension dissolves, and they plan adventures for their day off before turning in for the night.

Despite Hannah's previous reluctance to trust the Seelie Court, she wakes eager to explore. It's about time she met other fae—so far, she's mostly interacted with Lady Brigid and the twins, and even she must admit it's lame to befriend only the humans in Faerieland. Though the Lady is technically more human than the twins, she's also an immortal Seer, so she doesn't really count.

The Changeling leads the way from their treehouse, ready to take Hannah on a tour of all the places she's seen. First, she leads Hannah through a small clearing of grass and clover, surrounded by maples in their full autumn glory. Sugar maples, *Acer saccharum*—not the best for climbing, but Hannah's favorite for a different reason. In February, she could tap them for syrup. Hannah wonders if it ever becomes February in the Seelie Court, and if the syrup tastes as magical as it does when she pours it over chocolate chip pancakes at home. Quercu isn't waiting for the Changeling, so they move on. The coloring of the foliage in her hair shifts as she walks past.

They come across a fawn in the path, and though it's apart from its mother, it doesn't seem distressed. Hannah keeps a respectful distance and mutters, "White-Tailed Deer. *Odocoileus virginianus*. You're quite pretty."

The creature lifts its head and twitches an ear toward her voice, then takes a few steps closer. The Changeling's wings flutter behind Hannah, who holds her breath with anticipation. The fawn shows no fear as it moves forward, dappled light playing over its spotted hair. It shoves its nose into Hannah's pockets, just like any tame creature at a petting zoo looking for treats, and she dares to lift her hand and pat the tawny fur on the baby's head. It leans into the touch, and she can feel a hard bump under the softness. As she strokes its head, she realizes this is no ordinary deer. Instead of two bumps, as she might expect for a creature with antlers, she only feels one, positioned above and between the eyes.

A unicorn.

The cloven hooves have a metallic silver sheen, and the white-haired patches refract the light into rainbows. It has a mane and a small patch of beard under his chin, still growing into its fullness. It's still a baby, after all. The tail is long and strong, almost prehensile as it wraps around her wrist like a hand. There's a tuft of the shimmery white fur on the end, along with a rusted iron band. Hannah *tsks* at the device and cradles it, looking for a hinge or clasp. The baby whines and tries to skitter away, but she makes soothing noises and puts a firm but gentle hand on its snout, the same way she'd try to calm their miniature horse, Snubs, back home.

Eventually, she finds the lever she's looking for, and with a bit of wedging and scraping, she's able to free the creature's tail from the ugly device. It whips its tail away, dances in a circle around her. She can't help but laugh with joy as it frolics away to rejoin its mother. The larger creature gleams when she steps into the sunlight, and her mane ripples like a tapestry of diamond thread, throwing rainbow shards around the forest. The singular, twisting, spear-like horn glows. She gives a singular nod in acknowledgment and then wanders away.

Hannah sighs and returns the slight bow as a sensation of peace and relief washes over her, healing the aches and pains of the last six days of training and the journey to Seelie before that. She whispers thanks for the blessing. The Changeling puts a hand on her shoulder, shaking her out of her trance.

"You freed a unicorn," she whispers, still reverent in the creature's recent presence.

"It was a small favor. The poor thing was in pain."

"You can free them from the irons," the Changeling says, her voice pitching higher with excitement. "The Unseelie and their human wards nearly hunted them to extinction. Most of them bear scars or the remnants of traps. They live here, where they're safe, but none of the Seelie can help them, since the iron burns them."

"Oh." Hannah doesn't know how to respond to that. She didn't expect her mundane human nature would give her any advantages here. "Are there other creatures that need freeing?"

"Oh, plenty. Some irons are more complicated, though. Entire snaring mechanisms."

"Don't the other Powers help?"

"I'm sure some of them try, but a lot of them are part fae, like the twins, or changelings, like me. They're also busy, and they have to split their attention between here and their homes. Lady Brigid's stopping an Unseelie ritual right now; otherwise, I'm sure she'd do her part. There aren't enough resources to go around."

"Well, as long as we're stuck here, I want to help. I could probably fix them if I had tools. Hannah rubs her hands together, stretches them over her head, relishing the ability to move without stiffness or soreness. She can be a hero to these creatures in trouble! Heroism is about helpfulness, right?

The Changeling takes to the air and points down a different path. "Follow me. I have an idea."

They work their way down the hill, over rocks, tree roots, and burrows, until they reach a cave that smells of smoke and leather. Clangs of metal-on-metal echo from inside, and when Hannah ducks through the low entry and lets her eyes adjust to the dim light, she finds a dwarf working at a forge. He only comes up to her shoulder and has his long black hair braided away from his face so it doesn't impede his work. His bristly beard covers his nose and mouth, but it's stained gray from catching the forge's ash.

Annoyed as he is by being interrupted in his work, it takes some explaining to convince him to help, but the grumbling craftsman eventually concedes. Hannah peppers him with questions about metallurgy, as he creates a tool for her. She learns about all the alloys he uses: bronze and brass, tin and pewter, even titanium, anything other than iron. Then, equipped with a brand-new all-purpose screwdriver, she thanks him and sets out to explore.

The afternoon fills with adventures as Hannah releases various creatures from iron traps, storing the metal contraptions in her bag so she doesn't leave harmful litter around the Seelie Court. Some of the fae are distrustful at first because of her clanking satchel, but after the Changeling explains their mission, all are happy to accept her help.

The girls splash under a waterfall with mermaids and nixies. Hannah takes a running jump off a rocky ledge and plummets toward a mirrored lagoon, like leaping into the sky, until she shatters the smooth surface and sinks beneath the warm water. She's surrounded by silvery fish, tickling her toes and guiding her back to the surface. Faerieland knows no earthen boundaries, and the selkies say this lagoon will portal her to the shore of any ocean she wishes. Despite the marvels the Seelie Court offers, Hannah remembers the seashells she left in the woods to guide her way home, and she wonders if she'll ever collect them again.

The seafolk sing for them. It's nothing like the Piper's call; this song is gentle like the lapping of sea foam in the shallows. They share laments for their sister sirens, kept captive in the Unseelie Court to lure sailors to their deaths. The harmonies weave together into a lighthearted reel, bandying verses back and forth. They remember every shanty the girls know and every one lost to history. Hannah's delighted to hear the Changeling sing again, after the long drought of inspiration that left their home empty of both song and art. The melody transforms into a soothing ballad of farewell and well-wishes. Hannah leaves with a coral comb that tames the frizz in her curls as a thanks for removing a heavy ballista chain from a mermaid's shimmering green tail.

At the next stop, Hannah takes a few hours, gently prying a barbed net away from the delicate wings of a giant dragonfly. While Hannah works, the Changeling borrows her notebook and pencil to draw the creature for their nature journal. It looks like a member of the family *Macromiidae*, if one could grow to the size of a small plane. Though the Changeling hasn't drawn anything in nearly a year, the picture still comes out well-done. Hannah's untangling is painstaking work, but once the net is finally released, the bug buzzes into the air with a jubilant spin. An ancient mountain spirit runs the stable. His body is shaped of craggy stone, and moss grows on his head in place of his hair and beard. Glowing crystals glow for eyes. He shows them how the enormous insects serve as mounts for long journeys or fae with injured wings.

It takes some encouraging before Hannah works up the nerve to try flying on one herself. She stands with her toes on the edge of the platform, staring over the canopy of the forest below.

The Changeling sprints past her and leaps, soaring away. Not about to be shown up, Hannah takes a couple steps back, musters up her courage, and runs for the takeoff. As she flings herself into the air, the dragonfly zips from the staging ground below and positions itself to catch her. She shrieks as she falls a few feet, but lands safely on its back and soon, they catch up to the Changeling. Hannah clings to the reins, hair whipping across her face as it darts back and forth. She keeps up with the Changeling as she dives and flits through the air. It's the first time Hannah's seen the Changeling *fly*, and it's an incredible sight. This is the little girl who wanted to pet the wind. Hannah screams with delight and waves her arms as they skim over the clouds. The clouds wave back to her.

Chapter 27

The Namer

T THE END of the day, they return to the same maple clearing where they began. Hannah gives a long sigh of satisfaction. Maybe she was supposed to rest today, but she's more pleased with her progress in this new purpose. She can understand now why the Changeling wants to stay here—why she needs to stay here—why she can't leave the Seelie Court to rescue the Taken. This is a place for broken people to heal.

Today's the closest Hannah's come to recognizing her sister through the glamours. It hurts to watch, knowing she can't stay. Hannah wants to see the Changeling learn to be a new person, a happier version of herself, but fate has other plans in mind. For now, she savors the time they have together.

Repeating the ritual from the morning, the Changeling marches to the center of the clearing and spins in a circle, scanning the trees for something Hannah can't see. This time, she grins and then leans close to Hannah's ear. "Can you spot Quercu's glamour? Don't focus too hard. Look for movement in your peripheral vision and edges that don't line up right."

Hannah copies the Changeling's sweep of the clearing, following her instructions. It takes a couple tries, and a hint, but when she tosses her acorn into a bush, it stops in midair, and the bush in question stands up. The edges shimmer, and the leaves flatten at the edges, until Quercu stands before them, ruffling the Changeling's hair with a grin.

"I'm on strict orders from the Lady not to teach ye anything today, little miss, so if you think you're prying any secrets out of me, yer sadly mistaken."

"I know. We just wanted to check if you were alright."

"Right as rain," Quercu says with a forced grin. She's covered her bare arms with bandages. "My Taken didn't come up with a name, but I gotta give her points for scale. I've never seen her command so many mockingbirds at once."

Hannah shifts from foot to foot, curiosity warring with propriety in her mind before curiosity wins out. "I've been meaning to ask you. *Quercus* is the genus for the oak tree. Did you name yourself after a specific species of oak tree?" She crouches to pick up a stray acorn. "This looks like *Quercus rubra* to me, but uh... You don't have to share if you don't want to."

Quercu's eyebrows shoot up, and she leans forward into Hannah's face. Hannah makes a valiant effort not to squirm and meekly hands back the acorn she'd picked up. Quercu takes her time inspecting the satchel full of iron bands, though she's careful not to touch any herself, and checks Hannah's hands for blisters and scars.

"Changeling, you never told me your Seeker was a Namer," she says in a low tone.

Is that a good thing or a bad thing? Hannah knows names carry power in the Fae Realm, but she has no idea what the significance of scientific names means to these people. They come from human Latin, historical nomenclature customs. What could they mean here?

She feels her face flushing, and she casts her eyes toward the ground. She should have known better, to have held her tongue. Nobody likes when she rambles. Back home, only the Changeling matched her energy and willingly listened. Who would have thought the same unwritten rules applied here in Seelie? With all its connection to the wilds and the wonderful day she's had so far, some small, irrational part of Hannah hoped things would be different. She yearns for the times they would go hiking together in the Human Realm, her old sister asking at every turn 'What's that plant?' and 'What about this one?' so Hannah could indulge herself by info-dumping.

"She does that all the time. It's her special interest. She must have hundreds of them memorized," the Changeling says.

Through the glamours, Hannah can't read the expression on Quercu's face.

The teacher lets out a slow whistle. "This is the same Seeker that befriended the twins' wild critter?"

Hannah huffs, annoyed at being talked about while she's standing right here. "Yes, the same. That's not his name. "Critter" doesn't mean anything. He's a least weasel, *Mustela nivalis*, although the biologists who named him were also being rude. It just refers to them being the smallest of the weasel family, unlike stoats. His name is Kit-Kat."

Quercu breaks into a wild grin and slaps her palm on her forehead. "I should have known yer one of the Powers!"

Hannah shakes her head and crosses her arms. She's been called many things: weird, nerdy, even a dork, but she won't stand for someone assuming she knows all this through magical means. She's earned her nerdiness, fair and square. "I didn't ask Lady Brigid or the Monarchs for any magic, if that's what you're assuming. I learned these things on my own, before ever coming here."

Quercu laughs, and at first Hannah thinks she's laughing at her, but then she says, "Do you have any idea what wonderful magic you have?"

"I just said I don't have any magic."

"But you do! The best of magics! You're a Namer." Quercu puts a hand on her shoulder for emphasis. "Tell me, do ye got a green thumb?"

"I keep a garden every year, and houseplants. Mom says my bedroom is a jungle, because I mostly raise pothos, *Epipremnum aureum*, which are native to tropical environments. I don't see what this has to do with any naming magic. Plenty of people keep pothos. They're hardy plants, and pretty, too."

"And do you get along with animals? Not just Critter—Kit-Kat—but any pets or other wild creatures?"

"Well, yes. But anyone who doesn't get along with animals is a monster," Hannah answers with a shrug, trying to shake Quercu's tight grip off her shoulder.

"We have a dog named Willow, who always sits at her feet" the Changeling says with an impish grin. "She's the one who can always find our cat, Inky, when she's hiding, and Hobbes only lets her pick him up. And we have twenty-seven chickens that she loves and who love her, but Onii is secretly her favorite."

"That's just because I spoil them, and we've trained Willow since she was a puppy," Hannah protests. What does this mean if it's true?

Quercu laughs again, but this time Hannah can tell it's not meant in harm. Admiration, perhaps. "I know Lady Brigid said no lessons today, buuuuuut seeing as I'm not giving the Changeling the lesson, I can get away with this. Sit, child."

What else is Hannah supposed to do? She can't just run away from this awkward encounter without some kind of repercussion. Her curiosity overwhelms her too, and so Hannah sits. Quercu gestures to a white bloom between them.

"What would ye call this?"

"Clover. Their genus is *Trifolium*, but I don't know all the species. *Tri-* for three, *folium-*for leaves. Three-leaf clovers. Sometimes mutations cause four-leaved ones, but it's a harmless adaptation." Now that she inspects them, she realizes many of the clovers are four-leaved, lucky ones. Figures.

Quercu nods her understanding. "Right. Those are the two names—formal and common. Now, ye already know there's a third—a chosen name, like Kit-Kat."

"I don't know what I'd call this clover. I would need to find a name that fit it. Or I suppose if it already has a name, I would have to find it."

"Right-o. There's one part yer missing. Its song."

"You mean like how the Third grows her plants? She was humming something when the vines grew toward me. Or how the Piper controls the rats with his flute?"

"Exactly," Quercu says. "Each thing has its own song. Knowing the True Name of a thing means knowing each part of it, and understanding how each thing is more than the sum of those parts. Being able to speak to them requires the True Voice, which takes practice to develop."

It surprises Hannah to find this makes perfect sense to her. "So, I understand True Names, but I don't have the magic to manipulate plants or animals, not in the same way the Taken does. I don't have the True Voice, you mean."

"No indeed. The Piper's magic involves controlling a thing by stripping it of its name. It's a wicked practice."

Hannah pointedly avoids looking at the Changeling who used to be...what *was* her name? Dread rises in Hannah's throat as she realizes she can't remember. Quercu continues talking, but out of the corner of her eye, Hannah can see the Changeling practicing her glamours, trying to disappear.

"Naming is not an evil practice. The Piper twists things and throws them out. He makes them forget what they are. You, though, you remind things of what they are. You tell them what they could be."

"But how can I do that without the True Name? I don't know any songs. I can't carry a tune in a bucket."

"Ye already got two or three of the four. Yer magic might not be the most powerful, but it's a glorious start. Even more impressive because nobody taught ye or blessed ye with powers to make the process easier. Ye learn names out of love. That's a sacred magic, indeed. I'd be proud to count ye as one of the Court."

Hannah feels a flush rise to her face, and she stutters out a clumsy "thank you" as she struggles to accept the high praise. This could be useful in helping the Third come back, or in helping Cec—the name lags in her mind, and she can't breathe for a moment as her throat closes and her tongue grows heavy. She would not be able to say it, even if she wanted to call the Changeling her True Name.

Her True Name. She hasn't chosen another.

Quercu acknowledges Hannah's pause and moves on with the conversation, pivoting topics as quickly as they'd switched to naming in the first place. She jabs the Changeling in the arm.

"Quick, make yerself scarce. Don't ye want to show off what ye learned?"

"Doesn't that count as a lesson?" the Changeling says.

"Doesn't count if I don't critique ye about it or make ye practice to fix your mistakes. This is just a rehearsal. Might as well give the Seeker a taste of our craft so she can recognize it. I'll see Lady Brigid about bringing her in for a proper lesson of hide-and-seek at some point."

The Changeling grumbles something about homework but does as she's told. Once she's out of earshot, Quercu gestures for Hannah to come closer and lowers her voice to whisper into her ear.

"I can tell yer worried about the Changeling losing her name. No Namer worth their salt would be comfortable with that on any old stranger, let alone one's own sister, eh? Ye know better than to let that slide."

Hannah's voice catches in her throat as she watches the Changeling go. "How do I help her? I don't want to force her to be my sister if that's not who she wants to be."

"Is that what ye want her to be?"

Hannah thinks back to their fun adventures today. The Changeling still is her sister, despite their arguments and Hannah's own bitterness. She knows her sister by her joy when she pets the wind and takes to the sky on brilliant blue wings. By her laughter after being drenched by a cannonball in a lake full of mermaids. By her compassion for creatures bound in iron.

But her sister doesn't know her. Not anymore.

"Yes," she answers Quercu. "But what I want doesn't matter. She should be happy, and she'll be happiest here, being herself, with you and the others to help her get better."

"How do ye know she's being herself? She doesn't know her name," Quercu points out.

Hannah bites her lip at the somber thought. "How can I help her?"

"She's retreated into a shell to forget her guilt. Some changelings break themselves into pieces to see what bits don't fit anymore and assign a new name to the resulting creation." Quercu's face contorts in remembered pain. "Ye were right, by the way. Red oak. Some remember who they were and decide how they want to grow. She's still a good kid. A lot better than me. You can help her remember."

Before Hannah can respond, Quercu abruptly turns on her heel and yells out, "Fifty-eight, fifty-nine, sixty! Ready or not, here we come!"

She bats Hannah on the shoulder. "See if you can find her. She's become a right marvel in a few days."

Hannah gives a long sigh and walks into the woods, scanning each piece of foliage and hunk of rock as she does so. Quercu's words weigh heavily on her mind. How can she recall the Changeling to herself if she can't say her True Name? What kind of disaster will meet them if she can't help the Changeling before they leave? And even if she does, the Changeling still wouldn't be able to come home, or she won't come home, or she shouldn't come home. Would it be fair to remind her of what she can't have?

Hannah shakes her head. She needs to focus on the present problem. Can she persuade the Third to abandon the Piper if Hannah still calls the Changeling her sister? Won't she believe the Changeling replaced her? Hannah can love two sisters, just as the twins love all their siblings. She needs to convince them of the same. If the unfortunate meeting at the Tree is anything to go by, the Taken isn't likely to listen to a naïve human girl who's never experienced the Piper's horrors firsthand. But she might listen to another victim. She might listen to the Changeling.

The responsibility sinks into Hannah's shoulders, all the memories of the past week collapsing back on her, breaking the lighthearted bubble of forgetfulness the vacation had given her. She misses her sister. She understands now what she needs to do, taking her duties as a Namer seriously, even if she still isn't sure how to remind the Changeling who she is.

Focus on the present problem, Hannah. Not the Taken, not how to explain things to her parents when she gets home. The now. She's so lost in thought she forgets to look for glamours until she's been wandering in the forest for ten minutes and needs to turn back.

Find her sister.

Just like old times.

With a wry smile fixed on her lips and her plan fixed in her mind, Hannah scans the woods for the shimmer of glamour. She wanders longer, remembering the instructions, looking for movement or the telltale shifting of textures. It's difficult to spot a glamour once a fae has summoned it, but if she catches it during the in-between, she can narrow down the location.

Cecelia. She can't say the word, but she forces her tongue to make the right shapes, even though it feels leaden in her mouth.

Cecelia. She chants the name in her mind so it cannot slip away and hide from her.

"Cecelia," she calls, her voice coming out barely a whisper.

Something draws her gaze toward the treetops. She didn't hear any shuffling of leaves, nor did she see any shifting, but something like a tug, a thread, pulls her gaze upward and along the branches. Her sight doesn't flit around to spot something out of her peripheral. She knows exactly where to look.

There she is. Curled amongst the leaves, invisible but for Hannah's sense she must be looking at her sister.

Hannah whistles and points. "Ready or not, here I come!"

The Changeling grins and shifts back into her almost-human form as she drops from the tree. As Hannah stops focusing on the name, it evades her again, leaving her a little emptier than before. But as she sees the familiar smile, Hannah also sets her mind on this task.

The Changeling will come back to herself, even if she's not coming home.

Chapter 28
The Training

THE NEXT MORNING, at Quercu's request, the Changeling drags herself to the training ground to choose weapons. When her mentor had returned from the rescue mission, battle-worn and depressed, she'd claimed to have understood why the Changeling had run away from the mission.

"I don't blame ye," she had said, cleaning and wrapping her wounds. "After escaping the doom of the Unseelie Court, I can see why ye'd rather kiss a snot-faced toad than return to rescue a Taken brat." Her words drip with bitterness, projecting her own hurt, and she ties off the end of a bandage with her teeth.

"Hannah only cares about finding her real sister, not me," the Changeling had said, pretending not to care how much it had stung when Hannah had disowned her without a second thought.

That's another lie, another part of her argued. She had disowned herself when she'd run away, but she thought she had made her peace with that. Apparently not.

"She wouldn't want yet to come on the mission if she didn't care about ye, now would she?" Quercu had asked, "Besides, whether or not ye want to go on Hannah's mission, Lady Brigid's asked me to instruct you in more than just magic tricks. There's a difference between picking a fight and learning some self-defense."

The Changeling had groaned, and Quercu flicked an acorn at Changeling's temple with more force than usual in response for her sass. "Now scram. I don't want to see hide nor hair of ye until tomorrow."

So, this is how the Changeling finds herself studying the training field, simmering with dread and not a small amount of petty annoyance. Though she appreciates Hannah's apology about the glamours, she'd hoped the adventures yesterday would tempt the stubborn girl to abandon her fool's errand and stay safe in the Seelie Court. She could sense some connection drawing them closer again, but Hannah's iron determination burns away the nebulous camaraderie of yesterday.

The twins are missing at the moment, busy preparing protective gear. Quercu badgers a newcomer, who doesn't share the same blue-green lichen of the escaped changelings. She's a true Seelie warrior; despite her short stature, she holds her white and gray speckled wings in a confident posture. Her skin is a shade of grayish-green and she's pulled her long flowery purple hair back into a military bun to keep it out of her face. She's wearing the silvery chitinous armor of the Royal Guard, and responds to Quercu's friendly harassment in good-natured spirit. Hannah's glaring daggers, and the guard gives her a sheepish smile.

"Here for a rematch?" the guard asks, but there's no malice in the tone. The Changeling realizes this must be the guard who captured Hannah when she'd arrived in Seelie. Hannah doesn't have time to reply before one twin emerges from the armory and steps between them. "Iva volunteered to help train you. Please don't give her a hard time."

Hannah only nods, wary but eager to start. She's already carrying her falchion and starts her regular set of drills, while the twins call the Changeling to a side room that serves as an armory. Racks display assortments of swords and bows, axes and maces, spears and polearms with dozens of different heads. The Changeling doesn't know what she's looking for or how any of these are supposed to work. Should she have a preference? She doesn't belong here, surrounded by such capable warriors. If

Quercu weren't here to spot her, she'd glamour herself into the wall and avoid all this trouble.

Quercu, of course, notices her hesitancy and steps forward to heft a mace.

"You'll want something light, if you're going to be flying." She drops the mace with a *CLANG*, prompting an indignant cry from the twin, who rushes over to set it upright. Hannah had spent a few minutes earlier that morning explaining the twins' switching to her, and with some practice, the Changeling is learning to tell them apart. She guesses this one is Marco by his animated gestures whenever Quercu turns her back.

Quercu picks up a bow next and draws it, testing the weight. "This would allow you to keep your distance. It's tricky to master the timing between wing beats, though, and even more difficult to hit a moving target. This will be best for sneak attacks if you're stationary and concealed in the trees."

"Best not to give her the English longbow, though. That's got a draw weight of a hundred twenty pounds," Marco advises

"I'm sure she can manage," Quercu says, passing the weapon to the Changeling. As it passes from hand to hand, the bow shrinks to her size, and her palm slips into the grip. The magic preserves the energy wound up in the bowstring, but when she tries to pull it back, she reaches halfway to her chin before she gives up and releases it carefully to avoid a dry fire, which would damage the weapon.

Marco raises his eyebrows, impressed. "Cheater."

"What? What did I do?"

"Have you ever heard of the Square Cube Law?"

The Changeling only gawks at him, befuddled. No wonder Hannah gets along with him. They're both nerds.

"It's the reason ants can carry so much, even though they're so small," Marco explains. "Despite being human-sized, fae skirt that rule and benefit from it in ways we can't. It's a function of your wings too, allowing you to fly, despite all known laws of aerodynamics stating it should be impossible. It's all rather fascinating."

"Cut it out, Marco!" his twin calls from the other side, where he's correcting Hannah's form. "This is a fighting lesson, not a physics lecture."

"Physics is a battle of the mind, I'll have you know!" Marco snips back. He takes the English longbow from her hands and hands her a smaller bow with curved limbs. "Try the recurve. It'll distribute the draw weight, and its compact size is easier to maneuver in the trees."

Matteo comes over now, holding a quiver full of short arrows. "The Mongols used them on horseback, but many winged folks around here use them, as well. The English longbow was an infantry weapon."

"This is a fighting lesson, not a history lecture," Marco quips. Matteo sticks out his tongue at his brother.

This bow pulls back with effort, but the Changeling can draw it, and so she agrees with the choice. Matteo hands her the quiver, which straps on like a belt and rests at her hip so it doesn't get in the way of her wings.

"She also needs something to fight with. Melée, but something that allows her to keep her distance," Quercu muses. After perusing the long rack of polearms, she finally settles on a simple spear. "This will have the easiest learning curve."

It's a little taller than the Changeling and fixed with a wicked iron tip she's careful to avoid. Her weapons selected, the twins suit her up in protective gear, which make her feel silly.

Once everyone's prepared, Iva and Quercu pair up for a demonstration while the girls watch. They're not tracking points like a sporting match; rather, the two will spar until the sand runs out of Matteo's hourglass to simulate a real fight. Iva prepares some capsules from a satchel at her belt. When Quercu takes to the sky, her spear aimed downward for a lunge, Iva smashes one capsule on the ground and releases a high, clear note. A shower of seeds erupts, growing at rapid speed, twisting inward to tangle Quercu in their honeysuckle vines.

The air of friendly competition shatters. This is combat.

The Changeling screams, panicking despite the twins' warnings. Iva has the Piper's power! What's going on here? Hannah backs up too, grabbing her hand, raising herself on the balls of her feet, ready to run.

Quercu dodges and dives toward Iva, spear outstretched. A vine slaps it out of the way, just past her shoulder, as she comes in for the punch. Quercu recovers, flicks the spear to rap Iva's wrist and flies out of range again. The melody dips and weaves, and Iva's hands move as if she's a conductor, leading a symphony.

Marco puts a hand on the Changeling's shoulder. "It's alright. It's just a drill."

"Why are the vines—you're not—Iva—" she babbles, pointing frantically. That's *controlling*. This kind of magic shouldn't be in Seelie! She's supposed to be safe here! Was she ever safe here, or have they been manipulating her this whole time?

"The noises are different," Hannah says, watching the exchanges intently. "She's singing. The Piper and the Taken sound more discordant. This feels like a melody. It's not the same."

"What do you mean? She's controlling the vines!" the Changeling screeches, incredulous that Hannah can be even a little bit okay with this.

"The Piper's magic takes the True Name and twists it," Marco explains.

"Iva greets them by name and asks them for a favor," Matteo says, voice switching with his brother's.

"She gives them her own magic to let them grow and move supernaturally fast," Marco continues.

"It's a fair trade, not force," Matteo says.

"Magic is a tool, neither good nor evil."

"What matters is how we choose to use it."

This doesn't improve the Changeling's mood, but she forces her panicking mind to slow and observe. Quercu is agile and swift in the air, and though Iva stays grounded and fights in the same style as the Taken, she never hurts her partner. A tendril wraps around Quercu's ankle and flings her to the ground, but releases just in time for her to twist like a cat and land safely.

Matteo consults the hourglass and, after another couple seconds, calls time for the bout. The vines retract, Quercu lands with her spearpoint lowered to the ground, and she and Iva salute each other with a deft snap of their wings.

"Now, Quercu and Iva will both play the role of the Taken," Marco says. "Hannah, you'll be with me and Iva. Changeling, you'll go with Matteo and Quercu. We'll be switching between you to check on your progress."

Hannah nods and strides off, taking her place between her instructors and saluting them with a swish of her sword. When had Hannah shared her name with these two? When she'd arrived in Seelie, she had trusted nothing, but now she seems to have befriended everyone, while the Changeling's relationships are...strained, to say the least.

Regardless, she doesn't have time to wallow in her lonely awkwardness, because Matteo forces the spear into her hand and tells her to fall into a fighting stance. She stands as stiff as a post, strangling the weapon's smooth wooden shaft with a white-knuckled grip. He adjusts her feet, tells her to bend her knees, fixes the position of her hands, and pats her on the shoulder.

"Relax. I promise, you won't get hurt here. We're going to start with practice drills, no sparring. If you're less tense, you'll be able to move more smoothly."

The Changeling muffles a groan, dread rising in her stomach as she faces the grinning Quercu, who empties a seed packet and starts humming. Vines rise from the earth at the beckoning of her hand.

Run. Run. *Run!*

Some distant part of her mind registers the clatter of the spear hitting the ground, as her grip slips and the Changeling flits backward, hovering above the floor. She struggles to calm her breath. Matteo tries to hand the weapon back to her, but her hands are shaking too hard to hold it. She hovers further away. How can they expect her to do this?

Matteo sighs. "You're going to be afraid if you have to fight the Piper. It's just a fact. If you freeze up or try to flee, it'll cost you your life. You must learn how to fight through the fear."

"Warriors aren't supposed to be scared. I can't—I can't do this. You don't understand what you're asking me to do!"

"Nay, methinks I really do," Quercu snaps, holding up her arm, still wrapped in bandages from the battle with her estranged sister.

The Changeling doesn't care. Quercu's had years of experience to work through her fears.

Tucking the spear into the crook of his elbow, Matteo holds up his hands in a placating gesture. "Look, we're just your teachers. I'm not asking you to go on this quest, but I am asking you to take these lessons seriously. It's my responsibility to make sure you return in one piece. It's normal to be scared. In fact, I'd be worried if you were fearless. But I can't instruct you if you have a bad attitude."

With that, he holds out the spear again, daring her to take it or leave it. "What do you say?"

Chapter 29
The Departure

IS MATTEO KICKING her out? The Changeling wants to quit training but she doesn't want to leave like this, as a failure! She pauses, hand reaching halfway to reclaim her spear, fear of the Piper and fear of rejection warring in her mind.

The clanging swords cease across the field, and the Changeling glances at Hannah instead of answering the question. She sees her exchange a couple of soft words with Marco that she can't overhear. Hannah lowers her falchion and locks eyes with the Changeling. Her expression holds disappointment and resignation in equal measure.

"If you don't want to come, then fine. Don't come," Hannah says.

Something in the Changeling's chest snaps at the casual dismissal. She should be relieved. This is the permission she was hoping for, the excuse to avoid her fears. So, why does it hurt? Hannah doesn't want her company or her liability. Hannah still doesn't trust her. Is this how they part ways? The Changeling is surprised to realize she doesn't want that, despite everything. So she doesn't reply.

Hannah raises her falchion again. Iva gives a loud, clear whistle, ready to begin the drill, and enormous rats scamper forward from the bushes, each one the size of a large dog. The Changeling bites back a screech, but before she can warn Hannah, Matteo puts a hand on her shoulder.

"They're friends, remember? The rats have a choice if they want to play," he says, but it doesn't set her at ease.

"I've met the Piper," Hannah reminds the Changeling as she begins the bout. "I know what I'm getting into."

The first rat closes in on her. *Slash, slash!* She uses a training sword with dull edges for this bout, but Hannah still stops short of hitting the animal. It lunges. Hannah thrusts. There's a look of desperate determination in her eyes as the point makes contact, and the rat gives a yelp and scrambles away. The Changeling realizes by the way Hannah flinches that she's scared too, but she tries not to show it. The rat scurries back to Iva, who feeds it some fruits.

"I left home alone to look for you," Hannah says, wiping beads of sweat from her brow. "If I leave the Seelie Court alone to look for the Third, what's the difference? I'm more prepared this time."

Two more rats attack. Left. Right. Feint. Over. One falls, playing dead, mouth open to show its sharp front teeth. The other is too close to strike with the blade. Hannah motions slamming the pommel of the sword into its head, but doesn't put her weight behind the blow. It flops over, tail curling.

"I'd miss your company," she says as she waits for the next attack. "But no one is forcing you to come along, if distance makes the parting easier."

Another volley. Right, left, right, over! Three enemies scurry around her as she whirls. Hannah doesn't block the last one. Instead, she steps to the side and lets it pass her by. Before it can recover, she lunges and pokes the tip of the blade into the shoulder, then nudges it away with her foot in the stomach. If she'd put the force of her fury behind her foot, it'd have been devastating. The foe crumples.

"Stay in Seelie, where you'll be safe and free. I understand that's what you need."

The Changeling stands in slack-jawed wonder as Hannah parries and ripostes the next wave. She grounds her stance, holding her posture, sturdy and defensive, as she dispatches Iva's pet rats. Even though she's never seen Hannah fight like this before, she's still the same girl the Changeling always looked up to: capable and feisty, protective and resolute. It's the same strategy that scattered blocks around their room to deter invaders, and the same force of will that drove her to keep her promise.

I won't let him take you.

Hannah hadn't understood what she'd promised on that fateful night of the storm, curled up under the covers. But she'd listened when no one else did. She followed where no one else could. Coming here hadn't been stupid, because she hadn't known what was at stake. She didn't have to step through that portal after escaping the Piper. She could have turned home. For all Hannah had known, she could have been walking into the Unseelie Realm when she'd crossed the border. Only through wit and luck had she ended up in the Seelie Realm relatively unscathed. She'd fought monsters with a pocketknife. Hannah did these things for *her*.

Instead of guilt or anger, for the first time, the Changeling's heart swells with fondness and gratitude. How could she ever be angry with Hannah? She hadn't needed rescuing after all, but her sister, yes, *her sister*, hadn't known that. She came anyway. Now they know the Taken needs help, and Hannah will do the same for a girl who attacked them, despite the dread of knowing what's coming. It's integrity and devotion the Changeling both lacks and admires.

She's been a hypocrite.

The Changeling knows the danger better than anyone. Her actions trapped the Taken with the Piper. Shouldn't it be her responsibility to set things right, instead of letting Hannah mop up her mess? She knows the dangers of the Unseelie Court. Shouldn't it be her turn to protect Hannah from the perils that await her on this quest? She still doesn't know who she wants to be, but she decides at the very least she can't be a coward.

Hannah finishes her drill and straightens her back, saluting with a flourish to Iva, who responds in turn. She stows her blade, and the rats understand that's their signal to rise from their prone positions. Hannah fetches a handful of seeds from a container on the sidelines and feeds them the treats as thanks for their cooperation. She scratches them on their heads, murmuring names in her friendly way. One curls its tail around her shoulders, and Hannah doesn't seem to mind.

The Changeling is still sorting through her thoughts when a voice interrupts the moment. "I'm afraid the parting must occur sooner than we expected."

Lady Brigid emerges from the line of trees, looking haggard, a familiar pet perched on her shoulder.

"Lady Brigid! Merciful Monarchs, where have you been?" the Changeling asks.

"Kit-Kat!" Hannah yells, running to see her friend. He's not hurt, to the Changeling's relief, and the little weasel jumps from the Lady's shoulder to Hannah's and runs under her hair and around her sleeve as she giggles.

"Good morning to you too, Hannah," Lady Brigid says with a wry grin that doesn't quite reach her eyes. Her ominous greeting and the letter sticks she's still holding tell the Changeling something is very, *very* wrong.

"What's the matter?" Hannah asks, giving Kit-Kat a scratch on the head as the Lady steps forward to join the group.

"We've set our trap for the Unseelie in Carterhaugh Forest, but Kit-Kat brings grave news from their summit. Queen Mab chose the Piper's offering—either your sister delivers the both of you, or she will serve as the sacrifice herself. Hannah, if you don't recover her now, the Taken will die."

"But it's a trap!" the Changeling says. She tries to keep the despair from creeping into her voice. In all of her worst imaginings, she never considered this possibility. Now the Piper forces their hand, and she hates it. She hates him.

"Yes, it surely is," Lady Brigid admits, her face set in determination. "But the Piper is proceeding toward the offering place with the rest of the Unseelie and counting on the Taken to bring you after. He's distracted, and if he's treating it like a game, he's bound by his own rules not to interfere until you each play your course. The Tithe has been delayed. It's the best chance you have of finding your Taken and returning with her safely."

"It's rigged!" the Changeling protests. She can't let Hannah take this insane mission.

"It's your last chance." Lady Brigid says. "If you delay, the Unseelie will offer her."

As Hannah hesitates, the Changeling holds onto her hand. She says nothing, but gives Hannah her most pleading look.

"I won't ask you to come," Hannah whispers, before prying her hand from the Changeling and turning back to Lady Brigid. "I promised to rescue my sister. I will not betray her now."

Lady Brigid continues explaining her plans as the Changeling squirms. How can Hannah approach her worst nightmares with her head held high? It frightens and inspires the Changeling, sending a shiver down her spine.

Can the Changeling put her life on the line for a girl they barely know? How will she face Hannah's real sister, the girl condemned to a fate she didn't deserve?

It doesn't matter what she fears.

"I'll intercept the Unseelie hoards and attempt to stop the ritual. If—Monarchs forbid—you fail, the Piper will sacrifice the Taken. Perhaps she will listen to you since she is at the end of her rope," Lady Brigid explains.

Matteo and Marco share a look, unspoken communication crossing between them in a moment, before they step forward, hands on their swords.

"Let us go with you. We swore fealty to you when you brought us into the Court, and we're your best fighters," Marco says, his voice confident and unwavering.

"You'll be at the mercy of Queen Mab and all the Unseelie hoards once they realize what you're doing. Let us come to protect you," Matteo adds, voice more tinged with concern than fear.

Lady Brigid nods her assent and turns to Quercu, "Can you guard Hannah?"

Quercu squirms, torn between duty and family. "The Tithe will mean my sister's afoot. I'd prefer a chance to bring her back to the Seelie Court, but if the girlies need a friend—"

The Changeling shakes her head. "No. Go to your sister. We'll be fine." She doesn't sound very confident, but they all notice her use of the plural. "I won't let Hannah go through with this alone."

"Ce—" The name catches in Hannah's throat, and the Changeling's heart skips a beat. "Are you sure?"

The Changeling isn't sure of anything: not her name, not this mission, not her place in the world. But she knows Hannah needs her right now, and that's enough.

"I promised to help you rescue your sister. I will not betray you now," she echoes. Her dark eyes look into Hannah's, meeting her gaze intentionally. Hannah blinks slowly.

"Thank you," Hannah says simply, breaking eye contact first, and the Changeling realizes that she's scared too. They turn in unison to face Lady Brigid.

"What do we need to do?" the Changeling asks.

The rest of the day is a whirlwind of activity. The Lady disappears with the twins to gather items to avoid a repeat of the last mission. Quercu draws a map and plots out a course they can take to reach the Unseelie territory. She reminds them over and over that time moves differently in that realm, and they'll need to move fast if they want to get back before they lose years to the hungry clock. She can chart a route for them as far as the Piper's lair, but they'll need to navigate the maze of enormous rock formations and tangled thorn vines on their own.

The Changeling takes up her spear, and learns to fight. She only has time to learn a few basic moves with Quercu and

Hannah before they'll need to leave, but it will have to be enough. It takes several rounds of drills before the Changeling stops flinching at every strike, but eventually she learns to block, lunge, and how to dive from the air. Her aim still wavers, and her knuckles bruise whenever she mistimes an exchange, but when Hannah congratulates her on a strike well-made, she comes to appreciate the value in the lesson. All the same, the Changeling is grateful when Quercu says she's finished and teaches her how to glamour the spear into a walking stick for safekeeping.

Lady Brigid returns bearing supplies: food with healing enchantments, water to refill their bottles, tea for energy and restoring their strength, spare clothes, shoes for the Taken, and bedrolls, in case they grow too tired to continue without rest. She stresses they should only sleep if there's no other choice but to collapse from exhaustion. To sleep is to lose months, and time is not a luxury they have. She even packed woven straw crosses for protection, and lumps of soft cotton fluff they can use to plug their ears. These items put the Changeling's nerves at ease, just a little.

Hannah packs her all-purpose screwdriver from the dwarf, in case she needs to dismantle any iron traps. She lets Lady Brigid enchant her backpack to fit all the supplies with space to spare. It's almost bottomless, like Mary Poppins' carpetbag, but the Changeling's too worried to marvel at the new toy.

Lady Brigid and the twins take them to the edge of the woods, far from the comforts and beauty of the Seelie settlements, where they face the dark and wild unknown. The sun sets in the distance. The Changeling wonders if she'll ever see it rise again.

They embrace their friends one last time before they part ways. The Changeling only cries a bit.

"We'll see you soon." Marco says, patting the Changeling on the shoulder. He forces a smile.

"Godspeed—"

"And goodwill."

Chapter 30

The Argument

HANNAH AND THE Changeling move through the forest like a pair of foxes, clambering over rocks and fallen logs. The Changeling leads the way around near-invisible bends in the path, and Hannah follows her like an extra shadow, dark curls framing her face, green jacket good as any glamour.

Though the Changeling enjoys wearing this face, she considers it might be for the best if she appears more human when they encounter the Taken. Her hair flickers and darkens to match Hannah's, and instead of hiding the Piper's Plague with colorful flowers, she lets the illusion mask it. She keeps her wings, though. Quercu taught her to see through her eyespots, and it's a heady feeling to watch all around her at once. Once she gets over the disorientation, she feels safer keeping her guard up.

Hannah shivers behind her. They'd been comfortable in the Seelie Court, the Changeling knows. There, beautiful blazes of autumn leaves persist past their prime while the weather remains the perfect balance of warm sun and cool breeze. Here, the branches are almost bare, and the air has a biting chill. The starlight flickers out as they draw farther and farther away from the Monarch's influence, until the only light comes from the flashlight she carries.

The Changeling realizes she doesn't need the flashlight to see in the dark. She's spent too much of her life in the shadows, and they welcome her return. She shivers, even though she doesn't feel the cold, and tightens her grip on the disguised spear.

When they reach a steep cliff, the Changeling doesn't hesitate in throwing herself off it, her wings keeping her airborne. Hannah skids to a stop just before she slides over the edge. The Changeling hovers in the air, waiting for Hannah, heart leaping into her throat, blood pounding in her ears. They need to move fast, but no giant dragonflies can catch Hannah's fall here. Their mission requires stealth.

The human girl slides down the decline in an avalanche of pebbles and grunts as she almost twists her ankle in a hole. She limps forwards for a few steps, shaking off the pain, and tries to keep up the pace. Watching her struggle, the Changeling slows her headlong sprint, though she's anxious to be done with this mission. She offers Hannah the walking stick.

"You can take this, if you need it for balance. I don't need it, since I can fly."

"It's more than a walking stick," Hannah reminds her, voice hushed in case the Taken is listening.

"I'll take it back if I need it."

Hannah shrugs, and accepts the aid. They follow the map Quercu drew for them, walking side by side while the path is still wide enough for them both. The Changeling pretends not to notice as Hannah looks at her with a curious expression, looks away, looks back again, as if she's turning over words in her mouth, deciding if she should spit them out. The Changeling squirms under the scrutiny.

"What?" she asks when she can't take it anymore.

"What?" Hannah responds, surprised by the sudden outburst.

"Why are you staring at me?"

"Oh." Hannah tears her eyes away and pretends to look at the map again, even though their path is straight for the next mile or so. "It's...it's good to see you again," Hannah answers.

Again. The word both stirs up the muck in the Changeling's heart and makes her feel warm and welcome at once. It's confusing, and she shakes her head at the silly sentimentality.

"But I've been with you nearly this whole time," she says.

"That's not what I meant." Hannah's voice is low and wistful, and she's staring again, though she doesn't mean to.

The Changeling knows exactly what she meant. She's glad to see the face of her old sister again. It's familiar and deceptively comforting for her, but can't Hannah understand it's not true? "I just thought it'd be better to meet the Taken if I don't look like one of the Piper's lieutenants. If I kept my true form, I'd scare her off, like Quercu's sister," the Changeling says, shrugging as she tries to frame her actions practically.

Hannah sucks in a long breath. "I've already made a negative first impression on the Taken. Hopefully, you can win her trust by telling her about home."

Home. The Changeling avoids thinking about it as much as possible because it's not supposed to be her home. But as much as she loves the Seelie Court, something at her core aches for the comfort of familiarity. Unbidden images come to mind of her room, decorated with all her favorite things. Hannah's plant specimens strewn about the desk. Mama's cooking. Dad's bedtime stories. She scratches at the cheek where she knows the lichen lies and turns away from the unwanted memories.

"I can't talk about that," the Changeling says, trying and failing to keep the crack out of her voice.

"It was your home, too." Hannah stops walking and forces the Changeling to turn and look at her, free hand on shoulder. The Changeling refuses to meet Hannah's gaze and rolls her eyes in response. Is Hannah determined to have this conversation? Here? Now?

"I stole my place," the Changeling reminds her. If Hannah stays angry about the past, maybe she'll let this drop.

"That doesn't matter anymore. I forgive you."

"But if we survive this, you're taking your sister home. And I can't go back. And while I want to love the Seelie Court, I can't call it home if you're not here."

"But if you could come home with me, would you? Didn't it hurt to leave?"

"I'm not your sister." The Changeling's voice is scornful, and she tries to keep walking. "You said so yourself. I can't be that person anymore."

"I'm sorry." Hannah's voice bleeds with sincerity, and it catches The Changeling off guard. "I never should have said that. I was confused and angry, but I'm neither of those things anymore. Now, I'm just sad I don't know who you are anymore."

"That's okay. It'll be easier to go home if you're leaving a stranger in Seelie."

"I would rather bear the pain of losing a sister than the pain of making you a stranger."

The Changeling struggles with herself, her face transforming as she loses control of the glamours. She thought Hannah had pushed her away intentionally, but now she realizes they've both been grieving what they couldn't have—a return to their old life together. Sobs escape her lips as the pent-up frustration and remorse flood back into her. In running away, her only goal was to stay safe in Seelie, but now? Instead of shrinking away from Hannah's devotion, shouldn't she be grateful for someone who wants to know her for who she is?

When she doesn't answer, Hannah takes a step back. "I know you never planned to come home, but...losing your name? Did you hate your old life so much that you wanted to forget it completely?"

"No," the Changeling chokes out. "No, of course not. But I can't have that life."

"Then pick a new name. I'll accept it."

The Changeling walks away, ignoring the statement. She hates Hannah poking her in a vulnerable spot, and hates even more that they're vulnerable here, on the border of the Unseelie Court. "I don't know. It doesn't matter. We have a job to do. Stop getting distracted. We're in enemy territory, and we should keep moving and watching for threats."

"Ce—gaahhh! Changeling. Listen to me! We're going into the Piper's traps, and you don't have a True Name. He can control you in this state. The Taken needs to find her Name too. How can we convince her to come back with us if you don't know who you are?"

"He can't take my name if I don't have one," the Changeling counters, but as she says it, she realizes it's a lie. Hannah's hard logic sends a shiver down her spine. The Piper won't need to take her name if she doesn't have one. Without an identity, his song can slip into the gaps in her mind.

"I'd hoped we would have more time in Seelie to talk about this," Hannah says, "but it's too late now. You insisted on coming along, and I'm glad you did, but I draw the line here. I won't let you get hurt for me. Before we go another step, you need to tell me who you are."

"I can't do that, Hannah. You can't fix this."

"I came here to rescue my sister—to rescue *you*. I don't care if the person you are is someone different from the person I thought you were. I still love you."

The Changeling stops walking away and wraps her arms around herself. "What about your real sister?"

"I'll have two sisters. There's more than enough room in my heart for both of you. We grew up together. Nothing can change that."

The Changeling sinks down and wraps her hands around her knees as the weight of those words hits her. She trembles, wings shaking like leaves in an autumn storm. The shifting glamours make her nauseous as her vision splits, and the lichen itches so much. She's sick, and now she realizes just how deep the Piper's lies have worked into her mind.

Hannah steps forward, sets down the walking stick, and wraps her in a hug.

"What do you want?"

The Changeling wants to go home and stay in Seelie. She wants to play with Willow and keep learning from Quercu. She wants to see their mom and dad, and she wants Lady Brigid to say she's proud of her. Can't she have both worlds?

She doesn't answer.

"What is your name?" Hannah asks, still holding her tight. It's every bit as comforting as that last night she'd slept in her big sister's bed. What was her name? It's been so long since she gave it up, and she struggles through her cloudy memories to find it again. She hasn't looked for a new name, as nothing else would fit. She needs to find her True Name.

"What is your name?" Hannah asks again.

The Changeling took the place of Hannah's human sister and took her name. Is it hers to take back? Did she have a fae name before the switch? The Piper had taken advantage of her broken magic. The Taken was a baby. The Changeling took her name with ease...a borrowed word to describe her. She grew into it, like a tree grows its roots around rocks. The name was hers—and not hers. She can't give it back now. Without those rocks, she'd topple over.

Dangerously close to falling apart, she asks herself, *What do I want?*

She wants to be Cecelia again.

Cecelia the changeling.

Cecelia of the Seelie Court.

Cecelia the Sister.

Can she be all these things at the same time? It seems impossible, but here she is, held in the arms of her human sister, standing in the middle of the Unseelie woods, searching for their lost sibling. Hannah makes impossible things happen. They'll have to find out together.

"What is your name?" Hannah asks a third and final time as she tilts up the Changeling's head to look into her eyes.

Regaining control of the glamours, she lets her features settle. A flower crown covers the Piper's plague growing from her forehead. Wings exposed. Exoskeleton armor. Human face. The face Hannah knows. She can be both.

"Cecelia," she says, wiping away tears. She thinks back to the throne room, when Hannah had told the Monarchs her name was Maria. There might be many Marias who have a lovely name—and it served her well as a disguise—but it is not hers. There are a thousand Hannahs in this world, and they bear a good name—a brave, determined, confident one. But they are not Hannah Teagan. There may be dozens of Cecelias too, but they are not her.

"My name is Cecelia Teagan," she says, more sure of herself now.

"Your name is Cecelia," Hannah repeats, "and you are my sister."

"My name is Cecelia, and the Taken is our sister."

"The Taken is our sister, and we won't leave her behind," Hannah affirms. They fall into each other's arms again, and relief floods Cecelia's body as she clings to her big sister for comfort and support. Just like always.

"She'll have to find her True Name, or choose one for herself, since the one she was given..." Cecelia pauses and then amends, "Since I took the one our parents gave her."

"When the time comes, we'll try to help her," Hannah says.

"How can we do that?"

"I just helped you, didn't I?"

"That's cheating. You knew my name already."

A look of sorrow passes over Hannah's face and her shoulders slump with relief. "It was slipping away. When you gave it up, I struggled to say it or think it."

"Oh." Cecelia hadn't realized that, and the idea of Hannah forgetting her terrifies her more than the fact that she forgot herself.

"I was cheating, though," Hannah continues with a smug grin. "Quercu gave me a hint you might need a reminder."

Everything makes sense now, but Cecelia can't suppress a surge of indignance. Her friends had been scheming behind her back, even if it was in her best interest. "That meddler! That's why she was so caught up on you being a Namer!"

"Well, that, and because I'm so phenomenally talented at the magical art of biological taxonomy," Hannah says, shrugging.

Cecelia rolls her eyes. "Hey, what's that plant?" she asks, pointing at a random bush to their left.

Hannah, working on routine, walks over and inspects it with her flashlight. "*Lindera benzoin*, I think. Spicebush, because you can make it into a spicy tea or seasoning. She turns back to Cecelia and laughs at herself. "I missed you so much."

"I missed me, too."

Chapter 31

The Maze

HANNAH CONSULTS THE map, turning it this way and that, trying to see if they'd turned aside somewhere or if the map was just wrong. Maybe Quercu had accidentally given them one that was out of date? Or perhaps the landscape had just changed since they last charted it. Nothing in Unseelie can be reliable, and she's unsurprised but still frustrated at the tangle of brush that hedges off the path they're supposed to follow.

Frowning at the map, Cecelia opens her wings. In a shimmer of indigo, she shoots upward, following the angle of the vines and branches that block their way. Hannah sits down and shakes the pebbles out of her shoe. Back on the trail again. At least she had time in Seelie to let the blisters heal. At least she has her sister by her side this time. Cecelia's name is a relief, and she anchors it in her mind.

She's disappeared into the darkness above, and Hannah tries not to worry when she doesn't flit back into view right away. The silence suffocates her, worry causing the breath to tighten in her chest. The Taken might hunt both of them, but Cecelia is the prize. Hannah hates letting her little sister out of her sight, even if she can scout where Hannah can't go. She forces herself to breathe five times, then ten, then wait until the count of sixty, before the panic, loneliness, and oppressive dark grow too much to bear.

"Cecelia! What do your elf eyes see?" she calls softly.

"They're taking the hobbits to Isengard!" Cecelia's peal of laughter floats down from the treetops, and Hannah sighs with relief.

"To Isengard!" Hannah calls back.

There's a muffled grunt and scraping as Cecelia makes her way back down.

"I can't see much," comes the faint reply, serious this time. As soon as she's within sight of the ground, she lets go of the branch and flutters down to join Hannah. "Whatever this hedge is, it's too thick for me to fly through. There's a ceiling of sorts, where it reaches a branch up above. I can't climb over, and you can't reach either way," she says. "Do you think this is her doing?"

"Most likely," Hannah says. "If she knows the game, she'll want to lead us to a place where she can trap us while remaining hidden. I think she's trying to herd us off the main road."

Hannah can't shake the eerie feeling of being watched, the unsettling wrongness of these plants. In the Seelie world, the plants she didn't recognize were new, wondrous things. She found species that humans hadn't categorized yet. Here, familiar plants become warped and twisted; the bush in front of them might have been *Berberis thunbergii* once, but it isn't anymore. All the plants in this hedge look the same, invasive shrubs she thinks carry berries, until she gets closer and realizes the branches themselves bleed.

She paces the length of the path up to the hedge, looking for any side paths they might have missed in the dark. She scans her flashlight over the unfamiliar forest, searching for any beaten trail or gap between the cramped trees. Sets of eyes stare out at her, gleaming as they reflect her torch. She stares back, and they blink first.

After a few minutes of searching, they discover two paths, leading left and right alongside the hedge, like a T in the road. To the left is an archway made of curving branches. To the right, a narrow path leads upward; stones serving as steps almost steep enough to climb are crowded with thorns.

"There's a gap!" Hannah calls, pointing it out to Cecelia. "Which way should we go?"

"I don't like the look of either of these paths," Cecelia says, her nose wrinkling.

"We're not getting any closer to the Taken by standing here feeling sorry for ourselves, are we?"

Cecelia makes a long-suffering sigh, orients herself against the light of the moon trickling through the canopy of leaves far above them, and frowns at the path behind them.

"Left?" she finally decides, and Hannah raises an eyebrow.

"Are you guessing, or are you telling me?"

"Telling," Cecelia answers, sounding only marginally more confident. "The closest entrance to the Piper's compound is north of the palace, according to Quercu's map. And we set off in a northeasterly direction. So going west for a bit will get us back on track."

"Uh-huh," Hannah says. The logic is sound, but another thought occurs to Hannah as she squints at the map again. "Do directions work the same way in Faerieland, or is it just as backwards as time?"

"Look, we're not getting any closer to the Taken by standing around second-guessing ourselves, are we?" Cecelia echoes, and Hannah can't argue with that, so she sticks out her tongue instead.

Since the arching branches make it too low for Cecelia to fly, they walk along the left path. Hannah leads, and she's only taken a few steps when she kicks something hidden in the fallen leaves. Pain shoots through her foot as the iron jaws of a clamp trap lock around her boot. She steadies herself with the walking stick, and avoids falling face first into another trap, hiding in the leaves.

Biting back a shriek, Hannah shoves the walking stick into Cecelia's hands and whips the multi-tool out of her bag. The trap comes apart with a few quick jerks to unfasten the hinge bolt, and she retracts her foot. The spikes didn't pierce the tough leather, and she breathes a sigh of relief after testing her weight on the ankle and realizing it's not broken.

"I'm glad I wore my hiking boots," she says through a grimace.

"She's setting these to capture me," Cecelia says with a horrified expression. She's wearing laced sandals that she'd found in the Seelie court. They're flexible enough to let her work with glamours, but not tough enough to protect her from the traps. She shapeshifts again and readjusts the straps, reinforcing herself with exoskeleton armor that forms sturdy plating over her feet.

While Cecelia busies herself with that, Hannah assesses their surroundings, and comes to a decision. "Retreat. The other path is the one we want."

"What? Why? If she's setting traps, then surely she's this way."

"Think about it. She'll need a vantage point. That's the way she went after she finished setting these."

Cecelia flutters into the air with a beat of her wings, floating just high enough to keep her feet off the ground as they make their way up the other path. Hannah nods with bitter satisfaction as she notices the clue she missed earlier: thorns to block their path so they can't follow her. Thorns that match the Taken's style of attack, far more than the boring, indistinct branches of the left-hand path.

Hannah creeps along for a few paces before the beam of her flashlight lands on a flower, growing from the center of the path.

No other flowers dot the ground. Hannah leans down to inspect it: a yellow rose, like a beacon of sunshine.

"This is it," she says.

Cecilia whirls. "That wasn't there before."

"She's watching. It's a sign. Let's go."

Despite the flower, Hannah's doubts grow as they follow the path. It curves left, then pivots right, until she's sure they're going in circles. The ground turns swampy, and as Hannah struggles through the mud, a burst of fire spurts up at her. She shrieks and flails backward, but the flames lick at the hem of her jacket. Cecelia, hovering above, extends the walking stick. Hannah grabs it, and Cecelia pulls her free from the mud. They beat out the fire before it can spread.

Crisis averted, Hannah finds a large branch and carves it into her desired shape, then uses her pocketknife to whittle tinder. She finds some trees with sharp metallic needles and pierces herself a few times trying to collect sap on the end of her branch, hoping it'll catch fire as well as pine sap. Then she rolls it in the wooden shavings. The next time they hear the spluttering of the flames, she shoves the end of the branch into the burst, and lights the torch. It catches, and blazes blue.

They only have a few minutes before it burns itself out, so they'll need to work quickly. Hannah holds the torch high, and it reveals another crossroads before them. Left or right. They're pinned in on either side by enormous boulders. To continue down either path, they'll have to clamber over the rocks like goats. To the left, they're covered in damp slippery moss that reflects pale green luminescence in the light of the flickering blue torch. The humid, pungent air settles heavy in Hannah's lungs. To the right, the path rises sharply, making almost a sheer cliff. Cecelia could fly to the top easily, but Hannah would have to make the slow ascent on her own. Thorns surround them, blocking any other options, forcing the girls to play the Taken's game.

Cecelia groans. "Now what?"

"Right?"

"Back?" Cecelia says, hopefully.

"I think we're too far in for back."

Hannah considers their choices, shoves the torch and walking stick into Cecelia's hands, and pulls her falchion from her side. "I'm cutting through," she declares. If they can avoid taking either path, maybe they can reach the Taken directly! She imagines herself facing a mighty dragon of writhing woody stems and thorny horns, staring down a monster like the heroes in her storybooks. Heroism is about fighting, right?

And fight she does! Channeling all her frustration and urgency through the falchion, she slices through the shrubbery. Branches fall around her feet, and she tramples them underfoot as she beats further into the hedge. She feels a momentary surge of triumph as she makes headway, but then her ears flood with a low, angry humming.

The plants writhe around her. Panic rises with their growth, and she slashes, trying to thrash her way back to Cecelia's worried shouts. Through a gap in the fallen branches, Hannah catches a glimpse of the Taken, wearing a replacement mask, holding her sling. A stone flies past, narrowly missing Hannah's eye. Another stings her leg. Anger seeps from her heart into her hand as she cuts down more vines, but soon her legs and arms bleed with cuts from the thorns, and she almost takes off her own nose as she stumbles backward.

Hannah retreats and staggers onto the path, exhausted, ashamed, and more frustrated than before. Cecelia drops the walking stick and catches Hannah with one arm as she falls. Holding the torch out of the way, Cecelia gently lowers her to the ground, avoiding the sap-sticky blade. Hannah catches her breath, then frowns at the curling, overcrowded thicket closing between her and the Taken. She'd been so close!

"Are you ok?"

"Fine," Hannah grunts, pulling herself to her feet. She shakes her head regretfully, remembering the way Quercu had battled with her own sister. Hannah will fail if she keeps fighting the Taken every time they meet, even if she doesn't mean to instigate a fight.

"Do you think her plants get growing pains?" Cecelia whispers, picking up her walking stick again. Tiny leaves sprout from the seasoned wood, affected by the Taken's magic.

Hannah mutters an apology to the bush before turning back to the problem at hand. They can't reach the Taken directly, so they'll have to pick a route.

The left path chokes behind them now. The torch sputters out.

It seems they have no choice, so they keep marching as the path meanders between boulders that loom over them like tombstones.

Chapter 32

The Approach

CECELIA FLIES AHEAD with the flashlight to chart a path, then leads the way for Hannah as she climbs through the maze. They trade their equipment back and forth as the terrain grows more dangerous.

"This way, careful! It's narrow," she calls quietly.

Hannah grunts in response and squeezes through the tight crevasse, but no sooner than she does, a soft groan makes the plants grow up again, all sharp thorns and tough woody bark. Cecelia pulls Hannah through before the passage closes between them, and she reaches the other side gasping for breath.

"That was a close one. She's trying to separate us," Cecelia says, wringing her hands.

"How are we supposed to navigate a maze when the paths move? I wish I still had those seashells."

"I don't know how much good they'd do us now."

Hannah sighs in affirmation to Cecelia's point as they trudge along the fresh dead end. She tries not to look too often at the flickers of movement she catches between the stones and hedges—shapes that resemble blinking eyes, peering at them through eyelashes of fluttering leaves. Too many eyes. She remembers them from her first meeting with the Piper, and realizes they must be his spies.

Hannah hazards a glance over her shoulder at Cecelia to see if she's okay and notices that as she flicks her wings closed, the eyespots blink. She must be watching their surroundings for threats, too. Are there other creatures trapped with them? Hannah realizes by closing off the retreat, the Taken has also trapped herself.

In a wider stretch of the path, Hannah slows and leans close to Cecelia's ear. "You're right. She's watching, so we should try to set a positive example. Show her we're friendly. We need to bring her home. We need to win her trust."

Cecelia nods, pretending there's nothing suspicious about this forest, and keeps strolling along. They try to relax and take each change of the maze in stride, always working closer to the Taken. Cecelia spots ladybugs crawling on the underside of a large leaf, and they stop for a while to watch. The light shifts, tinting the forest in a pale wash-bin gray. The morning sun hasn't yet come over the horizon, but Hannah realizes they've been searching all night with no sign of getting closer to the Taken. She's still grateful for any light as her eyes strain.

They compliment the ever-shifting scenery and avoid hacking off any more plants as they scramble over enormous boulders the size of trucks. Cecelia sings Hazel's lullaby but makes up new words, a reflection of the verses Hannah had sung when she'd first entered the forest looking for the Seelie Court.

Merfolk play in mirrored streams,
Crystal caverns, dwarf forge gleams,
Freely roams the unicorn
Freed from bonds by the first-born.
Bonds of friendship shall we weave,
Hours away the Fae Realm thieves.

Creeping beetles, skulking rats
Squeaking, swarming, flapping bats,
Swarms of them obey the call.
All beware the Piper's thrall.
Rotting logs and molding thatch,
Leaves obscuring, light a match.

Hannah tells herself it's fine the ladybugs have skulls painted on their backs. The sound of cruel laughter from just behind the bushes isn't ominous in the slightest. They laugh right back, and play I Spy until Hannah gets sick of Cecelia beating her. Hannah tries not to think about the fact it's the next morning, or about her broken promise to return before dinner. She's not worried at all about what their parents must think. If it's Halloween in the fae world, who knows how much time has passed in the human world? Every minute they spend in the Unseelie world counts against them.

It seems Cecelia has the same thing on her mind since taking back her name. "What are you going to tell Mom and Dad if you get home safe?" she asks as they crawl up a passageway that's especially steep.

"When *we* get home," Hannah corrects, trying to find purchase for her foot to avoid slipping down the narrow stone shaft she's climbing.

"Do you really think I could go home?"

"Sure. Why not?" Hannah says. She hauls herself over the ledge and pants for a minute. If they survive the Piper, facing their parents' wrath will be as easy as dealing with Willow's slobbery kisses. Messy, but harmless. She rubs her hands on her pant leg. So much poison ivy. *Toxicodendron radicans.* Of course that's an Unseelie plant she can recognize.

Cecelia pulls her to her feet. "I don't know if I can go back to hiding after so long. And after everything we've seen...I'm still Cecelia, but I'm a different Cecelia than Cecelia the Runaway."

Hannah pulls herself to her feet, and they move again. They make it a couple steps before she notices the tell of rust-orange metal dust above them. She shoves Cecelia out of the way, but she's not fast enough. The massive trap falls between them and blocks the path, missing Hannah, but ripping open the sleeve of Cecelia's tunic dress as it rakes down her arm. Cecelia shrieks with pain. Her skin blisters where the iron scratched her, angry and raw.

Hannah dismantles the device with ruthless efficiency, just thankful the damage wasn't worse. When she reaches her sister, she pulls a salve out of her bag and dresses the burns before answering Cecelia's question. They can't risk it getting infected.

"I'm not the same Hannah either," she admits. "But I think that's okay. Truth be told, I don't want to leave this world forever either. I want to go home, but I also want to come back to visit our friends."

"Do you think that's allowed?"

"When we get back, we'll ask Lady Brigid. But I don't see why not. It might be hard to find the portal again, or we could only go through on certain days, but I'm sure it's possible. The twins have lives and family outside of their Powers work. It's dangerous, but no more so than what we're doing now." She ties off the end of the bandage and seals it with a kiss. "There, all better."

Cecelia gives her a smile and surveys their surroundings for more traps before moving forward again. "Ok, say we both go home, and say we still keep up my disguise as a human. How do we explain the Taken?"

"We will tell them the truth."

"They'll never believe us," she says, as if she's stating a fact like "the sky is blue."

The sky is not, in fact, blue, but a miserable overcast gray that blots out whatever weak sun had risen on their desperate morning.

"They'll have to!" Hannah says. "How else do we explain our long disappearance, why we're bringing home a third sister?" They come to a stream of greenish muddy water, which

Hannah recognizes from her misadventure with Quercu's sister. She warns Cecelia to fly over it, once again envious of her wings, and then picks her way over the stones, only splashing a little of the burning liquid on herself.

"They'll think I'm crazy. I'm mad enough as it is, and I'm a much better actor than you. It's outlandish. That's why I was so adamant about staying in Seelie. It only makes sense if two girls go home. If all three of us go back, it would be too hard to explain."

Hannah opens her mouth to protest, but glimpses the eye-spots on the wings watching her, and reconsiders what she was about to say. "What do you think we could tell them?" she asks instead.

"Half-truths, I suppose. I wandered off for an early morning hike and lost track of time. You tracked my footsteps, and on the way back, we found another girl in the woods, so we brought her back safely. Someone had kidnapped her, but she escaped. If they don't believe that, they'll assume she's a runaway. They'll call the police but won't find anything, and then, after a few weeks, they'll get used to it."

Hannah frowns. The idea of lying leaves a sour taste in her mouth, though Cecelia's logic makes sense. "Can't we try telling the truth first? You deserve to live the truth. Mom might believe us, at least. She lets us leave out food for Hazel and socks for the monsters under the beds."

They reach another rock wall. Cecelia flies up, then lies on her belly and reaches down with the walking stick. Hannah backs up a few steps, runs, plants one foot on the surface, leaps higher, and grabs the rod with both hands. The fae pulls her up with unnatural strength, until she can get a hold on Hannah's coat to pull her up the rest of the way. Hannah swings a leg over the ledge to find her footing and scrambles to her feet. It's a move they'd practiced a few times. Obstacle surpassed Cecelia lets out a sigh.

"I miss Hazel. I never thanked her enough for cleaning our rooms."

"*You* never thanked her enough? We were giving her crumbs. I owe her, like, ten batches of cookies. At least!" Hannah says.

Cecelia giggles. "At least," she agrees, before her face falls. "Come on, Hannah, admit it. Putting up with childish flights of fancy is one thing," Cecelia makes air quotes around 'childish flights of fancy,' and Hannah feels her face flush with embarrassment. "Accepting a faerie impostor or reasoning away an extra daughter is another matter entirely."

"The reason doesn't matter, as long as they let her stay," Hannah insists. "Truth first. Then your version of the story as a fall-back. I'll back it, keep up the act of the practical older sister who knows better, as long as you try to tell the truth first." Cecelia wavers and Hannah presses on, sternly but not unkindly, "You owe it to them, and you know it."

"I don't want to hurt them," Cecelia whispers, suddenly small and soft and still. She curls into herself like a hedgehog protecting its soft belly. "Not like I betrayed you. What they don't know won't hurt them. I can't break their trust, too."

Hannah shakes her head and takes Cecelia's hand. "I trust you. I love you. Mom and Dad do, too. They were mad with worry when you left, and they couldn't understand why you would wander off again, especially after last year..." She leaves the implications unsaid as her little sister shudders, remembering the encounter with the Piper she hadn't shared with the family.

"We've been gone a day now. They'll just be happy to know you're alive and safe. They'll want to know what happened. Dad left for town right away in the truck, and Mom is probably still walking miles all over the neighborhood with Willow for any trace of you. They want their daughter back. Faerie or not, you're still a Teagan. You got two names, y'know."

Cecelia smiles slightly, and Hannah gently punches her in the arm, turning jovial. "Or you're stuck with us. Take your pick. But if you thought running off into the woods was going to work, you'll have to do a lot better to get rid of me."

A genuine smile then, and Hannah feels a warm glow of triumph at cheering up her little sister. "Mom and Dad aren't the sort to turn their backs on a child in need," she continues. "Whatever we tell them about the Taken, I'm sure they'll help. It might be difficult, but she'll be safe." She hopes that somewhere, their lost sister is overhearing this. She hopes the Taken understands.

Cecelia nods and takes a breath to answer but cuts herself off. Her long ears swivel around to better hear something, and her wings rise to ready. Her eyes dart around the clearing. This time, Hannah hears the rustle in the leaves, and she realizes it's the first sound of life they've heard outside their own chatter in hours. Her hand drops to the hilt of her falchion. Is it the rats?

A swift, dark shape darts across the path and onto Hannah's foot. Cecelia stifles a scream and Hannah steps backward, kicking as she moves. The thing clings to her pant leg, and it takes a second for her mind to catch up to what her eyes see before her. Kit-Kat screeches, digs in her pocket, runs back down her pant leg, bites her shoelaces, and tries to pull her along. Hannah breathes a sigh of relief and delight and bends to scoop up her friend, who wriggles with glee.

"Kit-Kat! I've missed you! Where did you go, you little scoundrel?"

Kit-Kat nuzzles into her palm and replies with a happy chitter.

"Did Lady Brigid send you? Oh! Here!" Hannah rummages in her bag for the letter sticks and scatters them on the ground. This time, Kit-Kat only lights up two symbols.

Taken. Close.

"Thank you! Good boy!" That's a message she can't misunderstand. It's a relief to know they're near their target, and they haven't been on a wild goose chase this whole time.

Laughing at the interaction, Cecelia scratches the top of the weasel's head.

"Hannah, are you sure you didn't get a Power when you met the Monarchs, like animal companionship? That's a very fitting gift for the Seelie Court to grant. Even as a Namer."

"What?" Hannah puts on a tone of mock offense. "My natural charm is more than enough without your magic. I befriended him before I got to the Seelie Court, and besides that, I'm Inky's favorite."

"Are not!"

"Uh-huh. Hobbes' and Onii's, too."

"Maybe because Onii is almost as ornery as you are."

Hannah releases an overexaggerated, long-suffering sigh. "I'm so glad we fought the Piper's rats to rescue you, only to be called ornery and compared to a chicken, as upstanding a chicken as she may be. Kit-Kat and I will go save the Taken now. Have fun with the maze," she says jokingly.

Hannah sets Kit-Kat down on the path, spins on her heel, and starts marching down as Cecelia laughs and follows. Kit-Kat snatches at her shoelace to pull her back, and Hannah's stomach drops. He's trying to tell her something, something important, and she can't understand. She goes for the letter sticks, but instinct drops her hand to the hilt of her falchion instead, bracing for the worst.

That's when they feel the footsteps.

Ground-shaking.

Thundering.

Footsteps.

Chapter 33

The Troll

HE TAKEN IS running out of time.

The girl she fought—the girl who escaped into the Portal Tree—the girl who calls herself Hannah—is not the same unsuspecting fool who'd wandered into a faerie circle last time. As the human dismantles yet another iron trap, the Taken realizes her boldness doesn't just belong to her ignorance. If anything, her new capabilities only embolden the screaming, scampering person she used to be. She's formidable, but the Taken refuses to be cowed by her determination.

She doesn't know what to make of the runaway fae—the one who took the name Cecelia. The Taken eavesdrops on their conversations, knowing they're searching for her. Watching Cecelia find her name pulls at something in the Taken's mind. The plants slip away when the name takes hold, wrapped up in a more powerful magic than hers. This magic doesn't control, doesn't strangle and demand, and she doesn't understand why it works.

The name Cecelia rings with a familiarity the Taken shouldn't recognize. It bothers her, and she catches herself dwelling on it. Though she needs to capture the girl, she can't leave the name alone, prodding at it in her mind, like poking her tongue through the gap where a tooth used to be. Why? It feels strange to refer to people by names; she's so rarely met anyone who has one in the Piper's court.

And they used that word "sister" a lot, for themselves and for the Taken. She knows the changeling replaced her in the human world, but the Taken doesn't see why that connection should mean anything special. As far as she can tell, they want to capture her and bring her back to the human world. A mirrored mission. But the Taken can't indulge any curiosity today. She has too much to lose.

It doesn't matter, she tells herself, and she shuffles forward, breath hitching in her throat as fear creeps in around the edges of her desperation. Her grip tightens on the branch she's fashioned into a spear. The ground rumbles with a snore as she creeps around the edge of an enormous hand.

If the girls won't fall into any of her traps, she'll just have to provide a distraction they can't ignore. She double-checks her escape route, a clear path to the exit of the cave. She'll be fine as long as she's quick. Awaken the beast to chase the girls, and while they're distracted with a different foe, she can nab them with the vines. It should work.

It has to.

The Taken jabs the cave troll. Her spear sinks into the flesh of his belly, not deeply enough to wound him, but sharply enough to rouse him from his slumber. It sticks there, and the Taken lets it go. The monster howls with pain and thrashes awake. The Taken sprints away to cower behind a rock so she doesn't get smashed.

She lets out a loud whistle, and it draws his attention, but as he turns to strike her, the seeds she planted erupt from the ground and bind around his wrists. He towers over her—she'd fit into the palm of his hand—yet he strains against her bonds, even as her willpower overcomes his. They creak and stretch but hold firm.

The Taken grins with relief and wild adrenaline. She dashes out in front of him, loads her sling, and pelts him with stones.

They bounce off his leathery hide, but they get his attention. His bloodshot eyes snap to her and he *ROARS*.

"Come and get me!" She screams and flings another rock, taunting the troll as the vines pull him toward her. She can't control a cave troll through a song. Her True Voice isn't powerful enough to even have a rat of her own yet, but maybe she can puppet this thing to her wishes.

It stumbles forward, yowling and grumbling, but she keeps running ahead of it, tugging it along until they're clear of the cave. She ducks behind the bushes and scrambles up the big jagged rocks that make up the entrance of the hideout to get a bird's-eye view of the situation. The girls stand at the bottom of the path, exactly where she wanted them. After she realized they could avoid the traps, she started laying intentional bait so they would follow her here, into the best trap of all. Now that she's out of sight, she directs the troll toward his true prey with a quick jerk of the vines around his neck. He's a stupid creature who can't differentiate one small girl from another. They're all food to him.

The troll's fist smashes down, and the girls both jump into action. Hannah dodges the first blow and swipes at the enormous hand with her sword as it swings past, leaving a gash no more lethal than a paper cut on the troll's knuckle.

Cecelia takes to the sky, and what used to be her walking stick drops its glamour and transforms into a wicked spear. She dive-bombs the troll and sinks the tip into his shoulder, then transforms her feet into insectoid hooks, bracing herself against his neck to pull her weapon free. He tries to slap her, like she's a biting fly. Cecelia tumbles but throws out her wings, catching herself midair, twisting as she falls. The accident brings her face to face with the Taken's elevated hiding spot, and her eyes go wide.

"Hannah, she's here!" Cecelia shouts.

Sneering through her mask, the Taken shoots a vine toward her, aiming to grab her around the middle. Cecelia dodges, and the vine slips, wrapping around one leg instead. She screams for help as the Taken drags her into her grip.

Hannah grunts and rolls past the troll's foot, slashing at the heel tendon. The troll bellows and stumbles. Hannah runs clear, but the troll's flailing hand bats Cecelia away from the ledge just before she reaches the Taken. The vine stretched between them snaps tight and drags the Taken with her.

Screaming, the Taken falls and loses her control of the plant. It slips free of Cecelia, and without her wings struggling to hold the both of them in the air, the Taken crashes to the earth. Her vision goes fuzzy, and flashes dance as her head jars from the impact. The mask jerks askew. Her chest clenches as the wind is knocked out of her. Pain stabs through her leg, and she lies in a daze, distant screams ringing in her ears.

"The troll is free!" Hannah screams.

"Help! She fell!" Cecelia shrieks.

"Get...off of me!" Hannah grunts. There's a thumping sound.

The troll releases an inhuman roar. "GNNNAAHHHHHHHHHHHHHH!"

The Taken squints her eyes and readjusts her mask. She's lying in the beast's shadow. Cecelia crash-landed in the tree above and now hangs from a branch, tangled in the remaining vines. She had kept hold of her spear in one hand when she had flown, and now uses it to slice through the restraints.

The troll squeezes Hannah, but she's freed her sword arm and hacks at the soft skin between his thumb and pointer finger. The troll bellows and drops her. She lands hard. Cecelia, finally free, rushes to her side.

The troll turns from them, deciding a dinner that can cut him is a dinner he doesn't want. He pauses and looms over the Taken. *Mab.* He's spotted her.

The Taken tries to scramble to her feet, the desperate need to run pounding in her ears. Her head swims as she pulls herself up to a seated position and she tries to get her feet under her. After a single step, her leg buckles and causes her to stumble. She screams as pain and fear take hold of her mind. Her leg's broken. She's as good as dead.

"Beware the dawn! I'm warning you, the sun's coming up. It's still early, but if the clouds part, you'll turn to stone and die"

Is that Hannah's voice? The troll had raised his hand to strike the Taken, but he stops when he hears the shout. Hannah regains her feet and raises her sword in the air, pointing at the horizon. The troll looks over his shoulder in the direction that Hannah indicates. Why would she warn him instead of letting the daylight deal with her enemy?

Cecelia leaves her sister to face the troll alone. She charges for the Taken, spear in hand. No time to call the vines. The Taken raises her fist to strike Cecelia away, but the fae doesn't attack. She stands next to her, then turns her back on the Taken, planting herself in front of her, spear raised, stance ready. Leaving herself vulnerable to the Taken's attack.

Guarding her?

"Troll!" Hannah yells. "Do you have a name?"

Confused, the troll lowers his arm. "NAAAAMMMME?"

"What. Is. Your. Name?" Hannah pants for breath and, to the Taken's utter shock, sheathes her sword.

"I DONNN'T KNOOOOWWWW," the troll drones.

This is ridiculous. Everyone knows trolls are stupid creatures. They don't have names. If the Taken doesn't have one, he certainly doesn't.

"Can I call you Geoffrey?" Hannah asks. "You look like a Geoffrey."

This is the Taken's chance. With the troll frozen in curiosity and the girls' attention occupied, she could grab Cecelia and bind her now. If she could walk, she'd have been out of here already. She could still restrain the runaway changeling and use her as a hostage. The Taken reaches into her bag as Cecelia glances over her shoulder.

"We're here to help," she whispers. "We'll keep you safe."

What? Aren't they here to hunt her? But Cecelia doesn't point her spear at the Taken. She never had. And Hannah has put her sword away in front of a *troll*. What kind of crazy do they possess? Something in the air changes, the ambient magic of the forest tugging and shifting. It forms an ethereal connection between the monster and the small girl standing in front of him. A fainter bond reaches from Hannah to Cecelia and joins them at the wrist, where they both wear red bracelets.

And one reaches...to her? It dances around her fingertips but can't make contact. Neither girl seems to notice the golden threads hanging between them.

The troll squats to peer at Hannah more closely. "I LIIKEEEE GEOFFREY," he answers.

"Fantastic! Nice to meet you, Geoffrey."

Geoffrey glances at the horizon and raises his hand to shield his eyes from the first red light of day. The sky burns the color of hot coals. A weak sun struggles to pull itself over the horizon and bleeds gold across the streaky black clouds.

It's too late. The Taken's stomach sinks with the realization her last trap has failed. If she can't take the changeling, the Piper will sacrifice her instead. She redoubles her determination and ignores the faintly glowing strands of magic. Pulling a sachet from her pouch, she scatters seeds at the fae's feet.

"No! Don't look at the sun!" Hannah warns. "Please! Go home. I don't want to hurt you, but I will defend my sisters. You cannot eat them."

"YOUUUU ARRRRRE TOOOO PUUUUNNNYYYY TOOOO EAAAATTT! THE LITTTLLLEE ONNNNE WOOOKE MEEE." He points accusingly at the Taken, and she cowers back from an enormous finger as large as her entire head.

"I would be angry if she woke me too, but she won't bother you anymore," Hannah says. "Go back to sleep, Geoffrey. Before you turn to stone."

Nodding, Geoffrey lumbers away. Hannah slumps with relief as she watches him go, still leaning one hand on her sword, making sure he doesn't change his mind. Is she like the Piper? How can she control such a monster? She doesn't sing...but that connection. Even though she's human, the magic answered her with ease. It makes no sense to the Taken. The power fades as the troll leaves.

It doesn't matter. She has to act *now*.

Chapter 34

The Confrontation

ITH A DESPERATE whine, the Taken grows the seeds around Cecelia's feet, wrapping her in a cocoon of vines. The plants trap her arms against her sides, pinch her wings together, and root her to the ground. Cecelia screams. Hannah sprints over, but the Taken holds out a hand, brandishing it to show her control. With a flick of her wrist, Cecelia jerks to the ground and kneels, gasping with surprise and pain.

"Let her go!" Hannah demands. Though she'd been so level-headed facing the Troll, now fear and anger creep into her expression. *Good.*

"I need her."

"We just saved you!"

"Well, keep up the favor by letting me take her," the Taken says, through gritted teeth. Cecelia whimpers as they stand at an impasse.

"I will not let you sacrifice my sister," Hannah responds in turn. So she knows about the Tithe already. How much has she learned from the Seelie? The Taken's lost her only bargaining chip, along with her mobility.

"The Piper needs an offering. Don't. Stop. Me," she growls.

Hannah gives a sharp nod, looking over the Taken's shoulder. Is she giving in?

Then something jumps onto her neck, sharp claws digging into the thin fabric of her tunic. A rat? Cursing and screaming bloody murder, she stumbles back on her broken leg. She cries, crumples to the ground, and falls on her back. The creature twists around her shoulders and lands on her chest, staring her down. She's met this little monster before. Tears of frustration join tears of pain that prick at the corner of her eye and run under her mask.

"Good job Kit-Kat! Don't bite her, just keep her busy!" Hannah says. She surges forward and starts pulling the slackened vines off her sister. She disentangles them with a careful hand, peeling away the clinging tendrils as lovingly as detangling a knotted clump of hair. Cecelia takes it with a flinch and a grimace, but soon enough, she's free. The Taken tries to bat the weasel off her chest, but he only hisses at her, bearing tiny needle-like teeth.

"This is your attack weasel?" the Taken shrieks.

"He's our friend. His name is Kit-Kat," Hannah replies.

"You sent him to spy on me! He's been following me since the Tree! I thought I lost him in the Piper's caverns, but now you sic him on me!"

"I saved him from the Piper's rats, and he saved me in return," Hannah says evenly. She scoops up the little devil and puts him on her shoulder. "Thank you for your help, Kit-Kat. Can you scout around for the Piper and his rats? They might set an ambush. Come back to warn us if you see them."

Kit-Kat answers with an enthusiastic cry and scampers off. Cecelia stays behind Hannah now, having learned her lesson, but it doesn't matter. They've trapped The Taken. She's helpless. Her quarry has power over her now.

The Taken sits up and positions her back against a rock so the little devil can't sneak up on her again. Hannah shoves a bright-red water bottle and some bread into the Taken's hands. She recoils but doesn't throw the food away, confusion undermining her despair. Why are they giving her this if they're here to capture her?

Hannah backs up to sit with Cecelia out of reach and takes a bite of her own food to prove it's not poisoned. The Taken refuses to consume anything they offer. She can't trust them. They're from the Seelie Court, and that's a realm of temptation and madness.

"It's not enchanted," Cecelia says. Her wings snap, shoulders held tense, but she sets her lance aside. "It might taste bland, but it's nourishing and filling."

The Taken scowls at her, but her growling stomach betrays her. Hannah's face twists in sympathy.

"It's safe. I'm human, look," Hannah insists, taking a bite of her piece to prove her point. "We're not here to hurt you or trick you. We're here to help. The Piper's after all of us, so we're going to escape together."

Treasonous words. Impossible plans. Her fate's sealed. She's failed, and the Piper will kill her. The Taken looks over her shoulder, listens for any trace of the swarm. She can't tell if her Master is here, but she's sure he's watching, somehow.

"I can't escape. You broke my leg."

Cecilia rolls her eyes. "Your troll did that."

"I sent a troll after you!" the Taken says, thumping her fist in her hand for emphasis. Why are they treating her like this? "You defeated me! Escape, if that's what you want. Leave me for dead now."

"You're not our enemy, and we won't harm you. We came all this way to find you. We will not abandon you now, and we need to trust you won't hurt us in return," Hannah says. She reaches into her bag and pulls out bandages to dress their wounds.

The Taken gives a cruel, disbelieving laugh. "You're both fools."

"Eat. Please. You need your strength."

The Taken wavers, then sniffs the bread, exhausted. As long as her mouth and hands are full, she can't hum or sing or punch, which means she can't attack if they try to escape. Despite that, they seem determined to hang around, and she needs food, so...maybe she can risk it.

The mask only covers the top part of her face, so she can eat without removing it. The bread smells sweet, and she reluctantly takes a nibble. Before she knows it, the whole chunk is gone. Hannah hands her another slice, this time with some cheese and an apple. The Taken wolfs down the food. When had Rychtic brought her a meal last? Days, weeks ago? She accepts the water as well and drains the whole bottle. With the pain in her stomach satisfied, her aching leg reasserts itself. When she's finished her small feast, she doesn't return the bottle, but strangles it between her hands as a distraction and glares at the doppelgänger sitting across from her.

"Why are you still here? This is a war, and I'm your enemy."

"It's not your fault you got caught on the opposite side of the war," Cecelia says, wings trembling. "It's mine. Do you know who we are?"

This is the first time the Taken's come eye to eye with the changeling who reversed their places, their only meeting before now a wild chase on a dark and stormy night. She's the reason the Taken belongs to the Piper, and now the Taken sees her own face looking back at her. Despite the pointed ears, the watercolor eyes, and the pale hair woven with flowers, it's the same face.

She hates it.

"Sure, I do." The Taken's words drip with scorn. She doesn't remember a lot about her life before the Piper, but the events of the switching spell have always been clear in her mind, the void in her soul a nagging presence she tries to ignore, its edges long since scabbed over. The Piper always said he'd brought her to a better life. Maybe it's a better life than the other Unseelie wards, but she'd never believed he treated her better than...whatever she'd lost. He wouldn't have taken it from her unless he'd found it valuable, and somehow, she's never convinced herself a human life would be worse than his well-intentioned treatment. This changeling took that from her. It's a hollowness she'll never be able to fill. She can never go back to that life.

"You're the scheming, selfish fae who sold me to *him*," the Taken says. She turns to Hannah. "And *you're* the worthless, self-appointed protector and older sister who didn't even notice a liar and a scoundrel replaced me."

"That's not fair!" Cecelia protests. She springs to her feet, wings raised and open, eye spots glaring.

Indignance flares in the Taken. "You're telling me! Your voice never learned the True Voice! Your face never slept with the rats! You've never gone cold and hungry. Of course, it's not fair!" She's vaguely aware she's crying now and forces herself to turn her betrayal into fury. She lunges for Cecelia, teeth bared, hands curled into claws, leg curled up at an awkward angle. "Tonight, I'll send you back to where you belong!"

"Stop that!" Hannah throws herself between them and catches the Taken's arm. She flinches back. Cecelia's sobbing now. The Taken's words have touched a nerve. Good. The stupid fae should writhe with guilt.

Hannah motions for Cecelia to step back and keep her mouth shut. "We can't change the past. We're sorry. Really, truly sorry. But it doesn't have to be this way. You could escape, run away to Seelie, come home to the Human Realm with us. You'll have protection, a loving Mom and Dad, a soft bed every night, and enough food at every meal."

It's too tempting. It sounds so good, it can't be true. Why would they want the Taken to come back to that life, after the things she's done to them? Playing cat and mouse with Hannah and dangling her over the hollow of the Portal Tree? Hunting Cecelia relentlessly and torturing her with cruel words? Why would they offer her forgiveness after this? They don't know what she's done in the Piper's compound. Even if she could return, it wouldn't last. Unwanted memories flood back to her, and she squeezes her eyes shut, trying to block out the feeling of the Piper's disappointed gaze on her neck. The Masters await their offering.

The Taken's lip trembles. A million apologies won't make this decision any easier. "I can't. He's too scary. Too powerful."

"You can!" Cecelia says, despite Hannah's glare. "It's your choice and yours alone. You just have to confront—"

The Taken shakes her head so hard her neck hurts. They haven't given her much of a choice, not really, between failure and the one thing she fears more than anything. "You don't know what you're asking me to do. You need to come with me."

Hannah kneels before her and extends her empty hands. "I know you're hurt and confused, and we're strangers. You don't have to trust us. But you know the Piper wants to hurt you. And so far, all we've done is feed you. So can you work with us just long enough to escape him?"

If the Taken leaves, the game will end. The Piper will find them and sacrifice them *all* to Queen Mab's dreadful Tithe. She's babbling now, incoherent, desperate to make them listen. "It's impossible to leave the Unseelie Court! I can't tell you how many times I've tried! It's too late for me!"

Hannah sighs, tears welling in her eyes. "If you want to leave, we're giving you a chance! I can't force you to come with us, but I can't let you take us to the Piper, either."

Cecelia sighs, opens her mouth to say something, but thinks better of it. She takes Hannah's outstretched hand as curiosity and anger get the better of the Taken.

"Spit it out," she says.

Cecelia finally meets her eyes. "You're not the only one who ran away. Don't give up your only chance at freedom because of your fear."

Chapter 35

The Acceptance

ANNAH'S HANDS SHAKE as she holds them out to the Taken. They're so close. They've stuck the poor girl—literally—between a rock and a hard place. Will she have the strength to make the right decision? Hannah's mind races as the Taken denies her freedom again and again. She wants to escape, but she doesn't believe she has any hope of survival. If only they could get through to her!

Something in Cecelia's words hits home, and the Taken scowls at her as the realization takes hold. Her face is still partially hidden beneath the mask, but Hannah can understand that expression. She screams and kicks the ground with her unbroken leg, wailing her agony and making the plants grow wild and sharp. She growls and roars and screeches like a wild thing, slamming her hands on the ground until it shakes beneath them.

Hannah holds Cecelia close, sheltering her from the righteous fury of this tantrum but not cowering before its force. Sorrow stabs through her racing heart as she watches her little sister's anguish, but there's nothing she can do now that won't cause her more distress, so she only watches with a level, tear-filled gaze. Hannah understands meltdowns, but the Taken won't accept comfort. Cecelia's face presses into her chest, and as Hannah puts a hand around the fae's wings, she wishes she could hold the Taken, too. Has anyone held the Taken or loved her like Hannah loves Cecelia? She will love the Taken just as much, no matter what she chooses, no matter if she hunts them both for the rest of their days, because she's only a child, caught in a trap so much bigger than herself. It's not her fault if she can't claw her way out of it.

"This isn't fair!" the Taken screams.

"You're right, none of this is fair," Hannah agrees.

"It can't be that easy!"

"It won't be," Cecelia says.

"This has to be a trap!"

"We walked into your trap to have this conversation. We can survive whatever's coming, as long as we're together," Hannah tries to sound more confident than she feels, terror and hope mingling in the depths of her soul. The Taken sniffles and puts her face into her hands, wiping at her eyes under the edges of the mask.

"I'm scared," she says, her fury surrendering to the vulnerable little girl underneath.

"Me too," Hannah says, her voice finally breaking with relief. "We can do it scared."

"I can't follow you with a broken leg."

"I'll carry you."

"I'll just be a burden."

"Not to me. Never to me. You won't ever be heavier than what I can hold."

Finally, *finally*, the Taken relents. She calms enough to collapse in a tear-stained, shuddering heap. Hannah offers her a handkerchief to wipe her face. She takes it, but doesn't lift the mask. The sisters wait as the Taken scowls at the dirt and rocks, collecting her thoughts. When she looks up, Hannah hooks her pinky finger to the Taken's. At the touch, she gives Hannah a puzzled look but doesn't pull away.

"You're my sister. I promise, I won't let you down." Hannah never makes a promise lightly, but she hopes to all the Saints and Powers she can keep this one.

"Fine."

The Taken lifts off the mask, shaped like the face of a rat, and sets it aside. She scrubs at her eyes and nose with the handkerchief. For the first time since the Portal Tree, Hannah gets to see the face of her little sister. She *recognizes* her sister now.

Hannah feels a weight lift off her chest, and her heart races with relief. They're not out of the woods yet, but the hardest part is behind them now, and they can make their escape. She gives the Taken her biggest grin and holds out the medical supplies for her inspection. "Is it okay if I touch you to splint your leg? It might hurt at first, but this will keep it from getting more injured while we travel."

The Taken shies away at first but agrees once Hannah explains the process. She sends Cecelia to search for suitable branches for the splint, but the Taken grows impatient and uses her magic to craft straight ones in the perfect length. They work as carefully as possible and give her medicine to stop the pain, though she refuses to take it at first. Remembering how she refused to take any Seelie food when she'd arrived, Hannah doesn't blame her. When she notices the rest of the cuts and bruises on the Taken's arms, they use their water to wash the layers of dirt away, then set to work patching up her wounds, all the while keeping up a stream of friendly chatter.

Even though they've only just met, Hannah already overflows with fondness for this snarling, prickly little creature, recognizing all of her own stubbornness and ferocity in her younger sister. She hopes the Taken will learn to like them, too.

Here in the Unseelie Court, the bite of the late autumn chill makes Hannah shiver, and goosebumps show on the Taken's arms under her oversized, threadbare, short-sleeved tunic. Her cape has a huge tear from the fall. Hannah takes one look at her own cozy red sweater and drapes her big green coat around her younger sister's shoulders. The Taken is still for a moment, so surprised by the gesture, but soon recovers from her shock and slips her arms through the sleeves.

Chapter 36

The Reconciliation

WHEN CECELIA SEES the Taken's scars, she curses the Piper for his cruelty—curses him with every boast and bind she knows, and a few she makes up on the spot. Her illusion slips in her fury, and the Piper's Plague reappears on her face, mirroring a bruise under the Taken's eye. Digging in Hannah's bag for the lavender salve Quercu had packed for her, she offers it to the Taken for her own wounds, hoping it'll work the same soothing magic on the raw, irritated skin. The Taken accepts the salve and looks at her for the first time with an expression other than hatred.

When she looks at the Taken, she sees her own face, and she can't find it in herself to hate her counterpart in return. All she can see is herself without a name—hurting and ready to heal. Now she understands Hannah's desperation to bring her back from the dark place she was in. The Taken holds up a magnifying mirror to her worst moments, and Cecelia needs to have hope she can heal from those broken places, as well.

"He hurt you, too," the Taken whispers, eyes fixed on the flaking skin. "You...you actually understand what's at stake?

Cecelia presses her lips together into a tight line and nods, anxiety clutching around her heart, hyper-aware of her surroundings again as she scans for any sight of the rats. "You don't have to like me. Just know, I'm not asking you to do anything I'm unwilling to endure alongside you. All those years, he never let me go either."

The Taken turns to Hannah. "Have you met him?"

"Just once," Hannah admits. "I don't understand these things like the two of you."

The Taken scoffs and resumes her brooding. It's the same silent treatment Cecelia and Hannah gave each other over the last few weeks—an attitude Cecelia still regrets—and she wonders how similar they all are. They are sisters, after all, through nature or nurture.

Hannah tries to encourage them as she packs up the last of the first-aid materials, speaking as much for Cecelia's sake as for the Taken's. "We won't let anything bad happen to you. The Piper won't hurt you again. We're getting out of here together."

"Promise?" the Taken asks.

"Promise," Hannah assures her. "We came all this way just for you. Don't you see how special you are? We loved you before we even met you."

"How could you do that?"

"You're our sister." Hannah responds to her skepticism with wholehearted sincerity. "You're one of us, and you deserve a home."

One of us. Cecelia understands this truth now. Before, she had thought of the Taken as Hannah's sister, just like how she'd left behind Hannah's parents and Hannah's home. Until now, this mission had all been for Hannah's sake, repaying her out of a sense of duty and concern. But now? Since taking back her name, Cecelia realizes that's not true anymore. It's her home, too. Why shouldn't Cecelia also call the Taken *her* sister?

"Home..." the Taken says, trying the word on her tongue like a new food she isn't sure she likes. She briefly reaches for her rat mask again, hesitates, and then consciously leaves it behind.

"Home," repeats Hannah. She stoops so the Taken can lock her arms around her neck, then stands to carry her piggyback, lifting the small girl with ease.

As they're leaving the clearing, Kit-Kat approaches with the all-clear, and Hannah asks him to lead the way. The weasel disappears for a few minutes, scampering ahead, then doubles back and points the way to go. In this way, they set off on their return voyage. As they start their journey, Hannah and Cecelia tell the Taken all about their home—about the big old farmhouse with the secret passage in the closet, the squeaky spiral staircase, the sprawling garden with the prettiest flowers that bloom all summer and the sweetest cherry tomatoes on the street.

They tell her about the huge red maple in the front yard that's the perfect climbing tree, how Cecelia climbs to the top where the branches thin, and how their dad taps the sugar maples every February to make syrup. They tell her about how they toboggan down the hill in the backyard every winter. Now, the Taken's tasted human bread, but that's nowhere near as tasty as the fresh loaves their Mom makes and spreads with butter and honey. They can have some as soon as they get back, and maybe even help make it.

Cecelia's homesickness grows stronger as she speaks. She will always cherish the Seelie Court and love the friends they made there, but it's not the same as home.

Mom and Dad will be happy to see the Taken, Cecelia promises. They'll give her the bed in the guest room, and it'll become all her own. They'll tuck her in and tell her stories and give her a kiss goodnight. Brilliant teacher that she is, their mom will teach lessons with songs, and the Taken will get perfect scores on all her tests because she's so good at singing and memorizing already. Their dad loves old cars, animals, and the outdoors. She'll get to know the cats and chickens.

She'll have a family.

"You'll just love it there. And I know they'll love you," Hannah says, and the Taken, for the first time, smiles. She has the same smile as her sisters. Cecelia offers her a matching bracelet, and she accepts.

Chapter 37

The Escape

HE TAKEN FIDGETS with her new bracelet as she contemplates her situation. It's a few shades of vibrant red, twisted together in a braid, the brightest colors she's seen in the Unseelie Court. It's a symbol of the fledgling bond between her and the sisters, their promise to help her escape this cursed place. Their return journey grows more difficult as they retrace their steps down the mountain. Hannah struggles to stay balanced as tree roots twist under her feet and the rocks become jagged and sharp. She uses the spear as a walking stick again, and Cecelia does her best to warn her about the uneven terrain, but the Taken can't help but feel awful for weighing down the older girl.

Their stories of home fill her with longing for unfamiliar delights. She blocks out the voices in her mind whispering the hazards of trusting these strangers. She tells herself that if they wanted to hurt her, they would have done so already. At first, climbing on Hannah's back had left her feeling weak and vulnerable. Why would this girl choose to take on such a burden unless to trick her? The Taken half-expects the girl to turn into a kelpie, accepting a rider only to drown her in a lake. But Hannah carries her without complaint. The Taken can't understand this show of humanity, but once she grows comfortable riding on Hannah's back, she can't help but tuck her chin into the older girl's shoulder. She tells herself it's only to keep from falling. No other reason.

It doesn't take long for them to realize the landscape has grown more hostile than their first pass, and the Taken has the sinking suspicion the Piper watches them now, trying to catch all three girls in his web. Anxiety roils in her stomach, but she squashes it down. Somehow, these girls escaped the Piper once. Maybe they can achieve that impossible feat again. The Taken isn't sure what to believe, so she clings to Hannah's neck, because that's all she can do.

The sun hovers above them now. They reach a familiar slope, but it's turned from a steep hill into a sheer cliff. Before, Hannah might have been able to slide her way down. Now, she'll have to climb. Cecelia pulls the rope from their pack and ties it to a nearby boulder, testing the knot to make sure it won't break.

"Cecelia, fly along and spot me," Hannah instructs, handing her the spear. "Make sure I don't accidentally knock the Taken's broken leg against the ledge as I'm going down!"

It's the first time they've referred to her by a title instead of talking to her directly, and it probes at something deep in her mind, like a seed, planted deep beneath the earth, stretching for the sunlight.

"Sure!" Cecelia calls back, and Hannah begins the careful descent. Her arms shake, bearing double the weight. The Taken clings to her back for dear life, but readies her vines to catch her if Hannah loses her grip.

"You called me the Taken," she observes when they reach the bottom.

Cecelia's face goes bright red as she returns the spear to Hannah. "Do you have a name, or something else you'd like us to call you?" she asks.

The question flusters the Taken. "Oh...No. I don't know. I'm...me. Or 'You!' or 'Girl!' The Piper has never called me anything else." She'd been indistinguishable from the other wards, all wearing their rat masks, all one mistake away from being turned into rats in the swarm. Leaving it behind had been her single greatest act of rebellion against the Piper. Without the mask, she's an individual. She's free. It's a giddy, treacherous feeling.

"Since we didn't have a name for you, we've used "the Taken" for a couple of weeks now. I hope that's okay," Hannah says.

"I don't see why I should care," the Taken says, feigning nonchalance, but the conversation leaves her feeling irritable and un-whole.

Cecelia's face darkens, frowning as her eyes turn cloudy. "I lost my name, recently," she says, flicking her wings awkwardly, "Actually, I'd rejected it. But without a name, nothing about my life made sense. I no longer understood who I was anymore, or who I wanted to be. Hannah helped me find it again."

She looks fondly at her sister, and envy stings the Taken. They have a friendship based on years of something the Taken can't fathom. She had no one. Not the Piper. Not even the rats. Angry tears prick at her eyes, and she swipes them away with the back of her hand.

"Hey, Cecelia. What were some of the other names Mom and Dad wanted to use for us before they decided?" Hannah asks. "I remember we had a list, but I was really little. As the oldest, it's my birthright to help pick out names for little siblings."

The Taken squirms at the mention of parents she's never known. Will they hate the savage daughter they did not raise? And why should she respect them? Around the trail's next bend, they find a fallen tree that hadn't been there last night, blocking their path. The woods creak and groan as chilly winds whip through the branches. Cecelia flies into the air, assesses the possibilities, then calls down, "Maria?"

The Taken frowns, insulted by their attempts to force a name on her, as if she's less than them without one. She understands, on some level, that's not what they mean.

Insulted, then, that they think naming her could make up for all the years she's spent nameless.

"Not Maria," Hannah says quickly. "It doesn't quite suit her."

"Sophia. Bernadette. Catherine," Cecelia continues.

Each name sounds pleasant to the Taken, but out-of-place. "Not me. Go closer to the log."

Hannah obeys and steps closer. The Taken puts a hand to the tree trunk and hums a meandering tune, trying to find a key or tone. Cecelia shivers and backs up, looking over her shoulder. As the Taken settles on a low croon, toadstool stairs are coaxed from the rotting pulp. Though she worries this might draw the Piper's attention, ultimately, it doesn't matter. They need to overcome this tree trunk, and the stairs hold sturdy beneath their feet as they climb.

"Miranda," Hannah suggests as she makes it to the top of the log. "Eileen?"

"What about Theele or Sarina?" Cecelia says, landing next to them on top of the log. She scratches the lichen on her face as the Taken sings to another line of large brown mushrooms that grow down the other side. The Taken winces, but she can't help if her powers aggravate the plague. When she's done commanding the fungi, she considers the options presented before frowning again.

"No, no, no, no!" Her annoyance evolves as they continue offering names, now glad that they're trying, more frustrated that none of them work. How come she can't just choose? What's in a name?

"What about Theresa?" Hannah asks gently.

On this one, the Taken pauses. It feels familiar but not quite right. Still too soft around the edges, but Hannah's voicing sounds like a song. Not like the Piper's song, but a different True Voice, one that knows her as a person and not a ward.

"Maybe…" She tries it out, not quite saying the name but feeling around the sounds, "Teresa? Terese? Tessa? Tess."

Tess. A sense of peace settles over her, so profound her whole body shudders with joy. The shell that holds her soul cracks open. When Hannah had first asked her name, a seedling of self had started to grow. Now, that seedling's broken through the hardened earth of her identity to unfurl a new leaf. She can turn her face to the meager Unseelie sun and know it shines on a girl named Tess.

Is the Taken ready to accept this change? Can she abandon the safety of her nonexistence just yet? How can she choose who she's meant to be on such a whim? If they cannot escape the Piper, can she bear to lose such a beautiful thing? Maybe it's better not to take the name just yet.

Hannah seems to sense the change. "You can choose," she says.

"I know…I'm not sure I want to choose. It's a big decision."

"You don't have to pick just one, if it's scary. Most people have middle names, too. Sometimes more than one," Hannah says as they reach the bottom.

"A secret name?" All of this is so complicated, it makes the Taken's head spin.

"Kind of! It's part of your full name—your True Name." Cecelia explains. "So, you can just tell someone your first name, but they won't have all of it." Well, that sounds useful.

Hannah stops next to the mushrooms before they move on and inspects them. "I think this is dryad's saddle. *Cerioporus squamosus,*" she says.

The Taken looks from the mushroom to Hannah and back to the mushroom. It looks like a normal mushroom to her. "Huh? I've never seen a dryad before. I think they're Seelie creatures."

"That's the name of the mushroom. In our world, we give things scientific names to organize them. Maybe they got that name because a dryad sat on them. Different mushrooms have different names. Like those?" Hannah points at a cluster of brown ones growing in a ring around the trunk of the fallen tree. "They're named *Marasmius oreades*, but they're usually called fairy ring mushrooms."

"Why do you know the names of things? There are so many things to name. Isn't that a lot to learn?" The Taken leans over to get a closer look, so Hannah squats next to them and points out a few identifying features. They have white stems and spores, with bell-shaped caps.

Hannah straightens up with a grunt, using Cecelia's spear as a walking stick to help her get off the ground. "I enjoy knowing what they are called. It imparts greater meaning to me."

"Do names have to mean something? What do your names mean?" Did the Taken pick a name with meaning? She can't think of it as her name. Not yet. She's still nobody. Even that title feels too dangerous.

Cecelia taps her head as they begin walking again. "We know our namesakes— people our parents liked who went by the same names. Hannah was an old friend of our mother's. Cecelia was an ancient saint, a musician and a singer."

The Taken stares at her for a moment in disbelief before turning her gaze back to the uneven ground. Somehow, the singing association feels right. If the Piper hadn't taken her, she wouldn't have her plants and her powers, but what might her life look like with the name of a singer?

"My name would have been Cecelia?" she asks, her voice small.

"Yes. I'm sorry." Cecelia shifts her glamours to fade into the background, but doesn't disappear.

Hannah gives the Taken a cheerful bounce. "Hey, it's alright. You get to give your name meaning. Cecelia chose her name again because it fit her the best. I try to be the best Hannah I can be. Whatever you pick, it'll mean something to you. That's all that matters."

They walk along without talking for several minutes, though the forest never falls silent. The biting wind whips through the trees and rattles the dry branches until they sound like bones cracking. Hannah stubbornly hums a tone-deaf tune to herself. Cecelia flicks her ears around, listening for the sound of the Piper's flute. The Taken wonders what it would be like to grow up with a name. She can't imagine them with any others, not even Cecelia.

Eventually, the Taken speaks. "I think it suits you better."

Cecelia blushes. "I've had some time to grow into it." She lets her hair shift to the light blonde she seems to prefer. With each change, her appearance drifts further from the Taken's dark matted hair, dark eyes, and human features, though the face always stays the same. She's become her own person, no longer just a changeling.

"Haven't you named me already? Why didn't you choose any of the names you mentioned before?"

Cecelia only shrugs, so Hannah answers for her. "It's yours to choose. That's why we only used a title. Though I suppose we could call you by our family name: Teagan. Little Teagan."

"I'm not little!" She digs her elbow into Hannah's shoulder.

"Ow!" Hannah flinches, but laughs. "Tiny Teagan."

"Hey!" the Taken punches Hannah in the arm this time, but more gently. Hannah twists her head over her shoulder to give her a grin, letting her know she's joking. The Taken's heart melts a little at the idea of adopting their family name, but she doesn't feel like she deserves that yet. She still knows nothing about the human world, about being a sister.

"You're really not the littlest—you're technically Cecelia's twin, like Matteo and Marco back in Seelie. We'll tell you about them later. But you're both little to me," Hannah says, and she ruffles Cecelia's hair. Cecelia sticks her tongue out in response. The Taken sulks, but she hugs Hannah a little tighter.

"Twins, huh?"

"Yep."

The Taken eyes Cecelia's long pale hair. "If you're supposed to be a changeling, you're pretty bad at copying me."

Cecelia grins. "I know."

Chapter 38

The Hero

THERE IS A secret to being a hero. Not a glorious truth, kept hidden until the last moment when its light reveals itself to banish the evil things lurking in the darkness. Not a mystery for clever wit to unravel and wield like a weapon. Not a talent for swordplay or strategy, sweeping in to save the day.

No. Heroism is about none of these things.

At least, that's what Hannah decides as dusk descends without any sign of reaching the Seelie Court. She shivers uncontrollably as damp wind bites through her sweater and beads of mist form on her hair. The trees cast long shadows over their path as the burning sun slips below the horizon. They'd taken a few breaks throughout the day, but every muscle aches from carrying the Taken toward home. A pulse pounds in her temple, either from hunger or thirst. She hasn't eaten since breaking bread with the Taken this morning, and every fiber of her poor, exhausted being wants to collapse on the path.

The Taken had walked on her own for several hours by fashioning a crutch with her magic and using her vines as mobility aids. It worked for a little while, but the further they moved from the Piper's stronghold, the more her power and energy drained. Now, the exhausted, broken little girl sleeps on

Hannah's back. Even though she's a heavy burden, the Taken is her little sister, and Hannah would never, ever let her down. Cecelia droops too, her vigilance taking a toll on her nerves. The girls are counting on Hannah, so she trudges on. One foot in front of the other. The forest blurs together. Kit-Kat's occasional directions confirm she's leading them in the right direction, but she's long since abandoned Quercu's map.

Despite the chasms, which they had crossed by crawling across a swaying bridge of woven vines.

Despite the quicksand that had claimed the Taken's makeshift crutch.

Despite the writhing walnut trees that take pot-shots at them with their nuts, which split and rot when they make impact.

Hannah holds herself together by the tattered string of her friendship bracelet, the fraying red thread serving as a reminder of home. She is the leader of this small and broken family, and she will act like it for her sisters. So, she pastes on a smile and does her best to encourage the girls, even as doubt squirms in the back of her mind and fear burrows into her stomach. She beats back despair with the desperate hope that any minute now, they will emerge from gray purgatory into the light. She will lend her sisters her strength until she has none left to give.

She understands now. Heroism is about sacrifice.

They must keep marching, because Hannah knows, if she pauses for even a moment, she will collapse. No familiar sights greet her sore eyes, but she believes they must be close. That faith is all she has to keep going. One step. Two steps. Three. Four. She prays for a sign, the words forming a rhythm on her lips in time with the beat of their footfalls. Cecelia joins her, finishing the litany when Hannah's voice trails off. The murmur of their voices rouses the Taken, and she listens attentively, though she does not know the words. Hannah hopes she finds some small comfort in the prayer too.

They're finishing the rosary when Cecelia stops reciting, ears alert, eyes wide. The Taken tenses as she also recognizes a distant rustling. Hannah dreads the worst as she waits for her sister's verdict.

"The rats are following us," Cecelia whispers.

"He's coming for me. He won't let us escape," the Taken whines, clutching to Hannah's back, "It's too late. We were too slow."

Hannah shakes her head. It makes no sense. Why would he show his cards now, after all the anonymous but unmistakable barriers they've passed? He must be desperate. Hell demands an offering, and time is almost up—he's not playing fair.

"We're close. We have to be. Cecelia, can you lead us?"

She nods and pulls out the map, checking the sky and their surroundings, then pointing off the beaten track. "This way. It might be a shortcut."

Kit-Kat signals his agreement by bounding a few strides off the path in the direction Cecelia indicated and scratching an arrow in the dirt.

"There are no shortcuts in the Unseelie Court," the Taken protests.

"But we're leaving the Unseelie Court. If we're really close to Seelie, it might be a boon," Cecelia responds. "Lady Brigid and the twins might come for us."

"You have no way of knowing that."

"Neither do you."

"Shhh," Hannah says. "Enough. No bickering if we're getting out of here. Let me think."

She weighs her options as the now-familiar burden of decision falls on her shoulders yet again. Thankfully, her sisters wait in silence. Finally, she says, "Let's take the shortcut. The Piper might not be expecting us to leave the trail. Cecelia, lead the way. Tiny Teagan, hang on tight. This is going to be bumpy."

"No, let me down," the Taken says. "I can move faster on the vines."

"Are you sure?"

"Do it."

Hannah lowers the Taken enough for her to put one foot on the ground, then steadies her as she gets her balance. Cecelia raises her wings and takes back her spear. The Taken prepares her seeds, shifting her weight onto the ball of her foot so she can launch herself into the trees.

As Hannah takes one step off the path, they hear a thousand rodent voices screaming. Kit-Kat screeches a battle cry and sprints toward the sound to buy them some time. Hannah hopes to see the little critter again, but it's too late to regret his help.

Run.

Hannah bounds through the hostile muck of the late-autumn forest. She skids past patches of ice, vaults over slippery, lichen-covered rocks, and barrels headlong over twisted roots, where she would otherwise walk with careful steps. She can't look behind her, but she can feel the swarm closing in. Above, Cecelia flies faster than Hannah's ever seen before. Her glamours render her almost invisible in the dim evening mist, dodging trees as she fights the wind instead of dancing with it. Hannah catches flashes of her bright blue wings out of the corner of her eye and little else.

The Taken moves with acrobatic vaults, commanding the vines to lift her so she doesn't have to put weight on her broken leg. She launches herself forward, sling-shotting a stone as a counterbalance, then lands carefully on her good leg, just long enough to push off a boulder as she flings herself into the air again. Her keening creates growths out of the tree trunks to act as handholds, and she hangs in midair for a second before dropping again, trusting her plants to catch her.

As both sisters soar over the edge of a cliff, Hannah slides down in a clatter of shifting slate. She's too breathless, too afraid, too desperate to bother envying their abilities. She forces herself to keep up, if only to avoid being caught first. Urgency draws her down the path.

The forest changes as they sprint past, and Hannah realizes they've emerged from the maze, but they haven't reached the Seelie Court yet. The underbrush thins through a ridge of pines and a new path curves clockwise downhill around the mountain. The evergreens are a welcome sight, and though the sky's still overcast with clouds, it's an unremarkable sky. Frost coats the ground, but it dusts mundane brown needles and ordinary underbrush, not the alien plants they'd seen deep in the Unseelie Court.

"We're lost!" Cecelia says, worry straining her voice at the edges. "I missed our mark by a mile!"

Hannah only half-listens to her despair as she spins to take in the clearing and the familiar smell of *Pinus strobus.*

"We're not in Faerieland anymore," she says at last. "Can you feel it?"

Cecelia's eyes widen with realization. The Taken only wrinkles her nose and leans on a nearby tree for balance.

"What do you mean? I've never seen a drabber place in my life."

"We're in the backyard woods, in the Human Realm," Hannah says. "I came through here on my way to Seelie. It's still far from home, but I think we're close to the Portal Tree."

The Taken cringes. "Is it really safe for me to return there?"

"It's our best chance for escape," Hannah says, remembering their earlier fight. "I forgive you for our fight. The Seelie won't hurt you, I promise."

She nods. "I can probably tether to the plants I controlled when I attacked you. That could help us locate it."

"Great idea! Try," Hannah encourages her. The Taken pushes off the tree she'd been leaning on for support and holds onto Hannah's arm as she resumes her humming pattern. As she lands on a tone, she finds her bearings and leads the way as they make their final mad dash for freedom. Soon, Hannah glimpses gold-and-red leaves through the sleeping oaks and shady evergreens—a beacon for the weary travelers.

"There it is!" Hannah points, giddy with relief. "We're almost there! Come on, it's just a little farther. We can make it."

She is answered, not by the voices of her sisters, but by the haunting, unmistakable sound of a flute. A singular note pierces their hope.

Hannah whirls, fury and fear filling her at once. The Piper looms above them, as high as their house, sneering at her. She throws herself in front of her sisters on instinct, arms outstretched. She senses the swarm gather, surrounding them.

"Get back!" she shouts, reaching into the bag for the earplugs. She crams the fluff into her ears and then hands it to the Taken, who follows suit and hands it to Cecelia. It muffles the sound of the Piper's high, shrill laughter but doesn't block it completely.

Hannah's hand goes to her falchion. How dare he? How dare he play cat and mouse with them for so long?! How dare he show his stupid face right when they felt the first glimmers of hope? Whatever willpower held her temper in check, whatever patience she kept for her sisters, exhaustion and pain consume it all. She will not stand down.

"Leave us alone, or so help me, I will snap that cursed pipe over your head!"

"Heh heh heh heh heh! You're a funny thing. Found yourself a fighting streak, have you?"

"You can't control us," Hannah growls.

"Can't I?"

Her senses warp as the Piper's glamours cast a spell over their surroundings. They're standing at the edge of their backyard woods on a dark night. The smell of woodsmoke drifts from the chimney and clings to the falling leaves. An inviting light from the kitchen window streams into the darkness.

Hannah's heart aches as she sees her parents holding each other's hands, sitting together in a silent, old empty house.

In a moment, the vision is ripped away. Beside her, a sob escapes from Cecelia's throat. Hannah grabs her sister's hand as the Taken goes stiff.

The Piper should not have shown this to Hannah. It only strengthens her resolve to leave this infernal place. "Don't you dare start with your tricksy questions again! We're going home. You cannot stop us."

Hannah turns away from the Piper and marches toward the Portal Tree. She takes Cecelia's hand in her left and the Taken's in her right. She refuses to acknowledge the swarm, the ominous figure blocking their path, the thorns entrapping them on all sides. Kit-Kat is nowhere to be seen. She hopes he's okay, but knows with a heavy heart that he'd only stop fighting if the rats hurt him. Fighting her grief, she marches forward, trusting the Piper will bow before her will.

The Piper looms closer and raises the instrument to his lips. His tune still trickles in around the earplugs, muffled but working its way into her brain. Still, Hannah marches forward.

Cecelia stumbles with a cry of pain, drawn back by the sound of the music. Hannah hauls her to her feet. The ground transforms beneath their feet, becoming a steep hill, and Cecelia tumbles backward. Hannah's arm wrenches, and she struggles to keep her footing, but she tightens her grip on her sister's wrist.

"Hold on!" Cecelia screams.

Hannah grunts and tries to pull her up, but the Piper's hold still drags Cecelia away from her like the gravity of a black hole pulling her into its mass. The force flings the spear from her hand and tosses it harmlessly to the side. Her agonized sobs repeat Hannah's name with a nightmarish desperation. Without Hannah's support, the Taken loses her balance on the quaking earth and takes a step on her broken leg. It buckles underneath her, and she falls, landing prone on her back.

The swarm descends on her in a roiling mass of squirming gray bodies. The Taken screams. She tries to weave a barrier around herself with the thorns, but that power belongs to the Piper, and he denies her the ability to resist him. The rats chew through the twisted shoots and reach her before Hannah can react. Their long, skinny tails wrap around her arms and legs and twist together until she's entangled at the center of a rat king, a nine-bodied creature pulling her limbs in all directions as they drag her toward the Piper. She's stranded, defenseless, frozen in terror and living bonds. She doesn't cry; there's only grim resignation written in her expression.

Cecelia's grip slips. She tumbles toward the Piper, jerking in a strange dance through the air as her wings beat this way and that. She's out of reach. Hannah curses and draws her sword. She hacks the rats away from the Taken. One lunges for her. She sidesteps and blocks left. It jerks away, a line of blood forming on its side, but the movement yanks the next rat toward her as the tails tighten. Hannah jabs it in the face, and when it rears, she lunges forward and slashes through the tail. It squeals and scrambles away. Hannah raises her sword to slice through the next tail, but another rat curls around and bites her on the shoulder. Hannah shouts in pain and drops the sword. The rats retreat, taking the Taken with them, squirming amidst their snarl of bodies.

Hannah sobs. She's failed. She can't save them both.

Choose.

The Piper doesn't speak; the word comes on the song, and helpless, she listens. It worms into Hannah's mind, an evil voice, whispering all of her worst insecurities and fears. She doesn't stand a chance. Compared to Cecelia's grace and the Taken's powers, she has the coordination of a newborn. Since she left home, she has been out of her depth. What was she thinking, trying to be the hero from the fairy tales? She's a mundane human girl, and she's fallen into the Piper's trap.

Choose!

Who does she love more? The sister who grew alongside her—the changeling who betrayed her trust and threw away her own name and family? Will she choose the liar? What about the sister she never knew—the hostile wild thing who attacked her? Will she choose the stranger?

The Piper forces them to stand beside each other; Cecelia, her wings restrained by spiderwebs that cling to her wings like knotted puppet strings, lichen growing from her face; and the Taken, surrounded by a rat king. Neither speaks, but in that moment, Hannah sees them both as her responsibility. She made a promise to protect them. Her sisters, both entrapped by the Piper for so long, deserve to be free.

Hannah knows what's at stake in the Unseelie Court. She doesn't care.

The song ends. A deafening stillness falls over the forest as the Piper waits for her answer. Hannah's vision blurs with tears, but her decision is crystal clear.

She raises her sword and salutes the Piper with a flourish. "I choose myself for the sacrifice! Let them go. Take me instead."

The Piper's echoing laughter fills Hannah's mind. The bonds slip off her sisters. They're safe now. Her life doesn't matter, as long as they're free. There's peace in her decision. She didn't let them down; she didn't fail.

Cecelia shakes free of the webs, wings tattered, and runs to Hannah, horrified. The Taken shakes herself free of the rats and lies still, watching in stark disbelief.

"Hannah, no! You can't!" Cecelia sobs, clinging to Hannah in the tightest hug. "You wanted to go home!"

"I love you, Cecelia. Remember your name when I'm not around to remind you, okay? Promise me."

"Hannah, don't do this! Please!"

"I know you're strong enough to break the spell and get home on your own. Look out for her. Remember your name. Promise me."

"I promise."

Hannah gives Cecelia a kiss on her forehead. This is goodbye. She'll never pet Willow or Inky or Hobbes or Snubs or the chickens again. She'll never explain their disappearance to Mom and Dad. She'll never be able to comfort her sisters again. Hannah thinks, that's the only thing she regrets.

The Piper plays a note.

Her arm twitches. It's still holding her sword. The Piper's control takes root, and she's no longer in control of her body as her wrist rotates to angle the point of the blade toward Cecelia's back. Her mind still belongs to her, but it goes blank with horror as she realizes the Piper won't let them get away. Instead of honoring Hannah's bargain, he's following through on his promises to Queen Mab.

He's going to use her to kill them.

She rallies the last of her willpower to use her free hand to push Cecelia away from her as hard as she can. The small girl stumbles back, looks of confusion and terror flashing across her face as she sees Hannah struggle to lower the falchion.

"Run! Run away from here! Take our sister. Find her name. Go!"

It's all Hannah's able to say before her will breaks and her strength surrenders. She lunges for the Taken.

Chapter 39

The Sacrifice

"HANNAH! No!" Cecelia screams, throwing herself between Hannah and the Taken. The music quickens into a high-pitched warbling noise, but for the first time, she's free of its control. The relief isn't enough to temper the dread.

How could Hannah do this? Her stroke is shaky, her arm swings wide, intentionally sloppy, as she resists the Piper's control. Cecelia ducks to the side but doesn't move away from her sister. Her arms are still outstretched from the broken embrace, and her chest aches from heartbreak and the force of the shove. Hannah staggers from the missed strike, and the Piper forces her to do a backslash. She twists her elbow at an awkward angle and grimaces in pain, but it misses Cecelia's wing.

"Go," Hannah orders through gritted teeth.

Cecelia doesn't even think of flying away. They can't leave without Hannah. In all their schemes, Hannah goes home. There's no other option.

They circle each other. Cecelia stays just out of reach, the Piper toying with Hannah as he looks for an opportunity. A sudden overhead strike makes Cecelia jump back. Hannah executes a clumsy swing to her left. Cecelia shapeshifts with a thought, forming a pauldron of shell over her shoulder. The blow glances off.

"Cecelia, let's go!" the Taken cries, pulling herself up from the ground. With the reminder of her presence, the Piper turns his attention—and Hannah—toward her once again, playing a slow ominous note. The Taken shrieks and hobbles backward, trying to put distance between them. With her broken leg, she won't be a match for Hannah under the Piper's control.

Take me instead, Hannah had said. Cecelia cannot let the Taken die before she escapes. She needs to disarm Hannah. There's no room for Cecelia the Coward. No more running.

Her form shifts. She gives herself a full exoskeleton, like a beetle's suit of armor, and turns her eyespots on the Piper. Though her back faces his enormous form, she can see him in her mind, and he can see himself through her, and she can see him, and on and on the fractal goes. Tears spring to her eyes as sharp pain shoots through her temples and a ringing fills her ears from the feedback loop. It's maddening, but it disorients the Piper enough that he mis-fingers a note, creating a screech in his controlling song.

It's not enough to break his hold on Hannah.

"Fight me instead!" Cecelia screams. She grabs Hannah's shoulder and jerks her around, ducking under the swing that comes with it. Hannah's the better fighter between the two of them by a long shot. The Piper regains the song in a moment, and Hannah ripostes, slashes, lunges, all in time with the beat. Cecelia just has to keep the Piper distracted and evade the blade long enough for the Taken to get away. After that?

Hannah has forfeited her life. Cecelia has no hope left to hold.

"How am I supposed to live without you?" Cecelia cries. She keeps her momentum and grabs Hannah by the collar, then throws her with all the strength in her body. Hannah flies a good six feet and lands on her back with a thud.

Cecelia doesn't want to imagine returning home without Hannah. Her empty room. Beloved pets waiting for a doting owner who will never return. She remembers their devastated parents in the vision, looking out the window for their lost daughter. They won't even find a grave.

"This isn't protecting us! The Piper lies! Now you've thrown everything away. Your future. *Our* future!"

The Piper drags Hannah to her feet with difficulty. Tear tracks cut through the dirt stains on her cheeks.

Cecelia snatches her spear from where it had fallen earlier. They had dreamed about visiting Seelie to help their friends, training with the twins and Quercu, freeing more creatures from the irons, having tea with Lady Brigid. Hannah should study plants and collect samples for her field journal, not offer herself to Queen Mab's Tithe.

"Don't you see? I'm only Cecelia because of you. How can you give up your own future after you made me believe in mine?"

The attacks come in quick combinations. Left, up, lunge. Down, right, lunge. Cecelia takes several of the hits on her armor, knowing that while it's saving her now, they'll leave awful bruises. She uses her glamours to blur her edges, hoping it'll make her harder to hit.

Hannah had recalled Cecelia's name when she'd lost herself in the glamours. How can she use her powers or even look in a mirror without remembering Hannah? Without grieving her?

"Why must you choose a path where I can't follow? We can't go home and pretend we won't see your ghost!"

Cecelia blocks the falchion with the length of her spear, and they lock eyes. Hannah's still in there—conscious, but out of control.

The blade flashes. Her armor chips. Pain shoots through Cecelia's shoulder. They spar like it's a dance, trading blows and blocks, but it's not a true fight. While the Piper tries to wound her with every move he makes through Hannah, Cecelia can't bear the idea of injuring her sister. Her strength wears thin.

"I'm not the sister I should have been. I'm not the sister the Taken deserves. We need you, Hannah. She needs a Name, she needs you! You can't abandon us now! Fight *back*!"

Cecelia catches Hannah's elbow in the gut, between the joints of her armor. She topples back over Hannah's knee, landing flat on her back with a painful *CRACK* as the wind knocks out of her lungs. Her wings crumple beneath her weight. A knee digs into her chest, a blade resting at her throat.

This isn't how the story goes. This can't be how it ends.

Chapter 40

The Name

ESS TEAGAN.

Her name is Tess Teagan.

She is Tess Teagan.

Through all her wavering, she knows the truth of her name. It latched onto her soul and did not let go. Tess is the one that feels like her, the one that feels most right, the one that feels like home. A name offered by her sisters, but chosen by her and her alone.

Tess has sisters. Her sisters ventured into the depths of Unseelie for her. They have treated her with more kindness in a day than she's received in years. They love her, and she's not surprised to find that she loves them, too. The new, strange feeling settles in her heart, and like her name, it fits.

But she doesn't know how to love. The Piper raised her to be cruel and scared and suspicious. She belongs to the music.

The Piper does not speak words out loud to her. Speaking is a crude substitute for what they can do. The song fills her up, and she understands the meaning in each note.

"Are these your new friends, my little offering?"

"They are my sisters."

"Seelie Powers used them, and they've only used you to their own ends. They only do and say what they need to make you listen."

Tess does not answer. Tess. Her name is Tess.

"They had no real devotion, foolish child. See how they bicker now? Fake fondness cracks in the face of hardship. All love withers in the end."

The Piper plays without waiting for her answer.

"You're forgettable. Replaceable. Do you really think you could invade their home and expect a welcome? You'd only be an inconvenience. Think of their parents. They won't need another mouth to feed. All this time, it's as if you were never born, and that's what they want."

She's not the Taken. She is Found. Her sisters found her. Her sisters named her Tess.

Her sisters fight the Piper for her. Hannah thrashes like a wild thing, and the falchion spins in her hand like its an extension of her arm. She's his puppet, but she fights. Oh, how she fights! Hannah shakes off his music and twitches with the effort of battling her own body, blocking out the hypnosis. She will fail. But she tries.

Hannah lurches forward, slashes the rats away, loses control, and turns her blade on Cecilia. Exoskeleton forms from her glamour, and the blows glance off, but it's clear they pain her. She never attacks Hannah or flies to avoid the barrage of slashes. Her voice turns raw from screaming, begging Hannah to return to them. She is afraid, but she fights. Oh, how she fights! Cecelia strains against the power the music gives Hannah, but she falters with the effort of evading every assault. She will fail. But she tries.

They would not fight for her if they did not love her. They would not welcome her into their family and call her a Teagan if they did not love her. The Piper lies.

"Queen Mab desires these two living sacrifices," the Piper's song says, *"but only you are required. If this grows too troublesome, I will simply kill them both and take you to Carterhaugh. You're too weak to resist. Surrender and spare these brats the suffering."*

The request almost sounds reasonable, but Tess knows the Piper, his ways familiar to her since her youth. He is not safe. He is not kind. Accepting may sound easy, but it means returning to hunger, to cold, to sharing her sleeping quarters with the biting rats. She would become scared and nameless once again. Oblivion would be a welcome release.

But she has no reason to believe the Piper would let her sisters go if she surrendered. Not after he betrayed Hannah's deal. Tess must resist him, but how?

Hannah pins Cecelia to the ground, sword to her neck.

"No. NO!" Tess screams, barely aware of herself. She never realized until this moment just how much they mean to her. She cannot bear to watch Cecelia die at the hands of her sister.

She cannot blame Hannah.

Fury and fear war in Tess's heart.

She must claim her name and defy the Piper to break his curse over his sisters.

Now or never.

Tess calls her vines and fires them off at Hannah, the net of woven tendrils pulling her off Cecelia, wrenching the falchion away, and tangling her arms behind her. She manages a smile in a moment of blessed relief. The plants surround Cecelia and create a dome as a shield, keeping her safe from the Piper.

A new song starts with a low hum and rises to a roar as Tess sings her sorrow, a countermelody spilling out of her like a river undammed, loud and clear and mournful. It winds around the Piper's dissonant notes and strangles them as her thorns wind around the Piper's hands. She strangles the malicious music and seizes the pipe, wrenching it out of his grasp and dashing it on the ground. She uses the True Voice—*her* voice—not a borrowed power, but her own dignity, a gift her sisters helped her find. She sings the truth. The most powerful truth she knows. A truth that will set her and her sisters free.

"I. AM. TESS TEAGAN." Tess cries. "These are my sisters! I claim this name, and I claim them as mine! You may not have them, and you may not have me. I know what you are now, and your words are poison and lies. Get behind us and torment us no longer."

The words tear from her chest with an ache that reminds her she's alive. It's grief and fury for a stolen childhood, taken because someone else thought it best. She has never lived, not before now. If this is the last thing she does, it will be living.

"I am their sister," Tess repeats, "and they are mine. I love Hannah and Cecelia. These are names you cannot take. Our bond is BROKEN!"

With these words, she shatters the tether the Piper holds over Hannah, over Cecelia, and over herself. His music rests. The swarm scurries away. Illusions disappear. Fog passes from her sisters' eyes, and they rise. The Piper, furious in defeat, lunges for Tess, but he cannot even touch her. Powerless and humbled, he retreats.

They're finally free.

Tess collapses, exhausted, but as she gathers a crutch and stumbles toward her sisters for a hug, she knows without a shadow of a doubt that everything will be okay.

She is safe.

She is loved.

She is Tess.

Chapter 41

The Release

THE PIPER'S POWER releases Hannah when Tess takes her name, but the panic hangs over her, even as the fog fades from her eyes and the flute from her ears. While she couldn't control her body, her mind had belonged to her, aware of the horrors wrought with her hands. She lurches and falls, a marionette with snipped strings, silky spiderwebs clinging to her jacket, caught only by the vines holding her. The plants release her, and she curls in on herself, holding her traitorous hands close to her chest. All she can imagine is her blade hovering a few inches from Cecelia's throat. Heaving breaths wrack her body as she sobs. How could she...she was so close to...her broken promises...what if—

Gentle hands take her shaking ones and pull her out of her terror and shock. She tilts her head up and peers through her disheveled curls to see the Taken smiling. Her sister's smile. *Tess's* smile.

Cecelia emerges from a shield, shifting back to her preferred form—all blonde hair and flowers—then tackles her sisters in a frantic hug. Hannah clings to them, dizzy with delight and relief, desperate to feel their solid, grounding presence. She cries into Tess's hair as she embraces her younger sister. Tess. What a beautiful name!

Tess cries too, but also laughs. A joyful sound that fills Hannah's heart, and they hold each other like a lifeline.

"I'm sorry," Hannah whispers over and over again, "I promised—" Her voice cuts off in another strangled sob. She cannot banish the sight of Cecelia's terrified face from her mind. "I thought if I—"

Tess shakes her head. She holds Hannah's hand with a grip so tight it hurts in a good way. "You saved me! My name is Tess!"

"I know you would never hurt me," Cecelia says. Her voice is still shaky, but she grins just as broadly as Tess. "But don't ever scare me like that again."

Hannah's stomach churns. "He forced me to choose. I couldn't sacrifice you. Either of you. Maybe I could save you, but...I should have known. The Piper always lies."

"It should have been me," Cecelia answers. "It should have been me from the beginning. All of this is my fault, and I should have been the one to pay."

"I couldn't let that happen. Don't you remember, Cecelia, on the night of the thunderstorm? I knew nothing about the fae, but I promised I wouldn't let him get you. Tess, do you remember the Tree? I didn't know you were my sister, but I told you I would help you escape. When he forced me to decide..."Hannah shudders. "I had to. I can't regret my decision, but look at you. Look at your wings. How could I? Cecelia, I'm sorry."

Cecelia's arms darken with bruises and bleeding cuts. Her left wing hangs at the wrong angle, and a jagged tear splits the eyespot on the right. She might never fly again. When she moves, her actions are stiff and she hisses through her teeth. Despite this, she puts a hand on Hannah's shoulder.

"You don't need to apologize," she says.

Tess nods and squeezes Hannah's hand. "Your love let me find my name. You showed me how to be brave. Thank you."

"You did it." Hannah squeezes her hand back, then pulls her into an embrace, joy washing away the lingering fear and blame. Pride fills her from her head to her toes, not for herself, but for Cecelia and Tess, the heroes who deserve all the praise in the world. "You did it, Tess! I love you so much. What a perfect name!"

Tess melts into the hug, and when she lets go, she's glowing. "What do we do now?"

"We go home."

Hannah looks at their surroundings. The Portal Tree glitters in the distance, a speck on the horizon. Monarchs only know how far away they are from their friends. Cecelia needs a doctor. Are Lady Brigid and the twins ok? Did Quercu get to bring her sister back? Hannah doesn't think she can take one more step, but she desperately wants to check if their friends are ok. Her exhausted body cannot haul herself all the way home. All she wants is to go home.

Cecelia volunteers an idea. "Is it ok if we go to the Seelie Court first?" she asks Tess. "We have friends there. They have magic that can heal us. It'll take care of your leg. We can rest, and then we can go home."

"Is it safe for me?"

"Of course."

Tess hesitantly nods her agreement and picks up her crutch. Hannah helps Cecelia to her feet and leads the way to the Portal Tree. Together, they limp toward the Court in companionable quiet.

Tess changes. She smiles, a lovely lopsided grin Hannah has seldom seen since they first met. Her free arm swings as she walks, her posture now relaxed and open. Autumn leaves drift around them, and the last of the autumn flowers bloom beneath their feet at Tess's bidding.

Cecelia changes. She sings without hesitation, tunes as buoyant as the breeze. She deserves to fly and to pet the wind once she has the chance to heal her wing.

Hannah revels in the glory of her sisters learning to be themselves. She's changed, too, in ways she can't name yet. She hopes it's for the better, like them.

Cecelia tells stories about the Seelie Court, and Tess listens in wide-eyed astonishment at the tales of mermaids and unicorns, of Quercu's antics, of the Lady's kindness. Hannah sometimes interjects with her own corrections, but she's content to let them connect without her interference. Their chatter is a balm to her wounded heart, and she knows, despite their shared strife, they will recover together. Even if the Portal Tree seems a million miles away, she's happy they're heading toward one of their two homes. As she's dreaming of the bed in the little treehouse cottage, a familiar voice interrupts her reverie.

"Lady Brigid! I've found them!" Quercu materializes out of thin air, transforming into her usual form, red hair ablaze. She descends on the girls in a flurry of wings and questions. Tess screams in surprise and grabs Hannah's arm, but Hannah assures her little sister that the overenthusiastic faerie is a friend.

"Where have ye girls been? What happened to ye, Cecelia? Cecelia! Ye have your name! Hannah, ye wonder! Where's the Piper? Who's this young lady? By the Monarchs, ye look a proper mess." Quercu rambles as she checks their injuries.

"Tess broke the Piper's power over us! He ran away, back to the Unseelie Court, or I don't know where. Did you stop the ritual? Where are Lady Brigid and the twins?" Cecelia fires back, jumping up and down with excitement to see her mentor.

"Aye! Ye know we did. Ye should have seen it! They're on their way. Slowpokes."

"They tried to stop the ritual? For me? No wonder you're all so eager to sacrifice yourselves!" Tess sounds completely incredulous, but Hannah can only laugh.

Hannah sees the twins approach through the trees and waves to them. They shout with excitement when they see the three girls. Marco rushes forward and tackles Hannah in a hug. Matteo shakes hands with Tess, who looks a little overwhelmed by the exchange, but pleased nonetheless. When Quercu realizes the extent of Cecelia's injuries, she releases the longest, most creative string of curses Hannah's ever heard. Hannah cringes, feeling guilty, but she can't dwell on the painful memories because Lady Brigid follows only a moment behind, welcoming them with open arms.

"Who do we have the pleasure of meeting?" she asks the newest sister.

"My name is Tess," she replies.

"Lady Brigid, at your service." She gives a deep curtsy, and Hannah beams with pride. The Lady heals Tess's broken leg, stitches together Cecelia's wings, and binds Hannah's wounds on the spot. Determining the girls are too exhausted to walk any farther, Lady Brigid sweeps Tess into her arms to carry her back to the Seelie Court. Matteo picks up Hannah on his back, carrying her piggyback like she'd been carrying Tess, and Marco takes up Cecelia. Hannah, too exhausted to protest, accepts their care. The twins bear their burdens swiftly and smiling, and she remembers they, too, have younger sisters. She wonders if she'll ever see them again, after they go home, and then she drifts off to sleep, her head resting on Matteo's shoulder.

They awaken in warm beds in the familiar treehouse cabin. Clean clothes hang from a rack and there's fresh food piled on the table. Hannah cries with joy when she finds Kit-Kat sleeping at her feet, recovering from his wounds after a legendary battle with the rats. Lady Brigid reports that dozens and dozens of the beasts laid slain around him where they'd found his body, that he'd reduced their numbers enough, they hadn't eaten the girls alive. Hannah showers him with praise and treats. She knows she can't bring him home—at least for the sake of the chickens—and the twins promise to take care of him while he heals in the Seelie Court.

They eat a hearty breakfast that surprises Tess with every new food that isn't lukewarm, flavorless gruel. She loves it all—

eggs and bacon, fruit jams and butter bread, warm tea and chilled apple juice—and she eats as if she's been starving for years. Lady Brigid and the others only talk a little about their exploits in defeating the ritual, and none of the girls ask for more information. If they don't want to share, Hannah doesn't want to know; she's just comforted to know they won.

The fae don't press the girls for details about their adventure either, but the story comes out bit by bit, each of the sisters telling their part. None of them want to relive the experience, but relief comes in sharing the burden of the horror. Words cannot convey their true terror, but speaking allows them to process their past days.

Quercu hangs on every word. Hannah can't help but notice her sister still hasn't returned, and she squeezes Quercu's hand to lend her some strength. Despite the bittersweet homecoming, Quercu lets nothing impede her bombastic attitude, and makes plans to pursue her sister yet again, now that Tess "softened the Piper up for her."

The twins exaggerate every part of the story, calling their navigation a work of genius, plotting a course through a mythical labyrinth. They cheer at every turn of the troll fight, much to Tess's embarrassment, but they congratulate her on having such a clever idea, and beam with pride to hear how Hannah held her own against such a foe. Lady Brigid promises to check on Geoffrey and offer him a place in the Seelie Court, now that he has a name.

After breakfast, they approach the Monarchs for one last audience. Hannah protests, reminding Lady Brigid they need to go home, but she insists the time will be worth it, and so they enter the throne room hand in hand. Hannah refuses to be intimidated by the king and queen anymore. After facing her worst nightmares, it's easy to indulge their quaint eccentricities. When she'd first come through this room, Hannah had been too overwhelmed to appreciate its beauty. The alabaster walls hang with tapestries depicting the creatures of the realm. Chandeliers of sparkling crystals glow with a soft amber light. A soft violet carpet leads the way to the thrones, where the Monarchs wait for them.

Hannah's skin tingles as they enter the powerful magical presence. The Monarchs have transformed with newfound power since thwarting the Unseelie Tithe. The Queen's velvety blue dress drips with pearls, creating constellations in their patterns. Her eyes fill with nebulae and starlight. She stands at the window, surveying her domain, and Hannah wonders how far those eyes can see. The King's golden hair wreaths him in a corona of flame. He plays a harp while he waits, and the song layers over itself, creating a complex piece that resonates throughout the space. Unlike the Piper's song, this song fills Hannah with peace and joy. They survived. They escaped. It's a triumphant hymn of thanks. When they notice the girls' presence, the Monarchs stand, bow to them, and beckon them forward. A few notes ring out even after he sets down the instrument.

"Gifts! Gifts for the heroes!" proclaims the King, and Lady Brigid brings forward a chest. The Queen unlocks it with a key from around her neck and pulls out three medallions on leather strings. Each contains a glass bead about the size of a marble, swirling with more colors than Hannah had thought possible. Each bead spins at the center of a gold disc inscribed with faerie script. The queen places one around each girl's neck. The honors awarded, the Queen steps back and clasps her hands in satisfaction as she looks them over.

"These medallions will grant you safe passage back to Seelie. The Portal Tree remains locked most of the year, but these serve as keys. You may seek sanctuary here whenever you desire."

The sisters chorus their thanks, and the Lady gestures for Hannah to step forward.

"For the Seeker," Lady Brigid announces, "who faced friends and foes more powerful than she, with no more than a pen-knife and pluck. For the sister who would stop at nothing to defend those she loves, putting herself at risk so they may have a chance at escape. To the one who always sought the truth, even when the road grew rough, we give to you this spyglass."

Hannah gasps. Her old spyglass from home had broken when she'd first entered Seelie, and she'd been too frazzled to mourn its loss. They must have collected the pieces and remade it with a beautiful new casing. Telescoping bronze cylinders hold the crystal-clear eye-pieces.

"Not only shall it grant you the Sight," Lady Brigid says, "but you shall also be able to see your sisters when you look through it, wherever in the world they may roam."

Tears sting Hannah's eyes at the praise, and she retreats without a word. She hopes her sisters never stray so far away that she needs to use the powers of the spyglass, that they always stay safe and close to her, but she's thankful for the gift.

When Tess is beckoned forward, she looks the Monarchs in the eye with a confidence Hannah's sure has only come with her newfound freedom. Lady Brigid gives her a box wrapped in shiny paper, and Tess doesn't know what to do with it at first, so Hannah gestures for her to rip off the bow and open the present as the Lady begins her speech.

"For the Soldier, who survived torments and terrors. She who escaped one of our greatest enemies. For the sister who learned trust and love and freed herself with the help of those she loves, we give to you this compass." It matches the style of Hannah's spyglass, with a thorny rose engraved on its cover. "Should you wish, when you open it, the needle shall always point toward home, wherever in the world your heart may lie."

Tess slips her hand into Hannah's and clutches the compass to her chest. She whispers her thanks as her eyes well up with tears. She has no possessions of her own, at least until now, but Hannah knows this will rank among her most prized.

Finally, Lady Brigid calls Cecelia forward. "For the Spy, who lived an unwanted lie and fought deception to save her family. For the sister who sought truth, even when it most hurt, the Monarchs offer you a place among the Seelie Court. We can undo the switching spell. If completed, it will restore Tess in the minds of your family, as if the Piper had never taken her."

Hannah holds her breath, awaiting Cecelia's decision. They'd talked about going home together, but this offer would mean the world to her sister—finally, a chance to live a life where she doesn't have to hide half her identity. The freedom of flight, the fellowship of friends who know her story, a fate untethered from the Piper's plans. She deserves that, Hannah knows. Cecelia shouldn't ground and guard herself anymore. Even if all she wants is for her sister to come home.

Does Cecelia still want that? Something in Hannah breaks as she realizes this must be the point of the other gifts. So she can see her lost sister living in Seelie, so Tess can know where she wanders, apart from them.

Cecelia turns to the Monarchs and makes a deep curtsy. "Your Highnesses, thank you so much for your generous offer, but I cannot take it. Though I may be fae by birth, my true place is at home with my human family. May I ask a different boon?"

Hannah's heart leaps, and her breath catches in her throat as her mind catches up to what her ears are hearing. The Monarchs nod in unison, and Lady Brigid gives her a knowing smile. What does Cecelia have planned?

"It will be difficult for our parents to accept the truth, but I do not want to continue living a lie. Please, instead of reversing the switching spell, restore their missing daughter in their memories without erasing me."

"Such a thing is not easily done," the Queen says.

"But the things that are honorable and worthwhile are rarely done with ease," says the King. He gestures for Lady Brigid to step forward, and she brings with her a full-length mirror. The King and Queen trail their fingers along the edges and speak in their own True Voices. They ring like the peal of church bells, the blast of the organ, the chime of a clock. Then they give Cecelia a proud smile.

"Look upon yourself, Cecelia, and change," says the Queen.

"For this mirror will show the truth of anything that is reflected in it," the King explains, "You need only show your family, and they will see your story."

When Cecelia walks forward, the reflection shows her as Hannah remembers—the same dark hair, the same rounded ears, and a back bare of wings. The reflection's expression is confident, compassionate, and knowing. Her dark eyes are deep, like they hold the answers to all the world's questions and the truth of all the world's secrets.

Hannah wonders how she had never seen that before. When Cecelia looks back to her sisters, she's changed her appearance to match the human reflection.

Lady Brigid holds up the mirror, and it shrinks to the size of her palm. She presses it into Cecelia's hands. "Keep the truth with your secrets, and guard both carefully," she says. Cecelia nods solemnly and tucks it into a pocket. Then she moves to stand opposite of Tess and hold Hannah's other hand. Hannah squeezes it three times in endless gratitude and joy, and Cecelia returns the gesture.

I love you.

They say their final thanks to the King and Queen, and goodbyes to their friends. Returning to their cabin, Hannah and Cecelia change into their cleaned clothes from home for the journey back. They return their packs and gear to Lady Brigid, and the twins return their weapons to the armory. Cecelia locks up their little cottage and drops the key in her pocket. Then Tess pulls out her compass and leads them to the Seelie Court's border, through a series of caves and up the hollow trunk of the Portal Tree. They laugh about their first fight before stepping to the edge of the faerie ring.

Hannah fears what they might find on the other side. Will they emerge from the fiery forest of perpetual autumn trees to find a winter wasteland? Or maybe next spring? Maybe the seasons have passed into another autumn, decades from the one they left behind? What if they wander down the mountain into a foreign future? Tess has spent so much longer in Faerieland than Hannah, and heaven knows what the changes have done to Cecelia. Will they emerge to find themselves aged?

They have come too far for her to hesitate from fear. They fought for this very moment, so Hannah squeezes both sisters' hands and says, "Let's go home."

And with that, they cross the barrier.

Chapter 42

The Return

N THE OTHER side, the forest looks and feels exactly how Hannah left it. They retrace the steps she took in her flight from the Piper. She spots her footprints, still visible in the soft earth, dried but present. They can't have been gone long.

This thought fills Hannah with hope, and she sets their course down the mountain at a headlong sprint. Cecelia's injuries are still red but scarred over, and she moves without pain, telling Hannah dozens of times to stop apologizing. Tess keeps up with their fast pace, her leg healed overnight and stronger than ever, but she still uses a crutch for balance.

Soon, Hannah spots a shell she'd left to trace her path.

"Aha! This is it!" She snatches it up and cranes her neck to find the next one. Tess spots it, makes her way down the path, and collects the small conch. She marvels for a moment, turning it over in her hands as she admires the swooping curves and mottled colors. Hannah pauses for a breath and shows her how to hold it up to her ear.

"You can hear the sea."

She gives a small sigh of wonder and clasps it to her chest. "I want to go."

"We'll take you some day," she promises, then points out the next one, further down the path. And so they go, leapfrogging from one mark to another, following the trail home. Grinning at her older sister's idea, Cecelia sings the last verses of the song she's made, verses that tell of where they're going and how far they've come.

Blankets soft on my own bed,
Grounds I know and often tread,
Freshly baking loaves of bread,
Bookshelves stacked with tomes I've read,
Hearth fire blazing fills the heart,
Ne'er again from home I'll part.

Run—Run away, where you know your name.
Run—Run away so you can't be claimed
Run—Run away, where nothing is tame.
Run—Run away to a tree aflame.
Run—Run away from the hurt and blame.
Run—Run away, never be the same.

Finally, breathless and sore, they reach the last of the seashells atop a ridge. Through the bare trees and shrubs, they can see the open meadow of the pasture, the outline of the garden fence, and a plume of smoke rising from the stone chimney above the red roof. A joyful chorus in Hannah's mind sings, *Home! Home! Home!*

In the yard, they introduce Tess to Snubs and let her pet his fuzzy head. Hannah throws extra seed at the chickens and gives Onii a scratch under the chin. They hear Willow barking inside, and a moment later their parents emerge from the house.

Hannah charges ahead to tackle Mom in a homesick hug. Their mother is so bewildered by the sight of three girls running out of the woods that she tumbles backward in surprise. Hannah doesn't even notice. Dad picks up Cecelia and twirls her around before wrapping her in a bear hug. Willow barks in delight, and as soon as Mom lets go, Hannah throws her arms around the

Newfoundland's neck as she covers her in slobbery kisses. And she laughs, longer and harder than she's ever laughed before.

"Where have you been?!" Mom demands. "We were worried sick! The police are out looking for you right now! What were you thinking, leaving the house when we told you to stay put? And you, little miss!" She draws Cecelia into a hug, and Hannah sees their mother's face is exhausted and careworn, their father's eyes overflowing with relief. Her voice cracks, joy overwhelming the anger. "We thought we'd lost you."

"How long have we been gone?" Hannah falls into her father's arms and squeezes him tight around his waist, basking in the comfort of his arms around her shoulders, strong and safe. She's home. He's got her now.

"Three days. You disappeared on the eve of Halloween. It's All Souls' Day," their father answers. "Oh Hannah, we missed you." He buries his face in her hair, and she sobs into his chest.

"I missed you, too."

Hannah feels him raise his head, looking over her shoulder. His eyes fix on Tess, standing awkwardly to the side, frozen while Willow sniffs her.

Mom hasn't noticed the third girl yet. She spins Cecelia around in a circle, inspecting her for injuries. Cecelia glamours over the scars, and her mother doesn't notice.

"Thank God, you're home safe! Where were you?! Never wander off like that again, you hear me?"

"I'm sorry, Ma. I won't, I promise."

"Hannah, didn't I tell you to stay out of the woods? You're grounded, little lady."

"I found Cecelia, didn't I?" she protests. Mom makes a noise somewhere between a groan and a laugh, telling Hannah she's not upset but also clearly not in the mood for an argument.

Their father approaches Tess and kneels down, holding out a hand to her. Tess hides behind Hannah, who shows her little sister how to shake his hand. "Hello. Who are you?" he asks, keeping his voice low and gentle.

"My name is Tess."

"Tess. You look...familiar. Have we met before?"

Tess mumbles something about sisters, but Mom cuts her off. Lady Brigid had given Tess new clothes, a bath, and a proper haircut before they'd left Seelie, so she looks less bedraggled than before, enough that the resemblance to Hannah shows through. She's still wearing Dad's jacket that Hannah lent to her. A dozen expressions flash across Mom's face in an instant, but she composes herself upon seeing the strange child standing before her, wearing her husband's oversized coat. Then she leans down to look Tess in the eye.

"Tess, honey, how can we help you?"

Hannah steps in to take the pressure off her little sister, though Mom doesn't know that yet. "When I went looking for Cecelia, I found both of them in the woods. She needed help, so I brought her back here," she explains. "I told her she can stay with us as long as she wants. That's okay, right?" It's a bold ask, but they'll understand soon enough.

Mom straightens up, and she glances from Tess to Hannah, then to Cecelia, who is still in her nightgown, with the classic "I hope you have a good explanation for this" expression. Then she smiles and claps her hands. "Yes, of course, that's fine. I'm glad my girls found you. Why don't you come inside now, and you three can tell us your story over some hot cocoa, okay? It's freezing out here."

"Cocoa sounds wonderful, Mom," Cecelia says, and Hannah echoes the statement. As they enter the kitchen, Dad drags up an extra chair for their newest family member. Mom dabs extra whipped cream on top of the hot chocolate and places three steaming mugs on the table before the girls. Hannah shows Tess how to blow on it so she doesn't burn her tongue, and when the younger girl has her first taste, her eyes go wide.

Mom's expression softens as she watches Tess savor the sweets. Hannah can tell, even though their mother is confused by the sudden appearance of a third child, she's already fond of her missing daughter. Dad settles in next to Cecelia, holding her close, as if she'll disappear from under their noses again. There's a pile of police reports on the table from the missing persons search. Hannah pushes them to the side as Mom sits down across from her.

"Tess, where did you come from?" she asks.

Tess mumbles something about the Piper into her chocolate. Hannah gives Cecelia a knowing look. It's time for her to come clean, and she squirms for just a minute before she removes the mirror from her pocket and places it on the table. "I haven't been truthful with you," she admits. "It's hard to explain. I know it'll sound crazy, but if you look in the mirror, it will explain everything."

Their parents share a skeptical glance. Their father lays his hand over the mirror and scans Cecelia's face. Can he see the glamour? Have they learned about Hazel? Hannah doesn't see any sign of the house brownie.

"Last night, a strange woman came to our house," Dad says, rubbing his temples. Instead of hot chocolate, his hands grip a mug of coffee. "Long red hair. Dressed like a nun. Old-fashioned. Strange."

"Lady Brigid!" Hannah cries. "She's been busy!"

"You know her?" asks Mom. She doesn't even sound surprised.

"She's wonderful."

"She told us you would come home today. She couldn't, or wouldn't, explain where you were or how she knew these things. We didn't know what to think."

"Did you think she kidnapped us?" Hannah asks. She understands her parent's suspicion, but it's hard not to get along with Lady Brigid.

"No," Dad answers. "Somehow, we understood she cared for you. We never felt threatened. She told us you were safe. It was just so odd, we didn't know what to make of it."

"But here you are," Mom continues, taking Cecelia's hand. "She told us to keep an open mind. We're hurt that you would keep things from us, but we love you, and we want to help. We aren't angry, just glad you want to tell us the truth. You can tell us anything, and it changes nothing."

"Where did you go?" Dad asks.

Tears spring to Cecelia's eyes at her parents' acceptance, and she nudges the mirror toward them again, but looks away, unable to meet their gaze. "I ran away to protect you. I'm a faerie. Please. Just look."

The sisters watch as their parents gaze into the mirror. A minute passes, their expressions unreadable as they take in the full story. Tess squirms as she waits for their reaction, and Hannah puts a protective arm around her shoulder. Cecelia squeezes her hand.

When the parents look up again, Cecelia has revealed her faerie form. There's a long moment of suspenseful silence as they process the information they saw, and then both parents fold Cecelia into a hug.

"You're still our daughter. Always," Mom says.

"And this will always be your home," Dad finishes.

Cecelia bursts into tears of relief and clings to them while Hannah cheers. They turn to Tess, tears in their eyes, too.

"Our lost daughter! Tess. How could we forget you?" Their father keeps holding onto Cecelia, while Mom holds out an arm to draw her into an embrace. Tess freezes for a moment, but Hannah nudges her forward, and she accepts the hug. Mom holds her tight and rubs her back like she's comforting an infant, and Tess melts into the soft touch. "My baby's home!"

Hannah watches the reunion with a full heart and cradles her hot chocolate in her hands, basking in the warmth and comfort. It was worth it, all their hardships and sacrifices. Everything was worth it. They've earned their happily ever after.

Epilogue

HE NEXT DAY, Mom and Dad call off the search. Despite the paperwork and questions about adopting a third child overnight, the sisters don't have to worry about any of it. Hannah shows Tess around the home and introduces her to all the pets. Cecelia shows them all the secret passageways and even introduces them to Hazel, their house brownie. Tess takes to it all with both hesitancy and wonder. She's shy around their parents and often talks to them through Hannah, but they understand and do their best to make her feel welcome.

While the mirror's spell restored the whole story to their parent's memories, their adult minds struggle to accept certain parts, and it takes a lot more explaining before they understand the trials and nuances of the faerie world.

When officials poke around to verify Tess's identity, Cecelia keeps her human form and refills her room with artwork and music, remembering Lady Brigid's words about keeping her secrets and her truth close together. The family needs to know what she is, but the world does not, and she intends to keep the Seelie Court safe from prying eyes. In private, Cecelia shapeshifts as much as she wants. It only takes one broken lamp for Mom to instate a No Flying in the House rule, but she sews wing slits into all of Cecelia's shirts anyway.

HE NEXT WEEK, Tess troops outside to help the family rake leaves. By midafternoon, she's grouchy, and blisters have rubbed her hands raw. Cecelia jumps in the pile and playfully throws a handful at Tess. Startled, Tess pushes her into the heap with a cruel laugh. She kicks at the leaves, scattering them again and catching Cecelia in the leg. Hannah shouts at her to stop, the old defensive reflex kicking in as she grabs the younger girl by the shoulders to shake some sense into her. Tess rips herself away and runs to the woods.

Mom catches her with a gentle hand. Tess flinches, but her mother does not berate or strike her. She guides her wayward daughter home again, speaking in whispers, before nudging her toward the sisters. Tess approaches Cecelia, shamefaced and head bowed. She learns to apologize and feels the relief of forgiveness once again. They finish the leaves together, and Hannah kisses the pain of the blisters away.

THAT WINTER, A blizzard hits just before Christmas. Tess loves to make sugar cookies. She can't ruin the pliable dough. If it breaks, she can roll it out again, and everything is okay. And though the cookies come out just a little too crunchy, they're softened with icing and cocoa so sweet it hurts her teeth. She beams at her father's praise as he steals another one and ruffles her hair. The house is so warm from the wood fire that she doesn't even need her coat.

The sight of her very own red jacket hanging next to Dad's is a comfort. She looks out toward the woods and thanks her lucky stars she's not out there right now. She worries Father Christmas won't bring her anything. He never has, and she was bad for so much of this year. But her mother soothes her with a story, and she falls asleep on the couch, content. When she wakes up, the world is white; crumbs lay scattered on the cookie plate, and a pile of presents sits under the tree with her name on the label. She can read her name now.

IN FEBRUARY, THEY buy a new batch of chicks for their coop. Hannah and Cecelia share the time-honored tradition of naming the new members, and Tess takes the responsibility seriously. She consults books for reference and, after much deliberation, chooses a name befitting her chick: Henrietta. She's proud of the choice and of how much her mother laughs at the wordplay. Hannah calls her clever, and Tess accepts the praise with a smug grin as she sings her charge to sleep.

DURING LENT, MOM gives up sugar, which means the whole family has to give up sugar, though Tess feels that's unfair. Cecelia says they're twelve now, so they're practically grown-ups, which means they can stay up half an hour longer than usual. 10:00 pm seems like a daring hour to be awake and still be safe from the dark. The soft glow of the lamp isn't a halo or faerie glow, but she loves it all the same.

Hannah reads *A Wrinkle in Time* out loud, and when her older sister puts the book down, Tess pads over to the kitchen table to ask for dessert. Mom shakes her head, but Tess pouts until Dad goes, "Here, cub," and makes a special dessert from graham crackers with peanut butter and honey dabbed on top. Mom protests, but he laughs and argues honey is "God's sugar" so it ought to be allowed, and she can't argue with that logic, so he makes one for her, and Hannah, and Cecelia, too. Tess tries to eat it as neatly as possible, smug with her trophy and intent on savoring it. When honey spills over the sides, she scrambles to shove the rest of the treat in her mouth as it drips onto her hands. It takes two mugs of warm milk to wash down the peanut butter stuck to the roof of her mouth, but she goes to bed with a satisfied sweet tooth.

N SPRING, HANNAH recruits Tess in the garden, happy to use her skills to coax the seedlings from the earth. Soon she's using a shovel to attack the soft, wet earth with gleeful wild abandon. By the end of the afternoon, she's covered head to toe in dirt and grinning from ear to ear as she hangs upside-down from a beanstalk taller than their mother. Mom shouts at them to come down, and the look of bewilderment and amusement on her face is so shocking that Hannah almost falls out of the plant from laughing. Tess grows a tendril to catch her, and the tomatoes taste better than ever that year.

N SUMMER, TESS finds the best wild raspberry patch in the woods. Their parents begrudgingly allow them to explore, but their fresh paths explore only a tiny portion of their magical backyard. Buckets in hand, they set out with promises to bring home enough for jam. When Cecelia trips and falls into the thorns while reaching for the biggest bunch of berries, Tess laughs, but it's not a cruel laugh. She warns Cecelia be careful, then extends a hand to pull her out, and kisses the sting of the scratches away.

They fill their bellies and still bring home more than enough for jam, and their mother has Cecelia stir the pot. Tess envies the fun job; she's asked to knead bread until her hands ache, but the rhythm entrances her. Her father praises the combination of bread and jam as long as the supply lasts, and they glow at a job well done. Every time Tess feels angry, she asks her mother to fetch the flour.

HEN AUTUMN RETURNS, storms rattle the roof, and Hannah waits awake for Cecelia to sneak into her room. When she does not appear, fear tickles the back of her mind, and though she cannot hear the flute, she still worries the Piper will return to settle their score. She ventures through the trapdoor, but Cecelia's bed is empty. Fear turns to panic as she bolts down the hallway to Tess's room, where she finds the two girls huddled in bed.

They invite her under the covers and use their flashlight to guide her around the traps they set. Cecelia fetches the red embroidery floss from the art desk, and they replace the old tattered binds of last year with fresh new ones. Tess whispers "I love you" as they don their armor, and they fall asleep huddled together. The Piper has lost, and the sisters sleep in peace.

N HALLOWEEN, THE girls are eager to make a reprise after missing trick-or-treating last year, and introduce Tess to all the fun traditions. Cecelia gives Tess her own costume—a princess gown—and it fits like a glove. Tess protests, tries to push it back, but her fingers linger on the soft fabric, and Cecelia insists. So they trade. Cecelia proudly goes as a faerie instead, and gives Hannah a wink as she dons her wings.

Tess slips into her room to change, and when she emerges, Hannah, the stegosaurus dinosaur, bellows in approval. They take up their baskets and pile into the truck to meet up with friends. In town, the other trick-or-treaters either don't notice, or don't mention, how well Cecelia's wings blend into the buttoned back of her sundress. Tess laughs at the scary decorations and enjoys the way Hannah drags her from house to house. There's only one minor incident when an adult emerges, dressed akin to the Piper, and the roses in the garden grow out of control, but Hannah pulls Tess away and hugs her tight.

"He can't get you," she whispers in Tess's ear. "Not anymore. You're safe."

OVEMBER DAWNS BRIGHT and cold on the anniversary of their homecoming, the day the family decides they'll celebrate Tess's birthday. They throw a party and bake a cake. She cherishes her presents, but something's missing. They haven't seen their faerie friends in a year, and the girls grow restless to visit the Seelie Court. Instead of leaving unannounced, they tell their parents where they'll be going. It takes some arguing, but after Hannah leaves them the spyglass, they finally relent. Tess leads the way through the woods with her compass, and it's not long before they reach the Portal Tree, which opens at the touch of their medallions, ready to welcome them for another adventure. Together.

The End

Acknowledgments

This is an incredibly personal book. It's a story drawn directly from my experiences playing elaborate storytelling games with my siblings in our backyard wood, turning our treehouse into a fortress, a castle, a pirate ship, acting out dramas that only ended when the sun went down and mom called us in for dinner. It's drawn from the joy of watching my younger siblings rediscover the joy of books I loved when I was their age, and hearing updates about their games whenever I got back from school or work. My family is at the core of everything I write.

To my dad, who encouraged me to keep writing fantasy even while pursuing a STEM degree. To my mom who taught me pretty much everything I know and gave me time and space to work on my silly stories, even on blue cup days. ;)

To my sister Isabella, who's unwillingly listed to my ideas late at night since we were ten, who brags about my book to literally anyone who will listen, commissioned artwork for my Christmas gift, and supports me in more ways than I can describe.

To my brothers Patrick and Thomas whose adventures and antics constantly inspire and entertain me. You're both incredible young men and I'm so proud of you.

To my sister Annalise, who is even more of a bookworm than I ever was. I didn't think that was possible. I hope you love this story.

A million billion trillion thank yous to my wonderful best friend-turned boyfriend-turned fiancé-now husband, Eric. You patiently endured me rambling about this WIP through the several years in which our relationship developed, months of COVID lockdowns, graduating college, moving across four states, rewriting seven drafts, endless reformatting, countless nights of tears, and somehow wedding planning alongside a book release. I don't know how you put up with my nonsense but I love you and I owe you the world.

To my friends: Theele, Sarina, Misha, Stephanie, Ben, Greg, and Alex, who also listened to my ramblings and updates at every get-together, inspire me with awesome DnD games, support me with cheering, offer snacks, good advice, and answer random polls in the group-chat. You're awesome.

I must also thank all of the amazing people who supported the development of the story. This book came so far from the initial draft and I can't imagine how different it might have been if not for all your help.

To my illustrator and Writerfriend Quinn, you're truly such a joy to talk with and I love all of our rubber-duck-debugging sessions over discord. As one of my first friends in the writing community I owe you for the confidence, encouragement (and sometimes venting) that it took to continue putting my work online and to keep going with the publishing process. Not only is your art absolutely incredible, you're also an incredible friend and I'm so honored to have you in my life.

To our Graphic Design Consultant Lumi who helped design a new logo for me, double checked file formats, and sanity checked our artwork, thank you a million for your selfless volunteering.

To my other illustrator, Emma, I'm shocked with how quickly you read the book and how many drawings you created. They're all so adorable and I loved seeing your interpretations of my characters. Thank you so much.

To my beta readers: What would I do without you? The original version of this draft was supposed to be a "short, easy, kids book" but in reality it was shallow and underdeveloped. You pushed my skills in character development, worldbuilding, exposition, prose, and so much more. Whether you read a chapter or finished the novel, I appreciate your willingness to give this book a chance. I had two rounds of beta readers so without further ado, Thank You to...

Round 1 Readers: Arva Blake, Aiden, Angelle, Katie Koontz, Mimi, Sav, Sofia, Ink, Isabella, and Quinn.

Round 2 Readers: Sav, Quinn, Katie, Ink, Avra, Orianna, Moshke Palmoni, Lila Mary, Lee, Kaze, Hyba, Azulina, Aslan, and Sarah.

Thank you especially to all my beta readers who returned for the second round, and to all of my friends from Tumblr and Instagram who cheered me on at each milestone. You're a huge factor in the success of this story and I cannot say enough how much I appreciate your messages, asks, and tags.

Addison Horner of Avocado Tree Press did the line/copy editing for this book and I could not possibly be more pleased with his services. He was professional, timely, encouraging, respected my author voice, and provided useful resources including a style guide, an editorial assessment, and a video call to recap the whole process. His comments were super insightful and easy to process. I appreciate all his help and highly recommend his work.

Eva Campney proofread this story and I thank her for her time and hard work. One day I'll learn how to use commas.

Finally, thank you to anyone else I might have missed, and to you, dear reader. If you've read my blog or supported my work in any way during these past 4 or 5 years, I appreciate your time and your willingness to take a chance on this story. It really means the world to me since this is my debut novel, and I hope you enjoyed it.

Godspeed and Goodwill.

Glossary

Brownie: A small, helpful faerie that lives in a human home and helps with housework in exchange for offerings of food. If offended, a brownie can become a boggart and turn mischievous or cruel. The Teagan house is home to a brownie named Hazel.

Changelings: Faerie children that are exchanged for human children as spies for the Pied Piper. They grow up with a human host family until the time comes for them to return to the Unseelie Court upon completion or failure of their mission. These fae have the short lifespans of mortals due to the Piper's Plague, and are glamoured using the Switching Spell to allow them to blend in with their human families.

Dryad: A tree nymph or spirit; a type of fae found in the Seelie court. Birch dryads work as librarians in a living forest where the words are written on the peeling paper-like bark.

Fae: Any creature considered magical or legendary in our world which can be found in the Unseelie or Seelie Courts, including dryads, grungtuttles, imps, merfolk, giants, trolls, and other beings seen in the story. "Fae" can be used as a singular or plural term.

Faerie: A magical creature that can be humanoid in appearance, has wings and can fly, can perform glamours for disguise and shapeshifting, and can't explicitly lie but can bend the truth through omission, half-truths, and other trickery. Multiple members of this species are referred to as "faeries." Faeries can belong to either the Seelie or Unseelie Court.

Glamour: Subtle but powerful faerie magic that can disguise or transform their true form into anything they imagine. It can also act as a form of mind control over other people, creatures, or things, but without using one's True Name, using glamour cannot physically compel someone to do something against their will.

Grungtuttle: A dangerous and uncommon wild fae creature found in the Unseelie Court. Best avoided.

Imp: Troublesome and mischievous but not especially dangerous fae creatures which are commonly found in the Unseelie Court. They are often small, humanoid in shape, with forked tails, tongues, and horns. Imps are lively and chaotic fae that serve below the Masters but rank higher than Taken wards.

Master: Powerful Unseelie fae that have sworn allegiance to Queen Mab, including the Piper, the Monster, the White Witch, and the Penumbra.

Namer: Someone who understands True Names and can use them to compel or connect to other people, creatures, or things. This understanding can be actively sought out or more subconscious, but it requires a deep and often timed nuanced relationship with the named thing in question.

Piper's Plague: A curse laid upon changelings which takes the form of fungi or lichen growing from the skin. It reduces a faerie's lifespan from millennia to that of a mortal human. The growths are itchy, painful, and unsightly, but not contagious to other fae or humans. The Plague can be mitigated by Seelie medicine and enchantment.

Powers: A league of lost humans, ex-changelings, half-fae, and other misfits who wish to fight against the Unseelie Court. They are led by Lady Brigid and given magical abilities and supernatural aid from King Oberon and Queen Titania.

Seelie Court: The part of faerieland which is home to fae with benevolent or ambivalent attitudes towards humans. It is ruled by King Oberon and Queen Titania, two angelic fae that protect and bless their lands.

Sight: the ability to see through glamours, to recognize the true form of a shapeshifted being, and to notice the invisible things of the world. A human can gain the Sight by looking through a Hagstone or Seeing Stone – a stone with a naturally occurring hole eroded through the center. The Sight can be granted by a Fae to a human directly or by enchanting a specific object.

Switching Spell: A curse laid upon changelings and their Taken counterparts. This spell switches the abilities and memories of the two children. This allows the faerie to believe they were always a human and can grow up with the host family. The human child gains knowledge of the Unseelie Court, the ability to learn the Piper's magic, and a resistance to the time dilation in faerieland so they continue to age normally. The spell can be manipulated by the Piper to control his wards, but it can be broken if both children renounce the Piper and reclaim their names.

Taken: Human children that are stolen by the Unseelie Masters as infants and replaced with changelings. The Piper's wards are raised without names or identities, wearing rat-shaped masks at all times. Taken wards are isolated from others of their kind and trained to manipulate plants and animals by using the True Voice in a twisted way, like the Piper. Taken wards who excel may be promoted and given masks in different animal shapes that match the creatures they control. Taken wards who disappoint the Piper are turned into rats and join his swarm. Other Taken wards are described in Chapter 25: The Offering

Tithe to Hell: A ritual done every 7 years in which the Unseelie Masters compete to offer a sacrifice to Queen Mab, who in turn, kills the poor soul and binds them to hell. Whichever Master earns Queen Mab's favor gains a larger share of the power that hell provides. Most Masters offer Taken wards. If this ritual is thwarted, the Unseelie Court wanes in power, allowing the Seelie Court to gain the upper hand in their eternal war.

True Voice/True Name Magic: A true name perfectly describes something's essential nature. Using one's true voice is a form a singing, humming, or playing music that connects to the soul. Knowing how to use one or the other gives a Namer a small degree of connection or control over the named thing, but understanding both creates the most unique and powerful kind of magic.

Unseelie Court: The part of faerieland which is home to fae with hostile attitudes towards humans. It is ruled by Queen Mab and her four powerful Masters, which each seek to enslave others and gain more power for themselves. They collectively gain their power from Hell by making a sacrifice every seven years.

Widdershins: Walking in a counterclockwise direction.

Will-o'-the-Wisps: Tricky fae that take the form of dancing or flickering ghost-like lights. Often seen by travellers at night, often around bogs, swamps, or marshes.

About the Author

Etta Grace is the eldest of five siblings and grew up in rural Pennsylvania, where she spent her childhood exploring the woods in their backyard. Their (not so imaginary) adventures inspired Runaways. Etta also runs an active blog and YouTube channel where she hosts book reviews, writing advice, livestreams, and interviews with indie authors.

Etta currently lives in the Cincinnati metro area where she works as a sustainability engineer. When not writing, Etta can usually be found volunteering at her church, trying to read every book in the world, learning various hobbies from textile arts to martial arts, or spending time with her friends and family.

Follow Etta to Learn More!

If you enjoyed this book, please leave a review on Amazon, Goodreads, or Storygraph. Word of mouth advertising is a huge deal for small indie authors like me, so it means the world to me every time you tell your friends and family about Runaways.

Do you want to learn more about the real-world mythology and folklore that inspired the fantastical worldbuilding in Runaways?

Do you want to get special access to companion study guides on the foreshadowing, symbolism, and nature featured in the story?

Do you want to be the first to know about my next writing projects?

You can do all of this by joining my newsletter! I only send monthly emails so I won't spam your inbox and it's an easy way to keep in touch.

You can also follow my blog on my website www.ettagraceauthor.com or check out my social media.

Scan this linktree Code to find me online!

linktr.ee/ettagrace

Content Warnings

Runaways is a dark YA/Teen fantasy action-adventure. It is written for an audience aged 12-15 years old but this book has been enjoyed by young readers, teens, and adults alike.

It contains age-appropriate references to child abuse, abandonment, adoption, animal cruelty, animal-human transformations (think werewolf), blood/broken bone/violence/fighting, body-swapping, captivity, deals with the devil, emotional/physical manipulation, family conflict, loss of identity, over-stimulation/meltdowns, plant/fungi-based body horror, shape-shifting, skin-picking, and odd varieties of unpleasant magical environmental hazards.

Readers who may be sensitive to these topics, please take care, for faerieland may be both terrifying and wondrous at times.

Colophon

This book is typeset in the program Affinity Publisher 2. It uses the fonts Merriweather for body text, Lora italics for headings, and Acorn Initials for drop caps, Cinzel Decorative and euclidCP for the title. The paper used is White 50lb / 74gsm.